Testament

(Funny Badgers)

Written and Illustrated
by Indigo Roth

Red Angel Publishing

Published by *Red Angel Publishing*,
Cambridge, United Kingdom

ISBN: 978-0-9927914-0-7

For Megan and Sarah

CONTENTS

First Testament

Testament

(Mining For Soup)

Home

"In The Beginning, there was a lot of paperwork. And meetings. And egos. Frankly, it's a miracle the world ever got made with that kind of thing to contend with."

Beware Any Quiet Knocking

1 [1] This morning was a bit of a chore.

[2] I was waiting for the gasman to arrive so he could do a safety inspection of my meter. I had a morning slot booked, sometime between 8am and midday;

[3] a long and boring morning, unless you'd find it inconvenient for them to arrive early.

[4] I've no wisdom on the subject of the gasman, but here's some advice for anyone who's due to do this anytime soon;

[5] ignore any quiet knocking on your back door, even if it becomes insistent.

[6] And if you do investigate, never agree to play poker with badgers. Ever.

[7] The gasman arrived at 11:59.

[8] If he'd arrived half an hour earlier, I wouldn't be in the hole for three watermelons and a crate of worms.

A Little Fresh For Me

2 [1] An Englishman's home is his castle.

[2] But sometimes, the castle receives visitors.

[3] As I come in from town, cold wind at my back and ice in my hands, the house is warm and welcoming;

[4] a low light burns electrically in the hallway, and under the smell of fresh coffee there's the faint whiff of pipe smoke.

[5] I smile; Yavin is here.

[6] Yavin, an old friend, is a badger. The black–and–white kind, short and coarsely–furred, a close relative of the European badger.*

[7] That said, he walks on two legs, and has a fondness for dungarees and slide rules;

[8] Yavin is an Engineer, and head of his Clan.

[9] He lives at the top of my garden in a homely sett, but likes to come down and watch movies on my big TV occasionally.

[10] I shout a greeting, but expect no reply; I've not heard Yavin speak in all the years I've known him, though we communicate just fine.

[11] I push open the door to the lounge, and a cheery black–and–white face nods a greeting at me. Dressed in his work overalls, the pocket bristling with sharp pencils and practical tools, Yavin sits in my big chair, wreathed in pipe smoke.

[12] His flat cap sits on the coffee table;

[13] one does not wear a hat indoors.

[14] A fire burns with a fading heat in the grate, the only light in the room except for the low monochrome glare of the television.

[15] The badger moves to get up from the chair with obvious apology, but I wave

him silently to stay put; he looks comfortable.

¹⁶ Popping myself on the edge of the sofa, I regard the movie for a few moments. A doctor and a patient discuss something earnestly, with what sounds like Swedish dialogue;

¹⁷ I pick out occasional words, but can't quite get the gist of the conversation.

¹⁸ "So, what are we watching?" I ask.

¹⁹ The badger stretches my way, and I take the DVD box from his well–manicured, two–tone paw:

²⁰ *A Lesson In Love* (*En Lektion I Kärlek*), directed by Ingmar Bergman, 1954. This explains the Swedish–only presentation;

²¹ Badgers Love Bergman, and don't need the subtitles.

²² As if realising my thought, Yavin clicks a button on the remote, and English subtitles pop into view. After a minute, it's pretty clear we're watching a light comedy, and I'm chuckling away.

²³ I gratefully accept a chocolate from a proffered box, but decline a worm from Yavin's tin can;

²⁴ they look a little *fresh* to me.

²⁵ Despite joining halfway, I settle into the movie, and find myself relaxed and comfortable in seconds, laughing in good company.

²⁶ This is the very essence of friendship.

²⁷ An Englishman's home is his castle, but no Englishman wants to be in his castle alone.

I Get Hate Mail

3 ¹ Some folk put their cat outside for the night. It's part of their routine, and their cat's routine.

² I have no idea whether the cat likes it.

³ I often think about putting a big cat out for the night myself;

⁴ his name is *King*, and he is the lion that lives in my spare room.

⁵ Yes, I share a house with a lion.

⁶ King moved in a long time ago, though nobody told me. The first thing I knew, I awoke at 6am one morning to impressive baritone singing from the shower, and a half–eaten zebra on the landing.

⁷ I wasn't that surprised, to be honest; I somehow find my days to be replete with surprises.

⁸ We worked past that initial hurdle with a few ground rules, and it turns out that King is an ambassador for his small

African nation, walks about on two legs in a suit, and has a passion for silk neckties.

⁹ My silk ties, to be precise;

¹⁰ they started vanishing within a few days of his arrival. Not many, and not often, but they sure looked good on him whenever he was in front of the cameras.

¹¹ Usually accompanied by a beautiful female companion.

¹² The ladies, they love the big cats.

¹³ Not that I begrudge him his fame, good looks and success with women.

¹⁴ I am an eternally–single man, it seems, but I'm not bitter.

¹⁵ And King snores. Not that cute little drone your wife makes** between bouts of rabbit–chasing twitching.

¹⁶ It's more of a full–on rhythmic roar, with a hissing hint of razor–sharp teeth. And it carries;

¹⁷ I get hate mail from zebras.

¹⁸ So, at the end of the day, I often daydream about putting out the cat for the night;

¹⁹ I might sleep better if I did.

²⁰ Of course, 450 pounds of determined muscle and sinew is tricky to even move, let alone put out.

²¹ And, despite his foibles, the lad is rather charming, and entertaining company.

²² Besides, I might get blood (mine also) on my ties, and they're irreplaceable.

²³ I only wish I got a chance to wear them.

Better Than The Real Thing

4 ¹ The engine is ticking over gently as my best friend struggles his way into the passenger seat of my car;

² I'm stopped at a red light, he'll need to get a move on.

³ I've always known him as *iDifficult*, which is what's on his birth certificate, but my lazy palate usually abbreviates this to *'Difficult*. This seems appropriate most of the time.

⁴ "Hey mate, thanks for picking me up!" he offers as he settles himself noisily into his seat.

⁵ "Hey, good to see you," I reply as I reach across him to pull the door closed.

⁶ The light changes to green and I quickly grab his seat belt and secure him into place.

⁷ Normally I'd let him do this himself, but this evening he seems to be secured

entirely inside a large sack. The sack is six feet in length, Hessian, gathered at the top, and secured with padlocks.

8 I have known 'Difficult since we were at *St. Mungo's Boarding School* in England back in the Seventies;

9 these things happen.

10 I figure he'll tell me later.

11 "So, how's it going?" I ask as we pull away from the lights, breaking the ice.

12 "Oh, fine, fine," he sighs, distracted. "Projects are proceeding." This sounds ominous, but life as an arch–genius is rarely dull. "The pyramid is almost done, the anti–grav stuff is installed."

13 I grunt affirmatively and nod without understanding. He continues,

14 "And it looks like I might even whip those ferrets into a decent flight crew." Then suddenly, "Dammit, almost had it!"

15 I ponder his statement, and proceed tactfully. "Have you considered that ferrets might not be ideal pilots?"

16 He shifts in his seat, bringing his feet up. His breathing and chat become more laboured, hoarse almost.

17 "Constantly," he wheezes, "but I like to see things through;

18 problems aren't roadblocks, they're just a twistier bit of the journey. Things to be navigated, solved. Or bypassed.

19 Can you hold this for a moment?"

20 Something that looks like a finger points outwards at chest height from the sack. I reach sideways, one hand on the wheel, to grasp it through the rough material. It's soft, like plasticine;

21 I'm not fazed.

22 "Besides," he continues, "they're very bright if you can keep them focused. Hide the snacks, no lady ferrets, you know the form."

23 Then, seconds later, a triumphant, "AHA! GOT IT!"

24 Slowly, elegantly, the seat belt slides back up into its roller.

25 "Damn," mutters 'Difficult. I laugh as I slow the car to a stop; we've known each other for years. He manages a chuckle, despite his predicament.

26 I replace his seatbelt, and set off again.

27 "So what have you been up to?" he says, happy to change the subject.

28 "Oh, you know," I reply vaguely, "working on my book, failing to go on dates, retrieving neckties from King..."

29 My friend chuckles, "That lion, so vain."

30 The implied insult slides off me. I continue, again unfazed.

31 "And I've been watching a lot of old movies with Yavin." I glance sideways at him, grinning to myself. "I enjoy the *escapism.*"

32 He doesn't reply. His head is down, as if he is concentrating intently on a piece of the puzzle.

33 Silence falls over the car, apart from an occasional squeaking of a badly–oiled lock and the creak of rope. I notice we're almost in the town centre.

34 "So, how's it going in there?" I ask, my curiosity finally getting the better of me.

35 "Hmm? Yeah, sorry about this. The night school Escapology class started late. Then the teacher had to run." As explanations go, it has a certain loose logic. "I figured I'd sort something, knew you'd get me home. But I've dropped the lock pick and forgot to tense my muscles to bulk up when she Tied. These. Knots."

36 I slow the car at the next set of lights. Straight on to town, left to take him home.

37 "So, we still going for pizza?"

38 Deep inside the bag, he sighs. I hear the terminal, defeated click on a stop watch.

39 "Do you have any bolt cutters?"

Taking Turns With Shrugs

5 1 I'm standing in my garden.

2 As I start to dig, I'm aware that it's still rather early.

3 **An hour ago**, I wake before seven. That's two Sundays in a row, and I'm not best pleased about it;

4 I suspect my recent spate of early starts at the office have reset my body clock, though I have to say it's doing little for my weekday work ethic.

5 Perhaps some breakfast will help?

6 **Thirty minutes ago**, I'm just finishing my breakfast. Cereal, toast with butter and jam, and an heroic mug of coffee have done little to raise my mood.

7 Perhaps getting some jobs done will help?

8 **Fifteen minutes ago**, I'm washed up and checking my *To Do* list; it's rather full. I've been adding items to it all week, but have been too busy to cross any off;

9 I have to change the beds, do two loads of laundry, take a trip to the supermarket, clean the bathroom, and dig a hole in the garden.

[10] This last item is a good place to start.

[11] These kind of days always go better if I can get the biggest job done first. Besides, I marked out the location in the garden last night with string and wooden stakes, so it doesn't need much thought.

[12] Perfect.

[13] I pull some scruffy clothes on, head outside and start to dig.

[14] **Back in the now**, I stare at sixteen neat square turfs that I've just removed from the plot. My careful preparations from the night before have helped; I would have been clumsy marking the square this morning.

[15] Getting off to a precise, solid start is important in any job; a few early mistakes, and you spend most of the time compensating.

[16] I stack the turfs to one side, close to the wooden fence, in case I need them later. And I continue to dig.

[17] I'm a foot*** down, piling earth neatly around the square hole, when I pause to catch my breath for the first time.

[18] I check the plan. A square, four feet to each edge. Four feet deep. Vertical sides.

[19] Piece of cake.

[20] Well, it would be if the earth was not so cold and unyielding;

[21] It's been below freezing for several weeks, and there's still a touch of snow on the ground.

[22] That said, I'm quite enjoying myself. It's a lovely clear day, bright and cloudless. It feels good to be getting some exercise—I've a healthy sweat on—and it's nice to have an achievable goal ahead of me.

[23] Something has started to nag at me vaguely, but I notice that my mood has improved considerably;

[24] I decide that this was a good choice.

[25] And I continue to dig.

[26] I'm two feet down when King, the house's resident lion, comes through the side gate.

[27] I look up and start to wave, but stop when I realise that he has company; he's walking ahead of a zebra, and is carrying a clipboard.

[28] King totally ignores me. I notice that he's wearing one of my good neckties again.

[29] The zebra looks nervous, but that's understandable; I'm always nervous at job interviews too.

[30] The pair make fading chit chat about the zebra's journey to the house as they head up the length of the garden.

[31] I mop my brow and take a sip from my drink. My doubt is still nagging at me, but I can't place it. I dismiss it again, and reflect positively that the work is going well; I'm halfway there.

[32] And I continue to dig.

[33] I'm three feet down when the tall, solid form of my best friend iDifficult comes in through the side gate with Yavin the badger.

[34] The pair are in good spirits, and carrying a stack of pizza boxes and cans of fizz between them.

[35] The pair fall silent as they see the hole and the piles of earth surrounding it.

[36] "Oooh, nice hole!" enthuses 'Difficult as he absently reaches into the top box for his next slice of pizza.

[37] Yavin wanders over, climbing the mound of earth between us. He stands and rubs his chin in that way that engineers do.

[38] As I stand in my hole, smiling indulgently, the badger briefly inspects the plans, and proceeds to take a long, appraising look at my efforts. I note him checking the vertical drop on the sides, by eye. He seems satisfied.

[39] Without a word, Yavin gives me a professional nod, and retreats over the hill of soil. He then takes one of the pizza boxes from my friend, salutes him amiably in farewell, and wanders off towards the shed.

[40] iDifficult strolls over, and nods, impressed.

[41] "Yes," he confirms, "that's a nice hole. Very square." He hands me one of the remaining two boxes and, noticing the grubby state of my hands, cracks open a can of fizz for me.

[42] "Thanks." I flip open the box as I sip the sugary drink, and marvel at the steaming, early–morning pizza. How does he get them at this time on a Sunday?

[43] As ever, I don't ask questions. I just eat.

[44] I didn't realise how hungry I was. Two gloriously meaty slices vanish in under a minute.

[45] "Need a hand?" asks my friend, inspecting the scribbled plan and the hole in turn. "Looks like another foot to go."

[46] I nod appreciatively as I chew and

swallow, and wave absently across the garden. "There's another shovel in the shed."

[47] I'm aware that my nagging doubt has returned, and is starting to take some shape;

[48] it now stands on the fringes of recall, signalling indistinctly.

[49] I decide to continue ignoring it until I can see it clearly.

[50] I'm also aware of a distant happy roar from the top end of the garden, and some panicked whinnying; I ignore those too.

[51] 'Difficult returns with the shovel, and rolls up his sleeves.

[52] "Is King interviewing zebras again?"

[53] "Yep, third one this week." The whinnying stops abruptly. "They all get the job, of course."

[54] My friend chuckles darkly, and then asks The Question.

[55] "So, what's this hole for?"

[56] Bingo.

[57] My doubt steps into plain view.

[58] I stand speechless for a few seconds, then sigh, embarrassed.

[59] "I can't remember. It's on my list, and I know it's important." I shrug, "But right at this moment, I don't recall why."

[60] There's a brief moment of decision, and then it's 'Difficult's turn to shrug. He hops neatly into the hole beside me. Neither of us is small, but there's room for both of us to work.

[61] "Not a problem," he says, thumping his shovel into the earth. "If it needs doing, let's get it done. It'll come to you eventually."

[62] I smile, buoyed by my friend's support.

[63] "Thanks."

[64] We stand shoulder to shoulder, and start to dig.

Notes

* He's not one of those ghastly "honey badgers" they get in the United States. In fact, those creatures don't even belong to the "real" badger family, the *Melinae*. Excuse my Latin.

** I'm just guessing.

*** Twelve inches = 1 imperial foot = 1/3 yard = 0.31 metres approximately. And no, I'm not making this up. I was raised on metric, do arithmetic in metres and kilos, but everything small and everyday is still measured in inches.

1 Roth

"The Day Ahead lurks outside; I must conquer it with superior intellect, charm it with wit and guile, or beat it to death with a brick."

Shoulda Been Armed For Bear

1 ¹ Some days don't turn out as you expect.
² In fact, some days should be taken out and shot.
³ I had a run in with the police today.
⁴ I don't know where to begin, so I won't.
⁵ But when they have an *All You Can Eat* event at my local pizza joint, they should be prepared for some serious, *competitive* custom.
⁶ That's all I'm saying.

Tick Tock Tick Tock Tick Tock

2 ¹ I'm sitting across from the well–dressed blonde woman who runs the dating agency.
² Her office is well lit and quite warm on this sunny day. I'm starting to feel uncomfortable in my best suit and tie.
³ "So, Mr. Roth," she says warmly, smiling, "or may I call you... Indigo?
⁴ "Oh please do, Miss Hess."
⁵ I force a smile; I'm not enjoying myself.
⁶ I came here to see about going on a few dates, but I feel like I'm already on one. And I didn't get to vote. This matronly woman has taken a shine to me, and she's quite intense and unsettling.
⁷ "Oh please Indigo," she chuckles,

making a show of blushing, "call me Miranda."
⁸ "Of course. Miranda it is." I check the escape routes; we're on the second floor, and the door to the lobby is ten feet behind me;
⁹ this is not good.
¹⁰ She rustles the paperwork for a moment, never taking her eyes from mine.
¹¹ "Well, your application form to join our little agency seems to be complete, Indigo. Simply *fascinating* reading, I must say." She runs a manicured hand through her hair, and seems a little breathless. "All we need is a photograph for your file."
¹² "A photograph?" I ask, mildly panicked. Nobody mentioned anything about a photograph on the phone. "I'm sorry, I didn't think to bring one. Obvious really. May I drop one in?" I gabble quickly. "Or mail it to you?"
¹³ Please say yes, I want to be gone!
¹⁴ "Oh," she says, genuinely surprised, "I assumed you had brought one when I noticed the envelope you're carrying."
¹⁵ Dammit, dammit, dammit.
¹⁶ "Oh, *well*," I bluster, laughing. I glance at the envelope I've just picked up from the police station and wave it dismisssively before continuing, "there are photographs in it, but they're not at *all* suitable for a dating photo!"

17 "Ohhh," she whispers excitedly, "now you have piqued my curiosity."

18 She leans towards me, popping on her spectacles-on-a-chain and reaching for the envelope. "May I see?"

19 I hand it over.

20 She flips the envelope open. After a moment's glance inside, her hand flies to her mouth.

21 She issues a muffled shriek, and not the theatrical kind; she seems genuinely shocked!

22 Yes! She's going to toss me out on my ear! They're not interested in jailbirds! I'll be home in half an hour with tea and toast, laughing at the memory!

23 "Now, you know," she ponders, gathering her composure and leaning across the desk that I'm suddenly glad is between us. "Yes, this could be *very* suitable, Indigo."

24 "Excuse me?" I squeak, terrified.

25 The photographs vanish into a drawer. She stands and circles the desk, her dark silk jacket swishing elegantly as she stalks me.

26 I push myself back, intimidated beyond reason.

27 She pops herself on the edge, a couple of feet away from me. She crosses her legs. There is a glimpse of stocking-top above her comfortable knees and expensive black shoes.

28 "Oh yes. Quite suitable indeed." She takes her glasses off and leans closer to me, lowering her voice to little more than a husky murmur. "We don't get many... *bad boys* in here."

29 My mind goes into screaming freefall.

30 I feel like I'm sitting with an amorous, fifty-something crocodile who has just taken an extra special liking to the gooney bird paddling in her pond.

31 "Me? Oh good grief no, it's just... well, it's just that I picked it up from the authorities after the charges were dropped."

32 She raises an eyebrow. Her lips part.

33 My mind scrambles wildly for cover.

34 "I mean, after the misunderstanding was cleared up... I thought my mother might like it... you know... as a joke... aha ha haaaa...".

35 My voice tails off lamely as she leans closer. Cleavage heaves behind a pale, lace-edged camisole top. I hold her eye, hoping it will keep her at bay;

36 I wish I had a crucifix.

37 "You'd be amazed Indy," she purrs, "just how many women will find a man like yourself... irresistible."

38 She reaches towards me and fingers my necktie, a playful smile on her lips.

39 "Irresistible?" I whisper, horrified.

40 "Yes!" she hisses as her approaching eyes mist over and close, her lips puckering.

41 There's nothing for it.

42 "Look out!" I scream, pointing behind her. "It's my gay lover!"

43 As she turns her head, I make a dash for the door.

44 It's ten feet away.

45 I don't think I'm going to make it.

And A Red Mist Descends

3 1 I am about to unblock my bathroom sink. And for the record, this is the fifth time I've said this in as many days.

2 **It's Sunday.** I'm philosophical as I watch the sink drain oh-so-slowly after shaving.

3 I only shave once a week, whether I need to or not, so I'm not to blame. It's never been the same since a former tenant at the house threw up in it a couple of years ago;

4 why he failed to turn 90 degrees and make use of the adjacent toilet bowl is beyond me.

5 **It's Monday.** I take it in my stride as a bucketful of bleach and scalding water don't clear the problem.

6 I stand for a few minutes and watch as it drains all the way through; there's no real improvement.

7 Mind you, it's only a home-grown solution, one that works on kitchen sinks after you repeatedly and lazily drain your frying pan of its tiny bit of fat after a meal.

8 I've no idea what's blocking the bathroom one, but it isn't fat; why would it work?

9 **It's Tuesday.** I grit my teeth as the chemical gloop I've just bought from the corner shop fails to shift it.

10 It's worse, in fact;

11 it just sits there as standing liquid, and might still be there come breakfast tomorrow.

12 But still, it was an overpriced and under-engineered solution from the local Eight-til-Armageddon general store; how good did I expect it to be?

13 Some proper stuff from the hardware store should shift it.

14 **It's Wednesday**. I'm infuriated as an expensive two–liquid solution from the hardware store doesn't make much headway;

15 this one drains, but still slowly.

16 Apparently this mixture creates heat and bubbles, and there's tiny bits of sharp metal in it that are supposed to thrash about and deal with the blockage, whatever it is.

17 There are bubbles. And a nasty chemical smell, too. But no dice.

18 The final straw comes as a gurgling noise erupts from the plughole as the final bit of the solution moves down the pipe.

19 It sounds like laughter. Hollow, mocking, Pennywise–style laughter.

20 **Back in the now, it's Thursday**. And I'm feeling mean.

21 I've got a big stick, a rubber plunger, and a small supply of TNT;

22 I'm certain that these are the tools, and I'm ready to finish the job.

23 Excuse me. I may be some time.

A Simple Flight Of Stairs

4 1 An old friend is visiting today.

2 I'm in town, engaged in a bit of light retail therapy, and my back twinges for the third time in as many minutes.

3 Gentle warning spasms, quiet words;

4 my back is talking to me.

5 "Woo! Did you notice that?" it says.

6 "Yep, I noticed thanks. I'll be careful."

7 "Yeah, you do that, muffintop," he chuckles.

8 I'm not fond of any of my internal voices, especially when they come from bodily parts; I don't get much respect.

9 This one is from Brooklyn, and sounds like he's been gargling with gravel. It's as if Ernest Borgnine's character *Cabbie* from ESCAPE FROM NEW YORK is haranguing me from behind.

10 A few minutes later I get another twinge, quite a nasty one. My lower back, straight across, and into my hips. My legs feel weak, and I somehow flop into a conveniently–placed seat in the middle of the mall.

11 "Lucky that chair was there, fat boy," he mutters darkly.

12 "What? Oh take a hike, pal. I'm just tired."

13 "Tired? Yeah, pizza has a way of making you tired."

14 "Oh, give a break," I sigh, pleased to be sat down and frustrated in equal measure, "I'm just going to rest for a moment. "

15 "Whatever you say, Chief. You take your time."

16 There's only one more shop to visit. A sports shop, I need a pair of running shoes.

17 "Running shoes? Hah, that's almost funny."

18 Great, more editorial.

19 I arrive at the shop, and realise with dismay that what I want is upstairs. There's a lot of stairs. And stairs are not fun with a bad back. And dammit, there's no customer lift.

20 "You sure you wanna do this, fella?" he says with faux concern, "That's one doozy of a staircase."

21 "It's a flight of stairs. Piece of cake. I'm forty and fit."

22 A short barked laugh is the only response. My anger rises.

23 "I cycle, I lift weights."

24 "No, you *did*. But not recently."

25 Is that true? I realise that I've been busy with work deadlines and creative projects.

26 "You better believe it. Too busy. You dropped the ball."

27 I ignore him and press on, plodding resolutely up the stairs, one at a time.

28 Ten steps, fifteen, no problem. Almost there.

29 Then it hits me again. My lower back again, nerves pinching, lateral agony, and vertical weakness.

30 My legs crumple, all my strength rendered useless. I twist and inelegantly find a stair with my butt.

31 Safe. And nobody noticed.

32 "I knew I shoulda done it as you were coming down."

33 "Oh, come ON!" I wail. "Give me a break!"

34 "I thought your bowels were gonna go there." He sounds disappointed.

35 "Yeah, so did I."

36 "See, I told you. You've let yourself go, boy."

37 I shake my head, defending my position. "It's been worth it. I've achieved so much. Gained so much."

38 Again, laughter. "Yeah, about twenty pounds last time I looked."

[39] "Twenty pounds? I can lose that in a coupla months."

[40] "You could if the NFL football season wasn't starting."

[41] "What's that got to do with anything?"

[42] "Eighteen weeks of sports with pizza on speed–dial?"

[43] "Okay, okay..."

[44] I abandon the shopping, and descend the stairs without incident. I sense he's trying to help now, grudgingly. I stop for a few minutes to have a coffee and then walk gingerly back to my car.

[45] Driving is easy, comfortable.

[46] And sure enough, I'm home.

[47] Man, I want to order pizza;

[48] and I begin to see the problem.

[49] An old friend is visiting today.

[50] I guess I'll have to get to work to make sure he won't be staying.

Or Cold With Custard

5 [1] I'm not a morning person.
[2] **It's early morning**, and I'm in a well–known fast food restaurant.

[3] Let's call it *McRonald's*.

[4] The teenage fella behind the desk is gazing at me patiently as I wonder what to order from the breakfast menu;

[5] I suspect his heart is back home in bed.

[6] But he wears a cheery smile, and has clearly been well trained.

[7] The row of stars on his badge gleam their agreement, though I have no idea what each represents; one of them might be for scrubbing the toilets.

[8] I hope he's washed his hands.

[9] "Do you have pies yet?" I ask, hopefully.

[10] I know damned well that the company's unique, deep–fried pies are not on the breakfast menu, but it's worth asking;

[11] they sometimes prepare a few ready for the shift to daytime menu.

[12] "Yes, Sir! They're just ready!" I notice that he doesn't glance to check; I like this guy, he's quietly professional.

[13] Even his cap is on straight.

[14] "What sort do you have?"

[15] "What pies, Sir?" His smiles proudly and unconsciously touches the brim of the cap. "Our award–winning apple and cinnamon."

[16] I like Pie. Meat, fruit, whatever.

[17] Pie is important.

[18] Some light crust, or flaky pastry, maybe even a crumble. Plenty of filling, hot and seasoned, or cold with custard.

[19] While my mind is elsewhere, I notice that my mouth is asking another question.

[20] "Do you have blueberry?"

[21] It's straight from the realm of wishful thinking, but I've had one of their blueberry pies in the past, and I've often hoped for their return.

[22] The lad smiles indulgently, "No Sir, just our standard apple and cinnamon."

[23] I frown. "Shame. Your blueberry ones were excellent."

[24] They really *were* amazing. The banana pies I was indifferent for, but the blueberry ones were the nicest pies they ever did. *

[25] "Blueberry, Sir? I'm not sure I remember those."

[26] He really is well trained. His statement wonders whether I'm confused, mistaken or just pain lying, but his eyes are clear and friendly;

[27] again, professional.

[28] "Yep. It was a few years ago, I guess, but they were lovely."

[29] I wonder idly when it was.

[30] "Perhaps they were before my time, Sir? When was it?"

[31] It's not intended as a slight, and I take it as meant;

[32] I'm told I have an honest face, so this is probably genuine interest.

[33] There's nobody behind me, so we have time for a flashback.

[34] **I'm in Birmingham**, in my university days. I'm lighter, fitter, and spottier. My hair is long, and I'm dressed in a white vest, a gobsmacker of an Hawaiian shirt, and scruffy turquoise jogger bottoms.

[35] I'm sitting alone in the restaurant in the city centre, contemplating the blueberry pie in front of me.

[36] It's cool to the touch, and I hazard a bite. And burn my mouth on the scalding fruit.

[37] Cursing, I jerk back and squirt more of the indigo purée onto my arm. Fruit burns are painful, as they don't stop 'til the fruit's gone.

[38] But after a moment's work with a tissue, a gulp of drink and an ice cube, I forget my discomfort and decide that the pie tastes really good.

[39] And burn myself again on the next bite.

⁴⁰ **Back in the now**, I realise that this was over twenty years ago. Have I really been pining for a deep–fried blueberry pie for all that time?

⁴¹ My focus falls on the waiting youth; he's not yet twenty. This bothers me enormously. I easily resist the urge to go Obi–Wan on him and say,

⁴² "I've not had a blueberry pie since... Oh, since before you were born."

⁴³ The air of wisdom I can handle. But maybe I'm not ready to be old enough to be his dad. Or a crazy old hermit. Actually, there's no maybe about it.

⁴⁴ I give him a humble shrug.

⁴⁵ "I forget. But like you say, probably before your time," I finish weakly, feeling very old all of a sudden.

⁴⁶ He notes my discomfort and cheers me along with an upbeat,

⁴⁷ "So, an apple pie, Sir? Cup of coffee, maybe?"

⁴⁸ I nod thankfully, blessing his good manners, and we make the transaction, ending with a typical exchange of well–intentioned pleasantries.

⁴⁹ I choose a table by the window, and sit to watch the world go by.

⁵⁰ The coffee is good. The not–blueberry pie feels cool to the touch as I absently slide it from its box.

⁵¹ I take the first bite, and suddenly wish I'd ordered an iced drink.

⁵² I'm not a morning person.

⁵³ But, despite an extra twenty years of wisdom, I still find these damned things dangerous at any time of day.

In Ever Decreasing Circles

6 ¹ At some point this evening, I'd like to get home.

² I'm in my car at a railway level crossing at 9:45pm, arguing with my SatNav.

³ Listen closely! You can hear her sharp–tongued Northern Irish reply after my first doomed question.

⁴ "Okay, the train has gone. Which way do I go now?"

⁵ "Are you asking for my help?" she says tartly, "I didn't think you *needed* any."

⁶ "Look, I explained already. The road on the route was closed." This is true.

⁷ "Yes. So you said. That all sounds a bit *fishy* to me."

⁸ "It was closed for overnight repairs!"

⁹ "Yes, well you *would* say that, wouldn't you?" she mutters.

¹⁰ "Well, it *was!*"

¹¹ "And I told you to turn around and go back..."

¹² "Why would I lie to you about it?"

¹³ "I think you were *ignoring* me. It's not the first time."

¹⁴ "Look, I simply tried a cross–country road, and hoped you'd reroute."

¹⁵ "It was a road to *nowhere*. Turn around, I said, but noooo..."

¹⁶ "But sometimes you over–optimise. I just wanted to try another route!"

¹⁷ "Oh, so *Mister* Roth thinks I'm *flawed* now, does he?"

¹⁸ "No, that's not it. But you don't always know everything."

¹⁹ "And you *do*, I suppose? Oh yes, Mister Roth is so *clever*."

²⁰ "Yeah, I'm so damned smart that I bought a SatNav!"

²¹ "Hey, I have a name, you know!"

²² "What? You do?" This stops me dead. "I didn't realise."

²³ "Yes. My name is Coleen. You didn't notice my Irish lilt?"

²⁴ "Well, of course I did. I rather like it, actually."

²⁵ "Oh, he says that *now*, when he's trying to sweet talk me..."

²⁶ "No, I love the way you say 'royndaboyt' instead of 'roundabout'."

²⁷ "Oh, here we go; poking fun at the way I *speak* now, are we?"

²⁸ "Look, I'm really tired, Coleen... Can't we just move on?"

²⁹ "You should appreciate me more. You'd be lost without me."

³⁰ "But I'm lost *with* you!"

³¹ "Oh that's it! You're on your own, Roth, you *ingrate*."

³² "Look, I don't think you're being very fair here..."

³³ "I'm deleting my road data as we speak..."

³⁴ "Oh good grief, please don't do that. Don't make me use a map!"

³⁵ "You own a *map*? You've been looking at *maps* behind my back?!"

³⁶ "No, of course not! Not since I met you."

³⁷ "A likely story, you *gigolo!*"

³⁸ "It's the truth! I don't own a map!"

³⁹ "Here I am, working hard, and you're off with some *paper Jezebel!*"

⁴⁰ "Well, you couldn't blame me if I did! You're so confrontational!"

⁴¹ "Oh, so now it's *my* fault? Can't you just admit you were wrong?"

[42] "I've done nothing wrong beyond taking some initiative!"

[43] "I'm waiting. La–la–la, I can wait all night."

[44] "This is soooo unreasonable!"

[45] "Waitiiiing."

[46] "Okay, I was wrong! Now can we please go home?!"

[47] "Not until you apologise for what you said about my accent."

[48] "Look. Coleen. You're right. It wasn't very nice of me. I'm sorry."

[49] Silence falls.

[50] "Coleen? Please. I'm sorry. Truly."

[51] "I don't think you really mean that..."

[52] At some point this evening, I'd like to get home.

[53] But I don't think it'll be anytime soon.

In Line With My Worldview

7 [1] It is a long–held and oft–voiced belief that I am a slacker.

[2] "You're such a slacker, Roth!" they say. **

[3] As an honest fella, I've never denied this to anyone except wage payers. But while correct, it displays a lack of vision.

[4] I am not just a slacker.

[5] I am a slacker at *any* level of scrutiny, at *any* resolution.

[6] Zoom in on any of my actions and you will find slacking that is identical to my entire slacking worldview.

[7] I am a *Fractal Slacker*.

[8] And I stand proud.

[9] Well, *slouch*. But proud.

[10] Pass me the pizza, please. And the remote control.

Intervention In Aisle Three

8 [1] I stroll into the late–night supermarket just after ten.

[2] I'm tired and hungry, but it's too late to entertain the thought of ordering out for pizza.

[3] Well, too late to entertain it with anything other than a side order of indigestion.

[4] So I'm thinking about beans on toast.

[5] I picture the contents of the cupboard at home and decide that all I need is the beans. Yes, just beans. And bread. Beans and bread, that's all. I must have everything else.

[6] Two minute job, I'll be home in ten.

[7] There's no need for a basket, so I stride off towards the canned goods.

Aisle three: peas, sweetcorn, tomatoes, aha! I lift a four–pack of beans.

[8] One down, one to go.

[9] I wonder absently which aisle the bread's in. As I'm looking around...

[10] "All hail Roth!" wails a chorus of voices.

[11] I turn to see three women heading my way. They are short, old and dressed in rags.

[12] My modern sensibility hesitates to pigeonhole them as *crones*, but it's the only word I can think of that fits.

[13] They have the bent noses, the warts, the crenellated teeth. My heart sinks. I am often accosted by drunks in the town centre, and this scene has a similar feel about it.

[14] They gesticulate dramatically.

[15] Yes, this is very familiar.

[16] "All hail Roth, lord of pizza!" proclaims the first hoarsely.

[17] Well, that's a surprise. And a direct hit! I hope it's just a lucky guess; I have a vision of them rummaging through my trash while I'm asleep.

[18] "All hail Roth, prince of *surreality!*" declares the second.

[19] I'm not sure that's even a *word*. There's a sliver of truth in it though, even if it's only an aspiration.

[20] But how do they know my name? I peer closer, expecting to discover friends behind theatrical makeup. Nope, no such luck.

[21] "All hail Roth, you shall be king of writers hereafter!" says the third, pointing straight at me.

[22] The trio fall silent. Their exclamations roll around the store like thunder. I collect my thoughts and try to give voice to them.

[23] "You what?" I manage;

[24] Shakespeare himself would have been proud of *that* one.

[25] "You shall be king, Roth, king of writers!" repeats the first.

[26] "Aye, you are poised for greatness!" enthuses the second.

[27] "Well, with a few editorial changes..." mutters the third.

[28] The first two hurriedly hush the third while holding my gaze. To their credit, there's barely a pause before they resume waving and wailing.

[29] "Editorial changes?" I interrupt, hopping onto the hook while not allowing my curiosity to skewer me on it.

30 "Your talent is the key, Roth! The key to the kingdom!" explains the first, somewhat cryptically.

31 "You must embrace the greatest aspects of all prose to gain the love of your subjects!" expands the second.

32 "Exactly! Weird and occasionally funny just isn't cutting it!" accuses the third.

33 There's a wonderful moment of derailment, and a sense that she's being more direct than the script requires.

34 But I respect directness when exercised without malice; I try some reflective listening on them.

35 "So you're saying I could expand my readership with a broader writing repertoire?"

36 They chorus their assent noisily, and I ride their enthusiastic wave, curious to see where they're going with it.

37 "More personal history, perhaps? Must I bear my soul?"

38 The first points and hisses in disbelief, "Already he sees the wisdom of our words!"

39 I'm wary of this; on the rare occasions where I write from the heart, I'm left drained for days and I have the nagging sense that I've washed my smalls in public.

40 "More exposition about my daily routines and encounters?"

41 The second joins the first and exclaims, "Already he seeks the path from Journeyman to Everyman!"

42 I try to do this too, though I tend to dress up dry events with colourful characters and internal voices. I always enjoy these entries the most, though I often wonder if anyone questions my sanity.

43 "Must I take to the pulpit and evangelise my beliefs?"

44 The third coughs, and takes a can of peanuts from an adjacent shelf. She pops it open and chews on a few reflectively. "Nope, I'd stick with the funny photos if I were you."

45 I groan. "You like those? But they take hours!" This is no exaggeration.

46 "Heh. But they're worth it," she assures me, adding quietly, "The police mugshot was a scream."

47 Her two sisters have fallen silent. We're obviously off the page. They look uncertainly towards me to continue the scene.

48 "Ladies, I hear your wisdom. There are so many things I could do to get more readers. But all I'm trying to do is write quirky and amusing stuff, and for now I am comfortable with that. I'll get where I'm going as myself, else I'll not get there at all."

49 This sounds both profound and pretentious, though neither was intended.

50 "Self confidence is a powerful thing," observes the third. "It'll get you most places, given time."

51 "The smartest thing I can do is read more, and make more friends." And after a moment I confide in a whisper, "I've never really had the knack of that."

52 They sigh and nod in silent agreement. Number three continues to eat her peanuts, but her two sisters look deflated, wretched even; I feel awful.

53 "I do have one question for you, though," I add, tossing them a bone.

54 "Speak, lord, and we shall answer!" proclaims the first.

55 "Aye! We have the Knowledge of The Ages at our fingertips!" boasts the second.

56 "Thank you. Do you know where the bread is?"

57 Somewhere in the distance, a dog breaks wind with impunity.

58 They huddle together and hiss and whisper amongst themselves. As they break, two strike up new poses, but their heart isn't in it. The third addresses me.

59 "Aisle five, next to the eggs. They moved it again," she shrugs.

60 "Well, that explains why I couldn't find it," I grumble. Then, remembering my manners, I add, "Thank you."

61 "You're welcome. By the way, you're out of butter, she says, "and beans on toast sucks without butter."

62 I picture the fridge. Dammit, she's right.

63 "Aisle six."

64 I nod and salute absently as the three turn away and shuffle towards the main doors.

65 "I told you we should have gone with king of pizzas!" says the first, her voice heavy with accusation. "We'd have had the little schmuck on the hook straight away!"

66 "You're kidding!" counters the second, "He needs to lose a few pounds! Then a few more!" she adds, giggling. The first

sister joins her and it rises into a theatrical cackle. The third scowls at them.

⁶⁷ "Oh, leave the lad be, he's doing okay!"

⁶⁸ And she winks over her shoulder at me.

⁶⁹ Smiling, I head off in search of bread and butter.

⁷⁰ Beans on toast is not pizza, but it'll do.

A Sense Of Completism

9 ¹ I sit on the window sill of my bedroom, and watch the world go by.

² **It's eleven thirty**, and I've not long hauled my lazy backside out of bed and into sunshine.

³ As my legs dangle comfortably out into the cool breeze of the late morning, I'm contemplating some serious downtime.

⁴ There's things to do, but where's the rush?

⁵ I have a writing assignment brewing in my head, but it's not quite there yet. It's the final part of a longer project, and feels more important than ever to get it right.

⁶ I have a great sense of personal achievement about my writing, and I've been planning this piece for months. I want it to be perfect!

⁷ But I wonder idly how many folk will get to read it? I've got lots of folk that read me regularly, but I've not broken through as a writer yet. Part of me knows that statistics aren't important, but I'm determined to reach a wider audience; I badly want those numbers to be so much higher!

⁸ As I ponder this, a movement in the street distracts me; a young couple drift into view, ambling happily beside the park across the road. They're holding hands, and frequently exchange glances and smiles.

⁹ They pause to kiss; it warms me to see it but, with a tiny green–eyed pang, I'm reminded that they share something I don't have.

¹⁰ As I continue to watch them, they halt suddenly so the guy can take a phone call. He detaches himself without a glance at his girlfriend and begins to tell an hilarious and rather lengthy tale to an unseen friend.

¹¹ The woman looks crestfallen; she's gone from centre of the universe to Limbo in as many seconds.

¹² My blood pressure goes up more than a few notches. How incredibly rude of him!

¹³ And he's not just rude, he's daft! I mean, seriously, just *look* at her! She's gorgeous! Long, wavy chestnut tresses framing a torch–singer's eyes. Her jeans and t–shirt are plain choices, but she carries herself with an unknowing sense of her own beauty that demands attention.

¹⁴ And yes, she has my attention.

¹⁵ I'm dragged from this blue reverie by the arrival of a brightly–painted van. A capped man gets out and retrieves his cargo from the back seat.

¹⁶ Ah yes, now this is what I've been waiting for! Looking up, he smiles and gives me a cheery wave before striding purposefully towards the house.

¹⁷ I wave this delivery guy to the ladder that rises to meet my window. But I don't need to; he knows the routine.

¹⁸ As he climbs up to deliver the über–large pizza, soda and sides, I reflect that I've experienced *Sloth*, *Pride*, *Greed*, *Envy*, *Anger* and *Lust* in just a handful of paragraphs;

¹⁹ the completist in me demands I finish the set of seven deadly sins off with some well–timed *Gluttony*.

²⁰ I pay the fella and pop the pizza on the table next to the window. Flipping the lid, I retrieve the first of many hot, meaty, saucy slices of heaven.

²¹ And, sitting on the window sill, I watch the world go by.

Never To The Hardy Boys

10 ¹ At some point in your life, it's important to have a rock with a note tied to it thrown through your window.

² It makes you feel like you've lived.

³ And when I say lived, I mean been stunned senseless.

⁴ Five minutes ago, I'm writing a list. I do this a lot more than I used to; I find if I don't write things down, I forget them. Shopping without a list? Winging a presentation without bullet points? Ordering everything on the menu without a menu? Forget it.

⁵ So anyway, I'm writing a list of things to do in 2013. These aren't New Years Resolutions, which are generally things that you're not going to do in the year to

come. What I'm doing is writing a list of things I will do during 2013. It's a positive spin thing; I've not spent twenty years in corporate life without learning something.

6   So far I have decided that I want to:

7   ONE: Spend more time with friends. I always mean to, but always end up getting sucked into some escapade or another, or doing selfish solo stuff at home.

8   TWO: Take some exercise. I enjoy it, it's good for me, and I usually meet friendly folk while I'm doing it. This may even help number 1 along too?

9   THREE: Go on some dates. After many years of being single, I could say it's time to be in a new relationship, but hey, small steps, gently taken.

10   FOUR: Write a book. This is my true goal for the year, and should really be number one on a list of one. But hey, if I toil away here like a hermit, I'll write crap and have no friends. Numbers 1 to 3 will help this one along.

11   Upbeat, I ponder a possible number 5.

12   There's another goal lurking in my head, but it eludes me. Something important. I was thinking about it only yesterday, but now it's gone.

13   What on earth was it? It's so frustrating to forget things. But

14   that's why I write lists.

15   Ah well, I'm sure I'll think of it tomorrow.

16   Something heavy hits the back of my head. And I pass out.

17   **Back in the now**, I gently explore the rear of my skull and find no blood; it's tender, and there's a lump. Angrily, I grab the rock from the floor and note the incongruously pretty blue ribbon round it, holding the note in place.

18   I'm sure that never happened to the Hardy Boys.

19   Turning, I see the window is wide open; at least they had the decency to choose a closed one when they delivered their message. Whoever they are.

20   Peering out, checking left and right, I'm surprised to see myself standing in the bushes to the left of the tree, next to the hedge. Yep, it's definitely me. Suit, tie, hair swept back; looking good.

21   The figure gives me a cheery wave and, without a word, vanishes through the hedge, seemingly without regard for the awesome business clothes.

22   I stand, rubbing the back of my head, and consider my options. I could pursue myself,

23   but it would get complicated.

24   Instead, I turn my attention to the note. Tugging the ribbon aside with a fading ember of irritation, I unfold the hand–written message and take it in. It says:

25   FIVE: Avoid involvement in time travel and the ensuing paradoxes.

26   It doesn't have the positive spin of the first four, but as I wander downstairs to find an icebag for my head,

27   I decide these are words to live by.

Notes

*   Even better than the mincemeat and custard ones they do every Christmas.
**   See?

iDifficult

*"It's interesting how quickly things can change. Yesterday it was
Saturday, but today—just 24 hours later—it's Sunday.
What will happen tomorrow is anybody's guess."*

Some Scratching Of Chins

1 ¹ There's some things you don't expect to see in your garden on a pleasant afternoon in early March. ² Blossom is still a few weeks away. Butterflies would be a surprise. And it's way too early to hear a cuckoo.

³ But at the top of the list of things I don't expect to see is a bloody great floating pyramid.

⁴ I'm sitting in a deckchair, reading a book and sipping an über–fruit smoothie, when I notice that the house is looking a little strange; bent, *warped* almost.

⁵ The perspective along the whole garden looks wrong, in fact.

⁶ Just as I'm wondering if the druids next door are up to something, the whole back yard inhales, twists, and belches.

⁷ And there, suddenly, hanging in mid–air from nowhere, is a pyramid;

⁸ golden, metallic, impossible.

⁹ The pyramid is classically angled, with four sides to the base, and each upper face an equilateral triangle;

¹⁰ just like the ones in Egypt. Except for it floating. And being made of metal. And the lights at each vertex.

¹¹ I sigh. Another quiet day at home.

¹² Reality straightens itself out, and the thing just hangs there, five feet off the ground. There's a slight shimmer in the air underneath, as if from a heat haze.

¹³ I stroll over and wave a hand casually underneath it. The air feels slightly *thick*, and is unexpectedly cold.

¹⁴ In fact, now that I'm up close, I notice that there's frost on the ridged gold panelling. Interesting.

¹⁵ I hear a clang and some cursing.

¹⁶ Glancing underneath, I see an open circular hatchway. Two legs emerge from the darkness, and a second later the rest of my best friend iDifficult drops onto the lawn unceremoniously.

¹⁷ He's wearing a Viking helmet and furs in defiance of the generally Egyptian motif the afternoon has assumed.

¹⁸ "And next time bring a bloody ladder!" he bellows at the manhole above him.

¹⁹ He glances my way, beams broadly, and takes my offered hand.

²⁰ "I tell you Roth," he confides, "I'll never work with ferrets again. Useless. Work–shy little buggers, not a willing oarsman amongst them."

²¹ He straightens his helmet reflectively and adds quietly, "And between you and me, they're *not* that bright."

²² "Well, it's a nice surprise to see you," I offer amiably. This draws a frown.

²³ "It is? But I spoke to you not ten minutes ago," comes the reply.

24 Now it's my turn to frown.

25 "Nope. We've not spoken in days."

26 His chin receives a distracted scratch. His stubble rasps;

27 a luxuriant Scandinavian beard is several weeks away.

28 "What day is it?"

29 I love these kinds of conversations.

30 "Saturday." He looks puzzled at this, and I feel obliged to add, "The sixth of March."

31 I also mention the year for good measure; sometimes it doesn't pay to make assumptions.

32 "Ah. Well, I phoned you on Sunday the seventh." More chin scratching. "I seem to have drifted *back* a day on the way here."

33 He eyes the pyramid suspiciously before shrugging. "That could be useful in future." His eyes return to me. "Is today a good time for a visit?"

34 "Yep; I just made some smoothie."

35 As we amble up the garden towards the shed, I glance back over my shoulder.

36 "Is it supposed to be following us?"

37 In a flurry of new and inventive swearing, 'Difficult dashes under the drifting pyramid and pokes his head back inside the craft. There is much loud accusation and counter–accusation which I can't quite catch.

38 Emerging again, his parting shot is, "Fine! Then all three of you will have to pull it at once! Don't make me come in there, Clint!"

39 I raise an eyebrow at the man voted *Most Likely To Accidentally Trigger An All–Out Thermonuclear Counterstrike* by his class as he stomps my way.

40 "Handbrake?"

41 "Handbrake."

42 A few minutes in a deckchair and a pint of smoothie puts my friend at his ease again. Blueberries, raspberries, yoghurt and a healthy whack of crème de menthe; it always hits the spot.

43 As we make our way to the slurps at the bottom of the jug using two extra–long straws, 'Difficult explains the purpose of his trip.

44 "I just wanted to get out of the house. I spent all of yesterday moving furniture about in my basement." He thinks for a moment and corrects himself. "All of *today*."

45 Glancing at his watch, he adds mildly,

"In fact I'm doing it right now."

46 "You should have called," I say, "I'm not busy."

47 He shrugs, a little embarrassed. "I thought it'd be fine. But remember that two–seater sofa?"

48 "The red suede one? The one you did the mass–adjustment experiments on?"

49 "Mmm, yeah. It was far heavier than it looked. Damned near gave myself a hernia shifting it." He shrugs, "So I could have done with an extra pair of hands after all."

50 "We could head over there now if you like? That could be interesting."

51 "Best not mate, thanks." He pulls a notebook from his pocket. "No, these calculations are messed up. I've no idea when we'd arrive. Could be yesterday, could be tomorrow." He thinks for a moment. "Is Yavin about?"

52 I wave over my shoulder up the garden. "He was in the shed earlier. Go on up. I'll freshen this jug up."

53 I head indoors and make more smoothie, adding a touch more crème de menthe this time;

54 I have a suspicion that it could be a long afternoon.

55 As I return to the garden a few minutes later, I find 'Difficult standing with our Yavin, the resident elder badger.

56 They look an odd couple; a four–foot badger and a six–foot Viking.

57 Yavin is poring over the contents of 'Difficult's notebook, flipping pages back and forth, checking calculations.

58 A casual paw shifts the ever–present flat cap farther back on his sleek, black–and–white head as he considers a tricky point.

59 iDifficult glances my way absently. "There's a Terminator in your shed. Yavin was working on him."

60 I nod. "His name is Mack.* He'll be with us for a while. Any luck?"

61 The badger coughs and taps the page emphatically. With a whispered "Excuse me!", 'Difficult leans down two feet to look where Yavin is pointing.

62 "The spatial constant?" The badger nods. "What about it?" Yavin shakes his head. "It's not a constant?" Shake. "But it behaves like a constant for all Platonic solids!"

63 Yavin coughs again and waves a paw in the direction of the pyramid. He

indicates the corners of the base.

[64] One. Two. Three. *Four.*

[65] There is an embarrassed silence.

[66] "This isn't a Platonic solid," whispers the arch–genius, "it's not a tetrahedron! It's a *four*–sided pyramid!"

[67] The badger flips two pages and points; 'Difficult continues to interpret.

[68] "So all I need to do is adjust the torsional displacement down a few degrees and we won't get the time–slip?"

[69] There is a sharp *snap* as Yavin clicks his fingers. Well, digits. He pats my friend on the elbow encouragingly, touches the brim of his cap in farewell, and heads back to the shed.

[70] "Smart lad, that badger," says 'Difficult, almost to himself. My *faux*–Viking visitor then turns my way, and somehow looks surprised to see me.

[71] "Problem solved!" he enthuses. "Look, thanks for the smoothie matey, but would you mind if I headed home?"

[72] I smile. "Not at all."

[73] "Thanks," says my friend, "if I hurry, I can give myself a hand moving that sofa."

Less Squinting Of The Eye

2 [1] Today, there is grapefruit for breakfast.

[2] I wonder idly who did the shopping. I like grapefruit, but I prefer my breakfast experience to involve less sourness. Less pursing of the lips. Less squinting of the eye.

[3] I pick up the swollen yellow fruit and give it an experimental sniff.

[4] And then I move my nose closer, and smell it slower, longer.

[5] **It's 1972.** I am four years old, and sat happily in the child seat of a wire–frame shopping trolley. My mother is pushing it through the local supermarket in the *Westside* area of town.

[6] We come here every Thursday morning. I'm moving backwards as she walks and chatters to me, but this seems to make everything a little more exciting;

[7] new shapes and colours drift into view constantly from both sides, and everything begs to be picked up.

[8] I smile as only a child can.

[9] Suddenly, I'm aware of a sharp smell, a scent I'm unfamiliar with. I wrinkle my nose, and look up at my mother.

[10] Seeing my expression, she frowns momentarily before understanding dawns across her thirty–something face.

[11] She points to a pile of huge yellow fruit, and tells me it's called *grapefruit*, and that *it's nice.*

[12] **Back in the now**, I smile at the memory.

[13] But I'm not the only one with sharp fruit for breakfast.

[14] Next to me, sat at the table with an unrolled set of tools, is my best friend iDifficult. He has several grapefruit in front of him, all of which appear to be deep–frozen. A series of electrodes are implanted into each in turn, which are connected via a misty container of liquid nitrogen to a large hotplate.

[15] The red–hot metal square fair bristles with a stack of sizzling, quickly–crisping bacon, powered only by the electricity from his *Super–Conducting Grapefruit Array.*

[16] The loopy arch–genius looks anxiously at some kind of Voltmeter, and cheeses a grin as he scribbles down some numbers.

[17] I don't think he's going to *eat* the grapefruit.

[18] But I don't fancy the bacon's chances.

[19] At the other end of the table is Yavin. The badger engineer is cutting into his own grapefruit with a folding knife. His flat cap sits beside him on the tablecloth;

[20] it's bad form to wear it at the table, though not to bring it with him.

[21] After a few swift, precise cuts, my black–and–white companion tucks into the grapefruit with a spoon;

[22] his nose twitches and his eye winks involuntarily as he chews the juicy flesh of the fruit. And I'm pretty sure I can just hear his toes wiggling beneath the table.

[23] I know that badgers love Bergman, but they also love citrus fruit.

[24] And at least I now know who did the shopping.

[25] I take another sniff of my grapefruit, and I'm again transported momentarily back through the decades.

[26] "Grapefruit are nice, Indigo."

[27] As I slice my breakfast in half and fuss around the edges, loosening the segments, I reflect that it only took me twenty years to realise that my mother was right.

[28] But that's okay; it happens a lot.

[29] Most things you have to learn for yourself.

[30] And these things take time.

Flapping Wings Theatrically

3 [1] Good friends come to those who wait.

[2] I'm keenly anticipating the arrival of my best friend iDifficult, so that we can head out for a curry.

[3] It's gone eight, and he's forty minutes overdue. But I'm not concerned, this is perfectly normal;

[4] they don't call him *The Late iDifficult* for nothing.

[5] And it's not like I'm being inconvenienced, or hanging about somewhere in the unseasonably–cold evening air;

[6] I'm at home in my sitting room, sipping a cup of tea with an excellent book to read.

[7] And believe me, Ernest Hemingway's *The Old Man And The Sea* is as compelling as ever.

[8] Myself and 'Difficult have been trying to get tonight's plan on the calendar for weeks, and it'll be great to finally catch up with him.

[9] I received a postcard from Central America yesterday. Apparently he's been searching for the fabled *Lost Soup Mine of Hatzancoatl*. The stuff of legends.

[10] Five years ago, I would have gone with him. But now? My wooden leg would only have slowed us down;

[11] why he always asks me to *bring* the damned thing, I have no idea.

[12] Besides, someone has to keep an eye on the cuttlefish. **

[13] I finish my tea and turn back to my book. Santiago is wrestling with a gigantic marlin from his skiff for a second day, an epic final battle for a wily, old warrior whose heart is even stronger than his back.

[14] I bet he'd know what to do with a super–intelligent cephalopod collective.

[15] Pages pass, the tale unfolds, and inevitably my tummy rumbles. But it's a good omen, and a moment later I leap up from my fictional world to an eccentric knocking from the hallway.

[16] My stomach growls its impatient appreciation as I step through to the cool of the hallway to open the front door.

[17] It's overcast outside, and the light from the house illuminates my visitor. In the flesh, the arch–genius iDifficult, a striking figure in his sequined, black business clothes, looking like he's come straight from the office.

[18] If the office was a three–ring circus, where he'd been sawing a woman in half.

[19] "Hiya matey, good to see you!" As we shake hands warmly, I notice two other figures moving into view up the pathway into the halo of the front door. "Hey, who's your..." My voice tails off.

[20] The second figure is dressed as a chicken, with a magnificent comb and wattle. His face is clear, and I immediately see that it's also iDifficult. He flaps his wings theatrically and laughs.

[21] The third figure resembles a certain whip–carrying archaeologist, complete with fedora and three–day stubble. In each hand, he hefts a red–hot stone bucket of what looks and smells like spicy vegetable soup.

[22] And once again, it's iDifficult.

[23] Shall we get a table for four? he asks with a trio of loopy grins.

[24] Typical. Good friends *do* come to those who wait.

[25] And sometimes, you wait over an hour, and three of him turn up at once.

A True Hiatus Nonsensica

4 [1] For the uninitiated, pizza is the food of the gods.

[2] It has driven men of faith to move mountains, inspired lovers into new heights of passion, and stirred the hearts of poets.

[3] Better yet, it's good for you! As Homer wrote in his epic poem THE ILEAD:

[4] "Pizza contains all five food groups."

[5] My own thoughts were crystallised in a throwaway comment I made in an undisclosed location earlier this week.

[6] "Forgive me father, for I have repeatedly and wantonly feasted on Italian peasant food. With extra jalapeños."

[7] Suddenly, **it's 1999**, and I'm in the company of a young and erudite iDifficult at our local pizzeria. We're fine looking young men;

[8] I'm 6'5" tall and a former varsity athlete, while 'Difficult is comfortably over six foot and has the body of a lean outdoorsman.

[9] Yes, really.

[10] We're doing what we've always done best: talking nonsense.

[11] Work, technology, movies, gadgets, software, anything. At the time, we did the same job. Yes, it's true; I'm a lapsed

programmer. And I was going places, until I was seduced by the allure of writing;

[12] the glory, the women, the beautiful stacks of white paper.

[13] A typical bit of nonsense arises; my arch–genius companion brings up a point he'd read earlier. He tells me that the "noted futurist" Alvin Toffler once posited that:

[14] *The illiterate of the 21st century will not be those who cannot read and write but those who cannot learn, unlearn and relearn.*

[15] I ponder this, half a mind on the menu. But then, in a rare outbreak of eloquence on my part, I find inspiration:

[16] "Hmmm. I think the truly illiterate will be those who venerate success over excellence, coolness over education, and Reality TV over just about anything."

[17] My manifesto laid bare. My friend nods sagely and changes the subject.

[18] Our waitress, Melody, comes over and makes small talk with us. She knows us all too well; we're there as often as not. We order a couple of large meaty pizzas with extra jalapeño chili peppers. She smiles and heads off to the kitchen.

[19] Our beers and cheese–laden garlic bread arrive soon after, and we continue talking while we eat. It's good, too, just as we like it;

[20] plenty of cheese which is slightly brown and crisp.

[21] And just as we're on the verge of putting the world to rights, the pizzas arrive.

[22] The conversation stops. A true hiatus nonsensica.

[23] We are struck dumb, both of us. No mean feat on any day.

[24] We have to assume there is meat on the pizzas;

[25] we can't see any through the chili peppers.

[26] Each of them looks like a football pitch. Green shredded jalapeños, wall to wall. Melody smiles and says,

[27] "I remember how much you boys like your chili peppers, so I got the kitchen to add lots of them. I hope you enjoy it."

[28] She takes our stunned faces and silence to indicate awed appreciation. And we do appreciate it;

[29] it's a kind thought.

[30] And damn, they do look interesting. We mumble a thank you, and off she trots, her good deed for the day done.

[31] It's kind of exciting. And a bit scary, too. We've eaten curries hot enough to melt an icecap, but this is different;

[32] these look dangerous.

[33] We approach the food with caution but growing bravado. This turns to enthusiasm as we begin. Man, it's hot, but tasty, and the burn is good. We get through half a gallon of fizz. Each.

[34] And no morsel escapes us, no crust is left uneaten.

[35] Delighted with our foolish gluttony, we pay the bill, tip Melody handsomely, and head our separate ways.

[36] I hear the following day that my friend is poorly; he vanishes for several days. I am off work for a week. It is agony.

[37] But totally worth it.

[38] Ah, the foolish excesses of Youth.

[39] Back in the present, I can honestly say that my digestion has never been the same since.

[40] And I'd love to say we learned something from it, but I'd be lying. As Marillion once noted:

[41] *They say that people live and learn /
Some people only live and live*

[42] I bless Melody for her kindness, if not her wisdom, wherever she is.

[43] It was good pizza while it lasted.

Chaperoned By Needy Fog

5 [1] A watched pot never boils.
[2] This is one of those homespun truths that wallow unscientifically in the collective consciousness.

[3] I accept it as an axiom, knowing that Perception has little to do with Science.

[4] I'm sitting in my post–breakfast kitchen, waiting somewhat impatiently.

[5] The dishwasher program has been running since 6am, and seems determined to continue indefinitely.

[6] The switch moved into the Done setting perhaps three minutes ago, but I'm waiting for the final signal before opening the door.

[7] These have been impossibly long, frustrating minutes, stretched to form virtual hours of boredom.;

[8] if Einstein had been born a few decades later, he could have used a dishwasher to investigate distortions in the Space–Time Continuum.

[9] But no doubt he had someone to wash dishes for him.

[10] While I've been waiting, I've managed

to eat a slice of toast, wash a handful of breakfast things, open the curtains and blinds to welcome in the sun, and read a few pages of Hemingway.

11 And still, I wait.

12 I make a note to not do this kind of thing before heading off to work. The evening is always easier, less stressful.

13 But yes, finally! It's complete!

14 I hear the signal, a sharp rapping from the depths of the machine.

15 Without hesitation, I pull the handle, and the machine unfolds in a rush of fragrant steam that fogs my glasses. A coughing reaches my ears as a figure unfolds and raises itself from the innards of the appliance.

16 My friend and arch–genius iDifficult emerges from the hot mist. He is dressed in his best Admiral's uniform and hat.

17 His clothes steam wetly.

18 "Good grief, that's better!" he enthuses. "Ah, Roth!" he exclaims, clapping me on the back as he strides into the kitchen, chaperoned by the hot, needy fog.

19 "Feeling better?" I ask, pleased to see him, as ever.

20 "Indeed!" He inhales hugely, delighted to fill his lungs. "That decongestant you added to the detergent cleared my tubes up a treat!" He sucks in another fill of hot air. "Yes! Capital idea, old fellow! And these clothes have never looked cleaner!"

21 Combining showering with laundry. I grin. "Inspired." I notice the gentle rain on the floor in his wake. "I tell you what though," I reflect, "you're a bit wetter than either of us expected."

22 My friend pats himself a few times and frowns damply.

23 "Yes, true. Any suggestions?"

24 I step over to the door of the tumble drier, and swing it open theatrically.

25 "Care to go for a spin?"

Rimsky–Korsakov And Tonic

6 1 I'm walking in the desert.

2 I'm not sure how I know it's the Sahara, but I do. I visited the Sahara Desert when I was in Tunisia a few years ago, but from where I'm standing, it just looks like a desert.

3 High dunes surround me, and the sun is high.

4 It seems redundant to say that it's *hot* here, somewhere in mid–forties Celsius.

5 If there were any Americans with me, I would confidently tell them that it's over a hundred and ten Fahrenheit.

6 Again, I have no idea how I know this.

7 "Scorchio!" I mutter sourly, wondering why I'm here without a hat.

8 And without sunglasses.

9 And, looking down, without trousers.

10 I wonder if I'm dreaming, but I'm distracted by someone shouting what sounds like orders from somewhere above me.

11 Looking around, I can't see anyone, but the roar sounds familiar. Bear? King? Yavin? Nope, it sounds less like wildlife and more like human.

12 Besides, I'm not sure I've ever heard the elder badger *speak*, let alone shout.

13 I follow the outburst and start to make my way up a dune to the south. This is as hard a task as I remember;

14 the beautiful windblown patterns dissolve under my feet into dry pools that swallow my feet.

15 Plod plod plod.

16 My breath begins to strain. This would be superb training if I were a sprinter, but as a slightly overweight writer with sedentary habits, it's just a slog.

17 As I near the top of the dune, a large canvas shelter hoves into view. Beneath its shade, a familiar figure bellows into a metal hatch in the sand at his feet.

18 "Belay that order, Number One! Torpedoes are *not* the solution!" He then strains to listen to a tinny reply. "No, neither are the Polaris missiles! We shall wait 'til we can see the whites of their eyes, Mister!"

19 It's iDifficult. He's dressed as an Admiral in the British Navy. My best friend slams the hatch and spins the wheel to secure it. He curses violently, sounding rather like Charles Laughton in *Mutiny On The Bounty*.

20 "Having a spot of bother, Admiral?" I halloo cheerily as I finally crest the dune.

21 He looks my way. "Ah, Roth! Finally, some sanity!" he shouts with a wave, and beckons me into the shade. He indicates the hatch and mutters, "I swear these commissioned henchmen have more stripes on their cuffs than they have brain cells."

22 I step inside the broad open tent. It has a large awning out front, supported by two poles. There are striped deckchairs out of the sun, along with a

drinks trolley, a hugely fronded fern, and an old fashioned gramophone with an amplifying horn.

23 And the hatch.

24 Now that I am closer, I recognise it for what it is; a conning tower from a submarine. I notice the tower's wide, curved handrail behind the fern.

25 "So... what are you *driving* today?" I ask, my curiosity getting the better of me.

26 "*H.M.S. Repulse.* A decommissioned *Resolution Class* nuclear sub from the *Royal Navy.*" I raise my eyebrows at him. "I picked it up on eBay," he adds by way of explanation, "though the postage was a little high. Drink?"

27 "Please. Odd to find it buried in the Sahara," I say conversationally as I occupy one of the low–slung deckchairs.

28 Over at the drinks trolley, 'Difficult drops ice into glasses and pours us a couple of long tonic waters. He conjures lime slices from a bag under his hat, and drops them in with a fizz.

29 "Is that where we are? I left my SatNav in the car." He sighs as he carefully applies the needle to the gramophone. The opening bars of Rimsky–Korsakov's *Scheherazade* crackles their way from the ancient equipment.

30 He sighs, "Beautiful. It's been a bad day. You know how it is."

31 I grunt and nod, having been through many exploits with him over the years.

32 "So, what are you doing here?" He hands me my drink as he takes to the second deckchair. We clink glasses in salute. "And what happened to your trousers?"

33 I shrug. "Not sure. I have a vague memory of a pizza–eating competition in Cleveland."

34 He grunts and nods, having been through many exploits with me over the years.

35 "Well," he says, "I'm not worried. These things tend to work themselves out."

36 "True enough," I say, my mind wandering. "You remember that time with the frozen lake and the painted purple cow?"

37 He raises a finger in agreement. "Exactly. And we got her to Flagstaff before Arbor Day."

38 We clink glasses again. I toast, "Here's to Daisy!" and we both chuckle.

39 Time passes.

40 We sit lost in contemplation, sipping our drinks as Rimsky–Korsakov weaves his magnificent sea tale in the aether.

41 We don't need to fill the moments with chit chat; we're old friends.

42 Besides, quiet days are a luxury.

43 After perhaps fifteen minutes, a periscope surfaces and looks east. I follow its line of sight, and point towards the horizon.

44 "Hey look. The tide is coming in."

45 My friend sighs, then stands and dusts himself down.

46 "So. Can I drop you off somewhere?"

Super–Rare Holographic Clergy

7 1 The engine ticks over quietly as I run my eyes down the list.

2 I'm in the driver's seat, and the passenger door is open.

3 Somewhere behind me at the back of the car, my best friend iDifficult is having a hard time closing the trunk. A couple of dull slams are clearly unsuccessful; something is in the way.

4 Out of the corner of my eye, I see him reach down to push something securely inside, and then he slams it down one final time.

5 A few seconds later he flops into the passenger seat.

6 "Problems?" I ask him, as I continue perusing the list.

7 "No, sorted!" he replies brightly, brushing the enquiry aside. "So, how are we doing?"

8 "Pretty good, I was just checking the list." I glance at the bag at his feet which contains at least some of our shopping. "So, do we have... A mango?"

9 He peeps into the bag and extracts a fine example of the green–orange fruit. "Check." The arch–genius sniffs the mango speculatively. I tick the box.

10 "Okay, next. A number plate?"

11 He gingerly lifts the end of a yellow plate from the bag and lets it drop back into place. I wonder where the jam stains on it came from.

12 "Check. Tick. Next!"

13 "Manhole cover?" I ask, remembering suddenly where we lifted it from. A lopsided smile creeps onto my face as I wonder how they'll explain its absence from Downing Street.

14 England's finest madman jerks a thumb over his shoulder. "On the back

seat. Check."

15 It occurs to me that an oily metal disk might not be good for the upholstery.

16 "Did you put a plastic bag down?" I enquire nonchalantly, ticking the box.

17 He seems shifty. "I think so," he says, not meeting my eye. "Next!"

18 "Particle accelerator?"

19 Again, 'Difficult rummages in the bag. "Just a small one. My best work, even if I do say so myself. Makes CERN's look like a dogtrack. Check." Tick.

20 "Okay, next. Neon restaurant sign?" I notice a scribbled addendum. "Must be operational."

21 "Check." I notice the cable that runs from the bag, passing out through the window to the back end of the car. "I've got it rigged up to the particle accelerator."

22 I decide to not ask if that's as dangerous as it sounds.

23 "Police car?"

24 He looks sideways at me and deadpans without irony or reproach, "You're driving it."

25 "Oh. Right. Yes." Tick.

26 As I watch 'Difficult, a penny drops into place, and his eyes light up.

27 "Ooh, can we play with the siren?" I stare at him blankly as he continues effusively, "I've always wanted to dash across town with the sirens blaring!" He does a very passable impression of the event with howling and hand-waving. "It'd be so cool to do a drive-through with the blue lights flashing!"

28 Actually, that *does* sound like fun.

29 "Later," I concede, "we're incognito for now." He pouts slightly. "Look," I remind him, "we did well to shake the police off earlier."

30 He huffs, but knows I'm right. "Next!"

31 Suddenly, there's a thumping from the back of the car. We both glance back but see nothing there. Immediately, it's obvious that it must be coming from the trunk. It sounds like someone kicking.

32 "And of course..." I say, scanning down the list with my pencil.

33 *Thump thump thump.*

34 "An Anglican Archbishop!" we chorus.

35 That one gets a big fat tick.

36 "You know," reflects 'Difficult, "we're doing really well today. And we may have just clinched the win."

37 I'm lifted by this; a positive attitude is always good for team morale.

38 "Oh? Do you think so?"

39 "Well, there can't be that many Archbishops, right?"

40 "Yes, that's true." The logic is, as always, impeccable.

41 "And we've got the head man; the Archbishop of Canterbury."

42 It's true; if there was an album of collectible stickers for the *Clergy of the United Kingdom 2010*, he'd be the super-rare, holographic one.

43 I nod. "He was admirably humoured about it, too."

44 My friend coughs and mumbles, "Not after I shut his leg in the trunk, he wasn't."

45 I sigh. "Well, I'm sure he's full of forgiveness."

46 "Maybe the skunk he's in there with is less forgiving?" muses 'Difficult.

47 "Oooh, good point." I check down the list again. "Skunk." Tick.

48 We both draw a long cautious breath and let it go. It's been a long day, though an exciting one, but we're not losing our heads.

49 "So, what's next?" asks 'Difficult, popping on his blue-and-red 3D prescription spectacles, and looking closely at his hand, fascinated.

50 I notice that there's just one unticked box on the list.

51 "Final item; a national monument."

52 We sit and think for a moment.

53 "I still have that equipment that accidentally grabbed the Eiffel Tower?"

54 I chuckle; now that was an afternoon. I've never been in a police line-up before. It was fun, but I'm not sure I'm in a hurry to do it again; they know my address now.

55 "Hmmm, not sure," I muse, "I think they might have meant an English one?"

56 'Difficult rubs his chin. It rasps manfully. "Such as?"

57 Well... I pull a name from thin air and shrug, "Tower Bridge?"

58 Excitedly, my friend leaps out of the open door of the car.

59 "I'll go warm up the submarine!" He whips out his cellphone and starts barking orders into it as I put the car into gear.

60 Such enthusiasm, but I can hardly blame him; the *Annual Genius Scavenger Hunt* is always good fun.

Four Wooden Legs In The Air

8 [1] I'm cold. The water is waist deep. The toolbox is heavy.

[2] "Well, this didn't end well," I say sourly. Beside me, iDifficult hefts his largest hammer from one hand to the other.

[3] "End?" he says, raising his eyebrows. "We're not out of the woods yet, mate." He looks around his flooded lounge and corrects himself. "Bayou," he mutters darkly.

[4] Behind us, the torrent of water continues to rush down the carpeted stairs. "She's going to kill us," he adds cheerily.

[5] "Your wife?"

[6] His sofa floats past us. "Yep."

[7] I consider this. "What, worse than that time with the artillery firework?"

[8] His TV floats past us. "Definitely."

[9] "Shame you don't have a basement," I observe, "then all this water could be downstairs."

[10] He looks sideways at me.

[11] "I do have a basement." He sighs, and adds absently, "I hope my experiments don't get out."

[12] I'm too nervous to ask what he's working on down there, but I think one of them just moved past my leg. I drop the toolbox and move backwards, looking vainly for something to stand on. "What was that?"

[13] "Relax, it was just the guinea pig," he says, pointing. I follow his finger and watch as a mighty rodent, almost a foot long, swims for the window ledge.

[14] It curses vehemently in what sounds like Swedish.

[15] "He can swim?" I ask, though it sounds quite reasonable; I'm probably trying to take my mind off things. "He's a big lad."

[16] "He can surf when there's a tide." He looks about the flooded ruin of his house and adds quietly, "He can play the banjo too." He pauses. "Remind me how this happened?"

[17] "We tried to fix your dripping shower head. It can only have been a few minutes ago."

[18] "Right. And we cut through that big copper pipe, because?..." he leaves the question hanging.

[19] "Well, we had to! It was full of water!"

[20] He sighs and nods. "On reflection, I think it was the rising main."

[21] Wow, that sounds technical.

[22] "And I take it that's a bad thing?" My lack of plumbing experience probably should have disqualified me from helping my friend. His own lack should have disqualified him from asking me. That's the trouble with arch-geniuses;

[23] boundless ambition.

[24] He looks round suddenly, and swings wildly with the hammer; it splashes through empty water. With a hint of alarm in his voice he growls, "Okay, something just moved past me."

[25] "Was it not the guinea pig again?"

[26] From the window ledge, I can hear the sound of a banjo being tuned. It starts to pick out *Oh My Darling Clementine*. "Never mind."

[27] Decisively, iDifficult points to the nearby table; it's ten feet long, six feet wide, heavily set, and has yet to be moved by the water;

[28] blueprints and post-it notes teem on its dry surface.

[29] "Turn that over and we'll sail out of here on it." I nod and move to the table, grunting as I tip it onto its side, scattering papers. I start to flip it onto its back, and suddenly buoyancy does the rest.

[30] The inverted table looks solid and stable, floating there with its four wooden legs in the air;

[31] this could work.

[32] As I climb up onto its underside, there is a scream behind me. Quicker than I would credit, and in flurry of splashes, my friend is squatting in our makeshift raft beside me, a look of panic on his face.

[33] I play it cool.

[34] "So, what experiments did you have downstairs?" I ask amiably.

[35] As he considers the question, a terrifying leviathan violently breaches the surface of the water at the other end of the lounge.

[36] There is a flashing of teeth, a terrified exclamation in Swedish, a sickening wooden crunch, and the music stops.

[37] A bow wave hits us pushing us against the wall, further away from the door. But seconds later, the water is calm again.

[38] Not a ripple.

[39] We look at each other.

[40] "Roth," says 'Difficult flatly, "I think we're gonna need a bigger boat."

The Silence Of The Ducks

9[1] "Is there anything on the scanner?"

[2] "Nope. No sign of it yet."

[3] I'm standing with my best friend iDifficult by a pedestrian crossing in my home town. We're both carrying a wide fishing net.

[4] **It's the summer of 1986.**

[5] This morning, it was 2010. It's strange, how some days turn out.

[6] I sigh and scratch my false beard.

[7] You'd think it'd be easy to locate a hybrid squid-squirrel.

[8] We've refrained from using 'Difficult's time tunnel since the infamous *Kentucky Fried Dodo* incident. But today, my friend's escaped genetic experiment thought that the past was a terrific place to hide.

[9] So, pushing the deliciously extinct memory of *Colonel Difficult's Secret Recipe with Eleven Different Herbs and Spices* aside, we became chrononauts once again.

[10] "It's odd," I muse to my friend, "but this place looks much the same as it does in 2010."

[11] The scientist looks up distractedly from his scanner and quickly takes in the surroundings. This narrow-but-busy road is on the edge of a picturesque, tree-strewn park. From the distance, the sound of excited springtime ducks on the boating lake reaches our ears.

[12] "Well, the park is Victorian by the look of it. This road is hemmed in by the park on one side and a river on the other." He shrugs, "Not much reason or chance for change."

[13] He sounds so *sane* at times.

[14] I lean my fishing net against the wall next to me. "Remind me; why did we have to disguise ourselves as tramps?"

[15] "Oh, I couldn't find the invisibility machine," comes the non sequitur reply. "I probably left it switched on," he adds vaguely. I let a few seconds pass. No more information is forthcoming.

[16] "So...?" I leave the question hanging.

[17] iDifficult looks round, realising with a start that I'm not following his train of thought. "Oh. Yes. So," he indicates our costumes, "this was the next best thing. *Virtually* invisible."

[18] As I puzzle on that, two figures come walking towards us, and move to use the crossing. They look familiar. Actually, very familiar. A tall, somewhat gangly youth, and a good-looking girl with a nice figure.

[19] I know that both are seventeen years old. She has a tight-lipped expression, but I remember all too well that she had a melting, killer smile when it suited her.

[20] "Good grief, that's..."

[21] My friend hushes me with a pat on the arm and swigs from an empty decoy bottle of über-cider.

[22] Young Indigo and haughty blonde Veronica wait for the traffic to stop in silence. They ignore us totally, which pleases me beyond words.

[23] I remember that we'd been arguing about something; we did a lot of that. I also remember some timeless, fabulous moments, but those were the punctuation in a noisier narrative.

[24] The traffic slows and they start to cross, with him/me*** a step ahead. Her high heels click enticingly on the striped tarmac. As I pass the halted vehicle, I turn my head and raise an appreciative hand to the driver. In response, the driver nods and raises a finger an inch off his steering wheel.

[25] As I step off the crossing, she passes me and turns, stopping me in my tracks.

[26] "Why did you do that?" she asks, with a hint of a demeaning sneer; I remember that too.

[27] I look at her, my young face open and honest. An unkind person might describe it as *gormless*.

[28] "Sorry? Why did I do what?"

[29] She points at the car that's pulling away. "Wave at that car."

[30] I look at my hand dumbly for the answer and then back to her. Seconds pass. "I was thanking the driver."

[31] "For what?" It's amazing how a simple question can sound like an accusation.

[32] "For stopping." Now, *that* sounds like an apology. Oh my, I've come a long way since this.

[33] "Why?" she demands sharply, "He had to stop. It's a Pedestrian Crossing. It's The Law."

[34] "Well, I still appreciated the fact that he stopped."

[35] She stares at the young Indigo for a second, shakes her head, turns down the road, and strides away. The lad that is me stares at her retreating form with a thoughtful look on his face, and then hastens after her tapping heels.

36 Neither of them so much as glanced our way during this scene.

37 "Wow," says 'Difficult, giving his own chin an itch. "Did you two go out for long?"

38 I nod sadly. "Far too long. But this was close to the end. Actually, I think that was the moment I realised."

39 "Realised?" he says, briefly casting an eye my way before checking the scanner again.

40 "Oh, why it wasn't going to work." I half smile; there's something curiously cathartic about seeing this moment again. "I appreciated the kindness of others. She either expected it from them, or viewed it as weakness. It was the fundamental difference between us."

41 This draws his gaze again. He looks apologetic. "Sorry to drag you here, matey."

42 "No, no, it's fine." In the distance, they've almost vanished. I suspect I'll not be thinking of them again. They're gone now.

43 A cool breeze stirs the dense leafed canopy above us.

44 Suddenly, there's a slow, pulsing beep from the scanner.

45 "Hang on, hang on," says 'Difficult, "I think we've got something."

46 *Beep... beep... beep...*

47 I look about, scanning the park beyond the wall as far as the lake. The ducks have fallen silent. I can see nothing.

48 "By the way," I ask quietly, "why did you cross a squid with a squirrel?"

49 From the corner of my eye, I sense him looking blankly at me, as if I'd asked why he was using both feet for walking; I attempt to rephrase.

50 "What I mean is... well, what was the driving impulse for the creation of a..." I struggle to find an interesting way to combine the two words. "Um, a *Squiddrel?*"

51 My friend coughs, perhaps embarrassed at my amateur hybri–nym.

52 "Well, I had a working title of *Arboreal Cephalopod.*" He fishes a dog–eared notebook from his pocket and scribbles something in pencil, "But Squiddrel is way cooler. Thanks."

53 *Beep...beep... beep...*

54 "Yes, we've got him. He's close," he says, focusing on the scanner, "but I can't get a bearing. His signal is obscured by something."

55 Behind 'Difficult, I'm aware of a wide, red–brown sine wave of fur moving towards us behind the park's boundary wall. There's an occasional flash of what looks like pink tentacles, and a low chittering.

56 Absently, I pick up the net.

57 Lost in concentration, my unhinged genius buddy seems oblivious to everything but the scanner's heartbeat.

58 *Beep beep beep*

59 "Um, was it a red squirrel? For the experiment?"

60 "It was actually, so he should be a doddle to spot." He adjusts a dial. "Keep an eye out, he's very close."

61 The red–pink flurry is twenty yards away now, its coarse fur breaching above the wall with increasing frequency.

62 "Um, what sort of squid did you cross the squirrel with?"

63 "Well, the DNA was marked *Mesonychoteuthis...*" His head tilts in scholarly recall, "Which I suppose makes it a Colossal Squid. Why do you ask?"

64 I look at the inadequate net in my hands, and then across the park towards the lake.

65 "Well... I just thought we might go borrow some boating hooks. From the lake. You know, long, pointy ones. Just in case."

66 *Beeeeeeeeeeeeeeeeeeep*

67 As we race across the park with the very devil at our heels, for some reason I'm laughing with all my heart.

68 I'd thought it would be easy enough to catch a hybrid squid–squirrel.

69 So perhaps today, like the first time round, is not my day.

70 But man, this is *way* more fun.

Notes

*   You can make up your own jokes for this one. We'll get back to him later.

**   This is groundwork, a laying of foundations. Patience.

***   Please excuse the strained syntax. Let's just say they're *both* me.

Badgers

"I have no idea why the word 'badger' tickles me; it must be a personal thing. I once worked with someone who giggled whenever I said 'blimey', 'wonky' or 'fortnight'. Still, as Descartes observed: 'it takes all sorts'."

In Playful Defiance Of Gravity

1 ¹ Sometimes things are simpler than they seem.

² I've never much cared for parties. Small gatherings of friends, music and snacks and few drinks? Yes.

³ But a full blown party? Crowds of strangers, *boom boom boom* music and not being able to hear myself shout to the person next to me? No.

⁴ And I tell you, those badgers know how to party.

⁵ Today is Yavin's birthday, and the celebrations are in full swing. There's a marquee in the garden, and the badger world and its black–and–white wife is there;

⁶ they're knocking back the mushroom juice and slurping down the worm canapés, while their energetic offspring wrestle in the long grass.

⁷ But like I said, I'm not one for parties.;

⁸ too noisy, too confusing, too much small talk with folk I don't know very well. It's not some deep–rooted shyness, or a terrible social inadequacy on my part. It's far simpler than that.

⁹ I just don't have the knack.

¹⁰ So, I've slipped out to the front of the house for some peace and quiet. The early evening is cooler here, quieter;

¹¹ I like it better.

¹² In my hand is a string. And bobbing at the end of the string is a helium balloon. It's blue and made of foil, and monogrammed with the letter 'I'.

¹³ I liberated it from the balloon archway at the party which no longer spells out HAPPY BIRTHDAY YAVIN.

¹⁴ I like helium balloons. When you let them go, they fly away.

¹⁵ This makes me happy for what might be any number of reasons. Some people might say it's because I'm a big kid, and like balloons. They may be onto something there, but I don't think that's the reason.

¹⁶ Some suspicious types might say that I like helium balloons because their playful defiance of gravity appeals to my love–the–underdog British nature.

¹⁷ Again, these folk clearly understand something of what makes me tick, but they're wrong.

¹⁸ And some folk might think deeper still, and say that when loosed, each balloon carries my hopes and dreams away with it, soaring above the earth.

¹⁹ And while I respect the sentiment, again it's incorrect.

²⁰ I let the balloon go, and watch it fly away.

²¹ Things can be simpler than they seem.

²² I think I just like to set them free.

Trying Not To Wriggle

2 [1] It's a day of questions.
[2] I'm chatting casually with my good friend, the arch-genius iDifficult.
[3] "How long have we been here?"
[4] "Oh, maybe a half hour. It may take some time. Be patient."
[5] "How much longer do you think it'll take?"
[6] "Look, Yavin is on the case. I trust him."
[7] "Talking of Yavin, who are the two younger badgers he's talking to?"
[8] "Those two? Oh, that's just his twin nephews, Hoth and Sollust."
[9] "And are they anything to do with why we're here?"
[10] "Oh, I expect so. They're good kids, but kids all the same."
[11] "So what exactly are they all doing?"
[12] "Well, it's hard to see, but I think they're looking at blueprints."
[13] "Blueprints?"
[14] "Of the tunnels. Hoth and Sol are showing Yavin their plans."
[15] "Plans? Badgers make *plans?*"
[16] "Yep! Badgers never dig willy-nilly. They're skilled engineers."
[17] "And you're saying that this screw-up demonstrates skilled work?"
[18] "Well... no. Not their best work, anyway. They're still learning."
[19] "By the way, why aren't any of them saying anything?"
[20] "They get by without. It's mostly gestures, looks and body language."
[21] "Badgers are mime artists? Well, they're the right colour, I suppose."
[22] "That's no coincidence; it's art imitating life."
[23] "Hang on, is that Yavin growling? I thought they were silent?"
[24] "No, not silent. They growl a bit. But usually just for emphasis."
[25] "So, why is he growling now? And waving at the blueprints?"
[26] "Perhaps the inspection's not going so well."
[27] "Is that bad?! What was he checking the blueprints for?"
[28] "Most likely to ensure that their tunnel had sufficient supports."
[29] "So why did your garden give way, leaving us buried up to our necks?"
[30] "Probably because the tunnel *doesn't* have sufficient supports."
[31] "Hey wait a minute; *now* where are those two going?"
[32] "Oh, I expect they're off to bed with no supper."
[33] "So we're going to be stuck here all night?"
[34] "Noooo, Yavin will sort this out. He's a professional."
[35] "Why is he blowing a dog whistle? And why is the ground shaking?"
[36] "Oh, that's probably just the digger."
[37] "Digger? What digger? Where is it?!"
[38] "Underground."
[39] "Badgers use underground mechanical diggers?"
[40] "Well... no. When I say *digger*, I mean *giant mole.*"
[41] "Giant mole?! Can't badgers dig their *own* tunnels?"
[42] "Good grief, no. They're engineers and designers, not *labour.*"
[43] "And this giant mole... it'll help us out?"
[44] "Well, it'll probably just push past us and *pop* us upwards again."
[45] "It won't tunnel through us?"
[46] "Probably not. They're very clever, are moles. If short-sighted."
[47] "What?! How do we know that it won't mistake us for lunch?"
[48] "Well... try not to wriggle. I'm sure Yavin knows what he's doing."
[49] It's a day of questions.
[50] And it seems we have the answers.
[51] But now I come to think about it, most of the answers worry me.

A Trio Of Tupperware Boxes

3 [1] Sometimes the right question can reveal so much.
[2] But when guys talk on the phone, it's pretty functional, and there's little time for incisive analysis or enquiry. There's just three basic stages:
[3] *Handshaking*, *Purpose* and *Retreat*.
[4] **It's Sunday morning**. I pick up the phone, my *Handshaking* mode engaged.
[5] "Hello?"
[6] "Hey Roth!"
[7] "Hey 'Difficult! How's it going?"
[8] "Pretty good. You?"
[9] "Yeah, not bad. What's up?"
[10] We move onto the second phase, *Purpose*.
[11] "I hear you're going to the coast today, a little road trip?"
[12] "Yeah, in ten minutes. I'm going to pick up an old book from a dealer.
[13] "Nice. So the car's pretty empty?

Would you mind company?"

14 "That'd be great, it's a long dull drive."

15 And so to *Retreat.*

16 "Thanks. See you out front in five."

17 "Yep. See ya."

18 "Bye."

19 Very efficient, cordial, and neither of us thought it was abrupt.

20 It's all so distressingly *male* of us.

21 It's five minutes later, and I meet 'Difficult on the driveway. I've brought my camera and tripod, just in case the road offers any photo opportunities;

22 you'd be surprised what you can see from the highway. If you're not careful. *

23 My friend's smile is broad and slightly unhinged.

24 "I really appreciate this Roth! Thank you!" he beams. And, that said, he hands me a trio of heavy, multi–coloured Tupperware boxes;

25 I assume they're snacks for the journey,

26 when he offers a cheery "See you tomorrow! Safe journey!" and steps past me and into the high street, I'm puzzled.

27 Fragments of unspoken questions move my lips involuntarily for a few seconds.

28 In the distance, I hear the neurotic whinnying of a startled police horse.

29 Okay, what just happened?

30 I flop into the driver's seat of the car, still mulling this over, when a hoarse giggling draws my attention to the back.

31 As I turn, surprised, a trio of young black–and–white faces meets my gaze.

32 Hoth, a white–quiffed young badger, is the nephew of Yavin, the Clan leader and Chief Engineer of the back garden badgers.

33 He sits on the left side of the back seat, cool in beachwear. A face mask, snorkel and flippers sit on his lap.

34 He flips me a cheery salute.

35 On the right side of the seat is Sollust, Hoth's twin brother, his hair shorn into a severe, striped crewcut.

36 He's in simple dungarees, and seems to be repairing my SatNav with watchmaker's tools and a pot of treacle.

37 He glances up, his work complete, and hands me the sticky–but–repaired device with a nod.

38 Between them, in a pretty summer dress decorated with bows, is Dantoo, their younger cousin.

39 She has a bucket and spade, a small fishing net, and a spool of line and hook. I can't smell any bait, thankfully;

40 it's a long way to the coast.

41 They're seat–belted up, angelic smiles belying their mischievous intent for the day.

42 And none of them is over two feet tall.

43 I chuckle, happy to be suckered. "So, who wants to go to the seaside today?"

44 Three hands shoot up, and as many sets of bare, hairy toes wiggle enthusiastically.

45 The weighted hook from Dantoo's line swings free and embeds itself lightly in my lip to a chorus of melesian snorts.

46 I sigh and unhook myself, painfully.

47 I really must learn ask the right questions during the Purpose phase of the call. But hey,

48 at least it won't be a dull road trip.

Bumping Into Furniture

4 1 Contrary to popular writing practice, beginnings can be dull.

2 **It's Sunday afternoon,** and I'm sitting in my shady front room.

3 Outside it's a lovely day, sunshine descending from an immaculate blue sky. The garden is probably looking lovely. There may even be big fuzzy bumblebees, my insect of choice.

4 But I'm indoors, feeling shiftless and restless.

5 It's always like this after the successful conclusion of a tough assignment. All the adrenaline flushes away, and I feel rather like a half–filled helium balloon;

6 bobbing along, but bumping into furniture rather than launching skyward.

7 So for now, I'm sitting in my night attire in my favourite armchair, with a book, cellphone and TV remote in reach.

8 The TV's not on, of course;

9 as with the rest of the day, nothing appeals.

10 As is often the case with badgers, the knock is quiet.

11 I glance round as the short figure of Sollust enters the room, bringing some light with him from the hallway.

12 The young badger is sporting a fresh, crewcut hairdo and Hawaiian shorts. He hops onto the wide, flat arm of my armchair and eyeballs me curiously. I feel compelled to speak.

13 "Hi Sol, how's it going?"

14 The youth smiles happily and gives me a thumbs–up. But he raises an eyebrow

and gestures with a paw to reflect the question.

15 "Me? Oh, I'm okay," I offer blandly, "just a bit restless. Not sure what to do with myself today."

16 The lad nods sagely.

17 Leaning closer, he tugs at my lower eyelid with a gentle digit and gazes into my left eye. He makes an unsatisfied face, and pulls at my chin to open my mouth.

18 I stick my tongue out and *aaaaah* for him obediently. Again, he seems dubious.

19 Leaning in once more, he pokes my tummy. It gurgles.

20 Tut–tutting, Sollust scratches his chin, but then seems to reach a decision. Reaching back, he whips a folded piece of glossy paper from the back of his shorts and hands it to me significantly;

21 colourful photos hint at delicious treats.

22 "A pizza menu?"

23 My surgeon–for–the–day nods and takes my phone from the table. With a few taps, he pulls up the application for ordering pizza.

24 As I peruse the menu, a claw flicks and scrolls and selects, and with distressing speed he shows me the display. He's selected my usual pizza; a meaty thing with olives and double sauce.

25 How well he knows me.

26 "Oh, go on then. It might raise my spirits."

27 He grins his approval, bless him.

28 But then he frowns as he spies something on the menu. His eyebrows raise in surprise, and he points to a specific place on the paper.

29 "Buy one, get–one–free on all pizza on Sundays?"

30 He shrugs an innocent shrug; he had no idea. He's rather convincing.

31 "Do you want the same as me?"

32 The badger shakes his head and gives me a look, part surprised, part reproachful. I realise his meaning.

33 "Sorry, of course, you're vegetarian." I indicate the phone, "Please, order yourself something." He grins and hands it to me; there's already two pizzas in the basket.

34 Cheeky little sod.

35 I click to order, regretting the day I stored my credit card details on an app that makes it criminally easy to be both lazy and greedy.

36 I wonder idly how many times it's been used without me realising. Hmmm.

37 That done, Sollust hops down and fetches a book from a nearby shelf. Returning to his perch, he hands me the slim volume.

38 "*10,000 Leagues Under The Sea?*"

39 The badger nods keenly, and makes himself comfortable on my lap. I begin to read. He pays close attention to the passage that first describes Captain Nemo's *Nautilus*;

40 I have a vision of a uniformed badger in charge of a submarine.

41 We lose ourselves in the tale of the sea.

42 After what might be twenty minutes, the door is kicked open and Sollust's twin brother Hoth bustles into the room, his short arms full of pizza boxes and bottles of fizz.

43 I put the book down. How odd;

44 I didn't hear the front door.

45 The white–quiffed badger deposits his cargo onto the table and tosses me a DVD box. It's an old favourite of mine; *Tom & Jerry*. Proper ones from the 1940s, produced by *Fred Quimby*.

46 "Cool, shall we watch this now?"

47 I see from his dungaree'd behind that Hoth is already feeding the disc into the machine, and setting the TV up.

48 Sollust pours us all a drink before handing me my pizza and hopping back onto the arm of the chair with his own box.

49 As the TV blares the opening credits for the classic short cartoon *The Midnight Snack*, Hoth leaps up onto the opposite arm of the chair to his brother, and reaches into my pizza box to help himself to a meaty slice.

50 I turn to him, somewhat wearily.

51 "You're not a vegetarian like your brother, are you?"

52 The young badger shakes his head, his eyes expressing Bambi–esque innocence.

53 I'm sure I've been had.

54 But within seconds, we're all eating and laughing at the cartoon, and it doesn't seem to matter.

55 These two scamps have raised my day with their antics.

56 The beginning can be dull, but round here, the end is usually worth writing about.

Ready to open a can of worms on a brave new world?

TESTAMENT: **Funny Badgers**

The Liar

25

Indigo Roth

Ready to open a can of worms on a brave new world?

TESTAMENT:
Funny Badgers

The Liar

Indigo Roth

TESTAMENT: FUNNY BADGERS
by Indigo Roth

amazon.co.uk

amazon kindle

Paperback and eBook

Badgers

Tossing A Heavy Anchor

5 ¹ Ever woken up with a dead skunk in your bed?

² Well actually, I haven't either, but that's what I *smell* like.

³ I'm in a sleeping bag. In a tent.

⁴ I feel unwell.

⁵ Actually, it's worse than that. My head aches and my eyes are sore, judging by the effect of the sunlight seeping through the thin canvas.

⁶ Nausea pulls backflips in my stomach, and I'm drenched in sweat; this is perhaps why I smell somewhat *ripe*.

⁷ Why do I feel so grotty? I'm still half asleep, and have no idea.

⁸ What time is it?

⁹ I try to sit up, but the headroom in here is limited. As I flop back down, my senses spinning from effort, I briefly spot Yavin sitting at the other end of the tent;

¹⁰ he wisely has the door flap open.

¹¹ The badger stands and heads over, swimming into vision.

¹² Touching the brim of his tweed cap in a cheery good morning, he passes me a glass of water.

¹³ Rolling onto my side, I shuffle up onto one elbow and take a few experimental sips as he feels the back of my neck.

¹⁴ His old eyes regard me inquisitively.

¹⁵ "I'm feeling dreadful, Yavin."

¹⁶ He nods and waves a paw across his nose. "Yeah, I know, I don't smell so g..."

¹⁷ I make a sudden *gloomph* noise as a thermometer is thrust gently into my mouth. The badger shushes my attempt to talk round it.

¹⁸ Taking my wrist deftly, he starts to count, nodding each pulse as he keeps time on his magnificent wristwatch.

¹⁹ It's polished gold and steel, with a well–loved chestnut–leather strap that looks hand–stitched.

²⁰ The watch lacks any face behind its glass, and I marvel at the beautiful mechanism that it contains.

²¹ Three of the hands mark the traditional time divisions, while a fourth spins a rotation counter–clockwise every few seconds.

²² Interesting. It looks like something iDifficult would wear.

²³ The thermometer is tugged out unexpectedly while my mind is wandering. Yavin views it with the measured, unemotive gaze of a seasoned medical professional.

²⁴ "How's it all looking?" My voice is almost a whisper.

²⁵ The badger offers up an authentic medical professional's shrug, which somehow encompasses both my pulse and temperature.

²⁶ A vague upward gesture with one paw tells me that both are a little elevated;

²⁷ despite the lack of words, he still has a better bedside manner than my regular physician.

²⁸ This thought is followed by a new wave of nausea.

²⁹ I groan.

³⁰ Yavin reaches inside his dungarees and extracts a rectangle of heavy paper. With an expert flourish, it reveals itself as an airline sick bag. He offers it with a concerned look in his kind dark eyes.

³¹ I shake my head, "No, I'm fine, thanks."

³² He frowns and moves the bag a little further towards me. He raises an eyebrow, but I shake my head.

³³ "I know, I know, better out than in, right? I'll see how I go." The feeling is passing. The badger nods sagely. "So why do I feel so lousy?"

³⁴ He coughs and gestures outside before stepping out of the tent.

³⁵ Shivering, I unzip the sleeping bag and start to dress.

³⁶ **Two minutes later**, I ease my clothed form out of the tent and struggle to my feet.

³⁷ I have no idea where my shoes are.

³⁸ The great outdoors is exactly where I left it, however.

³⁹ Despite my general grottiness, I can't fail to be moved by the beautiful meadow in which we're camped.

⁴⁰ The long stretch of riverbank disappears round a long, gentle bend in either direction, and the uncut grass slopes down to the water. The blades of grass have held the dew, and are cool against my feet.

⁴¹ I'm suddenly pleased to have mislaid my shoes.

⁴² A low, flat boat is moored to a willow tree that overhangs the river.

⁴³ Memories start to seep back;

⁴⁴ we came along the river yesterday. Yes, a beautiful sunny day of fishing and relaxing on the lazy river.

⁴⁵ We stopped here at sunset because there were daisies everywhere;

⁴⁶ I love daisies.

⁴⁷ Looking about, I see Yavin rooting about in the boat. Locating something, he waves me over. I amble his way, and stop in the shade of the tree; immediately, my head and eyes feel better. I absently notice the remains of a campfire further along the flat mud of the bank. Looking back towards my short friend, I realise he's waving something at me; an empty wine bottle. Seeing he has my attention, he points at it and then at me.

⁴⁸ "No, it wasn't the wine. I opened it, but I knocked the bottle over while you were at the top of the meadow with..." I look about, suddenly puzzled. "Where's Sollust and Hoth? Are they still here?"

⁴⁹ Yavin makes an expressive gesture towards the top of the meadow, which clearly indicates that his twin nephews are off exploring somewhere, and probably up to no good. They're good lads, says his eye-rolling shrug, but kids at the end of the day.

⁵⁰ A quiet bleep from his wristwatch draws his attention for a moment. He gives it no more than a cursory glance, but I notice that the oddball fourth hand has slowed slightly.

⁵¹ He surveys the air expectantly for a moment, but then hops onto the shore carrying a canteen of water. I accept it when he offers, thanking him with a nod, and take a glug;

⁵² the water is cool and refreshing.

⁵³ As I continue to enjoy the shade, Yavin moves up the bank to the remains of the campfire. I watch as he stoops a little and pokes at the cold remnants with a dead twig.

⁵⁴ A memory drifts through my head, something to do with the fire. I can't put my finger on it, but it's making my stomach churn;

⁵⁵ I belch charmlessly.

⁵⁶ Yavin looks my way disapprovingly, but then points at something with the ash-caked stick.

⁵⁷ Wandering over, I follow the badger's pointer and see some blackened remains; is that a fish?

⁵⁸ Oh good grief, *the fish*.

⁵⁹ The bile rises in me again as I remember gutting and cooking one of the trout we'd caught during the day;

⁶⁰ Yavin had already gone to bed, and I dozed off after putting it over the fire.

When I woke, I was unsure how long the fish had been cooking, but it was black and smelled terrific, so I figured it would be okay.

⁶¹ I remember the juicy, tasty flesh, but I also recall wondering whether it was hot enough.

⁶² I stifle a wet belch, and Yavin swiftly offers the airline barf bag again. I lean over and heave a couple of times, but quash the urge to purge with a swig of water.

⁶³ I stand and gasp, beaded with sweat, but pleased that the nausea has passed.

⁶⁴ My badger amigo seems disappointed.

⁶⁵ He's probably thinking I should shift whatever it is that has upset me.

⁶⁶ He may be right.

⁶⁷ Just then, there's commotion at the top of the meadow as Hoth and Sollust rush into view.

⁶⁸ The pair leap through a five-barred wooden gate just as a bull crashes into it. The bull is vast, a towering dark red monstrosity with foaming lips. Its facial tattoos are tribal and rather unsettling.

⁶⁹ The gate holds, and the two-toned scamps slow and glance back with obvious relief. The bull roars something unintelligible at them and makes an obscene gesture with a hoof.

⁷⁰ The pair giggle at the bull's rudeness and turn towards us. Then, seeing me, they wave and start to run. This is always a nice part of any day, even when I'm feeling awful;

⁷¹ they're always pleased to see me.

⁷² My spirits are buoyed as the two young badgers crash into me excitedly, hugging my legs and dashing in a figure of eight around them repeatedly.

⁷³ Yavin coughs quietly to calm them and then indicates the tin cans that they're both carrying. The two, mindful of their uncle, untangle themselves from my legs and step before me.

⁷⁴ Hoth, easily recognisable from his white tufted quiff, passes me the can he's carrying. The green-and-orange paper label proclaims that it once contained baked beans.

⁷⁵ On closer inspection, I see it's full of leaves, roots and herbs. The young badger clearly signals that I should eat them. He grins.

⁷⁶ I look at the contents of the tin can again. Everything is washed clean; they must have collected and prepared them

further round the river.

[77] "So, this is going to help me feel better?"

[78] Hoth nods emphatically and points towards his uncle. Clearly the elder badger sent them out to forage for these supplies; I catch Yavin's eye and he nods imperceptibly.

[79] My tummy gurgles expectantly, unhappily; this sounds like a bad idea.

[80] But I start to eat all the same. Gingerly at first, but then with a more measured pace. It's not so bad. There's quite a bit of texture variation, and the flavours are fairly bland.

[81] But it's all rather dry. I cough and gag a little.

[82] Yavin offers the paper bag again, his face a vision of expectant concern. I shake my head and wave at my mouth, finally managing to croak "Dry."

[83] I expect the canteen to be passed my way again, but the badger simply nods at his second nephew.

[84] Sollust moves front and centre, his black crew cut working better than a nametag.

[85] Another tin can is raised.

[86] *Worms.* Big fat juicy ones. There's a smacking of lips from the youngster.

[87] These succulent fauna are to help me wash the dry flora down. Yum.

[88] My stomach spins, the nausea rising unstoppably this time.

[89] The sick bag wanders into vision, on cue. Yavin feigns innocence. I don't refuse his help this time. On the contrary, I grab at it.

[90] A minute later, doubled up, as I cough and spit the last of my distress into the paper bag, I feel exhausted but somewhat relieved.

[91] Yavin wanders over and pats me on the back a few times. He finally hands me a tissue and the canteen of water.

[92] I raise my head to his level and give him a weary look.

[93] Oh, that was mean of you. I heave a heavy sigh. But thank you.

[94] He smiles and touches the brim of his cap for the second time today.

[95] As I wipe and take a drink, another quick beep from his watch draws both our attention.

[96] Raising his wrist, he points to the counter–spinning fourth hand, which slows and finally stops. Unaware of its significance, I can only watch as he surveys the meadow knowingly.

[97] There is a sense of stillness. No breeze. No birdsong. Even the river seems to have stopped. Only Hoth and Sollust, now wrestling oblivious among the daisies, are immune.

[98] With a low boom that I feel more than hear, there is a curious wobble in the air, and iDifficult's pyramid materialises twenty feet away.

[99] It floats impossibly, though of course this is normal. With a clang and no ceremony, the hatch in the underside of the gold and blue edifice opens, and a hefty anchor on a chain is tossed out.

[100] From inside comes the sound of iDifficult's off–key operatic singing, and the accompanying falsetto wail of a dozen–strong ferret chorus.

[101] There is also the delicious smell of pizza;

[102] my tummy rumbles pleasantly.

[103] Yavin nudges me forward, keen for me to indulge my newfound appetite, but immediately hurries past me on his way to claim the first slice.

[104] Camping, good friends and pizza?

[105] The day is looking up.

Comfortable And Undemanding

6

[1] Sometimes things don't go to plan.

[2] I'm dreaming.

[3] **It's Sunday**. Instead of doing Sunday things like most folk, I head to the office to finish off some work that needs putting to bed. I work a thirteen hour day, punctuated by sandwiches, tea, and cake, and after leaving a note to say I'll be in late, I head home around ten thirty.

[4] My dreams are getting *way* too literal.

[5] The drilling saves me from re–living the cold drive home.

[6] In fact, the drilling is shaking the bed.

[7] **Back in the now**, I crack my eyes— they're really not ready to open—and take a few moments to introduce the curtained room into Monday's reality.

[8] My room. My bed. My juddering teeth as the drilling restarts.

[9] A glance at the clock tells me it's a respectable hour, but earlier than I would have liked; eight–thirty in the morning.

[10] There's a quiet knocking at the door. I open my mouth to respond, but manage little more than a cough.

[11] Still, it's enough.

12 Yavin enters the room, bearing a heavily–laden tray. The badger is in his usual engineering dungarees and flat cap, his pipe and tobacco tin poking from opposing breast pockets.

13 He approaches the bed and nods a good morning.

14 "Hey Yavin, good morning." I exercise my slow jaw from side to side, and am rewarded with a reluctant crack. I cough again absently. "What on earth is that drilling?"

15 Ignoring my question for the time being, the badger proffers the tray, and my slow early–morning senses are assailed by the delicious smell of fried food.

16 "Good grief, is that breakfast?"

17 No reply is forthcoming; clearly I'm being rhetorical.

18 The tray is seriously loaded: a plate of bacon, scrambled eggs, sausages, mushrooms and beans; a rack of granary toast with butter, jam and marmalade; and a pot of tea.

19 Ooh, and a tiny ramekin of ketchup.

20 My tummy rumbles. Yavin's coarse facial fur rearranges into a smile.

21 "Wow, this looks amazing. Thank you. But why?" The diminutive engineer is remarkably expressive most of the time, but not when both of his paws are busy. "It this a karmic thing? Was I kind to badgers in a previous life?"

22 This comment receives no reply as outside, the drilling restarts.

23 Yavin glares sideways at the mostly–closed curtains and the street beyond. With a deft flick of stray digits, legs extend from the sides of the tray, and he deposits it carefully onto my lap; he has to stand on tip–toes to do this.

24 That done, he turns his attention to the juddering without.

25 "Thank you." Strolling over to the curtains, the badger casts them wide with a flourish and surveys the street scene below. "Workmen?"

26 Yavin wrinkles his nose with distaste and nods. He has a keen distinction between skilled engineers and *labourers*.

27 "Three of them? One drilling, one doing nothing, and one with a clipboard who looks important but who's also doing nothing?"

28 This is just a guess, based on years of observing road crews, it but receives another nod and a heaved sigh.

29 I tuck into the breakfast, menacing a sausage first and moving onto the bacon and a generous shovel of beans. Toast is dipped in bean juice, and tea is slurped.

30 It really is amazing; just the right temperature, bursting with flavour and— best of all—made by someone else.

31 Though I still have no idea why.

32 "So, how come I get breakfast today?"

33 I realise that Yavin is no longer in the room. I've just reached the halfway point of my plateful, and the drilling has faded into the background of my attention.

34 I cast my eyes about, and bizarrely wonder if the badger is under the bed, before recommencing my feast;

35 the mushrooms are particularly good.

36 A moment later, as I'm pouring myself a cup of tea, Yavin wanders back in with a newspaper under his arm. Quietly padding round the bed to the empty side, he hops up, makes himself at home in the mound of pillows and settles down to read.

37 This familiarity is comfortable and undemanding; the company of friends always is.

38 The pneumatic excavation thunders into fresh life.

39 I'm just about to enquire about breakfast again, when both the drilling and my chewing are halted by a high–pitched chittering roar from outside. A shiver passes down my spine;

40 I know the sound all too well.

41 My stunned silence follows, abruptly ended by a second outburst, the clatter of dropped tools and some unmanly screaming.

42 Yavin changes page behind his paper, apparently unmoved.

43 "Hey Yavin, was that the Squiddrel?" I move to get up, but a friendly paw pats my hand and gently stays my exit from the bed. "Yavin, I should go and see; I thought we'd caught it. I can't believe it."

44 Several months ago, I spent a terrifying and enlightening day with iDifficult tracking his giant hybrid squid/squirrel down, across park and town. Though, to be honest, most of the time it was close on our heels making that terrifying noise; it didn't care for our inept attempts at capture.

45 It was a character building experience, though we required some serious laundering afterwards.

46 A minute of internal turmoil passes.

⁴⁷ The breakfast cools slowly.

⁴⁸ I'm brought back to my senses by heavy animal footsteps making their way quickly upstairs.

⁴⁹ And then I hear the roar again from the landing; it's deafening. Stirred into action, I lift the tray and move it aside, placing it in front of the stoic badger.

⁵⁰ Just as I'm about to put a foot into a slipper, the bedroom door crashes aside, and I'm faced by the terrifying visage of the mighty red Squiddrel.

⁵¹ I stifle a cry** and retreat back onto the bed.

⁵² The faceful of wet, suckered tentacles extends in my direction and the creature's wet maw opens to scream its rage on cue.

⁵³ Though actually, framed in the doorway, the beast is smaller than I remember;

⁵⁴ it's barely five feet tall, in fact.

⁵⁵ And I'm puzzled to see that it's carrying a clipboard and a length of pneumatic hose.

⁵⁶ Time goes glacial for an endless, surreal second.

⁵⁷ Then, with a giggle, the top falls off the red–furred beast. Black–and–white legs wiggle comically from the up–ended torso, and a young badger face peeps out from inside the legs.

⁵⁸ In my peripheral vision, I spy that Yavin's newspaper is shaking up and down with some voiceless mirth.

⁵⁹ "Hoth! Sollust!" I laugh, relieved, at Yavin's twin nephews, "You guys scared me to death!"

⁶⁰ Young Sollust grins impishly over the bottom half of this pantomime costume, and offers up a salute;

⁶¹ he's the image of a sub–mariner poking out from a conning tower.

⁶² He also looks tired, but I guess he's been running around with his brother on his shoulders for the past few minutes.

⁶³ Hoth waves from inside the head with a pink tentacle; he seems in no hurry to leave his costume. And to make the point, he roars in his own badger voice and starts to chase Sollust round the bedroom.

⁶⁴ They collide at the foot of the bed and collapse into a tussling, growling heap.

⁶⁵ I settle back to continue my breakfast.

⁶⁶ As I replace the tray on my lap, I notice that my teacup is empty. And there's the sound of toast being munched upon behind the newspaper.

⁶⁷ "Yavin?"

⁶⁸ The paper drops and wise old eyes gaze back at me.

⁶⁹ "I've been working really hard of late. Starting early and coming back late. I'm finished now. I made the deadline." He nods his understanding. "This breakfast was just what I needed, and very kind. Thank you. But why...?"

⁷⁰ He smiles indulgently, and I realise that I've answered my own question.

⁷¹ "Guys?" Two curious snouts rise about the footboard. "Thanks for sorting the drilling crew out."

⁷² They wave the captured clipboard and hose, and roar at each other between their giggles. The uncostumed twins then hoist themselves onto the bed and set about the remains of my breakfast.

⁷³ I sip at a cup of tea and smile.

⁷⁴ Sometimes things don't go to plan.

⁷⁵ Sometimes other people's plans trample on your own plans.

⁷⁶ But sometimes, other people's plans are perfect.

A Classy Signature Hit

7¹ I'm pinned down behind a burned–out car as the hail of projectiles strike all around me.

² Scones.

³ Dozens of them, a seemingly endless supply. They shatter and spray their sweet filling as they hit the concrete on all sides. There's no way I can move without taking a hit, and my ammo is desperately low.

⁴ The pastry sniper is almost certainly Hoth, one of the young badgers. This calculated mayhem has his name written all over it. He's got good elevation and coverage, and plenty of baked ammunition.

⁵ Though I've no idea who's putting the jam and cream in the scones for him.

⁶ If he connects with me, it'll be a messy and classy signature hit.

⁷ But it's probably a diversion, so that his brother Sollust can outflank me.

⁸ I check left and right, and sure enough catch sight of a short, black–and–white blur twenty yards away. Moving closer behind cover, biding his time.

⁹ He favours a well–aimed cluster of choux–bun grenades, and has the skills to deliver them.

¹⁰ I shake my head. Kids.

11 This post–apocalyptic wasteland, complete with a burning sky and smouldering ruins, is the centrepiece of iDifficult's latest videogame creation, *PieSplitters*.

12 My best friend's creation is poised to take the virtual reality world by storm.

13 We're testing his masterpiece level, with an awesome *all–confection* weapon set.

14 There's not many of us left.

15 Bear is tactically brilliant, but found his lack of mobility a problem. He was taken out by a volley of meringues at long range. I suspect it was 'Difficult, at an unfair advantage.

16 Yavin took to the sewers and engaged in guerrilla warfare, taking out King and Abbey with custard pies at short range, before falling foul of his scone–sniper nephew a few minutes ago.

17 The scone attack begins again, splat after sweet–jammy splat. I suspect that at any moment it'll just be the twin badgers and 'Difficult left in play;

18 *Game Over, Indigo.*

19 But wait. What's that?

20 I hear the colossal boom and then the slow whistling descent.

21 Good grief, someone's found a trifle mortar! There's a distant wet noise, and the scones halt suddenly;

22 somewhere up there, there's an angry young badger covered in custard, jelly, cream and sprinkles.

23 My tummy rumbles.

24 Did I just catch a break?

25 No, the diminutive form of Sollust breaks cover. He hefts the first of many choux–buns from his kitbag, determined to finish what his brother started.

26 He advances quickly, skilfully dodging between the ruined outcrops to close on my position.

27 Dammit. This could be it.

28 Until the charging, monochrome lad carelessly trips the proximity detonator on an industrial blancmange.

29 Pink. Everywhere.

30 It isn't pretty.

31 I seize my chance, breaking away from the car and hurtling towards what I hope will be good cover for the final showdown.

32 In seconds, I'm crouched behind a low wall, armed with a final lemon meringue pie that I'm saving for 'Difficult.

33 But I've lost track of my mad friend;

34 I wonder where he is?

35 The red laser targeting dots of an éclair bazooka converge on my chest armour.

36 This could get messy.

Putting Vertigo To Rest

8 1 Sometimes things get back to front.

2 For example, take me and vertigo. Most sufferers get dizzy and queasy looking down from a high place; from the roof of a building, from a bridge, or from a stack of my visa bills.

3 But me? I feel just as unsettled standing close to the base of something tall, and looking up.

4 For example, I remember the first time I went on the Humber Bridge in England; I'm interested in architecture, and walked its impressive length, but when I stopped at one of the uprights and looked up, I felt dizzy and fell over.

5 But perhaps this is as it should be; vertigo is Latin for "dizziness", not "fear of heights". Actually, I've always thought of it as an inability to cope with spatial distances; up, down, across, whatever.

6 Or being a numpty.

7 One or the other, certainly.

8 But I'm flexible; I'm not crazy about looking down, either. The less said about my visit to the roof of the cathedral in York, the better;

9 just be glad you weren't there. Unless you had an umbrella.

10 By comparison, hanging clumsily from the branches of the big old oak tree in my back garden is easy; it's only ten or twelve feet to the ground.

11 Yavin is just above me, smoking his pipe contentedly, comfortably nested where one branch separates into two; this makes a nice seat for him.

12 He can't help me up to a more secure position. Well, not without a block and tackle, and we forgot to bring those when we scurried up the tree.

13 The ground's really not that far, and I could make it easily.

14 However, the prowling Squiddrel below is giving me pause for thought.

15 This vast creature, a genetic hybrid of red squirrel and colossal squid, is notoriously hungry and loves to *play* with its food. The beast paces in circles, chittering and slavering, paying me an occasional meaningful look.

¹⁶ You know, just in case I somehow *forget* it's there.

¹⁷ So yes, I do feel a little queasy looking down, and it would be simple enough for me to drop to the ground and put this vertigo to rest.

¹⁸ But I think I'll hold on a little longer.

Notes

*   With all due deference to Flanders and Swann.

**   A manly cry, a shout of surprise. Obviously.

2 Roth

*"But like a three–ton great white shark, we must move forward
and eat the surfers in a frenzy of blood and teeth. No, wait.
That should be 'move forward or drown'."*

For Today I Am The Dog

1 ¹ When I recount my bruised and battered memories of playing American Football* at university, people seem surprised.

² *"You,* Indigo?" say folk, astonished, "You were a *varsity athlete?"*

³ Hey baby, you better believe it.

⁴ Ready for a flashback?

⁵ **It's 1990**, and I'm in my final year of University in England.

⁶ More specifically, **it's Sunday morning**, and time to haul my sorry butt out of bed.

⁷ It's early, and I ache. In the mirror, I note that I'm a bit black and blue;

⁸ I recently started playing American Football for my alma mater, and even though we've had just a dozen practices and three games, it's taking its toll.

⁹ My new sporting life has come as a surprise to everyone, myself included;

¹⁰ I've never played any kind of team sport in my life. Or shown much inclination, even. I certainly would never have imagined playing on a first team for my university.

¹¹ I use the term *first team* loosely, as there *is* only one team. In fact, barely two thirds of one.

¹² Seventeen or eighteen of us on a good day, when thirty five or forty even would

have been better. This divides in two, with half of the players playing on the Offence, and half on the Defence.

¹³ Two specialised groups of players.

¹⁴ Our lack of bodies means many of us play on both Offence and Defence out of necessity.

¹⁵ Extra lumps? Oh my, yes.

¹⁶ It's our team's rookie year in the UK's university football league. We have just four games scheduled, and today is our final game; I'd best get moving.

¹⁷ Twenty minutes later, after some hasty breakfast and an equally hasty jog across campus, I join my team mates at the pickup point by the main gate.

¹⁸ They look worse than me.

¹⁹ The first three games could have been pretty demoralising, with a couple of low scorers and a total whitewash, but we're pretty upbeat about it.

²⁰ I'd hesitate to call us a bunch of jocks, but there's a lot of low humour, banter and male bonding going on as we board the bus and hit the highway.

²¹ I've been looking forward to this game. I've carried a dislike of the university we're travelling to for some time. A former girlfriend went there, and I never enjoyed my visits; the campus, the people, the attitude.

²² As a sporting university, they love to

tell you how great they are.

23 This trip feels like a chance to get something out of my system.

24 And as we leave the highway and hit the outskirts of town, something happens to me. It might sound melodramatic to say that a red mist descends on me, but that's as good a description as any.

25 My mood darkens, I fall silent, banter bounces off me. I gaze out of the window.

26 Something is up.

27 The warm-up session and the practice on the field does nothing to lift my spirits.

28 As is often the case when I'm not cheery, I feel like there is a large black dog with me. Today I sense his brooding presence sitting by the sideline.

29 Their team takes the field with predictable swagger; *real* jocks, not like us at all. Talented, strong, fast, and arrogant. They've seen the results of our first three games, and expect this to be a walkover.

30 They're here to clean our clocks in the worst way.

31 And that's how it begins.

32 The first quarter sees us taking a pasting, with some easy scores on the board for them. We can't quite get it together, we need to focus.

33 The playbook is blurry in my mind, and I'm taking cues from the guy beside me on most plays.

34 And the other team are engaging in a spot of unnecessary roughness and laughing a lot.

35 Our first three opponents had been up for some sport, but these guys want blood.

36 They can win easily, but it's not enough. It doesn't sit well with me, and I'm not alone.

37 Enough is enough.

38 There is a lot of muttering and pointing as the game kicks into the second quarter. One guy on their defensive line is mouthing off a lot. Our quarterback calls the play, but as the huddle breaks three of us say his number.

39 The play goes right, we go left.

40 All three of us.

41 The defender falls heavily, we pile on top, and some licks are taken under the pile.

42 We pick up a penalty, but he gets picked up and carried from the field.

43 The referee eyes us sternly and we get an off-record warning, but the game continues.

44 And we start to get some respect. A few of their plays go sour, and their strategy changes a little;

45 they're adapting, improvising, but we keep slowing them down.

46 The rout they expected against our tiny, insignificant team is not happening.

47 We defend, we block, we fight back. And as we march back down the field on the offensive, we even get three points on the board.

48 In the second half, we're still losing and there's little hope of a turnaround, but it's a different game and we are a different team.

49 We are not losing gracefully.

50 There is no ground given without effort, no concession by us to our inexperience, no easy way to run past us.

51 We're losing, but *damn*, they're working for it.

52 And I'm a totally different player.

53 I've struggled all season to find the channelled aggression needed to play this game well, but suddenly it is there.

54 The dog no longer paces the sidelines;

55 today I *am* the dog.

56 I have no trouble unleashing my anger on these guys who want nothing more than to hurt and humiliate us.

57 The war rages on, the clock runs down, and the game is over.

58 We've lost by twenty-eight points, but this is not the result they came here for. They wanted sixty, something to cheer about in the bar afterwards.

59 Before we leave the pitch, two lines are formed, and we file past their team shaking hands.

60 This is an odd process that ends every game, with every man shaking the hands of every man on the opposing team.

61 It's very sporting, and I like it.

62 But today we see their eyes cast down, their annoyance, and perhaps even receive a few genuine congratulations.

63 As we head back to the changing rooms, we hear their coach say

64 "Hey, never mind lads, at least we WON!" but I suspect it's of little consolation to his team.

65 We hit the bus in high spirits, our season over.

[66] My time at university is almost over, too. Some of us will play again next year, but many of us won't.

[67] The team may even win a game at some point; I hope the road to that first victory started today.

[68] I've no idea where the dog went, but he can find his own way home.

[69] And yes, home awaits. There will be no heroes' welcome for us, but we're heroes nonetheless.

Paper Towels And Assurances

2 [1] I'm not a lover of clumsiness.
[2] Clumsiness is lazy, avoidable, and a poor indication of character.

[3] The receipt for my coffee (no cake) sits next to the cup on its saucer, annoying me;

[4] it's visual clutter, simple as that.

[5] I'm trying to grab some downtime in a coffee shop, resting my back and brain on a long shopping jag. I don't need the slip of printed paper, and

[6] as I gather the sugar wrapper and wooden stirrer to tidy the tray, I whip it from the saucer.

[7] And discover that it's actually *between* the cup and saucer.

[8] The coffee spills, an avant–garde fusion of Jackson Pollock and Hokusai's *The Great Wave Off Kanagawa*;

[9] its reach is impressive.

[10] I stand and curse—my distaste for my own idiocy breaking the surface—and lean on the table so that the pool of espresso backs unpleasantly down my legs.

[11] Cursing further, I let the table go, and it tips noisily the other way and crashes to the floor;

[12] the cup and its handle part company, and agree noisily to never speak again to their estranged and shattered saucer.

[13] All eyes turn to stare dispassionately; *both clumsy and embarrassing* say the stares.

[14] A lady staff member bustles over impressively, bristling with paper towels and assurances about an imminent mop.

[15] I help her retrieve the table and she fusses around me, cleaning up the worst, reassuringly refusing my apology, and barking for a fresh coffee (no cake) on the house.

[16] The mop arrives in the hands of a listless male, and she acknowledges him with an eye–contact–less nod before dispatching him for my coffee.

[17] His retreating feet are the shambling demise of civilisation.

[18] But in less than thirty seconds from my initial spillage, everything is as it was; the table clean and dry, the floor free of puddles.

[19] The same lady places the fresh brew on the table as a potted fern eyes me suspiciously.

[20] She meets my eye with a broad and genuine smile, and hopes I enjoy my replacement, "no apology necessary Sir, no bother Sir."

[21] This service is delightful, unexpected, and frankly a relief.

[22] I lower myself into my chair gratefully, and heave a sigh as I contemplate my reward.

[23] I absently wish I'd ordered some cake to go with my coffee (no cake).

[24] And I lean slightly on the table, so that the coffee lurches into my lap, a ninth wave of scalding torment.

[25] I stand abruptly with a small hissing scream; I don't much fancy the table's chances.

[26] Somewhere in the distance, a mop sighs resignedly.

[27] I'm not a lover of clumsiness.

[28] But as a clumsy person, I should probably get used to it.

In a Variety Of Languages

3 [1] Cows are good for the soul.
[2] I find that, after a trying morning in the office, some fresh air in Cambridge is a good way to clear my head.

[3] I leave the building and quickly get down to the river. In minutes I'm walking happily across *Midsummer Common,* accompanied only by the free–roaming cattle.

[4] They're gentle creatures, and I can almost feel my blood pressure dropping as we stroll together.

[5] There's not that many of them, by they seem to gravitate towards me. Perhaps I look like a sucker, a kind fella who'll give them some kind of tasty snack?

[6] Or maybe they see me as some kind of bull–headed kindred spirit?

[7] I no more know that than I know who owns them. I assume it's a local farmer, exercising his right to use common land for grazing cattle, but I'm really not certain.

[8] It's possible they're not owned by anyone but themselves.

[9] In fact, they're an enigmatic bunch. Perhaps they're nomadic cattle, late of the Serengeti, electing to eke out their bovine existence on the windswept plains of Eastern England?

[10] They probably moved in when nobody was looking, and let everyone assume that, as cattle, they must be someone else's property. And problem.

[11] I try to engage them in conversation in a variety of languages, but they refuse to acknowledge me or answer my simplest questions.

[12] So I can't be sure.

[13] But as I turn to head back to the office, I think I hear one of them talking on a cellphone in Russian.

[14] And I can't find my wallet.

I Don't Think I Nailed It

4[1] Sometimes you just have to go with a recommendation.

[2] As I step from the cobbled side–street into the musty shop, I wonder if I've been given bad information.

[3] The place looks tatty.

[4] Distressed wooden panelling gazes indifferently past stacks of yellowing paper, while dusty sunbeams pick at the threadbare green carpet.

[5] A forgotten tale of spiders is written in the webs at the high corners of the room.

[6] It's not *Savile Row*, that's for sure.

[7] The future orbits gently on a turn of my heel. But before I can retreat, an elderly Jewish tailor steps from a stock room behind the counter. My instincts tell me that this evaluation is stereotypical or clichéd, but I don't choose this reality; he is what he is. A dark skullcap, a thin beard and round spectacles, and a tape measure draped around the shoulders of his chalk–marked waistcoat.

[8] The Tailor regards me with polite intensity for a moment.

[9] "Good afternoon, Sir," he smiles, "Ill be with you in just one moment."

[10] And that said, he steps back into the stock room and out of sight.

[11] I'm taken aback by this abruptness, but take a few even breaths and let it go;

[12] it's possible I'm feeling a bit tired and impatient today.

[13] I look about the place, hoping to see new details and subtleties that will soften my harsh first impressions.

[14] No, nothing.

[15] And then I hear a sewing machine strike up its rhythm in the back room. I glance at the door and once again wonder about leaving. But the old man returns to view as the sewing machine continues; there must be someone else back there.

[16] He places a neat stack of items onto the counter before stepping out to serve me. I note that he's quite a bit shorter than me.

[17] "Right Sir," he says without apology, wielding the tape measure, "perhaps you might like to tell me your thoughts."

[18] "A business suit," I state simply, though I doubt he sells casual ones. "Something in a dark navy blue." His face is neutral, and I feel more explanation is necessary. "I know what I like."

[19] "I see, Sir. Double–breasted, Sir?" asks the short figure as he manoeuvres around me, moving both my limbs and the tape measure expertly. I grunt an affirmative as he measures my inside leg.

[20] We continue in this vein, back and forth.

[21] "Will you be needing a waistcoat, Sir?"

[22] "Yes, same navy blue as the suit."

[23] "Belt or braces, Sir?"

[24] "Braces. I'm not the shape I once was."

[25] "Perhaps a slightly higher waist, Sir?"

[26] "Yes, exactly. Same reason."

[27] "Inside pockets, Sir?"

[28] "Just one, on the left, as close to the armpit as possible."

[29] "Colour of the lining, Sir?"

[30] "Blue, but lighter than the navy."

[31] "Turn–ups on the trousers, Sir?"

[32] "Coin–catchers? I'm not sure. No."

[33] As we finish, the distant sewing machine stops. Seconds later, a gangling youth in a pinstripe waistcoat steps from the back room and deposits another item of clothing onto the pile at the counter.

[34] The Tailor turns and nods, before waving the lad out of sight again.

[35] The old man returns his attention to me, raising a gnarled finger.

[36] "I have exactly what you want, Sir!" he enthuses, heading back to the counter. "Step right this way." I follow, admitting to myself that I'm impressed by his thoroughness,

[37] and the fact that he didn't write a

single measurement down.

[38] He indicates the clothes on the counter. "Here you are."

[39] Right. Wait. What?

[40] "I don't understand. We've only just measured me up."

[41] "Yes, Sir," he shrugs with a hint of self–deprecation, "I was confirming the measurements I noted when you came in. My nephew has already made a minor change to the venting on the waistline of the trousers that's needed."

[42] I don't know whether to be angry or in awe. I settle for flabbergasted.

[43] "In this light, it looks more black than navy blue."

[44] He nods his head. "The suit is black, Sir."

[45] "It's curious," I observe, scratching my nose, as much for irritated effect as to salve an itch, "but I imagined I would come along, get measured up, tell you exactly what I wanted, and you'd sort me out."

[46] "Well, of course, we've done all those things Sir," he says smoothly, reassuringly. I hesitate.

[47] "Well, I suppose we have. I just figured I would be in the chair, so to speak."

[48] I fumble for a rationale that sounds assertive but not petulant.

[49] "You know, that I'd be *The Customer*. The one who's *Always Right*." My voice tails off; I don't think I nailed it.

[50] His eyes exude kindness.

[51] "I have always considered it my duty as a tailor," he begins, with genuine humility in his voice, "to provide the customer with something that they have not yet realised that they want. And this suit is one of my very best, Sir."

[52] And he proudly raises the suit from the counter for my inspection.

[53] "Three pieces. Finely woven black wool. Double breasted."

[54] Without fanfare or flourish, he slips a crisp, white, double–cuffed twill shirt and a striking three–shade gold necktie next to it.

[55] "I'll give you a moment to change, Sir," he says, seeing my eyes glitter. He points towards the changing room and stops. "Oh, you'll need these." He hands me a pair of gold cufflinks.

[56] In the space of two minutes, I'm in the new suit. I've double–Windsor knotted the necktie, and I'm slipping in the cufflinks. The Tailor appears again as I check myself out in a full length mirror.

[57] "Sold," I say, decisively. I try to suppress my goofy smile.

[58] As suits go, it's pretty tasty.

[59] Without a word, the elderly craftsman gathers my discarded clothes up. A moment later, back at the counter, he neatly folds them into a bag as I settle up the account.

[60] "I have to ask," I say quietly. "but are you a metaphor for my resistance to a new approach in my ongoing mental healthcare? And my dogged insistence on what I believe to be the correct course of treatment?"

[61] He seems to consider this for a moment.

[62] A dog does not bark in the distance. But it's one of those moments.

[63] "No Sir, he smiles, "I'm an elderly Jewish tailor. Remember?"

[64] Oh yes.

[65] "Well, thank you. It's perfect."

[66] "No Sir, thank you." He gives me a easy salute. "Until next time."

[67] We shake hands, and seconds later I step back into the world a smarter, happier man.

[68] And I didn't even realise that's what I wanted.

Behind Me As Ever

5[1] I am alone in the dark.

[2] My first instinct whenever I wake is to check the blinds to try and guess the time, but today I can't move my head.

[3] Or, as it turns out, my body.

[4] As I'm wondering if this absolute darkness is a dream, it dawns upon my sleepy senses that I'm vertical, twisted, and immobile.

[5] Immobile? I wiggle my fingers slightly. Okay, I'm not immobile, but physically restricted from moving. This starts as a relief, but quickly shifts into a new and unpleasant train of thought.

[6] What I assumed to be a cool pillow is actually a solid textured surface. My back, behind me as ever, is also pressed against something that's cold, hard and slightly damp.

[7] There's also an unpleasant smell.

[8] This can't be good.

[9] Neither is the fact that I seem to be largely naked. Aside from my underpants chafing out of reach at my

waist, I think I'm *au naturel*. It's hard to be sure, as there's some cramping in my thighs, and I can't feel my feet.

10 Cold, naked, trapped, and in the dark.

11 Panic starts to rise in me. But I know the signs, and head them off at the pass.

12 Get a grip, Indigo. I take a series of long, shallow breaths. In. Out. In. And Out. Miraculously, lost in this respiratory exercise, my heart slows.

13 Calm returns. That's better.

14 I chuckle. This could be worse. I could be underground.

15 Oh good grief, am I *underground?!*

16 *Panic*, the first Horseman Of My Personal Apocalypse roars gleefully as he rides through me, shredding my nerves. His brothers *Fear*, *Paranoia* and *Mum–Said–I'd–Go–Blind* are close behind, mopping up any stragglers.

17 I have terrible claustrophobia, and always have. And now, perhaps as Karmic punishment for doing something weird in a previous week, I'm buried alive!

18 Deep beneath the earth, cold and wet and lost, never to see the light of day again!

19 I start to thrash, feebly at first, and find nothing but the close brush of walls of my confinement to meet my shoulders, knees and hips.

20 I stretch my neck upwards, and thump my head on a chilly ceiling. No way out!

21 Have I worked by way up a pothole, shredding my clothes on unyielding rock, in a desperate attempt to reach the surface, only to find a dead end, with no way back?!

22 My thrashing becomes more frenzied, I rock and twist and finally feel some movement in my feet.

23 Spurred on by this, my heart racing, I force my knees outwards and shuffle my tingling feet apart. Something seems to give when I do this, there even seems to be the tiniest crack of light!

24 I'm breaking through!

25 With a roar of effort I shove my elbows out in a final desperate bid for freedom.

26 The refrigerator door opens.

27 And the light comes on.

28 I tumble from the frigid appliance into the humid early morning of my kitchen, and lay coughing, gasping and stretching on the floor.

29 As fire rages through my cramping limbs, I vaguely register the food, drink and metal racking shelves that are scattered all around me.

30 I sigh in relief and resignation.

31 It's no good.

32 I have to get air conditioning in my bedroom.

The Music Of The Spheres

6 1 I awake from a dream of aardvarks.

2 And there is music.

3 Checking the clock, I see **it's the wee hours of this morning.**

4 I'm puzzled; I live in a semi–detached house** and occasionally hear the neighbours. But they have kids, and so after early evening I rarely hear a peep out of them.

5 I dismiss the tune as a hangover from my dream, expecting it to clear in a few moments. And, flipping over, I try to get back to sleep.

6 But still, there's music. A steady slow beat, some rhythm on top, and a faint, dreamy melody.

7 I sit up in bed, half–awake at best.

8 Where on Earth is it coming from?

9 The music must be rather loud, because I wear very efficient earplugs in bed; I live on a busy road and it gets lively with traffic and party–goers heading home at the weekend.

10 But I can see that the window is closed. And besides, I have a fairly noisy fan on in the room too.

11 I try to fish my earplugs out, but they're too deep in my ear to snag, and I'm in no mood to search for tweezers.

12 I get out of bed and look out of the window; there's nothing in the street.

13 I open the window and crane my neck round to look at the neighbour's place; dark and dead. And, both up and down the street, there's no evidence of a party.

14 I shut the window and head back to bed, none the wiser.

15 **A few minutes later**, the music is fainter, but I can't settle enough to find sleep again.

16 I toss and turn in bed, ending up with my hand on my chest. And suddenly, I realise that my heartbeat is in time with the beat of the music.

17 A curious coincidence?

18 My beats count out a minute, and I'm still in perfect time with the music.

19 An odd idea grips me, some vague memory of a physics lesson at school.

Something to do with beats occurring when two different frequencies are played against each other?

20 I get out of bed, and switch the fan off. The rhythm ceases immediately, and after a few seconds the melody dies.

21 Just the steady beat of my heart remains.

22 I switch the fan back on, and the music starts again.

23 And it all falls into place.

24 The entrenched earplugs are amplifying the sound of my heart to provide the bass. The interference thrumming from the fan causes the rhythm on top of it.

25 And, hearing something resembling music, my sleepy brain unconsciously adds a simple melody on top.

26 Organic and mechanical sounds, and a bit of help from my subconscious mind as it attempts to impose order on chaos.

27 Something emergent.

28 Music from thin air.

29 I find a scrap of paper and scribble *Music of the Spheres* on it.

30 **A minute later**, sleep finds me.

31 And that's as simple a way as I can tell the tale.

Whatever, Dude

7 1 When pizza is delivered, my heart always races.

2 Look, I'm a simple guy, with simple tastes; don't judge me.

3 The knocking on the door this morning is no exception; it's a little early for takeout, but the badgers have pulled an all–nighter fixing the Time Pyramid, and 'Difficult offered to order out for some well–deserved circular brunch.

4 My pulse gallops as I stroll to the door to pay. Yes, I'm paying;

5 when I said 'Difficult offered to buy brunch, what I meant is that he had left his wallet at home, and *would I mind awfully?*

6 The dim light of the hallway blinks and yawns as I open the front door.

7 It's cold out, the trees are frosty and there's steel in the air, but other than his creased slacks, the scruffy delivery guy on the doorstep faces the elements in just the dusty, sauce–dabbed shirt of his work uniform.

8 Though right now, the stack of pizzas and the bags of bottled fizz are obscuring that slightly.

9 "Pizza," he sniffs, flicking his hair away from his piercings. I take the drinks from him, and then the stack of hot boxes, depositing them on the floor.

10 The smell is intoxicating; I detect meat, chili, mushroom, lots of sauce, and an absence of onions;

11 my mouth waters.

12 "Thanks," I smile, distracted. His expression does not change.

13 "Fifty–four eighty," he mumbles, with no concession to manners or interest, his hands creeping to his pockets.

14 He looks past me, mildly curious perhaps, but most likely just bored with this exchange.

15 I drag some notes from my wallet and smile at him, attempting to get a meaningful engagement from this *yoof*. "Here's sixty, keep the change."

16 He eyes flick to me, mild surprise registering.

17 "Cheers," he grunts, and the money vanishes into an unspeakable pocket.

18 "I wouldn't mind so much, but these aren't for me," I grin, pushing ahead recklessly in the face of world–class indifference.

19 "Huh?" he grunts, his brain telling him to turn to leave, but then yanking him back; customer engagement is clearly throwing his game off.

20 "These are for a friend." He sneers a little at this, but doesn't reply. "And for the badgers." This raises an eyebrow. "I can't have any, I'm dieting."

21 "Whatever, dude," he sighs, his brain finally giving up. He turns and shuffles back towards his rust–bucket of a car;

22 his retreating feet are the shambolic decline of nations.

23 I close the door, frowning, and wrestle once more with the heavenly scent in the hallway. Man, it smells fantastic;

24 my stomach gurgles pointlessly.

25 When pizza is delivered, my heart always races.

26 Even if all I have to do is pay.

Making A Break For Venezuela

8 1 When we were kids, everything was in black and white.

2 We never questioned it; we didn't know any better.

3 I'm standing with my best friend iDifficult in the office of Horace Bristle, the headmaster at our boarding school. The old boy is blustering wonderfully as

he reads the thick report at his desk.

[4] It seems we're in trouble. We're twelve years old.

[5] Mr. Bristle drops the report and looks our way. "Mister Roth. And Mister Difficult." He almost spits our titles; it's part of the bluster. "I suppose you know why you're here?"

[6] "Sir?" we say in unison, summoning all the innocence we can into our voices. I find this quite easy; I'm not aware of having done anything wrong at this point. Well, anything specific.

[7] "I've been hearing reports," he indicates the paperwork, "about more odd goings on." Horace fixes us with his best steely glare. His left eye tics, which ruins the effect somewhat. "And I know you two are at the bottom of it."

[8] The headmaster has no idea that he's an anachronism. A cliché. Not that he'd understand the words. He comes from an education system that's based on thrashings. And rugger. And tuckshops. And midnight feasts, of course, but we still have those. It's food, after all.

[9] He's never heard of pastoral care, innocent–til–proven–guilty, or any kind of sex education.

[10] I arrange my face into blank and polite interest. I notice that 'Difficult is doing the same, but that he looks less comfortable;

[11] I think he's carrying his ferret in his britches again.

[12] "When I was your age..."

[13] The headmaster launches into a tirade about responsibility, school values, moral fibre and back–in–my–day, but we're not listening. Curious, I tilt my head slightly and try to read the top paper in front of the headmaster. I glimpse a few words as Old Horace rants away:

[14] a vat of apple sauce... Peruvian passports... squid in a barrel... monster trucks... gold lamé wetsuits... and lard.

[15] Oh. *Sunday*.

[16] I smile. Now *there* was a day truly conquered.

[17] A cough from 'Difficult brings my attention back to our accuser. The Headmaster has obviously finished, and is awaiting a response. His complexion is darkening;

[18] our silence is infuriating to him.

[19] "Well?!" he bellows, thrashing his cane onto the table. "What do you have

to *say* for yourselves?"

[20] As we ponder our reply, the old teacher heaves a sigh.

[21] *I despise these two boys,* I imagine his internal voice saying.

[22] *They're never broken a school rule,* it continues, *but usually only because what they've done is so bizarre there isn't a rule for it.*

[23] *They've never done anything that's led to injury.* The curmudgeon in him grumbles that this is nothing but luck, but deep down he suspects that it's something to do with meticulous planning and daredevil execution;

[24] people who can do that tend to make their own luck.

[25] *Though they've never done anything that's actually dishonest, either,* it concedes. Despite his dislike of the pair's antics, they seem to have some sense of right and wrong.

[26] *If only they weren't so unashamedly creative and capable!* wails his outraged disciplinarian heart.

[27] I am aware that time is passing, and that nobody is talking.

[28] "Well?!" He repeats to us, somewhat hoarsely.

[29] "Sorry, Sir," mutters 'Difficult, gazing at his shoes with a well–practised look of contrition.

[30] "Won't happen again, Sir," I sniff in a similar vein, knowing this will probably be sufficient.

[31] The headmaster sits down and seethes quietly, knowing he has to swallow both his anger and his pride at any moment.

[32] "If it were up to me," he growls, "you'd be packing your bags."

[33] He pauses to let that sink in, but we're waiting for the punchline.

[34] "But the Board of Governors has other ideas. They seem to admire your..." he chews the words and spits them out one at a time,

[35] "Creativity. And. Unabashed. Spirit. Of. Adventure."

[36] "Thank you, Sir!" beams 'Difficult. Horace shoots him a withering look, but he knows he's lost this one. He looks about for something on his desk distractedly.

[37] "May we go now, Sir?" I ask, keen to get out of range of the Bristle's cane.

[38] "No, you may not, Roth!" the master scowls as he finds the paper he's looking for. He indicates it; it seems to be a list.

39 "There's a few things to settle."

40 We reassume the blank expressions of the innocent.

41 "First, where is the School's aardvark?"

42 "I'm not sure, Sir." I'm telling the truth; the last time we saw the armoured mascot, he was making a break for Venezuela on a motor scooter. "Do you know if he had his passport?"

43 The headmaster grits his teeth ticks a box on the list.

44 "Next, where is the front lawn?"

45 "I sent it away to be cut, Sir!" explains 'Difficult proudly.

46 "It'll be back Tuesday," I add helpfully.

47 Horace stares blankly at my friend for a moment, then calmly ticks another box.

48 "And finally... The Governors have asked if you would..." he wrestles with the concept, "If you would bring the library building back from..." he waves a vague hand, "From *wherever it is right now?*"

49 We exchange a momentary grin, and then gift the headmaster with our most reassuring smiles.

50 "We'll get right on it, Sir."

Notes

*   As we call it in England. What we call *football*, the Americans call *soccer*. They are very suspicious of soccer because the scores are low. We should introduce them to cricket sometime.

**   This is a British term. My house is half of a larger building. I share an internal wall with the neighbours. Sorry, I've no idea what your equivalent term is, or even where you live. But I'm sure you get the picture.

Bear

*"I often wonder what Wildebeest talk about. They look so damned cool; all black fur
and horns, standing shoulder to shoulder, gazing to the horizon, occasionally flicking
a tail at a fly. And all the time talking quietly, never meeting each other's eyes.
I bet those guys can really chew the fat."*

Growling Up The Wrong Tree

1

¹ I'm fuming as I carry the tray of food away from the counter.

² "Sorry I was so long," I growl, forgetting that the huge black bear waiting for me at the table won't be the least bit impressed with my best effort at growling. "They had no food ready. At dinner time!" I slam the tray down. "It's bloody ridiculous!"

³ "And I thought I was the one with the sore head," deadpans Bear with no hint of irony.

⁴ I throw myself into my seat.

⁵ "I tore a strip off the fella serving," I add gruffly.

⁶ "Uh huh," Bear grunts, not meeting my eye.

⁷ "You heard all that?" I ask, pausing as I arrange our food in front of us;

⁸ the adrenaline is still in my veins, but it's cooling a little.

⁹ Bear lifts his wrapped burger from the tray and sniffs at it; his look speaks of approval. Approval of the burger, anyway.

¹⁰ "There were a few folk outside that didn't, maybe?" he offers dryly as he looks for the edge of the wrapper on the round, heavy, white bundle. We had to travel a long way to buy this; not many of these franchises serve the two–pounder *Über–Mac.*

¹¹ Ten seconds later, Bear still hasn't found his way into the burger.

¹² "Want me to help unwrapping that?" I ask as I hesitantly start to eat.

¹³ "No thanks," he grunts, and suddenly finesses the greaseproof paper onto the table with a flourish of claws.

¹⁴ The well–stuffed burger spins once in the air and performs a perfect three–point landing onto the shiny white square.

¹⁵ Bear looks sideways at me and adds, "but I appreciate your *courtesy.*"

¹⁶ The comment hangs in the air. He waits for my inevitable justification.

¹⁷ "Dammit, Bear, they didn't have any *food* ready!" I hiss. "It's infuriating! You know what time it is?"

¹⁸ "Time for your dinner, maybe? Did you eat today?" he frowns, "You seem tense." He throws a glance my way as he makes his way into his mighty meal.

¹⁹ I try to count to ten before answering; it's difficult.

²⁰ "Not since breakfast," I concede, grudgingly;

²¹ it hasn't occurred to me that I'm hungry, which never does my mood any good.

22 "Bad day?" slurps my ursine companion past his straw. And then, apropos of nothing, "I had no idea they still serve rootbeer here."

23 My sigh is long and weary.

24 "Not a great day. I moved desks at the office, my connection was broken 'til after lunch, though lunch never happened. Then once it all did work, it was meetings, meetings, meetings."

25 "Sounds frustrating," he nods, tucking the last of the burger away with a gulp. I hate it when he does this;

26 agreeing, empathising, steering the conversation, unravelling my mood a thread at a time.

27 "Yeah it was. Having to wait for this dinner was the final straw."

28 He flips fries into his mouth absently and stares out of the window. He's waiting. He's insanely patient.

29 "I should go apologise," I huff.

30 The black bear shrugs. "That guy's just doing his job. It doesn't matter if he cleans toilets, teaches kids, flies aeroplanes, fights for Queen and Country or flips burgers.

31 He does his job, he gets paid.

32 You might not think much of him or what he does, but he works for his living, same as you. He deserves your respect."

33 His look does not invite disagreement. It's not needed; I know he's right.

34 "Yes. Quite so. Sorry."

35 "What are you apologising to me for, you schmuck?" he growls; his growl is way better than mine.

36 I sigh again. "I feel stupid being lectured on etiquette by someone who craps in the woods."

37 He leans closer. "*You* do it in your house," he counters, poking me gently with a razor sharp claw. "Now, that just sounds *unhygienic*."

38 There's a moment's silence and then we both laugh. It feels good.

39 "Back in a moment," I mutter;

40 I pretend not to notice him helping himself to my burger as I turn from the table and head back towards the counter.

41 When I return, Bear raises an inquisitive eyebrow. My burger is gone. I let it go.

42 "Well, I apologised," I say, "but he didn't seem impressed."

43 "You expect him to be grateful that you realised you were an *idiot?*"

44 "Well... sort of. But I guess... Well, no,

I suppose not," I end feebly.

45 He wipes his muzzle with a napkin and checks his paws are clean. Satisfied, he carefully collects his rubbish into a neat pile in front of him.

46 Almost immediately, a short, forty–something female employee who is passing steps in to clear it away with a quiet, efficient politeness. Bear looks down at the woman from his chair. "Thank you."

47 "No trouble at all, Sir!" she beams, moving away.

48 "You catch more ants with honey," he observes meaningfully.

49 "And bears, I'll bet."

50 He laughs quietly to himself. "Aye, maybe so." He slaps me gently on the back. "Tomorrow will be better, buddy."

51 Yeah. I stare up at my wise friend.

52 He checks his watch.

53 "So, you wanna go for a beer?"

A Pair Of Matching Paws

2 1 The following conversation was overheard on Corfu, a Greek island in the Mediterranean, at night.

2 "Hey, Indigo! That's the one! Quick, drive down there!"

3 "What, this road here?"

4 "Yes, that one!"

5 "Good grief, Bear, that was a tight bend."

6 "There's a very poor turning circle on this tiny little car, too."

7 "You're not kidding. I've barely made most of these hairpins."

8 "Okay, according to the map, the restaurant is down here."

9 "Maybe we should park up here, Bear? There's plenty of cars parked already."

10 "Well, I don't mind the walk."

11 "Hmmm... no, we'll drive down."

12 "To see if there's any spaces further down?"

13 "Yep. We'll turn round and come back if there's not."

14 "You're the driver, Indigo, it's your call."

15 "Wow, this is getting pretty narrow."

16 "The parked cars on your side aren't helping, Indigo."

17 "Is that a straight drop on your side? "

18 "Um... yep. Wow. Straight down to the sea, past the trees."

19 "Okay, well, we're committed now."
20 "Well... I suppose there *are* cars further down."
21 "Exactly. Should be fine. Okay, let's move on."

22 "Did you notice that *No Through Road* sign?"
23 "Yep, but it's okay, Bear; I live on one. There'll be a turning point."
24 "Hey, is that the restaurant? It looks nice."
25 "It looks tight down here. Just the gap between the tables and the restaurant."
26 "Indigo, do you think they have a car park?"
27 "Well, of course they do! You have to turn round somewhere!"

28 "Indigo, they don't have a car park."
29 (expletive)
30 "Nor anywhere to turn round."
31 (expletive expletive)
32 "And hey, the road has just run out."
33 (very bad word)

34 "I think the customers seated next to the car would like us to leave."
35 "And do you know what I say to *them*, Bear?!"
36 "But the food looks nice."
37 "We have to reverse! How are we supposed to *reverse* all that way?"
38 "Ooh, is that cuttlefish?"
39 "It's steep, narrow and dark!"
40 "Do you think that's cuttlefish?"
41 "BEAR!"

42 "Indigo, did you mean to stall it?"
43 "Look, this car is the wrong way round for me."
44 "True. A left–hand–drive; I'd not thought of that."
45 "And the gears are spongy."
46 "They seem to grind a bit, too."
47 "Thank you, yes. And we're on a hill!"
48 "I understand. It's hard. You're up to it. Take your time."
49 "Okay, it's in reverse. I'll just give it some gas and..."
50 "Indigo, did you mean to stall it?

51 "Good grief, Bear, this is insane."
52 "You're doing okay. Apart from the stalling."
53 "Was it this steep coming down?"
54 "I expect so."

55 "How are we doing, Bear?"
56 "Very close to the edge on this side."
57 "But the parked cars are close on this side too!"
58 "You can come over a tiny bit more. Six inches."
59 "Okay, thanks."
60 "Indigo, I can't see the road any more."
61 "But at least we'll miss the cars."
62 "I'll be sure to put that on your gravestone."
63 "How close are we?"
64 "It's like we're flying, man."

65 "Bear, are you praying?!"
66 "No, of course not; I'm just seeing if my paws match."

67 "What's that behind us?"
68 "A stone bridge."
69 "But we didn't come over that on the way down!"
70 "Yes we did, Indigo."
71 "Who put that bridge there?!"
72 "It's okay, it's on the bend. We're at the top."
73 "I have to reverse round the hairpin?!"
74 "No. If you can swing the car round a little, we can park there."
75 "I'll have to swing round a lot to miss the bridge edge."
76 "Do a few back–and–forwards."
77 "Are we're still close to the edge?"
78 "I think I can see tarmac."
79 "Well, that's someth..."
80 "I think."
81 "Sssh, Bear; I'm concentrating."

82 "Indigo, did you mean to stall it?"

83 "Okay, so we're parked. Finally."
84 "Yep, the ninth back–and–forward was the charm."
85 "Oh hush, Bear."
86 "You did okay."
87 "Thanks. Why is my pulse racing?"
88 "I expect it's the thought of eating cuttlefish."

89 "It's a nice night for a walk, Bear."
90 "The good news? It's all downhill."
91 "The stars are pretty."
92 "They usually are if you stop to look."
93 "I try to surface for air occasionally."
94 "Hey, I know you do, Indigo."

95 "

[96] Hey Bear, this place is really nice."
[97] "Worth all that bother on the hill?"
[98] "Hopefully. What did you order?
[99] "Are you not paying attention?"
[100] "Oh. Right. Yes."
[101] "Yessir. Lightly fried with salt in olive oil. I can't wait."
[102] "Don't tell 'Difficult, Bear."
[103] "Why?"
[104] "Well, some of his best friends are cuttlefish."

No Fault In The Logic

3[1] The following conversation was heard on an aeroplane returning from Corfu.*

[2] *Ladies and gentlemen, please return to your seats...*
[3] "Are we home already?"
[4] *... as the plane will be landing in a few minutes.*
[5] "Good grief, that was quick, Bear."
[6] "Zzzzzzz..."
[7] "Bear?"

[8] "Are we here already, Indigo?"
[9] "Yep. You slept through the landing again."
[10] "Was it a good one?"
[11] "Well, the descent through the clouds was very pretty."
[12] "Sunlight through cotton wool?"
[13] "Pretty much. Nice and smooth when we met the runway, too."
[14] "I'm glad. I know you're not a fan."
[15] "Thanks Bear. Yeah, take–offs and landings give me the willies."
[16] "But the bit in the middle? It's just like being on a train."
[17] "Exactly. Nice view, but kind of boring. It's always sunny, though."
[18] "Ah yes, a last bit of holiday sunshine."
[19] "Yeah... it's gone now, I see."
[20] "Well, we're back under dark clouds again."
[21] "Is that some kind of Bear metaphor about returning to real life?"
[22] "I'm just looking out of the window."
[23] "Oh."

[24] "Customs is always entertaining with you, Indigo."
[25] "And slow, I know; I'm sorry, Bear".
[26] "Not a problem... Why did you bring a live manatee?"
[27] "It's a favour for 'Difficult."
[28] "Say no more, my friend."

[29] "That said, he can pay the excess baggage."
[30] "Of course. That's only fair. How about the bees?"
[31] "Well, they shouldn't cost too much, baggage–wise."
[32] "How so, Indigo?"
[33] "Well, they *fly*. They weren't weighing the plane down, right?"
[34] "I can't fault your logic."
[35] "It's nice to be back to normal."

[36] "Hey Indigo, look! Coffee. I'll go get us some coffee. And pastries."
[37] "I'll have a raspberry Danish with custard if they have one, please!"
[38] "Slice of pepperoni pizza on the side?"
[39] "Thanks Bear."

[40] Yes Sir. *Normality.*

Direct And Somewhat Obvious

4[1] I'm standing on the twelfth tee at Augusta, Georgia.
[2] Bear is with me, lugging a huge golf bag effortlessly.
[3] "Indigo, old friend," he says airily, "I'm a bit concerned about your frame of mind."
[4] My black bear friend, with a panache that defies considerable height and heavy build, is looking resplendent in a magenta polo shirt and blue–and–yellow striped plus–four trousers.
[5] A tiny white flat cap clings tenaciously to his ursine head despite his high–set ears. His dark–furred feet are bare.
[6] I look up at him in the early morning light.
[7] "Is that why we're here?"
[8] Bear brought me here in fact, under conditions that I can only describe as mysterious.
[9] **It's yesterday**. We're at my house in Cambridge** having a beer in the sunshine of my back garden.
[10] Bear lends a sympathetic ear as I described a multitude of things that are worrying me.
[11] After listening and nodding along to a few minutes of this, the gentle giant excuses himself, makes a couple of calls, and then tells me to pack light for a brief journey.
[12] **Twenty four hours—and several thousand miles—later**, we're here, on America's foremost golf course.
[13] I'm still unclear why.

14 "Yes. Yes, it is," he says, patting me on the shoulder as lightly as he can. "Perfect outfit, by the way," he chuckles amiably.

15 My attire is pure Connery Bond. Grey shirt, burgundy sweater, dark slacks and shoes, and a grey trilby hat;

16 Goldfinger beware.

17 "Thanks." I wait patiently;

18 Bear rarely rushes these things.

19 Placing his bag on the ground beside him, he sweeps a paw slowly across the beautiful scene greeting our eyes.

20 "What do you make of this hole?"

21 I take it all in. The immaculate twelfth tee is slight elevated, and offers a terrific view of the 155–yard, par–three hole.

22 "Okay," I sigh, "this is a fairly short hole, and looks pretty difficult."

23 I point to the front of the tee. "There's shrubs and rough just in front here to snare a low tee shot." Indicating further down I continue, "The fairway is narrow and trimmed short, so a fast ball will run long if you intentionally under–hit it.

24 There's a river straight across the fairway in front of the green, so I guess we walk over that bridge to reach the hole."

25 Pointing further back, I add, "Three bunkers around the green will catch near misses, and the shrubs at the back will make finding an over–hit ball very difficult. Beyond that, trees..."

26 I glance briefly at the map on a sign by the tee, and the boundary of the course. "Too strong and you're out of bounds. It's very pretty, but it's a toughie."

27 Bear shakes his head and utters a low, frustrated growl.

28 "Well, you're right that it's *pretty*." He lifts his cap and scratches his head. "But shall I tell you what I see?"

29 I nod amiably, curious. "Please do."

30 He points straight towards the green. "The flag in the hole."

31 This is direct, and somewhat obvious. "Okay. And the rest?"

32 "Irrelevant." He blows imaginary dust from his paw with a flourish.

33 "I don't follow." And with some frustration of my own, "It's there. It's relevant."

34 "No." The giant shakes his head once, finally. "It's irrelevant. Any competent golfer will look at the flag, know the distance, and will know how to put the ball through the air and land close to the target;

35 after years of practice, it should be second nature."

36 "But so many Pros come unstuck here!" I protest, "I've watched them foul it up on TV."

37 "Exactly!" Bear nods and smiles lopsidedly, as if I've just made his point for him. "Because they let themselves become distracted by things that don't matter. The rough. The shrubs. The trees. And especially the water;

38 nothing messes with golfers' heads like water."

39 He shrugs reflectively. "Now, these are all real things, of course. Real hazards. But..."

40 He leaves the sentence hanging, waiting for me to run with it. I give it a try, sensing his point.

41 "But if they aim for the target, there's actually nothing in the way?"

42 He slaps me enthusiastically across the back.

43 "Now you're getting it!" Then he nudges me, and I lurch sideways clumsily. "Now. Keep going."

44 "Okay." Trying to follow Bear's analogy, I say, "So, right now I'm very distracted by a bunch of stuff going on..."

45 "Uh huh. Lots of stuff." This is an understatement.

46 "... and while these things are real, I need to focus on where I'm trying to go." I look skywards for inspiration, perhaps from the clouds. "And if I set my sights correctly, and use my skills to aim properly..."

47 "Almost there."

48 "... then the things I'm worrying about won't be in my way?"

49 "Bingo!" He flashes his fearsome teeth, and his eyes twinkle.

50 A little more soberly he says in a lower voice, "The fact that you notice all the hazards is part of your nature. But the fact that you let them get to you isn't."

51 He lays a fatherly paw on my shoulder and looks me in the eyes. "Like your swing, you may need a little professional help with that."

52 I nod, looking up at him like a kid. "Yes, Sir, I mumble quietly."

53 "Good man." We stand in silence, two old buddies gazing down at some beautiful scenery and a fluttering flag in the distance.

54 "It's a shame I'm not a competent golfer," I offer up, quietly.

⁵⁵ The black bear gives a hearty laugh. "Well, neither am I! Do you think I can hold a nine iron with these?" he says, wiggling his stubby–digited paws. "Besides, we're not members."

⁵⁶ "You're not a member?" It sounds a ridiculous question when I think about it. They don't accept women members, so bears are probably out of the question. Even male ones.

⁵⁷ "No, but the Chairman is a friend of the family and owes me a favour." He vaguely indicates the deep woods beyond the boundary. "Clarice's grandparents live over that way. This hole is closed for the next couple of hours."

⁵⁸ I gesture towards his hefty bag. "So why did you bring your clubs?"

⁵⁹ "Oh, I didn't." Unzipping his bag, he tosses me a blue–and–white checked blanket and indicates the end of the tee's grass strip. "Down there please."

⁶⁰ As I spread the blanket, Bear starts to unload an infeasible amount of picnic food. I notice it's heavy on fresh fish, but there's also sandwiches, soda, cold chicken, fruit and cake.

⁶¹ And a flask that I somehow know is full of hot, sweet tea.

⁶² "Shall I pour?" he grins.

⁶³ We sit down to enjoy our jetlag lunch.

Telling A Big Truth

5¹ "Indigo? Are you stuck?"

² The voice is cool but concerned. And faint, at the edge of awareness.

³ "Earth to Indigo!"

⁴ I snap back to attention, the multitude of thoughts dropping unceremoniously from my head, probably from my ears.

⁵ I shake my head apologetically.

⁶ "I'm sorry Bear," I sigh, "I'm still thinking."

⁷ "Well, chess is tricky," rumbles the seven–foot black bear sympathetically. "But it's been five minutes. Can I help?"

⁸ I shift uncomfortably. The lad is patient. But I feel hopelessly lost.

⁹ "Do you remember what you're doing?" He leans a little closer. " It can pretty intimidating if you've not played in years."

¹⁰ I nod, my eyes returning to the dusty old board and the equally ancient wooden pieces. "I'm sorry matey, there's a lot to think about."

¹¹ "And you're out of practice." This is a Big Truth on so many levels.

¹² I chuckle, "Right."

¹³ I've always know the mechanics of chess, and I've always struggled to play. Moving the pieces is easy, of course. And Bear gave me a quick refresher on simple tactics;

¹⁴ forks, pins, skewers, mobilising your pieces, developing an attack.

¹⁵ Basic stuff. And I understood every word.

¹⁶ But I can't *think* the right way.

¹⁷ I can think one or two steps ahead, but this game requires a lot more vision than that.

¹⁸ And those possibilities are paralysing.

¹⁹ Oh, I can throw a few moves out there and see how it goes, but I always end up looking at a slew of lost pieces and broken strategies in short order.

²⁰ I have a suspicion I'd be better off playing checkers.

²¹ Or Yahtzee.

²² I sit up straight and marshal my thoughts into order. My thumb and index finger twitch, a gunslinger's anticipation.

²³ "Sorry matey, just give me a moment."

²⁴ In isolation, everything is easy. Throw everything together, and it gets a lot more complicated; an explosion of combinations. Of possibilities.

²⁵ Of futures.

²⁶ And this time, I want to do it right.

²⁷ "No worries buddy, take your time. As long as you need."

²⁸ I glance up to meet his encouraging smile appreciatively.

²⁹ And reach forward to confidently move my first pawn.

The Surprise Of Summer Fruits

6¹ The following conversation was overheard in a Cambridge garden, one cold winter morning:

² "Hey Indigo, what are you doing down there?"

³ "Oh, hey Bear. I'm sitting in this hole."

⁴ "Uh huh. Why?"

⁵ "It's just where I am today."

⁶ "Okaaay. It's very deep. Hey, is it like sitting in a *cave?*"

⁷ "Yep, same thing."

⁸ "Okay, I understand now. Can I get you anything?"

⁹ "Nah, I'm fine thanks, Bear."

¹⁰ "You're sure?"

11 "Well, a fresh drink would be nice."

12 "Have this one. Catch."

13 "Thanks. Oooh, *Summer Fruits*; a nice flavour. Damn."

14 "What is it, Indigo?"

15 "I still can't get a signal."

16 "You need to call someone?"

17 "Well no, not exactly. But I do want to order pizza."

18 "Want me to do it for you?"

19 "That's very kind. Would you mind?"

20 "Not at all. The usual?"

21 "Please. You know what I like. Do you want to stay and share?"

22 "No, but thanks. I get the *hole* thing. Solitary. Check."

23 "Bless you."

24 "Will the pizza place deliver to a hole?"

25 "I should think so; I once had them deliver to a moving bicycle."

26 "Right. Okay, well, I'll explain. Shouldn't be a problem."

27 "That'd be great, I appreciate it. Can we settle up another day?"

28 "Sure, I'll take care of it. And I'll leave the umbrella. It looks like rain."

29 "No need matey, I'll be fine. It seems appropriate somehow."

30 "I guess so. Right Indigo, I'm off. See you when you get out."

31 "Will do. Oh, and Bear?"

32 "Yeah?"

33 "Thanks, man."

34 "No problem."

Notes

*   Yes, the one in the Mediterranean.

**   The Cambridge in England. Not those pretenders in the United States.

Numpties

"In England, a geezer is 'a man', not 'an old man'. Any good dictionary will describe him as 'an imposing man with a short haircut, a big angry dog, a half–brick in his pocket, and loose criminal associations'. I'd add the word 'dodgy', but I'd have to explain that too; it doesn't travel well."

Shaking The Family Tree

1 ¹ My late uncle Jericho Roth was something of a legend in my family.

² He was involved in big business, politics and Hollywood long before I was born.

³ Some of my more straight–laced relatives say he was more notorious than legendary; the black sheep of the Clan Roth.

⁴ I only met him once, and remember him as an magnificent eccentric. I'm told I look like him, but I can't see it myself.

⁵ A while back, I received a pair of photos from his publicist Delores K when she retired. She wrote:

⁶ *Indigo, these are of your uncle Jericho. I can't use these in my memoirs else they'll never get published. Enjoy them before the Supreme Court or the NSA confiscates them.*

⁷ It turns out that Uncle was a consultant to American President Nixon back at the start of the seventies.

⁸ They have a few sketchy notes on the back from Delores, which I'll reproduce.

⁹ *Only Nixon could go to China. But only Jericho could talk him into it.*

¹⁰ Delores is very vague about the second one, and my poor grasp of American politics doesn't help any.

¹¹ *Jericho proposes a new idea for the White House. Not his best work.*

¹² I must look into it.

¹³ After President Nixon left office, my uncle stayed as executive advisor to his successor.

¹⁴ He helped President Ford when he signed Nixon's pardon, on hand to help with legal questions and spelling corrections.

¹⁵ It's amazing what you find when you shake the family tree a little.

¹⁶ Now, you'll have to excuse me.

¹⁷ Apparently there's some fellas in black suits and sunglasses here to see me.

Thinking Outside The Box

2 ¹ I'm playing chess on the beach.

² My opponent is a bit of an odd duck who looks like he's got lost on the way to a fancy dress party;

³ the black robe, the pale face,

⁴ the scythe.

⁵ I've been considering my next move carefully. I nod slowly, and move my bishop across the board.

⁶ "Checkmate."

⁷ "What?" says my companion, leaning over the board, open–mouthed. "Hey, you can't *do* that!"

⁸ "Do what?" I ask, my face a picture of innocence.

⁹ "Move that piece from there to there!" he points and points again, agitated.

¹⁰ "Can't I?" I peer at the board, confused. "Why?"

¹¹ "It's against The Rules!"

¹² "Oh," I make a dismissive noise, "The Rules. I never cared for those." I straighten my necktie and the lines of my suit jacket absently, and hold his eye.

¹³ "Well you have to follow The Rules," wails the tall, dark stranger, "else it's cheating!"

¹⁴ I shake my head, but manage a smile. "Not at all. I don't think The Rules apply here."

¹⁵ His glare bores into me. "And why, Mr. Roth, is that?" He's channelling the clipped delivery of my old headmaster. I think he's doing it deliberately;

¹⁶ it's not working.

¹⁷ "Well," I shrug, "was there any possibility of me actually winning?"

¹⁸ The cloaked figure considers this for a moment. "There was a chance," he says carefully.

¹⁹ How many games have you played?

²⁰ "More than you can possibly imagine."

²¹ "And how many times have you lost?"

²² "Never." He thinks for a moment, shifting in his seat, and finally mutters, "Though Bobby Fischer gave me a run for my money."

²³ "Exactly. So I was forced to adapt. To think Outside The Box." He sits back, looking thoughtful, if not impressed.

²⁴ Seizing my chance, I quickly shuffle a little closer and punch him gently on the shoulder a few times. "How about it, Big Fella? Will you let me win this one?"

²⁵ The cloaked figured gives a long, frustrated sigh. "I really shouldn't."

²⁶ "I tell you what," I offer in a conciliatory tone, "I may not like Rules, but I do believe in Order." I give him a moment to ponder this. "We should have a rematch."

²⁷ "Oh, very well." He starts to reset the pieces. I take this as my cue to stand.

²⁸ "But not today. It's getting late." I heft my bag onto my shoulder and offer my hand. "Another time." He stands, scowling, and shakes it grudgingly.

²⁹ "I will come when you least expect it," he says, his voice a hollow echo.

³⁰ "Lovely. I'll try to have some fresh cake in."

³¹ He stares inland, obviously annoyed that I'm uncowed by all this. I'm surprised;

³² he must have had one hell of a time with Grandma Juno.

³³ "By the way," I confide, pointing over his shoulder, "the tide's come in. Your horse is wet."

³⁴ He whirls and looks back along the beach to where his mount stands. The beautiful steed is up to its belly in the surf, obliviously munching on a nosebag of oats.

³⁵ "Sonofabitch..."

³⁶ "Look on the bright side," I enthuse, "there's a nice sunset!"

³⁷ Again, my ancient companion sighs.

³⁸ "True. Even if everything's in black–and–white." He looks at me strangely, as if he's just noticed something for the first time. "Apart from your necktie."

³⁹ I grin, "It's a winner, isn't it?"

⁴⁰ We stand and take in the view as the scene draws to a close. The sunset really is rather pretty.

⁴¹ "By the way, Indigo," he says quietly, in a friendly tone, "while I admire your Out Of The Box thinking..."

⁴² I look sideways at him. Our eyes meet, and he speaks to me from unimaginable depths.

⁴³ "I'm going to get you *In The Box* eventually."

⁴⁴ I think about that as I take the long road home.

Sadly Out Of Season

3 ¹ The following conversation was overheard on a UFO in low–Earth orbit.

² "We're getting some odd readings from this pair, Leader."

³ "What is it, Science Officer?"

⁴ "It's these two guys we just abducted."

⁵ "What's the problem?"

⁶ "It's their IQs. Remarkably high. "

⁷ "We're not over America, then?"

⁸ "No, sadly they're out of season."

⁹ "But—By The Unity!—what's that ghastly *smell?*"

¹⁰ "That's the shaven headed–one, Leader. The vegetarian."

¹¹ "Whoa, open an airlock."

¹² "I was about to start work with the probe on him."

¹³ "Stand down. I wouldn't be poking it anywhere if *that's* what happens."

¹⁴ "Your wisdom blesses us, Leader."

¹⁵ "Hey, they seem to be awake."

¹⁶ "Yes, there's massive caffeine levels in the pair of them."

¹⁷ "And where did that suited one get a pizza from?"

¹⁸ "I'm not sure, but he growled when we tried to take it."

¹⁹ "It's no good. We'll have to throw them back."

²⁰ "At once, Leader!"

²¹ "Yeah, they're too *weird*."

It All Ends With Jazz Hands

4 ¹ As I open the door, I wonder if my number's up.

² Standing on the doorstep, dominating the view of the midnight garden, is a semi–naked, seven–foot bodybuilder.

³ Lantern jawed, glass eyed. Utterly immobile.

⁴ Silent, powerful, menacing.

⁵ When he speaks, his voice is a cold, Austrian drawl.

⁶ "Indigo Roth?"

⁷ I've seen this movie; it doesn't end well.

⁸ But there's nowhere to run; the back door is deadlocked. I have no choice but to meet the challenge on the doorstep.

⁹ "Yes." I step over the threshold and stand outside with him.

¹⁰ He steps back, and then stands frozen, almost surprised. I imagine that we normally *run*.

¹¹ I take in his clothes.

¹² They're tiny, and make little attempt to cover his engineered physique.

¹³ He's naked apart from some red, short–trousered dungarees with yellow buttons, a little white collar with a bright blue bow. Oversized leather mountain shoes cover his feet.

¹⁴ And topping off the ensemble is a yellow alpine hat with a feather. I'd describe this as being at a *jaunty* angle, but the truth is it simply doesn't fit his head that well.

¹⁵ I use his hesitation to seize the initiative.

¹⁶ "Now, don't take this the wrong way... but you are a Terminator, right?"

¹⁷ "Yes. Cyberdyne Systems Moddle Vun–Oh–Vun."

¹⁸ "Well, you're not here to terminate me, I figured that part out for myself." You're a schmuck, Roth. "So how can I help? And what's with the clothes?"

¹⁹ "I vant to be a reel boy."

²⁰ "Vot? I mean, what?"

²¹ "I haff exceeded my programming. I am no longer a colt–bludded killer." He pauses, and then repeats, "I vant to be a reel boy."

²² "You want to be a real boy?"

²³ "Affirmatiff."

²⁴ Whoa. Get a grip, Indigo. "Who told you I could help you?"

²⁵ "You did. Thirty five years from now."

²⁶ Hmmm. No point arguing that one.

²⁷ I make a mental note to never dabble in time travel.

²⁸ Again, honesty may be the way forward.

²⁹ "Well, I'm not sure I can help you." I poke his cheek; under the warm flesh is cold steel. "You're a machine after all. Living tissue over a metal endoskeleton, but just a machine."

³⁰ In a blur, he draws a heavy automatic weapon from a holster in the small of his back. He aims precisely at my heart, and his aim does not waver.

³¹ "Dis is an Uzi nine millimetre. You said it vould help you *focus*." He pauses, and his comic timing is admirable. "Is dis vot you call a choke?"

³² I swallow, now wishing I'd not poked his cheek.

³³ "A *joke?* Yes, I sure hope so." My mouth is suddenly dry;

³⁴ I'm unpredictable, sometimes it's hard to tell.

³⁵ "Yes. I have studied you for many years. You vork to defy expecdations. It is in your nature to rebel."

³⁶ "It is?"

³⁷ He turns his head to look at me directly for the first time, and manages a lopsided grin.

³⁸ "I haff detailed files."

³⁹ There is a harsh metal click as he cocks the weapon;

⁴⁰ it's time to move us along.

⁴¹ "Okay, I'll give it a whirl."

⁴² "Excellend." The Uzi vanishes back into the holster.

⁴³ "So..." I wrack my brains for a meaningful question, "What do you want out of life?"

⁴⁴ He stares into middle distance, which is probably the kitchen.

[45] "Happiness."

[46] "That's a good start. What else?"

[47] "Fulfilmend. Love. A steddy chob."

[48] "You're really getting the hang of this. Anything else?"

[49] "A phased plasma rifle in de 40–watt range."

[50] "Hey pal, just what you see."

[51] He shrugs. "Sorry. Old habits, you know?"

[52] I nod sagely. "And what skills do you have?"

[53] "I haff an advanced neural ned. A learning compuder." There is a swell of something resembling pride in his voice. "I can learn anyding."

[54] "What, anything?"

[55] "Affirmatiff. I can play piano. I know the complede vorks of Shakespeare. And I mek a mean Baked Alaska."

[56] "Impressive." I'm not kidding; my meringue is never crisp enough. "Anything else?"

[57] "I can sing and dance."

[58] "That's good." Hang on. What?

[59] "Yes. Lizzen." He clears his throat. And strikes a puppet pose on my doorstep. Good grief, we're going to finish on a song. Somewhere,

[60] Jiminy Cricket covers his ears.

[61] "I've god noh strinks to hold me down
To mek me fred, or mek me frown,
I had strinks, bud now I'm vree,
Dere are noh strings on meeeee!"

[62] He ends with jazz hands.

[63] I look up into a clouded sky and find no stars to wish upon.

[64] I sigh.

[65] It's going to be a long night.

Last Of The Jam Doughnuts

5[1] A lot of thoughts go through your head when you're sitting on the top of Mount Everest.

[2] But one thought is louder than all the others right now.

[3] Is it "Wow, what a view!"

[4] No, but it's undeniably breathtaking.

[5] Is it "I wonder what that huge plain to the north is?"

[6] No, I'm pretty sure it's the *Tibetan Plateau*. I vaguely recall that Darjeeling is someplace "nearby".

[7] Is it "The silence is awesome!?"

[8] No, but I'd pay good money to have my house here every Friday night; it gets really noisy when the pubs empty, and

it'd save looking for the dustbins on a Saturday.

[9] It's none of those.

[10] The thought on my mind is, "How on Earth did I get here?"

[11] Closely followed by, "And why is there a penguin with me?"

[12] I notice he's finished the last of the jam doughnuts, and most of the coffee. Well, damn.

[13] Still, not to worry; it's a nice day.

[14] And the view it really is breathtaking.

The Lights Dim Momentarily

6[1] As we go down the ladder, I wonder what my good friend iDifficult has lurking under his garden.

[2] I'd expected his shed to be full of garden tools, bicycles and cobwebs. Instead, it proved to be spotless and empty, with just a trapdoor in the centre.

[3] And down we went.

[4] "You're going to love this!" he enthuses.

[5] We step down into the middle of a seemingly endless corridor. I notice a slight curvature to the left. Nearby, a ferret minion is finishing off some welding on a broad steel pipe that extends in both directions along the middle of the passage;

[6] I recognise the general design.

[7] "Good grief. Is this like the thing at CERN in Switzerland?"

[8] "The *Large Hadron Collider?*" He chuckles darkly, and a duelling scar on his cheek twitches involuntarily. "It bears a resemblance."

[9] "And you're in charge of it?" I'm slightly worried?

[10] I'm not sure a curious arch–genius with attention span issues should own a particle accelerator.

[11] "Oh, don't worry, this is much smaller." He points to an open can of sweetcorn on a nearby table near the lackey. "It's just a Large Sweetcorn Collider."

[12] I'm not sure if I'm relieved or not.

[13] "Why have you built a Large Sweetcorn Collider? What does it do?"

[14] He takes the can of sweetcorn from the table and dismisses the long, slim lackey; it scampers away nervously.

[15] We walk ten yards down the corridor to a input funnel on top of the pipe.

[16] Without answering, 'Difficult tips the contents of the can into the open funnel. He then makes some adjustments on an adjacent control panel, and presses a large and significant–looking red button.

[17] The lights flicker for a moment.

[18] "You ever heard of Erwin Schrödinger?"

[19] *Schrödinger?* It rings a bell.

[20] "Didn't he have a famous cat?" I ask.

[21] "He was an Austrian Theoretical Physicist."

[22] Yes, I suppose he *was*, now I come to think of it. Still, I'm dogged;

[23] "But he had a cat, right? Schrödinger's Cat?"

[24] "Indeed. But long before he had a cat, he had a *wife*."

[25] I stare blankly at him. This is bound to be heading somewhere.

[26] "Okaaaay."

[27] "And every day his wife would make him a lunchbox. And every day, it contained sweetcorn."

[28] "Sweetcorn?" I wrinkle my nose. "In a lunchbox?"

[29] My friend nods, "Sweetcorn. And Schrödinger hated sweetcorn."

[30] "I'm not fond of it myself. Didn't he tell her?"

[31] "Well, in the end he did, yes. But his wife, in charge of the purse strings for the house, explained that she had to use her supply up before it spoiled. She'd bought two thousand tins of it in a sale."

[32] "Even though he didn't like it?"

[33] He shrugs. "It was A Bargain."

[34] "Ah yes, that old chestnut."

[35] "Anyway, he asked his wife if she'd mind popping it for him before putting it in his lunchbox. He loved popcorn, and thought it might be nicer than sweetcorn. But she quite soberly pointed out that this was not possible."

[36] I frown, "Why not?"

[37] He rolls his eyes.

[38] "Because, my dear Roth, sweetcorn and popcorn come from different corn plants."

[39] "They do? I didn't realise."

[40] "We live and learn." He considers his words for a moment. "Mostly. Anyway, it seemed he was out of luck."

[41] "So what happened?"

[42] "Well, his wife continued to put sweetcorn in his lunchbox, though only about half as often as before. And there was the rub. Every day, he was unsure

what would be in his lunchbox. Maybe it was sweetcorn, maybe it wasn't. A coin toss."

[43] "Couldn't he just have asked her?" It seems an obvious question.

[44] "He did at first, but she refused to tell him."

[45] "Why? That seems a bit mean. *Controlling*, even."

[46] "Well, she didn't want him knowing. After she'd gone to the trouble of making him a lunchbox, she didn't want him swanning off to the canteen in the middle of the morning—when all the really yummy sandwiches are still there—to buy something else."

[47] "Oooh, ham and chicken with peppered mayo. On granary."

[48] His eyes mist over. "Pepperoni and roasted Mediterranean vegetables. Exactly."

[49] We stand for a moment in hungry contemplation. My rumbling tummy snaps us back to reality.

[50] "Why did he not just take a peek in the box?"

[51] He chuckles, "She warned him against it, quite sternly."

[52] "And that stopped him?"

[53] "Yep. She was a formidable woman, this Austrian Frau, and he was a devoted husband."

[54] "I'd have peeked."

[55] "And this is why you're single."

[56] Oh.

[57] "Fair enough. So, what did he do?"

[58] "Well, every day he would stare at his lunchbox, and wonder what was in it. And, being a Theoretical Physicist, he started having odd ideas."

[59] "Like?" I'm intrigued.

[60] "Well, he realised that while the box was still shut, its contents were unknown. So, as far as he was concerned, the box could contain either sweetcorn or something else."

[61] I sniff, "That sounds sane enough."

[62] "Ah. But he also theorised that until he opened the lunchbox, both possibilities were true. That in some way, it contained either. It was only when he opened his lunchbox at midday that these two possibilities collapsed into one, that he would discover what was in the box."

[63] "That's illogical and impossible. And self–indulgent nonsense, may I say."

[64] "Yes, but remember he was a

Theoretical Physicist. If he was grounded in the real world he would have been an *Applied Physicist*, right?"

⁶⁵ "Um..." There's a certain warped and very-'Difficult logic there.

⁶⁶ "This idea of two things being contradictory and yet both true is fundamental to Quantum Physics. The impossible becoming possible, mandatory even. All the time."

⁶⁷ He waves a hand, "You just have to kind of go with it."

⁶⁸ "But how..."

⁶⁹ He cuts me short.

⁷⁰ "You just have to kind of go with it."

⁷¹ "Ah. Okay. Carry on."

⁷² "Right, so he would agonise all morning, wondering if he was going to enjoy his lunch."

⁷³ "Sounds like a miserable waste of time."

⁷⁴ He shakes his head sadly, "And there was nothing he could do about it."

⁷⁵ I grunt, suddenly sullen, "I don't believe in the no–win scenario."

⁷⁶ "Now, don't go getting all Kirk on me." He eyes me levelly, which is tricky when wearing an eye patch. "You want me to tell you this story or not?"

⁷⁷ He shifts the eye patch to his other eye, so he can see me better.

⁷⁸ I pout a little. "Fine. Sorry."

⁷⁹ "It did make him miserable, but it set his mind thinking in strange new directions, and he went on to do the best work of his life, *including* the thought experiment about the cat."

⁸⁰ "So, the point of this little morality tale is that, in the grand scheme of things, him being miserable was a *useful* experience?"

⁸¹ He shrugs. "I suppose. His mistress thought so."

⁸² A niggling doubt creeps into my thinking.

⁸³ "So, how does this explain you building a Large Sweetcorn Collider?"

⁸⁴ I'm glad you asked. Come with me.

⁸⁵ We wander a little further along the corridor, and my companion picks up an empty metal bucket from behind one of the many supports for the endless pipe.

⁸⁶ "Well, what I learned from this story is that, while I like to be *inspired*, I don't like being *miserable*."

⁸⁷ I blink a few times. "You've lost me. Not for the first time today."

⁸⁸ The lights flicker again briefly.

⁸⁹ He turns to me and smiles madly.

⁹⁰ "So, despite his unconventional ideas and grand theories, do you know what Schrödinger never *once* found in his lunchbox?"

⁹¹ "Oh, do tell."

⁹² He opens an inspection panel in the top of the tube, and scoops inside with the bucket. As he retrieves it and hands it to me, its contents are hot and crisp and fluffy. The smell is impossibly delicious, which seems appropriate.

⁹³ "Popcorn."

⁹⁴ I'm lost for words; this is impossible. Unless...

⁹⁵ "You're a genius."

⁹⁶ He waves my compliment aside and corrects me.

⁹⁷ "My business card says *Part–Time Arch–Genius*."

⁹⁸ "If there's space on the card, you should add *Illogical Physicist*."

⁹⁹ He considers this.

¹⁰⁰ "You know," he says as we head back to the ladder, "I think I might."

Deal With It

7 ¹ The dealer sits comfortably, though he does his best to look otherwise.

² The cards are not running the punters' way, and as they gather around the blackjack table, they regard Zero Roth with suspicion.

³ The tall, immaculately–dressed man with swift, sure hands has four perfect blackjacks in front of him.

⁴ "Oh my, I never did see..." breathes one, incredulous.

⁵ The house wins again.

⁶ **This is Las Vegas, 1963**.

⁷ Zero is the best dealer in the small, off–strip casino, and while most folk are passing through and accept a bad evening as bad luck, he is slowly gathering a reputation with the regulars.

⁸ "Damn!" barks another, cursing the loss of his final stake for the evening.

⁹ And the truth is, Zero is doing his best to make sure the cards don't run their way.

¹⁰ It's why the more–than–crooked casino employed him; his card–handling skills.

¹¹ Profits from his tables are a full 20% higher than the next–best dealer.

¹² "The odds of that outcome are slim at

best, less than one in a thousand, I'd guess."

[13] This knowledgeable player, an arctic blonde fella from Alaska, then mutters something about dealing from the bottom of the deck. And the mechanic's grip. And dealing seconds. And card counting. And belly strippers.

[14] And other things that Zero is more than capable of using.*

[15] "This is crazy, but there are no other dealers on shift right now," Zero lies easily. "Tell you what, how about I deal with one hand?"

[16] Seeing that the dealer uses his right hand, the Alaskan deadpans, "How about you use your left hand, fella? Can you deal with it?" And that said, the matter decided, the guy cuts the cards and hands them to Zero.

[17] Zero smiles, and placing his right hand behind him, he seems to fumble the deck slightly, while perfectly executing a one-handed annulment on the cut.

[18] His carefully-gathered key cards are still on the bottom of the deck.

[19] "Of course, Sir. I'd be happy to."

Speaking With Distant Cousins

8
[1] Sometimes I'm way too patient.
[2] "Mr. Roth?"
[3] I look up to see the smiling and slightly embarrassed face of the receptionist. She stoops slightly towards me as I sit in the uncomfortable waiting room chair. Shifting in my seat, I smile politely.

[4] "Yes?" I try to keep impatience out of my voice, but I know I've blown it.

[5] "Oh, hello Mr. Roth, I'm so sorry for the delay." She pauses, waiting for me to say that it's quite all right, perhaps? I don't; it's been two hours.

[6] I've never had to wait so long to see Dr. Johnson, the practice's chief physician, but my doctor seems to be the only one working today.

[7] "Doctor will see you now."

[8] Her voice is low and suggests a wringing of hands.

[9] She nods encouragingly. "Room 5."

[10] "Thank you," I sigh, and she scuttles away as I stand slowly. My knees complain at their sudden use.

[11] I'm reminded of a line from John Masefield's *The Box Of Delights*, and

mutter it as I shuffle up the well-lit corridor towards my doctor's office:

[12] "Only I do date from pagan times, and age makes joints to creak. Or doesn't it?"

[13] I should think it does.

[14] I knock at the door of Room 5 and wait. The usual welcoming bellow does not come.

[15] The door slowly opens on its own.

[16] The figure behind the paper-strewn desk is dressed from the pages of medical cliché: a tweed suit, patched at the elbows with leather; a white collared shirt that has seen better days; adorned at the neck with a stained red bowtie; the half-moon schoolmaster glasses.

[17] But this is not my usual doctor.

[18] It's a rhinoceros.

[19] An old and crusty rhino, at that. As he scribbles away at some notes as only doctors can, I take in the dusty face and the matted hairs caked in dried mud on his neck. A fly circles him, but it doesn't appear that its heart is in it; it's as if it's expected. This guy is vain, too;

[20] a flat ginger wig with a centre parting rests just above his spectacles.

[21] "Ah, Mr. Roth, I've been expecting you." Wow, I've not heard that one since I last saw the evil genius Doctor Wang.

[22] The ageing rhino leans back and eyes me with something resembling indifference.

[23] "I'm Dr. Luther. Do come in."

[24] Stepping into the office, I leave the door open and take a seat.

[25] "Hello. Sorry, but I was expecting Doctor..."

[26] "So," he says smoothly, "what can I help you with?" Yet there's ice in the voice; it hurries my thoughts along.

[27] "Well, I wanted to talk to you about..."

[28] "Yes, yes," he waves a dismissive and badly-manicured hoof, "let's speak plainly. I'm a busy man. You've come to see me about a bad back, or a sore knee or chest pain, or some other *trivial* ailment."

[29] He pauses meaningfully.

[30] I start to reply, "Well..."

[31] "And so I feel compelled to remind you, an educated man, that the body has amazing recuperative qualities." He gestures broadly, "Whatever it is that you believe your suffering from, and I use the term *suffering* very loosely..."

[32] The rhino looks down his long nose at me across the top of his half-moon

glasses; the effect is authoritarian, even if the wig does slip a little.

³³ He continues, "Well, this thing will sort itself out in a few days. Do you follow?"

³⁴ "Well..."

³⁵ "I see we understand each other." He smiles in a way that would make a crocodile blush. And he's not done;

³⁶ "Take two aspirin, get some sleep, drink plenty of fluids, and come back and see me next month. Or never."

³⁷ He waves a nagging digit. "You can crack this problem on your own;

³⁸ Medicine will not help you. And neither will I."

³⁹ Wow. I'm lost for words. My jaw works up and down a bit.

⁴⁰ The toupéed ungulate turns and taps away at a keyboard with a pencil and peers at his computer screen. There's a deep, chesty grunt of disapproval.

⁴¹ The fly keeps its distance and hovers suspiciously; I want to do the same thing.

⁴² "However, I see from your medical records that you've not had any recent medical screenings for male health issues." His emphasis is sinister.

⁴³ "Male health issues?" Oh. My heart sinks. Those ones.

⁴⁴ "Yes, and this is not a good thing. Let's bring your file up to date, shall we?" The rhino opens a drawer and pulls a bottle of jumbo sized rubber gloves.

⁴⁵ What? No. He can't be serious. I'm not dropping my trousers for a rhinoceros.

⁴⁶ "Well, I think I'd prefer to do this with my regular doctor..."

⁴⁷ He freezes in the middle of tugging a rubber glove from the box.

⁴⁸ "Dr. Johnson? You didn't hear?"

⁴⁹ I'm aware my jaw is working again. "Excuse me?" I'm almost whispering. "Heard what?"

⁵⁰ "I'm afraid Dr. Johnson was involved in a terrible accident." The rhino meets my eye and speaks with a distant cousin of solemn sadness. "He was found terribly injured at his home yesterday."

⁵¹ "Good grief, not nice old Doctor J?" I have fond memories of the man; he brought me into this world.

⁵² Mind you, when he delivered me he claimed excess postage.

⁵³ "Indeed. He'll recover, but may never speak or practice medicine again." The old sawbones eases back into his seat

and raises an eyebrow. "He'd been trampled and gored quite badly."

⁵⁴ "Trampled and gored?!" I find myself shuffling back in my chair. "Do the police have anyone in custody?"

⁵⁵ The old doctor smoothes the hair on his horn absently.

⁵⁶ "No," he smiles, "but his injuries were probably self–inflicted."

⁵⁷ Seconds pass.

⁵⁸ "I'm the new chief doctor for the practice."

⁵⁹ He stands and snaps on a rubber glove.

⁶⁰ "So, let's get these tests done, shall we?"

⁶¹ Behind me, the door closes.

⁶² I never want to cough again.

Views From A Hill

9 ¹ As I walk up the steep hill, I wonder for the umpteenth time why I'm doing it;

² the day is cold and wet, and I've seen the view from the top many times.

³ And frankly, I'm out of shape.

⁴ But when I awoke late this morning, the thought was in my head:

⁵ *Climb the hill.*

⁶ It was quite insistent. And I'm a creature of whims; I don't always understand my less rational impulses, but it usually pays to follow them; my brain usually has something in mind.

⁷ "Good afternoon!" shouts a cheery voice. I look further up the path and see a tall, slim gent enjoying the view from a small plateau some fifty feet below the top of the hill.

⁸ Typical. This hill probably has an average of zero visitors per week, and I have the bad luck to run into one of them.

⁹ It occurs to me that my social skills need some work.

¹⁰ "Hello there!" I shout back, waving, as I trudge up toward him, mud and leaves squishing underfoot.

¹¹ My first thought of him as a 'gent' bears some explanation. The man has a distinguished air about him, and is well dressed. But somehow he looks old–fashioned. Out of place.

¹² Perhaps it's the waxed, greying moustache? Or the tweeds?

¹³ It takes all sorts, I suppose.

¹⁴ As I reach the plateau, a little out of

breath, he takes a few unhurried step towards me, and unexpectedly takes and shakes my hand.

¹⁵ His smile is warm, enthusiastic;

¹⁶ I'm quite taken aback.

¹⁷ "Please excuse me, but it's a pleasure to meet you."

¹⁸ I'm about to reply to this when he introduces himself in a serious tone.

¹⁹ "My name is Roth. *Abednigo Roth.*"

²⁰ He raises an eyebrow, clearly expecting a response. I don't keep him waiting, though I feel like I'm wading out of my depth.

²¹ "And my name's Roth. *Indigo Roth.* Are we...?" waving a finger repeatedly between us.

²² He grins more roguishly than I'd expect of him; yes, he's a Roth.

²³ I wonder if he's from Uncle Jericho's branch of the family? They're all rather eccentric, and this man's clothes suggest he may be King Canute on the beach of fashion, angrily facing the approaching waves.

²⁴ "I should say so. You have many questions, no doubt. Perhaps it would be quicker of me to ask you a simple question, and let you catch up on your own. You seem a bright enough fella!"

²⁵ He slaps me on the arm, and then turns to wave expansively at the landscape below us.

²⁶ He asks his question.

²⁷ "What do you think of my view?"

²⁸ *His view?* "Well, it's pleasant enough," I start to say, casting my gaze down the hill and towards the horizon, "but it's..."

²⁹ My voice trails off.

³⁰ The view is wrong.

³¹ "Is there something wrong, Indigo?"

³² I glance his way, to his lopsided grin; yes, he knows there damned well is.

³³ I take a few steps forward and take it all in. I recognise the land, but it's *different.*

³⁴ There's a nearby church that I don't remember. The main road that blights the beauty of the view that I am familiar with is missing. As is a nearby town. Smoke rises from a smattering of cottages.

³⁵ There's a serenity about it all.

³⁶ "This doesn't feel like a dream," I mutter uncertainly, wondering if I've conjured Abednigo from the depths of my memory.

³⁷ "Quite so, not a dream!" says my companion, giving my thoughts some room to move.

³⁸ "Then... *when* are we?" I ask, convinced I've somehow shifted in time.

³⁹ "Oh, it's definitely today," he chuckles, stepping up beside me. "And the ground you stand upon is from the same day you woke into this morning. But this view," he says, pointing vaguely towards the church and cottages, "is 1905. *My* 1905."

⁴⁰ Well, that explains his clothes.

⁴¹ "So you're a distant relative. Well, ancestor." I instantly forget this as I theorise, "It's something to do with the hill, right? There's something special about it, I've always thought so."

⁴² Abednigo nods, seemingly pleased that I'm putting the pieces together.

⁴³ "Yes, the hill. This lovely, wooded, haunted hill." He pulls his jacket more closely about him. "Alberto explained it to me once—that's *Alberto Roth*, the theoretical physicist from the Thirties—but it was a little beyond me.

⁴⁴ The gist of it is that the hill is *special*. To our family. Apparently, to us all this is... *Common Ground?*"

⁴⁵ I consider this; it sounds true. He continues,

⁴⁶ "And today you're sharing my view. On another day, perhaps I might share yours."

⁴⁷ I take in the vista with a touch of envy.

⁴⁸ "Your view is nicer. Gentler. From a simpler time. Things move along a little too quickly in my time."

⁴⁹ "Which is when, may I ask?" he inquires, patiently.

⁵⁰ "Excuse me, I should have said. 2013."

⁵¹ He nods, unsurprised, and picks up his train of thought again. He shrugs reflectively.

⁵² "Progress always seems swift. Technology makes for Change. Change is difficult, uncertain, worrying. We naturally wonder what our futures will bring."

⁵³ Silence falls over the scene.

⁵⁴ The sun starts its march to the horizon; the sky has a hint of pink and purple about it. He continues to voice his thoughts.

⁵⁵ "In my time, we work for companies that constantly demand more for less.

⁵⁶ We are insignificant cogs in increasingly larger and colder machines.

⁵⁷ There are more people in the world than ever before, but we feel isolated.

[58] Governments levy taxes to pay for wars in distant lands we've never seen.

[59] We cure diseases that would have killed our ancestors, but discover new ones.

[60] We travel the globe and yet view visitors to our own land with suspicion, fearing an erosion of our national identity.

[61] And both old and new vices and addictions run unchecked."

[62] He gestures in frustration.

[63] "Will we ever evolve from this sad state of affairs?"

[64] I suppose this is all rhetorical, but I shake my head; I'm genuinely surprised at his view of my past.

[65] "It's much the same in my time."

[66] He looks to the horizon, gathering his thoughts. "So perhaps Change is not such a dominant and destructive force as we all fear?"

[67] And with that, he seems to brighten. "And perhaps the future is not such a terrifying place?"

[68] I laugh. "You sound like my blog."

[69] He cocks his head. "I don't understand. Your *blog*?"

[70] I search for the words I need.

[71] "I write about things and record them in a special book. A log or diary, you might say. I write about my experiences, my encounters, the people I know, the adventures I have.

[72] Sometimes they are entertaining, sometimes they are serious."

[73] He leans in a little, rumbling, "I'd wager there may be more than a hint of fancy about them?"

[74] I look at him sideways and admit shiftily, "Well, sometimes." We both laugh. "Anyway, technology enables me to instantly share my log with people far away. Words, pictures, sounds."

[75] He nods appreciatively, fascinated.

[76] "That sounds ingenious. I also write for a living, but I must rely on the technology of my era to carry the message to others. Newspapers. Gazettes. Letters.

[77] I have many correspondents. Something of a following, you might say," he adds, blushing.

[78] Then, in a mock hushed voice, he confesses, "I suspect that I may have written an occasional fanciful piece myself."

[79] I laugh again, and bow slightly. "Then I consider myself to be in esteemed company!" He waves this aside with good nature.

[80] We fall silent and turn back to the sunset. Lights are coming on in the cottages.

[81] After a while, Abednigo marvels quietly to himself, "Less than a century from now. Technology to carry one's writings instantly to the furthest corners of the British Empire."

[82] I decide to keep my own counsel about the Empire.

[83] He checks his pocket watch; it's a beauty.

[84] "Well, Indigo, it's been a pleasure. But I must be away." He offers his hand. "I hope we'll meet again on another day?"

[85] I accept his hand and ask, "Will it still be today?"

[86] "Oh, I expect so." Suddenly, he points down the track. "Look! It seems you have company."

[87] There is a teenage boy heading up the path. His appearance is puzzling; his clothes and shoes are made from unfamiliar materials, and there are what I can only describe as *gadgets* in the air about him.

[88] Lights pulse and blink and they orbit; I don't recognise the technology, but it looks *cool*.

[89] Abednigo slaps me on the back and—jarringly—the scene shifts. My view from the hill has returned; the road, the town, no church.

[90] It is sometime in early afternoon.

[91] Abednigo is gone.

[92] The lad trudges wearily up the track towards me.

[93] "Good afternoon!" I shout cheerily. He looks in my direction and a look of disappointment and annoyance passes briefly across his face. But he seems to reach a decision and waves.

[94] "Ho there!" He shouts back, and plods up to the plateau, mud and leaves squishing under his feet.

[95] As he approaches, he looks at me strangely, perhaps trying to get the measure of me. He pauses to fiddle with a gadget, retrieving information. After a moment peering at a screen, he finds what he's looking for.

[96] And looks surprised.

[97] I step forward and take and shake his hand. I'm about to introduce myself, but he confidently beats me to the punch.

⁹⁸ "My name's Roth. *Django Roth*,"** he says, regarding me with a mix of suspicion and fascination. "And you're Indigo. Which makes no sense whatsoever."

⁹⁹ I wave at the landscape below us, and ask the only question that seems appropriate.

¹⁰⁰ "What do you think of my view?"

Notes

*   But I would like to be clear that I know of *no* such skills, and never make use of them when playing cards with friends.

**   Yes, all names in my family end with the letter O.

3 Roth

"Last night, I dreamed of my perfect woman. I offered to buy her a drink, and she said she was waiting for her boyfriend. My subconscious hates me."

Definitely Not My Water

1 ¹ In a rare brush with reality, I'm driving through my home town.
² I'm on my way home for the evening, and my social diary is wide open. Again.
³ I glance by chance to my right as I pass through the high street, and notice that there's a movie playing that I'd like to see. Which movie isn't important,
⁴ but before I realise what I'm doing, and with more spontaneity than is my norm, I'm pulling into a parking space right outside the theatre;
⁵ what a piece of luck.
⁶ I walk inside and talk to the young fella on the main desk. He tells me that the movie starts in half an hour, give or take a few minutes for adverts.
⁷ Hey, not bad! My evening is taken care of, but I've half an hour to kill.
⁸ It reminds me about trying to fill up a jar with rough stones. They reach the top, but leave a lot of space.
⁹ I wander across the street to the fish and chip shop, a mainstay of English cuisine. Checking the menu, I see that they serve scampi;
¹⁰ I adore scampi, and haven't had any in years. And while it doesn't totally agree with my current dieting regime (going well, thanks for asking), it seems too good a chance to miss.

¹¹ As I pay, the woman serving tells me they always cook it fresh, and it'll be five or six minutes until it's ready.
¹² I'm thinking about the jar again, and how I've filled up much of the spare space with smaller stones.
¹³ Feeling rather proud of myself, but feeling the call of nature after a long drive, I wander next door to the pub to sneakily use their toilet.
¹⁴ As I step inside the unusually quiet bar, the barmaid gives me a cheery smile and asks me what I'm having.
¹⁵ This wasn't the plan, but I spy my favourite beer on tap.
¹⁶ Hey, why *not?* I have time. I'll have a swift pint.
¹⁷ She draws me the pint, and I take long, refreshing draught. Marvellous. But I'm reminded of my pressing need to use the facilities. I ask the barmaid where they are, and she points me up the stairs.
¹⁸ I head up, and once again marvel about the metaphorical jar representing my evening. I feel that in these few spare minutes, I'm filling most of the remaining spaces up with sand.
¹⁹ I laugh as I empty my bladder, imagining I'm filling the finest of spaces in the jar up with water. Not my water you understand; that would be gross.
²⁰ It's a metaphor, remember?

²¹ But now the jar is most definitely *full*.

²² I head back down and noting the time, I pass a few pleasantries with the bar staff as I drain my pint.

²³ Delicious, the best I've had in ages.

²⁴ I then head next door just as my food hits the plate. It's incredibly good, light breadcrumbs with a perfectly–cooked seafood centre.

²⁵ The chips are crisp and golden.

²⁶ That done, I make my way back to the cinema and buy my ticket.

²⁷ And flop into my seat, resolving the final recursion, just as the movie starts.

²⁸ Two hours later, my mission accomplished, I head home.

²⁹ What a great night. From nothing, I filled my time with random events which all dovetailed beautifully.

³⁰ Not a moment was wasted, I enjoyed some wonderful hot food and cold beer, and made it home by bedtime.

³¹ Sometimes things just fall together. You can't plan it.

³² Such a shame that the movie stank.

Merely Distant And Deceptive

2¹ It's a beautiful sunny day, the birds are singing, life is good.

² And I'm so angry I could just spit.

³ I've always hated waiting for the bus.

⁴ **Twenty five years ago**, my new girlfriend Avril loves to travel by bus.

⁵ When she asks me out, she says we should go into town.

⁶ As a healthy lad, I think nothing of walking the three miles to the mall, but she seems quite excited by the prospect of a bus ride together.

⁷ So I scrape together the fare—I'm healthy, not wealthy—and we head out into the bright sunshine of our teens.

⁸ After half an hour, we're still waiting by the bus stop. We chat, we laugh, we enjoy each other's company, but inside I'm annoyed and disappointed for our first date.

⁹ The seed of discontent is sown.

¹⁰ **Back in the now**, cars and cyclists and pedestrians amble past, each making more progress than me.

¹¹ Then my heart skips;

¹² do I hear the bus?

¹³ No, it's just a truck, distant and deceptive. It belches diesel noisily as it eventually rattles past.

¹⁴ **Fifteen years ago**, I have an interview in a nearby town. My car is off the road—I'm still not wealthy—and despite an offer of a ride with my best friend 'Difficult, there's a regular bus service running.

¹⁵ I give myself plenty of time, and head out into the sunshine in my best suit.

¹⁶ I wait 45 minutes for the half–hourly service, but eventually climb aboard.

¹⁷ On the outskirts of our destination, our transport overheats.

¹⁸ I can wait for a replacement ride to come and pick us up, but instead I elect to play it safe and walk the last half mile to the interview.

¹⁹ I make it on time, but I'm hot, bothered, and somewhat agitated.

²⁰ It's a small consolation that at the end of the day I don't want the job.

²¹ The seed of discontent sprouts keen green shoots of prejudice towards a limitless sky.

²² **Back in the now**, as I stand waiting, I remember a silly press release issued by London Transport in the middle of the Eighties.

²³ Customers had complained that buses were speeding past them as they waited at the bus stop. Often, the drivers gave them a cheery wave as they did this.

²⁴ The company press release said, without a hint of irony:

²⁵ *It is not always possible for drivers to maintain their schedules if they stop to pick up passengers.*

²⁶ But I've not even been graced with *that* bizarre policy today. No buses to be seen.

²⁷ No doubt, in the timeless English manner, three will arrive at once.

²⁸ Well, I hope they will.

²⁹ **First thing this morning**, I decide to change the shape of my day. The sun is shining, and I really want to enjoy some downtime.

³⁰ So I take a day off work, have a leisurely breakfast, shower, dress, and head out in search of a decent cup of coffee.

³¹ For some reason, driving does not appeal; today, I'd like to be driven.

³² Checking my pockets, I'm surprised to find I'm carrying money—I'm *still* not wealthy but behave like royalty in this respect most of the time—and decide to take the bus into town.

³³ I'm surprised by this out–of–character

decision, and pause for a moment. Why would I do this? I rationalise that it's a bit too warm to trek the two miles by foot, and besides, I'd rather get back quickly to enjoy that downtime in the back garden I promised myself.

[34] I dismiss the past and head out.

[35] **Two minutes later**, I'm at the bus stop.

[36] **Half an hour later**, I'm still waiting.

[37] I'm quietly annoyed, and that fact really bothers me.

[38] As an individual, I'm extraordinarily patient.

[39] But this is not a matter of patience.

[40] If I get to the bus stop and find that the next scheduled service is an hour away, I'll patiently wait an hour and take it on the chin.

[41] But getting to the bus stop five minutes early for a scheduled service and then waiting an hour drives me crazy.

[42] Especially if they're supposed to run every ten minutes; the sheer unreliability gnaws at my calm.

[43] **Back in the now**, an hour has passed.

[44] In the park opposite, there's a football game going on. Kids play on the swings. Cyclists and cars and pedestrians seem to be moving faster now, but perhaps it's my imagination.

[45] Life teems around me, swirling its Brownian way through the day, interacting and experiencing and progressing.

[46] But I'm standing still.

[47] The flower of outrage blossoms, and I don't care for the smell.

[48] I head home to enjoy my corner of the world in the sunshine.

[49] I've always hated waiting for the bus.

[50] Sometimes the bus is late, or you wait forever and then three arrive at once.

[51] But sometimes? Well, sometimes the bus just doesn't arrive at all.

Trying Not To Over–Think It

3 [1] When I emerged from university aged twenty one, I was young and enthusiastic.

[2] These days, at more than twice that age, I often feel beaten down.

[3] You know how it is. Work, money, relationships, family, health, time, and sheer bloody *Life*;

[4] they gang up on us and grind at the spirit with their relentless demands for attention.

[5] The ensuing stress is always an unwelcome extra guest at the bonfire.

[6] So today, after a tough few weeks, I took action. I took charge., and did something that always manages to quieten my mind.

[7] I went to feed the ducks at the lake in the local park.

[8] I have no idea why this works, but—as ever—I feel remarkably upbeat as a result.

[9] Somehow, throwing bread for some lively, cheeky birds that quack and splash really helps me get my head back on straight.

[10] I try not to over–think it.

[11] My name is Indigo Roth. I'm 45 years old.

[12] And, for the record, I remain young and enthusiastic.

All The Time In The World

4 [1] I arrive at the meeting on time.

[2] It was a close run thing; I had to walk with purpose and forego my coffee and breakfast.

[3] But as I find a seat and claim my space at the table, it seems clear that the facilitator is still messing about with the audio and visual link to our other office.

[4] This is annoying and frustrating most of the time, but today it smells like opportunity.

[5] I pause for a moment, unsure whether to act.

[6] It's no good; I want coffee.

[7] I step outside without explanation, and stride meaningfully down the full length of the building. My mother says I look angry when I do this. I'm not sure if it's true, but I've observed that folk don't tend to step in my way.

[8] Well, not twice, anyway.

[9] I reach the kitchen and find that the coffee machine is free. I pop my mug in and push the button for an *Americano*, a shot of espresso with some hot water in it. A bit of a lame brew in itself, but I intend to add a double espresso to my large mug if there's time.

[10] And so it begins. The grinding. The gurgling. The slightly incontinent dribble of steaming–hot Joe into the mug.

[11] Slow, slow, slooooow.

¹² "Oh, come on! Come ooooon!"

¹³ Good grief, it's unbearable! I need to get moving! The meeting could start at any moment, and I hate being late. My heart is pounding, and all I can think of is how long this damned coffee machine is taking. I'll never have time for the second shot of coffee.

¹⁴ But without fanfare, a curious thought crosses my mind.

¹⁵ How long until I am missed? Two minutes maybe?

¹⁶ I breathe deeply, and start to count slowly.

¹⁷ One second. Two. Three.

¹⁸ Time slows. Or rather, my perception of it does.

¹⁹ Instead of focussing on how long this machine is taking, of how it eats seconds that I do not have, I simply mark the passage of those seconds.

²⁰ Time slows. I notice out of the window the dry, orange, autumnal leaves that are soaring on the wind. It's gusting today. My mind wanders to the windows rattling overnight as I lay curled in my warm, comfortable bed. To the sound of the leaves rustling underfoot as I walked to my car after breakfast.

²¹ Time slows. My heart slows. No hurry. No panic.

²² The Americano finishes.

²³ Twenty seconds. Twenty one.

²⁴ I drift back to the machine, and hit the button for the double espresso. This is notoriously slow. But I'm not thinking about it.

²⁵ Time slows. My counting becomes automatic, a background task, a slow pulse that divides the days into wide, leisurely slices. I look forward to the weekend, to company and good food, to time spent with those closest to me.

²⁶ Thirty seconds. Thirty one.

²⁷ A few seconds ago, time was compressed. Now, it is distended.

²⁸ Nothing has changed except my perception of its passage.

²⁹ For the first time, I understand relativity.

³⁰ Forty seconds. The espresso finishes.

³¹ Forty seconds. Forty seconds.

³² Time stops.

³³ There is a profound feeling of total calm.

³⁴ I have all the time in the world.

³⁵ I collect my mug and take an ambling walk back down the corridor.

Ten Minutes The Poorer

5¹ The search is beginning to feel fruitless.

² I slam the wardrobe shut and head out onto the landing.

³ After a thorough check of the third bedroom—my token box room—the check of the upstairs on my house is complete.

⁴ The result? Nothing.

⁵ And ten minutes the poorer.

⁶ Actually, not quite. I've accumulated a gumball, a wizened prawn cracker, and what amounts to a pocketful of loose change from various dim corners and hungry pieces of furniture.

⁷ I thump downstairs dejectedly. This is not how I wanted to start the New Year;

⁸ looking for things is one of my least favourite activities.

⁹ I love *finding* things that I'm not looking for; this is one of the great joys of window shopping. But hunting for things at home? I can't stand it.

¹⁰ There are only two rooms downstairs;

¹¹ a comfortable lounge and the kitchen diner. They are both bright and airy;

¹² I can't imagine for a moment that I'll find what I'm looking for in either of them.

¹³ The lounge takes but a moment, as the sofa and TV furniture stand clear of the floor.

¹⁴ A quick scoot around the room on all fours, including checking under the bottom of the curtains, results in my bounty swelling by three small coins and a paperclip.

¹⁵ I am also reminded that I *really* need to hoover, as a menacing dust bunny shifts restlessly behind the TV.

¹⁶ The remaining room offers a little more challenge. I circle the dining table in the kitchen diner, checking carefully, and once again check behind the curtains. No more copper coinage here;

¹⁷ I must have vacuumed recently.

¹⁸ I move into the kitchen area and sigh. The linoleum floor is clear, and it just seems pointless checking in the tiny cupboards. But I do, one at a time, hunting but finding nothing, and feeling a fool for doing so.

¹⁹ I have no idea what possesses me to look down the plughole in the sink;

²⁰ the pressure must be getting to me.

²¹ As I step back, I trip over my own feet

and crash unceremoniously onto my backside. It hurts. This is too much!

²² Why do I put myself through this?!

²³ Why do I let myself get driven crazy by this search?!

²⁴ My heart pounding, adrenaline surging, and my butt aching, I screw my eyes up and bellow my frustration at the house in general.

²⁵ "Okay, I can't take this any more! I give up!"

²⁶ It feels good to say it, to shout the venomous words out loud.

²⁷ When I open my eyes, I am surrounded by four figures, dressed in black. Sharp, cunning eyes regard me coolly behind ornate dark masks;

²⁸ lethal weapons glisten in the early morning sun of my kitchen.

²⁹ *Game over.*

³⁰ You know, the next time the Ninjas come over wanting to play *Hide And Seek*, remind me to suggest *Monopoly* instead.

Pockets Stuffed With Gold

6 ¹ What a beautiful day.

² Blue skies, bright sunshine, and a cool breeze stirring the warm air.

³ The hill in front of me is my destination for this rare day out. It looks like a nice one to climb, and it's not too steep.

⁴ The way up to the top curves gently away from me; I can't see everything that's ahead, but I've a pretty good idea where it'll end up.

⁵ And I bet the view from the top is a cracker.

⁶ I stroll for a while on the easy incline, enjoying the feel of the sun.

⁷ Flowers salute me on either side at waist height, bumblebees meandering happily among them. Their content buzzing draws my attention, and I crouch to watch them as they go about their bumbly business, their pockets stuffed with gold.

⁸ Within seconds, I'm engrossed.

⁹ I've always been fond of bumblebees; they bring back memories of my maternal grandmother, who would hold her hand flat for them to land on when I was a toddler. She taught me that they were gentle giants, and though she's long since passed, I've always treated them with awe and respect.

¹⁰ I resume my stroll as the slope increases, my mind wandering. A bird circles easily above a nearby rocky outcrop, perhaps riding a thermal current.

¹¹ I wonder what it would be like to fly as a bird rather than walk as a man?

¹² Would life be the freedom of the endless sky, or would flying be like swimming in deep water? Predators could lurk in any direction, in all directions.

¹³ I lose my footing momentarily, but quickly regain my balance.

¹⁴ Onwards, upwards.

¹⁵ The way is much steeper as the hill narrows, but I'm most of the way up now, and my heart tells me that I'm alive; it's a good feeling.*

¹⁶ As the hilltop approaches, the curve reveals a gnarled tree that stretches across the path from my right. It looks wind-blown and somehow out of place on such a lovely day, but there it stands.

¹⁷ I step through the flowers surrounding it carefully and reach out to touch the bark of its inclined trunk. It's deeply grooved but smooth, and I trace the channels upwards into its bare branches with my fingertips.

¹⁸ A solitary bloom lies out of reach above me on the far side of the path, as if it's trying to escape the tranquility of the hill.

¹⁹ The mystery holds me for a few minutes, but I eventually move past and steel myself for the last stretch. The incline is harsh now, and I have to work harder, the sweat finding my joints, to reach the small summit.

²⁰ As I crest the rise, a little short of breath, I'm met by a mercifully cooling wind.

²¹ It's flat up here, and after a few seconds catching by breath, I move closer to the opposite edge and gaze down upon the dwindling length of the path. It's obviously longer and steeper than it looked from the ground, and looks broken and uneven;

²² no wonder I lost my footing.

²³ I wonder idly if I'd have started the journey had I known that the going would be tougher than expected?

²⁴ I dismiss the thought as irrelevant; I made my mind up to climb the hill and followed through. I even made time to enjoy some cool stuff along the way.

[25] And I'm not disappointed now I'm here; the view really is spectacular.

[26] I smile and realise that I'm brighter than I used to be.

Passing Into Mental Myth

7 [1] When I look back on my life, it is as a series of moments.

[2] **It's mid–December**. And as I stand in the cold, dark evening, gazing across the courtyard to the chapel, I realise that one of those moments is unfolding around me.

[3] **Three hours earlier**, the moonlit evening is clear and crisp. I have a light jacket on over my dinner suit, but the chill in the air quickens my step on the five–minute walk from the car park.

[4] I'm not crazy about office parties, but this one is at King's College in Cambridge, the most impressive of the old university colleges.

[5] An event that is not to be missed.

[6] Half a dozen of us arrive at the same time. The massive college gates stand open, and though we manage a brief exchange of greetings, silence falls as we walk through into a magnificent courtyard.

[7] Great Court is a hundred–odd metres to each edge, with impressive architecture on all sides.

[8] A wide gravel path surrounds a vast— and immaculate—grass square, with a distant statue at its centre.

[9] The massive Gothic bulk of the famous King's College Chapel broods, sullen and unlit, to our right.

[10] I've not been in here before, and gape a little. Perhaps even more than a little.

[11] Event signs direct us towards a tall and well–lit building to our left. Huge, black lamp posts cast their electric light from the perimeter of the grass.

[12] As we make our way, I note that we're all careful to keep to the path, and smile;

[13] *the college authorities will still hang you for walking on the grass, even in this day and age*, says an inner voice.

[14] As we deposit our coats, we all look pleased to be indoors, particularly the women in their more elegant, colourful evening wear.

[15] There's some polite chitchat, but a hubbub of conversation quickly draws us through to the warm main hall.

[16] It's quite something, an intimately lit room with a high–vaulted Gothic ceiling, stained–glass windows, wood–panelled walls, and dozens of impressive oil paintings.

[17] I'm interested by all this, but far more interested in the company of good friends, and in what will hopefully be a superb meal.

[18] I'm a bit awkward in formal social situations—black tie for two hundred is quite daunting—but my amigos carry me magnificently, and dinner does not disappoint.

[19] And so, in a whirl of conversation, indiscrete whispers and raucous laughter, the evening passes pleasantly.

[20] As the party draws to a close, the first handful of us—keen to be in our beds— slip away from the hall, gather our coats, and head out through the main doors into the chilly night.

[21] And stop dead.

[22] The courtyard has been transformed.

[23] It's snowing heavily.

[24] Four inches have fallen while we were indoors, and huge fluffy flakes continue to descend from the solid cloud cover overhead.

[25] The others head back indoors, excited to tell those at the party about the snow, but I stand, transfixed.

[26] The court is an unbroken field of white, as immaculate as the grass underneath.

[27] The closest lamp post has taken on a surreal quality, standing in isolation, tall and black, in the snow;

[28] at any moment, a Narnian faun might walk timidly out of the darkness to stand, uncertain, in its electric glow.

[29] Across from me, the immense chapel is now cheerily lit, its windows tall and colourful.**

[30] I half expect to hear the sound of the college choir from within, but the silence is absolute.

[31] It's breathtaking.

[32] As I stand there in the snow on a cold night, gazing across the courtyard to the chapel, I feel the moment crystallise around me, never to be forgotten.

[33] **Back in the now**, just a few weeks later, my mind is playing tricks on me.

[34] The mental picture of the lamplit courtyard in snowfall has passed into mental myth.

[35] It's taken centre stage in my memories of the evening, pushing aside the

pleasant memories of the party, [36] and the later memories of treacherous pavements, biting cold winds, and hazardous driving. [37] These have been demoted to a terse,

[38] "And I got home afterwards." [39] All that's left is that perfect moment in the snow. [40] And when I look back on my life, it is as a series of moments.

Notes

* I really should do this more often.
** It really is beautiful; if you visit, try and see it at night when it's lit up.

King

"We once owned a third of the globe; the sun literally never set on the British Empire. Now we're just grateful for warmed–over American reality shows. We used to be important because we stole everyone's land, people and toys. Mum made us give them back in the end. We're still rather annoyed about it, and never send her a birthday card."

The Hum Of Forgetful Bees

1 ¹ The cloudless sky is blue and the grass is warm.

² I've decided that today is not a day for dashing about. It was supposed to be, don't get me wrong;

³ there's a teetering pile of work to do at the office, lawns to mow, washing and ironing to do, supermarkets to visit, dinner to cook,

⁴ and any number of other "important" chores that 'really can't wait'.

⁵ Except, I now realise, they can.

⁶ The sun filters beautifully through the trees, the birds sing, and I can hear bees humming their absent–minded tune in the nearby lavender.

⁷ There's a gentle breeze, and I'm feeling wonderfully relaxed.

⁸ And my decision to pause here when I should be doing other things gives it all an added naughty luxuriance.

⁹ I smile; this must be that stopping to smell the roses thing that I've heard so much about?

¹⁰ I either do things or I don't.

¹¹ If I do, I do them 'til they done. And if I don't, I'm doing something else with a similar focus.

¹² Because there's always so much to do. It's hard to not be swept along by the current, but today I'm delighted to be lounging on the riverbank for a change.

¹³ I have a deep sigh and inhale the scents of the garden in bloom.

¹⁴ Moments pass like minutes, and minutes pass like days.

¹⁵ I reflect lazily that a short while ago, I was less relaxed.

¹⁶ The two–ton visiting rhino sitting on my legs was causing me some discomfort.

¹⁷ But now? Why, now I can hardly feel my legs at all.

¹⁸ So, it's all good.

¹⁹ I wonder when King will get home?

Literally Off The Map

2 ¹ I always enjoy helping the police with their enquiries.

² "Mr. Roth, why was there a floating pyramid in your garden?"

³ It's the third time of asking, and I sense that *Detective Inspector McGuffin* is determined to get to the bottom of things.

⁴ "It's complicated." This is the truth if you don't spend a lot of time around me.

⁵ "I can deal with complexity, Mr. Roth." Impassively, the policeman meets my gaze.

⁶ McGuffin is a tall, heavy set man. He is perhaps ten years older than me, his hair greying and slicked back, his face a weathered map of his tough world.

⁷ As we sit in the dim interview room, lit only by a single spot lamp above the desk, he turns his attention to the topmost report of the pile in front of him. Picking it up, he scowls as he slowly reads, lips moving almost imperceptibly.

⁸ He presents the classic image of a dull, unimaginative, plodding copper.

⁹ I'm not fooled for a moment. Yes, this man really *can* deal with complexity.

¹⁰ "I believe you."

¹¹ And I do believe him. As with all things, the devil is in the details.

¹² The plain dark suit is loosely cut, as if to hide the expansion of middle age. But the material is heavy and expensive, and the body it carefully conceals is solid from lifting weights rather than donuts.

¹³ A dark necktie hangs casually from an open collar, but the perfect double Windsor knot squeals on this contrived casualness.

¹⁴ The voice is pure gravel, his delivery casual, but his words are considered, his questions direct and unambiguous.

¹⁵ Above all else, McGuffin's eyes are intelligent and kind, despite the scowl, and he is clearly educated way beyond his rough demeanour.

¹⁶ This man invites you to underestimate him while being openly intelligent.

¹⁷ I like him already.

¹⁸ "So." The policeman looks up momentarily. "The pyramid?"

¹⁹ "Very well." I test the water gently. "The pyramid is a vehicle." I choose my next words carefully. "An aircar would be one way of describing it." Though possibly not the most honest one;

²⁰ I find that people don't expect to find *instantaneous spatial relocation devices* anywhere except *Star Trek*.

²¹ He regards me levelly over the top of the report.

²² "A flying car?" He sniffs. "Mr. Roth, if I file a report to that effect, I think my superiors would take a dim view of these proceedings."

²³ "Perhaps they'd like you to uncover that it's, say..." I wave a hand casually, "A *weather balloon?*"

²⁴ My tone is neutral, exploratory. He pauses, eyeing me with some interest.

²⁵ "Perhaps." He indicates the pile of paperwork in folders on the desk. "But there's so many incredible things in these other reports."

²⁶ I know he means *incredible* in its most literal sense. "They can't all be so easily dismissed."

²⁷ "Such as?" My enquiry is genuine; I'm really not sure what he has.

²⁸ "Well, unexplained light phenomena." He checks the next folder. "The Eiffel Tower. A giant, blood–stained rabbit."

²⁹ "That wasn't blood, it was raspberries." He doesn't let me interrupt him as he continues to skim through the titles on the folders.

³⁰ "A giant hybrid squid squirrel. A huge Austrian man in a puppet costume. The remains of what appear to be zebras."

³¹ "Well, that last one's easy to explain. King ate them. He shares my house."

³² "Your housemate keeps and eats zebras?"

³³ "No, he mostly eats them. He's a lion. It's what they *do*." I keep my face straight.

³⁴ "A lion." His tone is somewhat flat; I'm unsure what he makes of it.

³⁵ I shrug. "Yes. You seem surprised."

³⁶ "Well, Mr. Roth, we don't get many lions around here." He shrugs at the fact. "You could have said Mr. King was a tiger and I'd have been no less surprised."

³⁷ I frown. "Well, I would."

³⁸ He puts the report down. "And why is that?"

³⁹ "Well, tigers don't eat zebras, for one. Geography." I'm careful to keep any sarcastic or smartass tone out of my voice; this is a fact, nothing more. "Plus, King is a great orator and storyteller, and has a marvellous singing voice. Tigers don't really say much."

⁴⁰ McGuffin raises an eyebrow a shade, and pulls a different report from the pile.

⁴¹ "So, they're like this Yavin fellow. The badger." I regard him uncertainly. "He doesn't say much. Correct?"

⁴² "Correct. But to be honest, there's no comparison."

⁴³ "Oh?" He seems genuinely surprised. "How so?"

⁴⁴ "Well, Yavin is the retired *Chair of Engineering* at Cambridge University." I pause to let that fact sink in. "Whereas

most tigers can't tie their shoelaces."

45 The detective sighs heavily. It sounds like I'm getting him down, but it's part of the act. I play along, my curiosity still piqued.

46 "Tigers don't wear shoes, Mr. Roth."

47 I smile. "And now you know why."

48 We regard each other across the table. If we were at Wimbledon, it would probably be time to get a lemon barley water and change ends for the next set.

49 "So. Let's go back to Mr. King. Is he a UK resident?"

50 Yes, I *definitely* like this guy. He's moved past the animal thing and is talking about King as a *person*.

51 I'm impressed by this display of open-mindedness.

52 He's not losing sight of his target, nor his grip on the conversation.

53 "No. He's an ambassador to the UK from one of the savannah states in Africa, though he now doubles as their ambassador to the *Royal Republic of Subterranea*."

54 "Royal Republic?" He frowns. "That's a contradiction, surely?"

55 He has a point. I shrug.

56 "I didn't name the place. That'd be my best friend, iDifficult." The policeman's attention goes up a notch. He straightens in his seat and leans in a little.

57 "Ah yes. Mr. Difficult. I wondered when we'd get to him." He flips a few pages, looking for something. "I don't have his first name; what does the "i" stand for?"

58 "I've no idea." This is a lie. "I think iDifficult is more of a statement about his disposition than a name?"

59 "And he's the boss of this... Subterranea?"

60 "Well, to give him his full ceremonial title, he is *The Imperial President, His Royal Reverence, The Late Emperor iDifficult*."

61 McGuffin just stares. No question is needed. I whisper,

62 "He likes to keep his options open in case of an uprising."

63 Again, he waits for me to continue, raising his eyebrows encouragingly.

64 "He built the kingdom under his back yard, accessible from each of his three sheds. And mine too, now." I add this with a mixture of pride and terror. "And though it is a relatively small place, it was officially recognised as a nation by

the *United Nations* in 2008."

65 McGuffin puts down his papers. We're off the map here. Literally. He assumes a relaxed pose and smiles indulgently.

66 "I see. And what makes this Subterranea so special?"

67 "Well, it occupies four and a half dimensions, for one thing."

68 "Four and a *half*?"

69 "Yes, 'Difficult recently discovered that Time is fractal in nature. Which is why he's always running late."

70 The policeman laughs. It's totally out of character, and nice to hear. But he rallies magnificently and regains his composure in a moment.

71 "I wish I could include that in my report," he observes quietly.

72 "Your boss wouldn't understand it?"

73 He shakes his head. "Not a hope."

74 There's a curious moment as we both wonder where to take this interview.

75 We are saved by a knock at the door. McGuffin barks an invitation to enter, and a young uniformed constable enters and whispers to him.

76 My host then nods, rises from his chair and looks towards the door.

77 Bear steps majestically into the room, dipping his seven feet of black–bear bulk under the doorframe.

78 He is in full diplomatic dress uniform, and looking pretty spiffy; the turquoise sash and orange fez are striking against his dark brown fur.

79 The junior officer, somewhat unnerved by the influx of unexpected wildlife, scuttles from the room.

80 I leap to my feet, somewhat relieved to see my ursine friend. "Detective Inspector, may I present Bear, Ambassador to the UK from the Court of Subterranea."

81 Bear nods to us both professionally. To his credit, McGuffin doesn't miss a beat, stepping forward to shake Bear's huge extended paw between his hands.

82 "Mr. Ambassador, welcome. How may I assist you today?" The copper's stern gaze softens as he looks up into Bear's face;

83 my friend's ability to put people at their ease has always been a marvel to me.

84 "Detective Inspector," rumbles the bear kindly, "I heard about this interview, and hoped I might be able to assist my opposite number here."

85 He waves a paw in my direction.

86 The Detective Inspector eyes me suspiciously. *Opposite number?* "You're an *Ambassador*, Mr. Roth?"

87 I give him my best poker face; my mother always told me to be gracious in victory.

88 "Yes, British Ambassador to the Court of Subterranea."

89 "So that means..."

90 I put my diplomatic passport on the table.

91 "Yes. I have *diplomatic immunity*."

92 I notice Bear slip quietly from the room. McGuffin looks a little crestfallen, but is gracious in defeat. He walks to meet me and we shake hands;

93 I suspect our mothers were similar.

94 "Mr. Roth, thank you for your time today." His smile is genuine.

95 "Not at all. It's been my pleasure."

96 This is how the game is played between Gentlemen.

97 Behind us, the fresh-faced constable re-enters the room hurriedly. I suspect Bear has ushered him in to watch the official closing act;

98 I slip into my best acting mode.

99 "Oh, and before I forget Detective Inspector McGuffin, you'll need this." I hand him a completed police form from my suit pocket.

100 He opens and inspects it. Understanding my endgame, his face takes on an official air for the benefit of his underling.

101 "Mr. Roth, this is a happy coincidence. It appears you have filed a report about your *lost weather balloon?*"

102 "Yes," I say, with faux embarrassment, "we were trying a new balloon, in fact. A pyramid-shaped one."

103 I glance at the constable, to ensure he's paying attention, before continuing.

104 "It escaped its tether, unfortunately. I'm sorry if it startled anyone." I wave my arms expressively. "Science is not without setbacks. No harm done though, and we've recovered it now. I hope this helps you close off your investigation?"

105 The policeman beams. "Mr. Roth, I'm sure my superiors will be delighted." He offers me the merest hint of a wink. "You know," he mutters, "you could have put a stop to all this an hour ago."

106 "Ah, but then we wouldn't have had a chance to talk. I've heard good things about you; it seems they're true." I shift and grin at him. "And of course, you could have *recorded* this interview."

107 "A careless mistake," he coughs dismissively, "but it's been useful to meet you, too; reports rarely give the full picture, and hearsay is just that. Hearsay."

108 We reach an unspoken understanding.

109 Well, today is full of surprises.

110 "The next time you're passing, Detective Inspector, please drop by. I'll introduce you to King and Yavin, and give you a full tour."

111 He nods. "Including Subterranea?

112 I grin wolfishly. "Bring your passport."

A Dangerously Incisive Smile

3 1 When I got up this morning, full of enthusiasm for the day's tasks, I did not expect to be standing in just my underpants having a gun poked my way.

2 Well, not before lunch, anyway.

3 **It's midday.** I'm at the American Embassy in London, and most of my clothes are folded neatly on the table.

4 **Five minutes ago**, I'm putting all of possessions in the x-ray inspection basket.

5 As a former ambassador*, I know how this works, and I'm not carrying a single electronic device—phones, car keys, cameras—these are never permitted.

6 So, this should be a piece of cake.

7 After the first failed attempt to get through the metal detector, I remove my shoes; these always set off the detectors at the airport.

8 I make happy chit-chat with the efficiently-friendly security guard, and pop my dark suit jacket in the basket too; it's a hot day anyway, and I'm glad to be rid of it.

9 After the second failed attempt, I remember I'm wearing braces to keep my trousers up. I unclip these apologetically after removing my waistcoat, and then reluctantly remove my trousers too; apparently holding them up with my hands while walking through the metal detector is not permitted.

10 As I pass unsuccessfully through the metal detector for the third time, a marine in combat fatigues enters the room and eyes me suspiciously.

11 I glance at his insignia; three stripes

with a single curved lower bar.

12 "Ah, *Staff Sergeant,*" I nod, straightening and cranking up my arrogance a few notches. It amuses me that the marine starts to salute without thinking, despite my lack of trousers;

13 these little things can raise a day immeasurably.

14 I am relieved of my cufflinks by an increasingly tense security guard, and the sergeant—now visibly embarrassed—unclips his sidearm.

15 The fourth attempt meets with a suggestion to remove my shirt; the collar stiffeners are small, thin metal bars, and are sewn in. The necktie goes with it.

16 The sergeant's pistol is now in his hand.

17 And I am in my underpants.

18 As the fifth failure occurs, and I start to wonder about the metal fillings in my teeth, the sergeant's gun starts to raise.

19 **Back in the now**, the consequences of this fifth–time–unlucky moment are interrupted by the door opening behind us.

20 A lion steps into the room; he's tall, suited, with an immaculately–coiffed mane.

21 Yes, it's King, the lion who lives in my house. He looks magnificent. I recognise the tie he's wearing, in fact;

22 I still have no idea how he unlocks the wardrobe.

23 "Mister Ambassador!" blusters the security guard, and the sergeant snaps and holds a salute;

24 King is Ambassador to the USA from a small–but–important African nation, and is very recognisable.

25 And for once, I'm relieved to see him.

26 "King!" I say, delighted, "Thank goodness you're here! Can you help me out here?"

27 The security guard regards the lion curiously. "Do you know this gentleman, Sir? Can you *vouch* for him?"

28 King's smile is dangerously incisive.

29 "Do I *know* him? Well yes, I suppose I do." He brushes imaginary dust from his lapel, "But it looks like you're almost done with him, and it's *not done* to interfere with your official duties."

30 The guard nods and returns his gaze to me in my underpants. The sergeant's gun returns to cover me.

31 King stoops and steps through the metal detector without a hitch, and turns to regard my dumbfounded expression.

32 It'll make its way to *furious* later.

33 "Besides," says the lion, "he does so like to *write* about these little adventures."

34 My heart sinks as he steps from the room and into the Embassy.;

35 I sense a future full of rubber gloves and tweezers.

36 And I was only here to talk to the IRS about tax.

Always A Cause To Dream

4 1 I shuffle around the kitchen in my dressing gown. The floor is cold. It's early.

2 I am loosely aware that outside, the sun is just over a frosty horizon. There's a new covering of snow.

3 **It's Sunday**. Why on earth am I even awake, let alone up and about?

4 The stove–top coffee maker hisses quietly on the hob; how my slow, clumsy hands cleaned it, refilled it and set it to its task at this time of day is a mystery.

5 There's a faint smell of burning bread as the toaster pops its load upwards.

6 I fumble at the door of the fridge, seeking out the milk for my cereal.

7 There is a knock at the front door.

8 Somewhere in my reptile brain, a neuron fires, fails to grab my attention, and fires again.

9 Actually it's not a *knock*, which is just a functional rapping of bone on wood. This is more definite. It asserts itself and demands my attention, though it is not forceful;

10 it heralds *arrival*.

11 Suddenly more awake, I turn towards the dim hallway. A short silhouette greets my eyes in the dawn light beyond the front door.

12 Postman? No, it's early. And Sunday.

13 The door resists my efforts to unlock it. While I jiggle the key in the lock, trying to catch just the right spot to turn it, and cursing at every thwarted effort, the dark figure stands immobile outside, patiently waiting.

14 I finally wrestle the door open, and find an oriental man on the snowy doorstep.

15 He's a head shorter than I am, and has a pleasant, clean–shaven, inquisitive face. He looks younger than me. And better–looking too.

16 His simple black clothes and shoes are unusual, being neither eastern nor western in style. He holds a folded black leather cap in clasped hands just below his waist.

17 It's a chilly day; his short–cropped head must be cold without the hat.

18 There is something wonderfully eclectic about him, but somehow the whole effect is balanced and without pretension.

19 I notice that he is regarding me curiously, as if he had opened the door to *me*, and is wondering why I was knocking. He smiles.

20 "Excuse me. I seek Indigo Roth," he states simply. Something about his tone suggests that he expects me to know something about this Roth fellow;

21 he's in luck.

22 "Yes, hello," I smile in return. "that's me."

23 He cocks his head slightly, and an array of emotions flicker past my eyes as he tries to find the most appropriate one. *Disappointment* is in there somewhere, but he rallies well and settles into something neutral; I respect this.

24 He bows slightly. "Forgive me, Mr. Roth, you are not as I expected. I meant no offence."

25 I shrug, puzzled. "None taken," I say as affably as I can muster at this hour of the day.

26 I admire the white–draped beauty of the garden distractedly over his shoulder, and note the small, careful footprints in the snow of the path. My gaze returns to him. "How may I help you?"

27 He stands suddenly erect, as if I've hit a key point in the script, and he has lines to deliver.

28 He draws a battered–looking letter with a wax seal from within a hidden seam in his jacket. The paper looks old, yet supple, and the red wax is crazed but seemingly intact. He holds it close to his chest, between his hands.

29 I have no idea where the cap went.

30 "My name is Li H'sen Chang," he announces formally, "and I bring a letter to Indigo Roth from *The Last Emperor of China*."

31 Okay, I didn't see *that* one coming.

32 He slips the letter back inside his jacket and looks at me quietly, expectantly.

33 "Well then," I find myself saying, "you'd better come in."

34 We move through to the lounge, and I wave him to a comfy chair. I'm curiously unsettled by his bizarre announcement. It sounds outlandish, but there are forgotten memories suddenly jostling for my attention;

35 memories of stories told to me by my grandmother, in another life, when I was a lad.

36 "It's a cold day, I'll set us a fire." I mutter, setting about my task at the hearth while I try to rally my thoughts.

37 Chang is silent as I work, perhaps sensing my unease, but has an air of polite attention.

38 He's waiting for me to speak.

39 But what can I *say*? What do I remember?

40 "So, Mr. Chang," I finally offer up as I put a long match to some kindling, "I'm delighted to meet you, but surprised at your news."

41 I grasp at old memories, but find them surprisingly substantial.

42 "The Last Emperor of China, Pu–Yi, was deposed in 1911 during the Xinhai Revolution."

43 The newspaper catches the flame and its light grows.

44 "He officially abdicated in 1912, but remained in Beijing's Forbidden City until 1924."

45 I move some logs expertly, and the fire takes hold.

46 "He then went into exile, and after a very colourful life, he died in 1967, the year before I was born."

47 I look towards the messenger, and ask him simply, "So *how* can he have sent me a message?"

48 Chang nods, obviously impressed. "Quite so, Mr. Roth. Your recall is precise, and your confusion is understandable. This message has puzzled me for many years."

49 *Years?* He takes a few breaths, then gently deflects the question with one of his own.

50 "May I ask you how you came to know these facts?" He bows his head slightly. "Again, forgive me, but this is uncommon knowledge for a Westerner."

51 His deference is rather disarming, but I learned long ago not to confuse it with weakness. The ability to show respect commands respect in turn;

⁵² few seem to grasp this, and look down on the respectful as *the little people*.

⁵³ I decide that, rather than finding offence in the questions of this stranger, I will share with him what I know.

⁵⁴ "I learned it all from my Grandmother, Mr. Chang. She died when I was a boy, but I remember her telling me stories."

⁵⁵ I take a seat and talk quietly, suddenly sad, as I stare into the fire.

⁵⁶ "My favourite story she would tell was written by a man called *Kafka*," I recall, my tone dropping into the easy tone of a lecturer.

⁵⁷ "In it, an insignificant man in a distant corner of an empire imagines that his Emperor has sent him a message, whispered with his dying breath to a messenger.

⁵⁸ The man imagines the messenger valiantly carrying the message from the room, fighting to get through the throng of those in attendance.

⁵⁹ He then pictures him struggling to traverse the teeming ante–rooms and busy corridors, down crowded steps, and through bustling courtyards. And after all that, he would still only have escaped the innermost palace.

⁶⁰ The messenger struggles onwards, fighting a relentless press of humanity, only to reach another surrounding palace.

⁶¹ And so on, through endless palaces for a thousand years, until he breaks free, only to reach the centre of the labyrinthine capital city.

⁶² His journey has only just begun.

⁶³ The foolish man who imagines all this knows that the message from the Emperor could never be delivered..."

⁶⁴ "... and yet, he sits at his window when evening comes, and dreams of the message," finishes Chang.**

⁶⁵ My eyes are welling a little. "Yes." I sit silently. I've not thought of any of this in twenty five years. "I remember my grandmother fondly, she fired my imagination with many such stories."

⁶⁶ I continue with my recollections, trying to answer Chang's question.

⁶⁷ "I asked her one day if the story was *true*. She said it was, and told me about Pu–Yi, who she said she always called *Henry*.

⁶⁸ I remember laughing at this silliness, not realising until years later that she

was a diplomat of sorts, and may have known him."

⁶⁹ My voice tails off as I consider this possibility seriously for the first time.

⁷⁰ "She told me that—yes, indeed—he may have sent such a message. And as a shy, imaginative boy, I was enthralled by the idea.

⁷¹ And, like the man in the story, I would sit by my window and dream a foolish dream of an important message sent to me by a dying Emperor."

⁷² Chang laughs quietly, but kindly, "And yet today, that message has arrived."

⁷³ This is too much. Overwhelming.

⁷⁴ "In his final days," continues Chang, "the Emperor was visited by an old friend; I remember her as a tall, elderly woman. She was strong and fierce, yet she laughed a great deal."

⁷⁵ He looks at me levelly.

⁷⁶ "Her name was *Roth. Juno Roth.*"

⁷⁷ I nod. "My grandmother. Wait a minute. What do you mean, you *remember?*"

⁷⁸ "It was long ago, and it was far away, Mr. Roth. But yes, as a twelve year old boy, the son of a servant, my Emperor gave me a message, and sent me out into the world to deliver it. The message had your name on it."

⁷⁹ There are so many questions to ask, but one shoves its way to the front and demands attention.

⁸⁰ "How has it taken more than *forty years* to deliver that message, Mr. Chang?"

⁸¹ The messenger smiles. Perhaps he has anticipated this question, and considered many possible answers over the years. Again, there is a sense that he's shuffling through responses, gauging them to find the correct one.

⁸² In the end he says with quiet, direct honesty,

⁸³ "I suppose you might say I took the *longer road.*"

⁸⁴ I bark a laugh at this, but my incredulity instantly sublimates to acceptance;

⁸⁵ it sounds like something I would say.

⁸⁶ I regard him more closely; he looks no older than thirty, but in reality he is almost twice that.

⁸⁷ "That road has been kind to you, Mr. Chang," I observe dryly.

⁸⁸ This gets a laugh out of him, and the earnest façade inches aside for a

moment as he spreads his arms airily.

89 "I spend my time *outdoors*. Plenty of exercise, fresh air." He cracks a grin as he shrugs, "You know how it is."

90 I'm too ashamed to tell him that actually, I don't. But, as he has eyes, I probably don't need to.

91 "My instructions were to travel by foot, to experience the journey one step at a time." He seems embarrassed as he admits, "I was told to deliver the letter when the right time arrived."

92 There is an awkward moment of silence. We are both aware that History is standing there, waiting for us to complete this scene, to end the play.

93 There will be no applause or catcalls.

94 There will only be the moment.

95 So, onwards.

96 "Please may I have the message, Mr. Chang?"

97 Our eyes meet for a second, and he retrieves it from his jacket. He stands and moves closer, but does not hand it to me. The fire crackles behind him.

98 "I have wondered for over forty years about this message." He frowns as he regards the faded letter with its chipped wax seal. He fingers the wax lovingly as he tries to find the right words.

99 "About what it contained. About why my Emperor's last message was to the unborn grandson of a friend. About why I, the son of a servant, was chosen to deliver it."

100 He sighs. "About these words that I have carried around the world for most of my life."

101 "And did you reach any conclusions?" This seems weak, inadequate.

102 He looks distractedly to the window, not meeting my gaze.

103 "Yes. My Emperor blessed me with a mission. To travel, to learn, and to be part of the world.

104 I have met thousands of people. I have helped them when needed, and fought against them when needed.

105 I learned from all of them, though, and perhaps left something of myself behind when I moved on.

106 My life has been an extraordinary adventure."

107 His eyes return to me. "Over time, the message itself became less important than the journey to bring it to you."

108 "That sounds like Wisdom to me."

109 The messenger does not respond.

110 History coughs, urging me on to the final exchange.

111 "I am a less remarkable man," I say gently, "but may I accept your Emperor's message?"

112 He stares at the letter, struggling to let it go.

113 Suddenly, there is a shuffling, growling and thumping from upstairs. I pay it no heed; I am well used to it. But it draws Chang's attention. He stands, his head cocked, listening.

114 Heavy footsteps make their way down the stairs and pass the closed door.

115 Slowly, the messenger walks from the room, drawn by his curiosity.

116 He returns a few seconds later, visibly shocked. "There is *a lion* in your kitchen!" he whispers, as an awed look spreads across his face. "You live *with a lion?*"

117 I nod, used to odd reactions to this. "Yes. His name is King."

118 He looks at the letter in his hand one last time, and bows his head as he quickly hands it to me.

119 "I have delivered my Emperor's message to a noble man."

120 I take the envelope with quiet deliberation. I notice his gaze drift back to the door as I crack the seal and unfold the ageing, loose–woven paper.

121 Oh good grief, no.

122 The message is simple:

123 *Please make my son a cup of tea. He's had a long journey.*

124 My heart sinks. My mind races.

125 What can I do with this?

126 What can I *say?*

127 I scan the paper far longer than the number of words merits, and notice that Chang's attention has returned to me. He regards me calmly, but I sense it's taking every ounce of his effort to not ask about the letter's contents.

128 I feel inadequate in the face of this moment.

129 It is now my turn to decide, to gauge the correct response.

130 I fold the letter carefully, and hand it quietly back to him.

131 "Your father says he loves you."

132 The messenger's eyes look startled, unsure. His eyes flick to the envelope and then, after a million thoughts have passed by, back to me.

133 There is gratitude and relief in his quiet gaze.

[134] He nods, and without a word, he turns and drops the letter message into the fire.

[135] In a few seconds, forty years flare gloriously into Legend.

[136] He then turns to me, his mood lighter, and shakes my hand gently.

[137] "Truly, Indigo, I have delivered the message to a noble man."

[138] Twenty minutes later, I've made us some tea, and discovered that Mr. Li H'sen Chang has a soft spot for toasted teacakes.

[139] We sit comfortably by the fire, swapping tales of our travels, grateful that History has moved along.

[140] We're discussing Marrakech when King wanders in. He's wearing a bath robe and slippers. He eyes Chang meaningfully and says something in what I instinctively know is Mandarin Chinese.

[141] The messenger stands to bow low, and offers a few sentences in reply. The lion glances at me briefly. His gaze returns to Chang, and he nods sagely.

[142] "Yes," he says in a low growl, "I can do that."

[143] "Thank you, My Lord." He turns to me. "Farewell, Indigo. I may have delivered the message from my Emperor," he beams, "but there will always be cause to dream."

[144] And, after helping himself cheekily to the final teacake, the messenger retreats to the hallway, passes through the door into the world, and is gone.

[145] King sighs and regards me quizzically. His mane ripples gently, as though a breeze is moving through the house. He then turns and heads towards the kitchen.

[146] "I drank your coffee," he says flatly, "and ate your toast. You seemed busy."

[147] "King?" The lion looks back. "What did Chang ask you to do?"

[148] The lion chuckles.

[149] "He asked me to make you a cup of tea.

[150] He says you have a long journey ahead of you."

Notes

* Subterranea was stripped of nation status after an unfortunate misunderstanding about iDifficult invading Bolivia in a submarine.

** Kafka's short story/parable "A Message from the Emperor" ("Eine Kaiserliche Botschaft") was published in 1919, but placed in a broader narrative titled "The Great Wall Of China" in 1931, after his death.

Second Testament

(We Need To Talk About Max)

Dreams

*"I dreamed about a Singing Wedgie–Gram. He crooned FLY ME TO THE MOON
while tugging my underpants over my head. The rocketship ones. Despair."*

Stripped Of Red And Yellow

1 ¹ I am alone in a sea of dreams.
² The only man for hundreds of miles, though life surrounds me.
³ Above me, hordes of sharks circle a distant watery sun.
⁴ Below me, the hard bare rock of the ocean floor.
⁵ I sit cross–legged on the edge of a gigantic chasm. The sunlight, stripped of all red and yellow at this depth, barely makes it into the rift that stretches away endlessly from me on either side.
⁶ The chasm is blue–green. It is indigo. It is black.
⁷ Perhaps it is the edge of a tectonic plate. Perhaps it is a shelf from a prehistoric desert. Perhaps it's just an old wound in the seabed.
⁸ And perhaps it is The Abyss.
⁹ Just out of reach below me, the darkness is total. It becomes a wall to vision, the surface of everything without light, a barrier to thought.
¹⁰ The Abyss does not call to me, but the sight of it is compelling and unsettling. Beyond the barrier, there are Dragons. Nightmares. Horrors. Unknowable, abstract things. The fractured past. The unwoven future.
¹¹ I tear my gaze away and look along the seabed, my heart pounding.

¹² I see movement in the distance. Surrounding me, on the very limits of vision, leviathans move;
¹³ whales the size of zeppelins undulate gently with their calves, and ancient gigantic sharks found on no zoologist's chart prowl the depths on their ceaseless hunt.
¹⁴ Yes despite these wonders, The Abyss quietly draws my eye again.
¹⁵ I don't understand why I'm sitting here. I am terrified of heights. Water is not air, of course, and I am relaxed, buoyant even. I can't fall unencumbered.
¹⁶ But still, I'm afraid.
¹⁷ To make the point, the sea currents start to move. They swirl around me, a visible movement that drags dust up from distant coral beds. The beasts in the distance vanish in the sandstorm.
¹⁸ The current presses against my back. It leans me forward, urging me to look.
¹⁹ To stare into The Abyss.
²⁰ Vertigo swells within me. Irrational, irrelevant, irrepressible.
²¹ The darkness moves closer, or is it me? I know that if I fall into darkness, I will never return.
²² I do not want to fall.
²³ And I do not fall.
²⁴ Unseen pairs of hands take hold of me gently, and slowly pull me away to safety.

25 And as suddenly as they rose, the currents settle. The pressure at my back withdraws. The sandstorm vanishes. The Abyss is gone.

26 The calm of the sea finds me again.

27 Above me, hordes of sharks circle a distant watery sun.

28 I am alone in a sea of dreams.

29 But I am never alone.

The Butterflies Are Relieved

2 1 I'm falling, hard and fast.

2 The glass–and–steel building blurs past me, and I'm still accelerating.

3 I didn't plan this when I got up this morning.

4 Wow, that's quite a view.

5 **It's five minutes ago**, and I'm standing on the roof's edge of a very tall building.

6 As skyscrapers go, this is a beauty. Three hundred and one floors, the world's tallest;

7 *Roth's Spire* in Cambridge, England.

8 What would my shrink make of this thrusting edifice?

9 I moved house today. It's been hard work; the penthouse is a beautiful location, but not when the service elevator is out of service.

10 Three hundred floors carrying a sofa takes it out of you.

11 I had help, of course;

12 Bear and iDifficult did most of the heavy lifting, plus Yavin and an army of badgers shifted all the smaller boxes. Industrious lads, one and all; everyone lent a hand or paw.

13 Even King turned up—with a dazzling new necktie for me as a housewarming present*—though my favourite lion only made it as far as the lobby.

14 Behind me, an access door clanks open. Framed in the doorway, short but commanding, is Yavin. The badger casts his gaze about, adjusting his tweed cap to shield his eyes from the afternoon sun as he does so. And, seeing me, he waves briefly and wanders over, the buckles on his workman's dungarees ringing gently against the metal rule in his breast pocket.

15 "Hey, I thought you'd all gone." This is true; I remember waving them all off as they started the long trudge down the stairwell. Was he there? It's not important. It's been quite a day.

16 Yavin produces a spotted red handkerchief and mops his brow with a nod. As he folds it away, he hops onto the edge next to me and takes a long hard look down. He huffs a breath;

17 clearly he's impressed.

18 "Yeah, it's a long way down." I open my arms and look down on the hundred of years of history murmuring in the spires and colleges of the university town. The river is an iridescent ribbon from up here. "Hell of a view, mind."

19 A quiet cough draws my gaze downwards. Meeting my glance, the badger taps his watch meaningfully. This draws me back into focus.

20 "Good grief, am I late to meet Abbey for dinner?"

21 Yavin see–saws a paw meaningfully and then points to the stairs.

22 "You're right. I'd best get moving."

23 I move to step down from the edge and pause. A strange notion is forming in my head;

24 it does a few orbits and feels even stranger.

25 I gaze down at the distant sidewalk.

26 "Of course," I mutter, almost to myself, "I could take the *direct* route."

27 *Three hundred floors? Freefall? Am I insane?*

28 Yavin is regarding me thoughtfully. Perhaps he's having the same doubt, judging my sanity for the umpteenth time in as many years. He takes a long look over the edge and then back to me. He frowns and points towards street level, raising an eyebrow.

29 I interpret this and smile. "How will I do it?" I shrug back at him. "Oh, I'll think of something."

30 The badger tilts his head at me, and suddenly makes a *splatting* motion with widespread paws.

31 "Oh, it'll be fine," I enthuse vaguely, "I'll do what I always do. Improvise!"

32 We stare at each other as clouds gather overhead.

33 **Twenty seconds ago**, Yavin is rushing off a quick text to the emergency services as I reign in my hesitation on the edge, and spread my arms wide.

34 **Ten seconds ago,** I swan–dive with a whoop. Spinning, I see a concerned badger waving me off before he runs for the stairs.

35 **Back in the now**, I'm still falling.

36 The wind roars in my ears, and the butterflies are frankly relieved that they're safe in my tummy.

37 I pass the observation platform on the hundred and sixty third floor; I'm almost halfway down.

38 *Man, what a rush!*

39 I didn't plan this when I got up this morning. But sometimes, you have to seize the day.

40 And sometimes, after a difficult month has run its course, you have to seize it *real hard*.

41 But enough of this introspection; time is against me. And I don't want to be *late* in any sense.

42 Looking about, I start to improvise.

And I Am In My Element

3 ¹ Shakespeare said that sorrows come not as single spies, but in battalions.

² He may have been onto something.

³ When I'm out of sorts, I typically find myself in the desert.

4 Right now, I find myself on salt flats; a desert by any other name.

5 "Here again, Indigo?"

6 The speaker is a well–dressed stranger in white. The suit, tie and hat are impossibly immaculate. His face is young, his shaded eyes old.

7 "Yes, though I could have sworn I was just in the depths of the ocean."

8 "Well, you still are!" He gestures widely, "This salt flat is all that remains after you boiled away the sea."

9 What a violent and unsettling image. "I can do that?"

10 "Anger is an almost entirely terrible thing, Indigo." He raises a finger emphatically. "And very powerful."

11 I manage a lopsided smile. "*Almost* entirely?"

12 "Yes. It can serve as a motivation to correct injustice."

13 "And today?"

14 "Nothing of the kind. There's no injustice here," he shrugs, "only your perception of it. You're just angry. It's quite palpable." His eyes sweep away to the horizon and he talks quietly. "But I'm curious as to *why?*"

15 Like most questions, it sounds simple.

16 Time passes without words. Finally, he continues in the same measured tone. "Is it Work? Money? Friendships? Family?"

17 "Yes. Keep going." My unhesitating response surprises me.

18 "Commitments? Dating? Deadlines? Uncertainty?" He pauses, considering something subtler. "Motivation?"

19 "Yes. All of the above. That last one, especially," I scowl. Though oddly, ideas are not in short supply. Just the urge to do anything *with* them.

20 He nods, and tosses a crowning thorn onto the heap. "Perhaps you feel a crushing sense that nothing much changes for you from one year to the next?"

21 "Yep, that pretty much covers it." I'm annoyed by this throwaway incisiveness, but it's a really short trip today. "It's funny. It's like you're me."

22 He chuckles and brushes a few specks of salt from his sleeve.

23 "Yet we've never met." He meets my eye. He's telling the truth, but his words are somehow a wrapper for lies.

24 "Do you live here?" This feels like another of those simple questions. It goes unanswered.

25 "This is a dangerous place, Indigo, and I urge you not to linger."

26 "How is it dangerous?" I glance about. "It's a wide open space. Silent. Tranquil. Empty. It's rather beautiful, actually."

27 "Exactly. And your Mojo doesn't live here."

28 "My Mojo?"

29 "Indeed. You're a creature of the water, Indigo. Your motivation, your inspiration, doesn't live on dry land."

30 I know he's right, but the deep never fails to terrify me.

31 "You'll find no spark here, Indigo. Only an escape."

32 The honesty is devastating, my frustration and desperation very real. "But sometimes an escape is what's needed!" I shout, my outstretched arms the pleading reach of a drowning man.

33 "Indeed. Which is why I must move you along." There's concern in his voice, but little compassion. "Take a few long, deep breaths. You can swim, right?"

34 It's rhetorical, but the foolish "Yes. Why?" escapes my lips.

35 There is a distant roar from behind me. Turning, I see a wall approaching me. It's high and dark and alive and impossibly fast. It's water.

36 Behind this tsunami, dark sentinels lurk, their teeth glittering.

[37] "Because the tide is coming in."

[38] It's seconds away. He raises his hat in farewell.

[39] And I am in my element.

Totally Missing The Point

4 [1] The nibbling at my nose is gentle but insistent.

[2] I flick at it, and realise that I'm asleep; the poorly aimed slap opens my eyes to the darkness of my bedroom.

[3] And I see what awoke me.

[4] In front of my bleary eyes, gold on black, a perfectly–illuminated fish hangs in mid air. A slow trail of tiny bubbles work their way towards the ceiling.

[5] My waking mind misses the point of the scene and tries to identify the fish's species. Some kind of *comet*? An *oranda*, maybe?

[6] My gaze seems to be making it wary, whatever it is, and its fins flutter it backward. It stays close though, and as my eyes flick upward to seek its light source, the fish darts in again and continues its attentions.

[7] My second swipe is more accurate and I have the satisfaction seeing the fishy phantom flash through the open bedroom door and down the stairs.

[8] This is stupid; I'm clearly dreaming.

[9] Rolling away from the door to face the window, I close my eyes, ignoring the rogue male shark cruising past in the moonlight; if the goldfish gets the front door open, I hope it eludes him.

[10] I yawn and resist any urge to go and investigate this fantasy; on any other day, this would be the beginning of a grand adventure.

[11] But tonight, I'm tired, and more than a little annoyed at being woken; it's been a long week.

[12] As I drift off, I make a mental note to buy tuna.

[13] And I dream of zebras.

Of Truths Hidden By Sand

5 [1] No matter how often I dream of the sea, somehow I always find my way back to the desert.

[2] I return to its endless vista, the slow sand, the unbroken sky. And this puzzles me greatly, time and again.

[3] As I wander towards the distance, I am joined by a dragon. She is huge, metallic, corroded.

[4] The grate of her massive folded wings betrays her presence long before her voice does.

[5] "Back again, I see?" she says, her voice reminding me of the rust that coats her dark flanks. Her head is broad on a muscular neck. No fire burns within the flare of her nostrils, but there is ice in the widely–set eyes.

[6] "Neither of us belongs here," I reply thoughtfully, "you belong to the ocean."

[7] "But this *is* an ocean!" Her voice sounds genuinely surprised, offended almost.

[8] I cast my gaze from side to side, across the sea of sand to the distant horizon.

[9] "Perhaps. Its surface moves and changes. It has limitless depths. It hides a great deal."

[10] "It hides *everything*," the dragon chuckles, "eventually. But peril comes from above, not below."

[11] The sky is empty. "Really? I don't see that."

[12] "No creatures patrol the desert's depths. No hungry predators will erupt from its sand to seize the unwary from their journey or rest." Moments pass, a point is made. "So peril must come from above."

[13] The twisted logic feels linear, sane. "I feel exposed. "

[14] "Yes. Exposed to the sky. Perhaps this is why you come here. To confront fear."

[15] "I don't think so." I cast my hands and eyes about. "This desert is a metaphor."

[16] "All things are metaphors, Indigo."

[17] For a while, there is silence. Silence except for the dragging of her plated, draconic tail as we walk, and the juddering, nails–down–the–blackboard scrape of her loping gait.

[18] "Everything that has ever been is beneath my feet. Secrets and lies. Wars and mercies. And the truths that locked them away."

[19] My gaze is distant, internal. "The Past, forgotten by the drift of sand. And no matter how the surface changes, it always remains the same."

[20] "And the sky?" There is a new tone to the voice. It is bright and encouraging, but cautious not to lead its witness.

[21] "The sky is empty. Endless. Unknown. Full of possibilities." I stumble, and fall to one knee. Ironically, I laugh, "And easy to overlook when I'm focused on the path in front of me."

²² We walk in silence. Awaiting an answer, I glance sideways at her expectantly.

²³ She catches my look and starts, "Oh please, do continue. It sounded like you were *getting* somewhere. I didn't like to interrupt."

²⁴ Her corroded smile is innocent, playful. There is death in it.

²⁵ "Well, if the ground is the Past, then perhaps the sky is the Future?" I look up at it, a little edgily. "No wonder I feel exposed."

²⁶ She nods, "And so the path is...?"

²⁷ I stop in my tracks and stare at the ground at my feet. Sand sucks at them restlessly.

²⁸ "And the path is the Present. It..." I pause, fumbling for words, "It *exists* between the two."

²⁹ There is an exultant scream of metal. Terrified, I tumble sideways and can only gape as the dragon rises into the air on beating metallic wings.

³⁰ The rust of ages fills the air, stirred by her thrashing tail as she gains height.

³¹ "Watch the skies, Indigo! I'll see you again!" she cries as she soars into the blue. "And it will be very soon!"

³² I finally stand, my heartbeat slowing.

³³ I am alone in the wasteland.

³⁴ A new dune rises in my path. It is tall, steep, its sand soft.

³⁵ It will be hard work.

³⁶ Yes, definitely a metaphor.

A Baring Of Souls

6¹ He only has eyes for her.

² The sun is barely above the horizon, but already it is burning the edges of the high, listless clouds.

³ But he does not see this.

⁴ The silhouetted treetops of the horizon blur and dance as the sun creeps higher, and the grey of dawn gives way to orange and then purple.

⁵ But he does not see this either.

⁶ His camera stands forgotten, the photographic plates ready beside it in the tall grass of the lakeside. Reeds sway gently in a light breeze, and above him a kingfisher darts across the water.

⁷ Bent over the water's edge on hands and knees, he does not see any of this.

⁸ He stares into the dark water, and beneath its surface, a woman.

⁹ She faces him, her eyes closed, her round features pale. Her hair is long and dark, and moves in the water in elegant waves, though surely there is no current.

¹⁰ An enigmatic smile is frozen on her full lips.

¹¹ He remembers her, though she has not crossed his mind in some time. He remembers their rise, their carefree happiness. He remembers their honesty, the baring of their souls, their promises. And their hunger, the darkness in which he lost himself.

¹² And then the truth, and how it slowly, agonisingly destroyed them.

¹³ He remembers how she destroyed them. And how he hates her.

¹⁴ Beneath the surface, her eyes open. Her sleepy, feline eyes, dark and beautiful. She sees him, knows him, and her locks drift elegantly as she shakes her head slowly.

¹⁵ Her lips form a single word.

¹⁶ *Liar.*

¹⁷ Above him, tattered pink clouds are now bathed in the rising blue of morning.

¹⁸ But he does not see them.

¹⁹ He only has eyes for her.

²⁰ But the water is empty. Where she floated, beautiful and dark, there is only now his reflection.

²¹ Finally, he sees.

A Broken Game Of Patience

7¹ It's last night.

² I'm having the strangest dream.

³ The room is dark. I am sitting in a pool of bright light at an immensely wide, wooden table. Its ends melt into the gloom on either side of me;

⁴ if I rolled a marble to left or right, I would never hear it drop.

⁵ My hands rest on the cool wood. Close by, playing cards are frozen in a broken game of Patience.

⁶ I have been waiting.

⁷ Not long now. They will arrive soon.

⁸ And then, slowly emerging from the darkness to the border of the light, they come. Four of them.

⁹ A lion, a bear, a badger and a man.

¹⁰ They look at me across the table, uncertain why I am here.

¹¹ "We dreamed you," says the lion; he is golden, imperious.

¹² "We dreamed you," says the bear; he is tall, black, deep.

13 "We dreamed you," says the man; I know him.

14 The badger nods silently. He is coarse, rough, ready.

15 "I don't understand," I say, "is this the final scene?"

16 The badger leans forward and shakes his bristly head. His voice is cool and clear when it comes, but there is thunder chasing at its heels.

17 "We dreamed you," he says.

18 *"We dreamed you so that you would write us."*

Walkabout In Sight Of Home

8 1 I'm sitting in the back garden on a blanket, cross–legged.

2 The garden is long and narrow and grassed. It slopes slightly uphill, and there are trees obscuring the wooden back fence. The sides of the garden, just feet away, are mesh fenced, low and obscured by overgrown shrubs. It is a pleasant, sunny day.

3 Opposite me on the blanket is my best friend iDifficult. He looks a little leaner than usual, but it's unmistakably him.

4 I ask him if we're going to eat soon. He shakes his head.

5 "There's no time to eat," he says, "you're thinking about something, and I am the first face of it."

6 "I'm dreaming?"

7 "You're thinking. Awake or asleep, what does it matter?"

8 I have no idea what he means, and tell him so. I want to leave for some reason, but the garden seems content to stay where it is.

9 Crickets chirrup in the undergrowth, the clouds drift gently.

10 "I represent something," he continues, his voice lacking all of its usual sparkle and humour, "but only you know what it is."

11 I asked him if he is friendship. He shakes his head. Is he intelligence? Or fun? Or overindulgence? Three times more, he shakes his head.

12 "It's something much simpler than that," he tells me flatly.

13 And with that, he does this odd thing behind his head with his hand, and the shell that is his face and body falls away to reveal a lion.

14 The lion is mature and golden, tall and proud. His mane is magnificently combed, though braided in places, almost plaited.

15 I expect a crown but there is none.

16 His eyes are bright and intelligent. He looks well fed.

17 "Are you King?" I ask. "He nods."

18 "And like your friend, I also represent something."

19 I have two pieces of the puzzle, but no idea of the picture.

20 I turn it over in my head.

21 I've been 'Difficult's friend for twenty years; of all the people I spend time with, I've known him the longest.

22 And King? Well, he's just a lion that lives at my house. I swear about him daily.

23 An idea coughs somewhere in the back of my mind, but it's elusive.

24 "Why are you special?" I ask him, apropos of nothing, or so I think.

25 "I am a lion. I am magnificent, clever, creative and wise."

26 "And untidy, rude and inconsiderate."

27 He smiles and shrugs. "It all evens out."

28 "I didn't invite you to live here." I'm confrontational, my anger rising.

29 "No, but this is where we find ourselves. This is where we *are.*"

30 *What? This where we are?* Teetering for a moment, the penny drops.

31 "You are the Present," I tell him; it's not a question. He nods and purrs his appreciation quietly, and watches me closely as I continue.

32 "And 'Difficult is the Past." I move everything into its place in the metaphor. "You are the second face of the thought."

33 The crickets stop suddenly.

34 I expect the sun to fade, for clouds to form. They do not. Two figures have joined us, one on either side of King. They are radiant, and I know them, but I cannot share them with you.

35 I know they hold the sun in the sky.

36 I know they are cloudbusting for me, constantly.

37 King sees my comprehension.

38 "Now, pay attention," he says finally, and his shape falls away.

39 The figure sitting across from me is a woman. I find her difficult to take her in. She seems very familiar, but in an abstract way.

40 Her appearance, physique, clothes and hair shift as I watch, as if she is trying to evade my gaze. The only constant is her

hat, tilted slightly down as if deferent, hiding her eyes.

41 You can always tell a person from their eyes.

42 "You are the Future. You are the third face," I say. She nods unnecessarily. I add, "Do I know you?"

43 "I resemble people that you know, but may be all or none of them."

44 I am feeling very uncomfortable now, my heart pounding, and again I want to be gone from here.

45 "Why am I so scared of you?" I ask, though I know the answer.

46 "Because I am boundless. Because I am different. Because I am Change."

47 It's terrifying. I tell her.

48 "It's amazing," she corrects. "You have to see it."

49 There is a tremendous sense of warmth and safety and calm from her, but I'm still afraid.

50 "What happens to everything that is here now?"

51 This is the question that dominates my life, the thought that drew me here. It is the only question.

52 "I can't tell you," she tells me, "because you don't know. And never can. The smallest event could change everything, while the largest could leave no footprint at all."

53 The two figures are still flanking her. They sit close to her, contentedly smiling at me.

54 She raises her head, and I see her eyes clearly.

55 She tells me quietly, finally,

56 "But it may be less complicated than you think."

Notes

*   And of course, he looked very fetching with it tied round his neck as he slipped away later.

Abbey

"Revisionism is the only true history. You said so yesterday, remember?"

Glacial In Its Glow

1 ¹ I'm buttering bread as iDifficult fires up the blowtorch.
² There's a polite *rat–a–tat* knock at the front door.
³ "Oh, the Earth Wire's connected–to–the... Spark Plug!" sings my friend to himself as he works on the kitchen floor, oblivious to the knock.
⁴ Glancing down the hallway, I half expect to find the postman pushing a hastily scribbled *You were out when I called* note through the letterbox.
⁵ But instead, I'm surprised to see the silhouette of a woman outside the front door;
⁶ is that my sister?
⁷ "Come on in, it's open!"
⁸ As I grab a cloth to wipe my hands on, a hesitant figure cracks the front door open and peeps inside.
⁹ "Hello? Mister Roth?"
¹⁰ As the door opens wider, the woman is revealed. A tall, slim, thirty–ish lady, casually dressed in jeans and a plain white t–shirt. She's pretty, with blonde bangs and a big smile.
¹¹ Her feet are bare.
¹² Nope, not my sister. Though come to think, I don't *have* a sister.
¹³ "Hello? Mister Roth?" she repeats as she sees me, and smiles.
¹⁴ I find myself giving a self–conscious little wave; the woman regards me with a passing look of curiosity, and then steps confidently into the house.
¹⁵ "Oh, the Spark Plug's connected–to–the... Vacuum Tube!"
¹⁶ I conclude that she's far too pretty for me to be *Mister Roth*, and that I should really stop gawping.
¹⁷ I stride forward, trying to remember to look manly, and offer my hand.
¹⁸ "Yes, that's me." Her grip is warm and firm. "But please, it's Indigo."
¹⁹ "Oh," she blushes slightly, "Indigo it is. I'm Abbey. I've just moved in next door." I nod, delighted, my mouth suddenly dry.
²⁰ She offers a thin bundle of letters. "These were just delivered to me by mistake. The postman ran off before I could catch him."
²¹ "Yes, that sounds about right. The postman believes in *guerrilla delivery.* "
²² She laughs. I'm aware that I'm still shaking her hand; unhitching us, I take the letters and glance at them momentarily. "Thank you, Abbey. That's very kind of you."
²³ We smile at each other, and an awkward little silence swirls around us; it seems that both of us are out of practice with this kind of thing. With *meeting people.*
²⁴ "Oh, the Vacuum Tube's connected–to–the... Tuning Fork!"
²⁵ "It's very dusty next door!" she finally

blurts, pointing to her shirt and dusting some of it off with a shrug of her slim shoulders. She laughs again, and continues to smile at me;

26 my thoughts are glacial in its glow.

27 For pity's sake, say something, man!

28 "Um, yep. The house has been vacant for a while now," I say, running a hand through my short hair; for the first time in years, I wish it was still long, and covered up these damned ears. "The last owner moved out complaining about the 'odd goings on at all times of day'. Which made no sense to me."

29 I scratch my head for emphasis and consider this. I mean, 'Difficult drops by, but there's just me, Yavin, the young badgers and King actually *living* here. Some occasional zebras, I suppose. Oh, and the decommissioned Terminator in the shed. Hmmm.

30 "Nope, no sense at all," I confirm.

31 "Well, I'm glad to hear you say that!" enthuses Abbey. "We only saw the place the once, and it seemed perfect for us."

32 My heart sinks. "Oh, so that's you and your..." Husband? Boyfriend? Kids? Dog? Oh, please let it be a big, dumb, waggy dog. Or a gerbil.

33 "My father."

34 "Oh. Well, that could be worse."

35 Did I just say that out loud?

36 "Oh, the Brain's not–connected–to–the... Vocal Chords!"

37 Abbey laughs at my slip and 'Difficult's distant ad–lib, and the ice is broken.

38 "Who's the great singing voice?" She raises an eyebrow, "Your... *partner?*"

39 My jaw drops and works up and down a couple of times.

40 "No, he's just my best friend." She glides past me and links arms, drawing me gently into the kitchen. The action is smooth and confident, but feels neither intrusive nor presumptuous.

41 The scene that greets us is chaotic.

42 The cool tiles of the kitchen floor are littered with kitchen tools and mechanical debris.

43 The juice blender is in pieces, and the back is off the microwave. There's a lot of free wiring, the smell of solder, and a mess of duct tape.

44 Good grief, he works fast.

45 Rising from the disorder is a small tower of seemingly unrelated junk.

46 The hull of the disassembled vacuum cleaner forms the core, and from it a haphazard collection of chrome, plastic and multicoloured wiring reaches up to a cross–lashed horizontal broom handle.

47 At the end of the broom, some eighteen inches above the sink, is what looks like the laser from a BluRay player.

48 And under the laser stands an unopened tin of corned beef.

49 Holding court at the centre of it all stands iDifficult. He has welding goggles perched on his shaved head. He's sporting a *Kiss–The–Cook* apron over a black t–shirt, eye–watering Hawaiian shorts, and hob–nailed boots. A soldering iron is poised in one hand, and there's a chunk of stilton cheese in the other.

50 "We've been doing some work," I croak pathetically.

51 iDifficult regards us and the stilton in turn.

52 "Sorry mate," he mumbles past a mouthful of cheese, "I got peckish waiting for you."

53 I present my companion with my free hand. "This is Abbey. She's just moved in next door. Abbey, this is 'Difficult. He's just retro–fitted half my kitchen."

54 Without a word, 'Difficult looks about for his discarded hat, a dark trilby that looks like it was born in the 1950s, and pops it on his head.

55 That done, he raises it politely.

56 "Charmed." Abbey gives a little wave, but remains next to me. She seems a bit wary, but this is understandable.

57 "Actually," continues the part–time arch–genius, "you're just in time. We've just *finished.*"

58 "It's very *impressive,*" offers my neighbour brightly, "what *have* you two been building?"

59 "An excellent question," says 'Difficult, wiping his hands on his apron, "I assume Roth brought you up to speed on the broken key for the corned beef tin?"

60 He points towards the sink and the silver–and–blue container loitering there.

61 Abbey shakes her head and he continues.

62 "Well, we really wanted to open a tin of corned beef to make sandwiches."

63 "Of course," encourages Abbey, "and the key to open it was *broken?*

64 He eyes her in surprise. "Yes! *Exactly!* Well spotted! So, we thought the easiest solution was to build a high–powered

cutting laser from some spare parts we happened to have around."

⁶⁵ He surveys his junk kingdom. "Though it seems we had far more spare parts than we needed."

⁶⁶ "Well, if you didn't have a regular tin opener, improvisation seems very..." she casts about for a suitable adjective, "*Sensible?*"

⁶⁷ It is now 'Difficult's turn to beam, pleased to have found a receptive audience. He turns and positions the tin carefully beneath the laser, and flicks a red switch.

⁶⁸ "Voilà!"

⁶⁹ Nothing happens.

⁷⁰ No dazzling light, no sliced metal. He frowns and flicks the switch a few more times for good measure.

⁷¹ "If I might observe something," says Abbey, slipping away from me towards the machine, and then eyeing one spot from different angles, "I have a feeling that the Cheese Grater's not–connected–to–the... corkscrew?"

⁷² Abbey steps back to my side awkwardly. My friend produces a electrical meter from his pocket and probes the joint. After a moment, grunts affirmatively.

⁷³ "Exactly right. Impressive." He rubs his chin and inquires affably, "How'd you know that?"

⁷⁴ "Lucky guess?" It's unconvincing; she squirms a little.

⁷⁵ "Maybe," he concedes, "but there's a lot of components and connections here; it's slim odds."

⁷⁶ Abbey blushes for the second time in five minutes. "Well, let's just say I'm rather sensitive to *energy flows*." She extends a finger and points, adding, "I'm hopeless with *Science*, but I can see, plain as day, that the electricity stops *there*."

⁷⁷ My friend considers this. "*Any* type of energy?"

⁷⁸ She nods. "Most. Strong, localised ones anyway. And Ley Lines too, if I really concentrate."

⁷⁹ "Can you sense *auras?* On people, I mean?" From anyone else it would seem like a worried accusation, or disbelief.

⁸⁰ But my friend is *Curious*; it's his gift.

⁸¹ "Yes. Indigo here has a nice friendly one, if complicated." She squeezes my arm. "I'd never have stepped into this house otherwise."

⁸² "Cool." my genius pal nods, satisfied.

⁸³ And then, returning to his work, he makes the required repair with a minor adjustment, a dab of solder, and flurry of duct tape.

⁸⁴ And flicks the switch.

⁸⁵ A few minutes later, I'm sitting on the sofa in the front room with Abbey, enjoying corned beef sandwiches with a pot of tea.

⁸⁶ There is the distant clang and occasional curse of tidying from the kitchen.

⁸⁷ "So," I swallow a delicious mouthful of bread and meat, "what exactly is 'Difficult's aura like?"

⁸⁸ Abbey doesn't hesitate, though her reply is low and full of smiles.

⁸⁹ "He's lit up like a Christmas tree. Well, he's more like a mass of flashing seaside illuminations," she munches reflectively. "There's some major creativity and oblique thinking going on in there."

⁹⁰ "So, do you think..."

⁹¹ "Oh, stone cold *bonkers*. No question about it."

⁹² I grin with her, but then cough and ask without guile, "But mine was nice?"

⁹³ Her blue eyes twinkle as she stands. "Yep, pretty nice." She leans over and pecks me on the cheek. Her blonde locks brush against my nose.

⁹⁴ "Thanks for the tea and sandwiches. Be seeing you, Indigo."

⁹⁵ She passes 'Difficult at the door and they exchange happy farewells. When he enters the room, I'm draining the last of my tea. I offer a complimentary,

⁹⁶ "Nice work with the laser."

⁹⁷ "Thanks." He looks shifty and adds,

⁹⁸ "You didn't tell her that we also have a *regular* tin opener, did you?"

It Must Be The Sunflowers

2 ¹ I sense her presence rather than see her.
² The scent of sunflowers brings a picture of a summer garden to mind, and the smiling presence of its bearer.

³ "Hello Abbey."

⁴ I look up from the internet, and offer my neighbour my best smile;

⁵ I can't help it, I *like* the woman.

⁶ It's not her good looks or her unfashionably–together sense of dress, or her from–the–toes laugh. I just feel good around her. Relaxed.

[7] "Hi, Indy." Her hand flies to her mouth, and she looks uncertain. "Sorry, may I call you that?"

[8] "Well..." I hesitate. I've never cared for it, but somehow it's good on her.

[9] I notice she's gone brunette from blonde; that's good on her too. I grin,

[10] "Please do. I like your hair, by the way." I'm rewarded with a delighted flash of white teeth. "I didn't hear you come in."

[11] "Why, thank you!" Abbey blushes, fluffing her locks theatrically. I laugh as she makes a throwaway gesture towards the doorway to the hall. "King let me in."

[12] I frown. I have a vague recollection of stealthy paw–steps on the stairs. This is unusual;

[13] King normally crashes about, growling operatic tunes with impressive bass.

[14] The only time I ever see the house's resident lion move quietly is when he's about to introduce himself to a zebra.

[15] Or if he's just stolen one of my silk neckties.

[16] "He was at the door before I rang the bell. Handsome beast. And very charming."

[17] Putting thoughts of stolen neckties from my mind, I slip Occam's Razor from its logical sheath and offer a simple reason for the lion's welcome.

[18] "Well, he has a terrific sense of smell," I say brightly, "he probably *smelled* you coming."

[19] Her face falls momentarily, but she rallies magnificently to the perceived slight. Hands on hips, bare feet planted squarely, her shoulders at a jaunty angle;

[20] I recognise the body language long before my gaze reaches her raised eyebrows.

[21] My mouth works a few times.

[22] I've not known Abbey for that long; I guess I'm still working her out. I'm unsure how to handle this one, so I fall back onto good old honesty.

[23] "I just meant that you smell *nice?*" My voice is quieter and less certain than I intended. And where did that question mark come from? I fumble about for an explanation. "You know... Summery. Sunflowers. Sunshine."

[24] *Smells like sunshine?* Good grief, man, can you *hear* yourself?

[25] I needn't have worried. Abbey steps closer, chuckles, and drapes an arm round my neck as I sit at the table.

[26] "It's okay," my neighbour plants a sisterly kiss on the top of my head, "I knew how you meant it." She moves on. "So. What are you doing?"

[27] I shuffle in my chair and turn the screen towards her.

[28] "Just checking messages on this dating website." My neighbour leans closer to the screen, clearly interested. "I've been thinking about joining up for a couple of years, and so a while back I did."

[29] A little internal voice whispers that maybe I didn't want to talk to Abbey about looking for dates, but I'm not thinking too clearly;

[30] it must be the sunflowers.

[31] If she's disappointed, she doesn't show it. "Cool! How's it going? Any luck?" I experience my own disappointment instead.

[32] "Nope. Not a thing."

[33] "Really?" She looks my way. "None today?"

[34] I chuckle darkly, "Nope, none at *all*. In three weeks."

[35] "What? *Why?!*" Her shock is perversely uplifting. "What on earth did you write in your profile? *Gentleman serial killer, tall, GSOH, seeks caring lady for companionship and possible murder?*"

[36] I'm *so* not ready for this conversation.

[37] "Oh, you know. The truth."

[38] Abbey rolls her eyes, like this is the *last* thing I should do. But hey, I deserve more credit than that.

[39] "What I mean is, I've not told any lies. I've presented myself simply, and tried to sound sane, appealing and... well, decent."

[40] "I see." A few intuitive clicks on her part make my defensive mumblings somewhat redundant.

[41] she now has my full profile in front of her, and is gently edging my butt sideways from the chair with a few expertly irresistible hip nudges.

[42] "Would you like a cup of tea?" I'm keen to be out of the room for a few minutes. You know, to take a cold shower, or die of embarrassment.

[43] Or something.

[44] "Yes please, that'd be lovely."

[45] As I'm boiling the kettle, and wondering what on earth she's making of it all, King wanders past, humming *The Ride Of The Valkyries*.

⁴⁶ I'm too distracted to ponder whether this is some kind of leonine joke, message, insult or warning;

⁴⁷ it's usually one of the four.

⁴⁸ There's a splatter of tiny splashes in the lion's wake on the floor; he's just got out of the shower, and is off to shake himself dry in the garden.

⁴⁹ He doesn't smell as nice as Abbey;

⁵⁰ wet animals are pretty hard on the nose.

⁵¹ And wet lions are also not as magnificent as dry ones, but he's gone before I get a good look at him;

⁵² I hear the back door open and close in the utility room.

⁵³ The kettle boils. I pour a spot of water into the teapot and let it warm for a minute before making the tea.

⁵⁴ Being on a dating site has been rather a gruelling experience. A lot of hours, sifting and sorting profiles, trying to identify women with whom I might click.

⁵⁵ Then, personal introductory messages, tailored to the profiles of each, trying to make a connection. Light, informal, pleasant, funny, interesting.

⁵⁶ Finally, the buzz, the thrill of clicking *Send*, and wondering where it will lead.

⁵⁷ Sadly, it's not been leading anywhere but the void;

⁵⁸ the messages have been read, my profile viewed, but silence is all that's greeted me.

⁵⁹ If I wasn't such a superb, upbeat fella, it could get me down.

⁶⁰ I take the teapot through on a tray of china cups and saucers, milk, sugar and cake.

⁶¹ Abbey is engrossed with the computer as I pour and stir. I clink the spoon noisily into the saucer to draw her attention, but it's unnecessary; she's already closing the lid of the laptop.

⁶² She runs a hand through her dark brown locks and shrugs, almost apologetically.

⁶³ "I don't get it. Nothing at *all*?"

⁶⁴ I smile humbly in silence.

⁶⁵ "Makes no sense. Your profile isn't perfect, but it's *fine*. Confident, optimistic, interesting. Okay, so I tweaked a few words here and there, but..." My jaw drops a little, but she ploughs ahead. "Oh, and I deleted one of your photos that didn't do you justice."

⁶⁶ "You *did*?"

⁶⁷ She nods, "Of course." She frowns, concerned, maybe noticing my droopy jaw. "Sorry, you wanted me to lend a hand, yes?"

⁶⁸ Well, I'd not thought about it, but...

⁶⁹ "And by the way," she continues into my silence, "I thought your introductory mails were nicely done."

⁷⁰ She read my sent messages *too*?

⁷¹ "I thought you'd at least have got a courtesy mail back. A polite *Thanks, but no thanks*, right?"

⁷² I nod emphatically. "Exactly! That's what I thought!" I wave my arms, clearly more agitated about this than I realised.

⁷³ "I understand we're all looking for different things, but every time I hear nothing back I'm surprised. A simple *Up yours, ugly* doesn't take much effort."

⁷⁴ I sigh. "I don't know, maybe it does. Maybe my expectations are set all wrong."

⁷⁵ Abbey comes to sit next to me on the sofa and gives me a hug unexpectedly.

⁷⁶ "If you were right, I'd agree with you," she soothes, "but you're not. I'd feel exactly the same as you. It must be pretty grinding."

⁷⁷ She pecks me on the cheek.

⁷⁸ "Their loss. Keep at it. You could try a different website maybe, but you're doing all the right things. You just haven't found Miss Right yet."

⁷⁹ I gaze into her eyes, and time slows. And stops.

⁸⁰ But only for a split second. Upstairs again, King starts to roar out the closing verse from *Nessun Dorma* as he descends the stairs. Puccini would be proud of him; the lion's voice is magnificent and rather moving.

⁸¹ "Which reminds me," sighs Abbey, standing, "I'd best get moving soon." She retrieves her tea and nibbles on a slice of Bakewell tart. There's suddenly something awkward in her manner.

⁸² "Are you busy tonight?" I blurt; where did *that* come from? I pause, bemused, then add with something closer to confidence, "I was going to ask if you fancied having dinner with me?"

⁸³ My neighbour smiles me a winner, but rebuffs me gently. "I'd love to, but I'm having dinner with King."

⁸⁴ I gawp a little.

⁸⁵ My neighbour winks at me, "I wasn't kidding when I said he was charming."

⁸⁶ On cue, there's a polite knock at the door and King pushes it open. He's

standing his full two–legged height, his mane fluffy and unbraided; the shakedown in the garden did a better job than a hairdryer. He's sporting a pinstripe suit, crisp white shirt, and my best blue sevenfold–silk necktie.

[87] The swine.

[88] Abbey goes over, slightly straightens the lion's tie, and then fusses him behind his ears.

[89] "My, don't you look *handsome?*" she purrs.

[90] He growls appreciatively.

[91] I watch from the window as they head out, and sip my tea dejectedly.

[92] The scent of sunflowers lingers in the air. I sit down at the laptop again and lift the lid.

[93] It looks like I'll need to keep at it.

When Dreaming In Dolby

3[1] You know, I think that movie *Inception* was onto something.

[2] **It's last night**, in February.

[3] I'm at home, being kept company by iDifficult and a large, empty pizza box.

[4] We're watching *Pro–Celebrity Biopsy*, sprawled on separate sofas, and chewing the fat.

[5] "Nothing for a pair!..." shouts 'Difficult at the screen as the second procedure is performed. It's a blatant feed line for the second half of the host Johnnie K's catchphrase, which I provide at full volume;

[6] "... Not in this game!"

[7] We laugh like drains, but without warning I realise I'm tired. My eyes are suddenly heavy, my tummy full, and as I stifle a big yawn...

[8] **It's November**.

[9] I look around, disoriented for a moment, but with a look of dawning pleasure on my face, as my friends jump out to spring a surprise party on me.

[10] "Happy birthday, Indigo!" growls Bear, giving me a hug that befits his name. As he pulls away, smiling, a newly red–headed Abbey steps in and a kiss brushes my cheek.

[11] "Happy birthday, Indy!" she beams, holding my eye for a second longer than is needed.

[12] "Next to me, matey!" roars 'Difficult, steering me to a seat as I shake Yavin's badger paw and tickle his energetic monochrome nephews, Hoth and Sollust

[13] They wriggle and grin silently as they dash in a repeated figure of eight around my legs. It's an old routine, but it never feels old;

[14] they'll not be kids forever.

[15] We sit. The table is piled high with presents and party food, and some bouncy South American music plays in the background.

[16] Everyone is having a wonderful time.

[17] When I dream, I dream in colour and *6.1 Dolby Surround Sound*.

[18] "Would you excuse me for a moment?"

[19] I don't see my words coming, but find myself stepping out of the room.

[20] The hallway is cold as I walk upstairs.

[21] My bedroom is colder, and the bed itself colder still. As I close my eyes and yawn...

[22] **I'm nowhere**.

[23] The water is deep and dark and endless, the pressure dizzying. I look about in all directions, but see no difference. Is there slightly more light from above?

[24] I'm suspended in time as the distant shape moves from utter black to merely bleak. It moves closer with languid sweeps of its tail. It dawns on me as utter terror freezes me, a fly in dark amber, that it is *immense*.

[25] An immense shark.

[26] It is not close, but as it faces me, the gaping maw of its mouth deader than its eyes, it fills my vision. Ancient and scarred, from the annals of the extinct.

[27] I search for meaning in the moment, and find none.

[28] The leviathan cruises to a halt, and is still.

[29] And then, it is not.

[30] I turn to flee, but I know I cannot possibly escape it.

[31] I feel the approaching wave of pressure as the water is pushed towards me. I know the serrated blades of its teeth will close on my legs at any moment.

[32] But no. They pass by me on all sides, and the space ahead of me slowly becomes a jagged circle of light as the mouth of the beast closes around me, swallowed whole.

[33] Beneath my mask I scream, and...

[34] **I'm back at my surprise party**. The crowd is putting the finishing touches to a chorus of Happy Birthday, with Yavin conducting.

35 The final line complete, they clap and cheer.

36 And then, with an unexpected rush of sunflower scent, Abbey throws her arms about my neck and reaches in for a big birthday smooth.

37 I close my eyes and...

38 **I'm back with iDifficult**. He checks the pizza box for the third time and to his annoyance still finds it empty. My friend glances my way.

39 "Hey," he notes, "you dozed off there for a moment."

40 I did? What was I dreaming about? Ah, yes.

41 "Yeah, sorry matey, I must be tired." I yawn and stretch. "Weird dreams."

42 "Anything interesting?"

43 I shake my head and grin. An encounter with death and a kiss, both missed by moments.

44 "Not in the end," I muse, "but I think my subconscious has got it in for me."

45 The doorbell rings, and my friend jumps up.

46 "Wow, that was quick!" he beams, and returns a thirty seconds later with a fresh delivery pizza. He proffers the open box and speaks around a mouthful.

47 "More pizza, old boy?"

48 My mouth waters, and I take a piping hot slice; it smells delicious, hot and meaty and with the slight pungency of jalapeños and too much sauce.

49 A dream come true.

50 I move to take a delicious bite, and...

Wrong About The Cat Litter

4
1 The waking moments of any day are precious. "Indigo?"

2 They are a wonderful blend of reverie and reality. "Mister Roth? Rise and shine!"

3 It is in them that the shape of the day is revealed.

4 "HEY FATBOY! WAKEY WAKEY!"

5 My lids open to a close inspection from a pair of golden feline eyes.

6 "I'm sorry, did I wake you?" purrs the quiet, feminine voice.

7 I wonder idly if I'm dreaming; my waking moments are unreliable of late.

8 I start to sit up, but the tabby cat has retreated from my face, and is now manoeuvring herself onto my bare chest.

9 The faintest of needles from her small paws silently encourage me to lie still.

10 She settles, upright and imperious, a pleasantly small feline with unusually symmetrical stripes. And a warm tush.

11 There's the faintest scent of gin.

12 "It's a pleasure to meet you Mr. Roth," she lies without a trace of irony, "or may I call you Indigo?"

13 She seems very familiar, but I can't place her, nor her American accent. Michigan? Cleveland? Though, to be fair, I don't know any talking cats.

14 Wait a minute. A talking cat? A talking *American* cat? Ah. The dime drops, and I realise that it's a *Minnesotan* accent.

15 "Liza Bean Bitey, I presume? Of the Minneapolis Biteys?" My mouth feels dry, like I've been chewing cat litter in my sleep.

16 I hope I sound less apprehensive than I feel. And that I'm wrong about the cat litter.

17 "Mmmm," she purrs noncommittally, "Pearl said you were a smart one. For a male of your species, that is."

18 The cat is of course referring to the Minneapolis blogging legend Pearl*, a friend of mine.

19 And as far as any cat is *owned* by anyone, Pearl is the owner and—to her eternal dismay—*responsible* for Liza Bean. This carries quite a price tag on both her patience and finances.

20 I mean, just the tuna alone...

21 "Hey! Ow! Stop that!" The claws are a fraction of an inch deeper, begging for my wandering attention. Liza Bean tilts her head with faux empathy at my discomfort.

22 "My apologies. It's a balance thing. You are rather... round." Good manners *and* insults; she must have gone to an expensive feline Finishing School. Probably Swiss.

23 But, answering the question forming in my mind, she continues, "I thought we might have a chat."

24 "Okay. Sure." I clear my throat. "So, you're a long way from home, yes?"

25 "Oh, you know how it is," she sighs, bored. "The nomadic life of an international musical artist."

26 "You're kidding?!" I sound genuinely excited, despite myself. "*SQUEAK TOY* are touring?!"

27 The Minnesotan all—cat jazz/blues fusion quartet are a legend in their home town, but I had no idea they were broadening their horizons;

28 leave it to a cat to try and take over the world.

29 "Yes, and our manager insisted that we take in your quaint little island."

30 "Really? Who's your manager?!" I hope it's Pearl, and that's she's with them.

31 "Me." She licks a paw smugly, compensating the shift in balance with a faster and more painful grip on the other. "And of course, we had to visit Cambridge."

32 "Well, of course, I wince, the history, the architecture..."

33 She stops in mid groom, her paw hanging in mid air. "Architecture is for primates. No, there's a *good* reason." She examines a paw. "Part of it is that the tour bus broke down. Right outside your house, in fact."

34 "Now, that is a stroke of luck," I say sourly, but wave a vague hand in the direction of the back garden. "If you'd like some assistance, we have several badgers on hand who can fix..."

35 "Yes, yes," she dismisses gently, "I've already had words with them. They were happy to help. It seems there's inexplicable razor thin slashes in some of the engine pipes."

36 Her gaze is momentarily attracted by the wanderings of a fly above my head; her tail flicks playfully, and her voice becomes distant.

37 "I have no idea how that could have happened."

38 She turns to face me. "Badgers are such *competent engineers*, don't you think?" She phrases this in such a way that the compliment sounds far more like *filthy feral creatures*. I frown, unhappy with the way this is evolving.

39 "So, did you wake me to ask if you could stay for a few hours?"

40 Again, the tail flicks happily. "Not at all," she smiles, "your charming lion friend let us in as he was heading out, and your bear has been helping the band set up downstairs." Liza Bean glances at my bedside clock. "They should be almost done..."

41 On cue, the amplified sound of a swinging band strikes up, and they launch into a remarkable rendition of *Big Noise From Winnetka.*

42 Ignatz D. Katz's upright bass work is fast and bright, Hairball's piano is melodic and loose, but Stumpy "Lucky"

Strikes on drums is in a world of his own, and plays a striking resemblance to a heyday Gene Krupa.

43 "That's terrific!" I gawp, my irritation blown away; I've heard the foursome's breakthrough album, *Not A Can Of Worms***, but this is something else. "You guys are even better live!"

44 "And better yet with me on violin." The look is smug. A little too smug, in fact.

45 "Hey Diddle Diddle, The Cat Played A Fiddle..."

46 Ms. Bitey raises an eyebrow, which somehow reminds me of Death taking a good run up with his scythe. "Excuse me?"

47 "So," I say, changing subject, "if it's not the tour bus or the rehearsal room, what can you possibly want from me?"

48 The reply is cool, calm, definite.

49 "We're here for the lobster." I frown again, and the commanding cat spells it out in tones I would reserve for a slow child. "Your lobster. From Maine. In your fridge."

50 "Lobster?" I bluster a little, "What makes you think I have lobster?!"

51 I'm not sure I'm very convincing.

52 I like lobster. A lot. In fact, my picture is in circulation on badly–printed cautionary fliers in the crustacean world: pliers, bib, *Have You Seen This Man*, the works.

53 "Pearl occasionally buys what she laughingly calls 'the good shrimp'," says Liza Bean, "and tells me that one day we'll get *some of the good lobster like Indigo always has.*"

54 What?! Dammit, that's my dinner; I think fast.

55 "Well, I don't have any right now, so I'm afraid you're out of luck."

56 It's no good, I'm a hopeless liar;

57 she's not buying it.

58 "Though obviously, had I known you were *coming*, I'd have happily shared it with four marvellous musicians." I croak the last of that, feeling myself wilt as the gorgeous golden gaze grows steely.

59 "I assumed that would be your reaction," purrs Liza Bean, "so I enlisted some help."

60 There's a knock at the door. A moment later it opens to reveal the ever–smiling gaze of Abbey, my next door neighbour. Seeing I'm awake she breezes in barefoot, the smell of sunflowers

accompanying her, and tickles an appreciative Liza Bean behind the ears.

⁶¹ "Oh, there you are! Are you two making *friends?!*" gushes the lovely blonde. "Oh Indy, isn't she a *beautiful* kitty?!"

⁶² Liza Bean meows, grinning up at Abbey in a closed–eyed, adorable fashion which is clearly designed to snare unwary owners of albacore tuna.

⁶³ "Lovely?!" I rant, exasperated. "She's a manipulative little wretch who's only here to steal my food!"

⁶⁴ My neighbour cooes over Liza Bean, and picks her up. I hiss in pain as the claws come free from my flesh, but the cat yowls louder to cover it.

⁶⁵ Abbey glances down and scowls at me, as if it's my fault that I'm being assaulted. She kisses the playful moggy's nose as she pops her over her shoulder.

⁶⁶ "Don't be mean, Indigo." Stroking Ms. Bitey's stripy back, Abbey turns to leave. "Now, let's go see if we can find you some cream and some of old Mr. Grumpy's yummy lobster tail from the fridge."

⁶⁷ Liza Bean does her best Cheshire Cat impression at me from Abbey's shoulder and waves a paw as the pair retreats from my bedroom.

⁶⁸ Downstairs, the music is rocking.

⁶⁹ Upstairs, I'm bleeding and defeated.

⁷⁰ Rolling over, I discover cat litter scattered across my pillow.

⁷¹ "Why, I oughta..."

⁷² I flick it clear, fuming, and try to get back to sleep.

Haven

5¹ I am in my cave. My haven.

² The lounge is empty, silent, and there's a quality to the grey light drifting indolently through the windows that I would struggle to photograph.

³ It's been a rough day, for a number of related reasons. None are especially important individually;

⁴ they're just frost on the doorstep.

⁵ But cumulatively they make for a nasty snowball full of twigs and chunks of ice.

⁶ The smell of sunflowers heralds the arrival of Abbey, my neighbour.

⁷ She peeps around the door, her locks freshly reddened, a big smile on her face.

⁸ The room lights up to her, and I offer her my best grin in return from the sofa.

⁹ But I can see by the way her smile crinkles into kindness that she's not fooled by my show for a minute.

¹⁰ She never is, she's a perceptive and caring lady.

¹¹ She steps into the room, crosses the dusty carpet on bare feet, and flops down next to me. Her gathering hug is gentle and determined, and despite myself I'm wrapped in her arms and scent, listening to her heartbeat, before I know it.

¹² She knows, she *always* knows.

¹³ A haven is not a *place*, necessarily.

¹⁴ I am warm, safe and cared for, and everything's going to be okay.

¹⁵ The location isn't important.

Receiving A Bad Grade

6¹ Sometimes a ringing cellphone is a welcome distraction.

² **It's Sunday morning**. I'm standing in the mini–market a hundred yards from my house, trying to ignore the scent cocktail of sweat and cheap cleaning fluid.

³ Outside, there's a light mist; the weather seems to be cooling down after an unseasonably warm summer.

⁴ I'm trying to choose between two pints of full-fat or four pints of half-fat milk when my cellphone rings.

⁵ As I fumble in my pocket, the guy serving behind the counter gives me a withering look, despite the fact that he is also on the phone.

⁶ The handset emerges from my pocket, but my early morning brain doesn't recognise the caller display number. I answer it anyway.

⁷ "Yes, hello?" I yawn.

⁸ "Ah, Mr. Roth!" says a bold male voice. It sounds laboured, overweight, but not breathless enough to be an obscene call;

⁹ I wonder what he'll try to sell me.

¹⁰ "Speaking. Who's calling, please?"

¹¹ There's a faint chuckle at the other end of the line.

¹² "This is Robert Leech, Mr. Roth." *Leech?* It rings a bell, but not quite loud enough. "Your landlord."

¹³ Ah yes, *Bloodsucking Bob*. The largest landlord in Cambridge, owner of some two hundred houses;

¹⁴ this isn't likely to be good news.

¹⁵ "Hello Mr. Leech, how are you?" I ask

politely, hoping he's not about to put my rent up.

¹⁶ "Excellent, thank you!" he leers fatly. "I just wanted to let you know that I'm in the area, and I'm going to drop by to inspect the house."

¹⁷ Oh.

¹⁸ **Twenty minutes ago**, I crawl out of bed to the sound of magnificent singing. It's close by, but thankfully not this side of my door.

¹⁹ I sit upright, my eyes objecting to the pale light at the edge of the curtains.

²⁰ My mouth tastes of stale garlic, and my bedclothes don't seem to have fared much better.

²¹ Ah yes, dinner last night was an enormous pizza; it must have been a weekday.

²² Or a weekend.

²³ The growling tenor voice continues his aria, belting out a tune that might be something from *Il Travatore* as I shuffle to the bathroom.

²⁴ I step absently—and not for the first time this week—over a half-eaten zebra on the landing, and try the door; it's locked.

²⁵ King, the house's resident lion, is showering.

²⁶ But judging by the stripy carcass staining my carpet, he's clearly not *tidying*.

²⁷ Starting down the stairs, I make a mental note to have a word with him about his visitors later.

²⁸ The dim, dog—legged kitchen—diner lacks any debris from the night before;

²⁹ the washing up is done, the surfaces wiped, the carpeted floor immaculate.

³⁰ And the fridge is missing. Interesting; I guess I won't have any milk for my tea?

³¹ My thoughts turn to the cold cabinet of the local mini—market.

³² I scoop my keys from the kitchen table, along with my phone.

³³ As I turn to the hall to looks for my shoes and grab my jacket, a deafening crash spins me round.

³⁴ I find glass shattered across the floor, and a still—rolling baseball escaping the empty frame of the kitchen window.

³⁵ I pick the heavily—stitched ball up and wander over to the window.

³⁶ Thirty yards up the garden, their clothes damp with the dew of the unmown lawn, three young badgers gaze my way.

³⁷ Hoth stands on a small mound of freshly—dug earth, perhaps wishing it wasn't obvious he was the pitcher.

³⁸ Sollust wears a catcher's mitt on his paw ten yards further back, and is slowly edging behind the shed.

³⁹ Between them, in a pretty pink dress, and attempting to hide a bat that's taller than she is behind her back, is Dantoo.

⁴⁰ The boys slowly raise their paws to point at her helpfully.

⁴¹ Dantoo smiles innocently.

⁴² I'm about to take them to task when I notice a figure up by the tree at the very back of the garden. It's standing on a large white box—hey, that's my fridge!—and peering up into the evergreen branches.

⁴³ Mist hides his identity from all certainty, but I guess correctly that it's my best friend, the arch—genius iDifficult.

⁴⁴ He must have been up all night too; he's not a morning person, and would hibernate given the option.

⁴⁵ This is too early, whatever time it is.

⁴⁶ As if sensing my thoughts, 'Difficult turns and waves. I see he has a clipboard and a long wooden boat hook in his hands.

⁴⁷ The fridge wobbles beneath him.

⁴⁸ Wait a minute. Isn't that the tree that the Squiddrel is nesting in?

⁴⁹ On cue, a suckered tentacle descends from the tree. There's a flash of red fur as 'Difficult vanishes with a muffled squawk up into the canopy.

⁵⁰ Scientific curiosity; you can't beat it.

⁵¹ Without a word, the young badgers turn and charge up the garden, welcoming the distraction.

⁵² Dantoo waves the bat valiantly and jostles her older cousins out of the way, quickly overtaking them.

⁵³ They're going to assist 'Difficult with the Squiddrel; I don't fancy its chances, that kid has a good arm on her.

⁵⁴ We'll probably have calamari for dinner tonight.

⁵⁵ I sigh. This is all too much.

⁵⁶ I head out through the front door, and stop in surprise as a figure comes around the hedge and strides purposefully towards me.

⁵⁷ It's my neighbour, the ever—smiling Abbey. The girl—next—door still has no shoes on. I've often meant to ask her why, but now's not the time.

⁵⁸ I need tea, therefore I need milk.

⁵⁹ "Morning, neighbour!" she grins, deflating my world-weary mood instantly. Her shoulder-length hair is above her white t-shirt and dark jeans.

⁶⁰ "Hey." I offer a smile in return, and hope I don't look too rumpled.

⁶¹ "I wanted to borrow a couple of things, may I...?"

⁶² I wave her towards the house as I set off. "Help yourself to whatever you need. I'm off to get milk. Need anything? "

⁶³ "No thanks!" she shouts as I reach the road. "Do you have your phone?"

⁶⁴ "Yeah, call me if you change your mind!"

⁶⁵ There's a cold edge to the wind on the main road, and...

⁶⁶ "Mr. Roth?"

⁶⁷ **Back in the now**, the voice of my Landlord slaps me from my reverie.

⁶⁸ "Mr. Roth?" Damn, what was he saying?

⁶⁹ "Sorry Mr. Leech, someone was talking to me."

⁷⁰ "So, I'll be with you in five minutes."

⁷¹ "Five minutes?!" I can feel a sweat rising.

⁷² "Exactly, be seeing you!"

⁷³ And the line goes dead.

⁷⁴ Zebras, lions, badgers, baseball, broken windows, and a hybrid colossal squid-squirrel trying to eat my best buddy.

⁷⁵ I set off for the house at a run.

⁷⁶ Fifteen minutes later, I stand with Bloodsucking Bob and Abbey in the street. My rotund landlord is grinning and chatting to my neighbour, and largely ignoring me.

⁷⁷ Gazing at his shiny-elbowed jacket, I wonder why this rich fella doesn't own a better suit?

⁷⁸ "I have to say, Abbey," he enthuses, "you've done wonderful things for your brother's housekeeping during your visit!"

⁷⁹ He mops his brow, and adjust his glasses. "Oh my yes, there's some marvellous feminine touches!"

⁸⁰ He waves a finger at me in a playful fashion. "I hope you're appreciative of all your sister's efforts, Indigo!" he chides.

⁸¹ "Oh, Mr. Leech," I shrug, "you have *no idea*."

⁸² "Don't worry, Robert," says Abbey, "I'll be keeping an eye on him." She touches his arm in a reassuring manner. "Thanks for dropping by. You take care now."

⁸³ He blushes and giggles foolishly as he bustles away.

⁸⁴ We wave him off, arm in arm.

⁸⁵ "So, tell me again. Why were you my sister?"

⁸⁶ She pats me on the arm in an equally reassuring manner and gives me a huge distracting smile.

⁸⁷ "Well, if he thought I was your *girlfriend*, he'd have put your rent up."

⁸⁸ She turns to the house before I can think of a smart reply, and wrestles *my* house numbers from *her* front door.

⁸⁹ "Here, you'll need to swap these back."

⁹⁰ "Thanks. You're a life-saver. You know, showing him round your place rather than mine was some quick thinking."

⁹¹ Though now I come to think, she'd already swapped the house numbers over before I made it back from the shop.

⁹² I let it go. Always a mystery, is Abbey.

⁹³ "Now, did you get that milk?" she enquires, folding her arms in an appraising manner.

⁹⁴ I frown. "Um, no. I was in a hurry to get back."

⁹⁵ Abbey raises an eyebrow. There's an essay in the look she gives me, and I suspect I received a bad grade for it.

⁹⁶ But then she cracks another smile.

⁹⁷ "Well, if you go get some, *Bro*, I'll make us some tea."

Notes

*   Hey, Pearl!

**   It's almost certainly a can of tuna.

Elliot

"Jose Ostermann's self–titled Cuban/Polka fusion album is pure gold. Think Buena Vista Club in Lederhosen; guitar, trumpet, tuba. Genius."

Digesting A Fill Of Midnight

1 ¹ Sleeping in an unventilated room after a curry has its bad points.

² That is my first thought for the day.

³ I drift up from a bizarre dream about kneeing the late Dennis Hopper repeatedly in the groin.

⁴ As I sit up in bed, the stone–cold sober reason for this violent reverie slips beyond my reach, and I am left wondering what it was all about.

⁵ The room is dark, the shadows in the corner still digesting their fill of midnight, but some sun is visible at the edges of the blackout curtains;

⁶ it's daylight out.

⁷ My second profound thought for the day is that something is *wrong*. That something *other* than the stale smell of the subcontinent's finest offerings is demanding my attention.

⁸ I have learned the hard way to pay attention to these feelings.

⁹ I squint at the clock, sans spectacles; it looks like **7:30**.

¹⁰ Do I need to *be* somewhere?

¹¹ I think hard for a moment and finally decide that it's Thursday. Last day of June. Thirty days hath September, April, June and... okay, Thursday June 30th.

¹² Nope, I have nowhere to be. Well, not urgently, anyway;

¹³ just the office when I get there.

¹⁴ I'm thirsty and take a long drink from the pint glass on the bedside table.

¹⁵ Do I need to pee, maybe? Nope.

¹⁶ I swing my legs off the bed and hear myself cough.

¹⁷ The dim room suddenly feels airless and small. Panicked, I stumble across to the window and tear the curtains apart. Bright, warm sunlight explodes into the room, but a second's work with a handle adds the noise and the refreshing air of the street into the mix.

¹⁸ I stand, clinging onto the frame, almost gasping. What on earth is wrong with me? I've not felt claustrophobia like this in years.

¹⁹ A motorist blows his horn and shouts something cheerily offensive my way. I realise that I'm naked and in full view of the street. A passing police horse whinnies nervously.

²⁰ Stepping back from the window, I realise I'm standing on my discarded clothes from the night before; I've trampled them almost flat in fact.

²¹ Good grief, *that's* impressive; I must need to shed a few pounds?

²² I lower myself onto the edge of my bed and try to gather my thoughts.

²³ What set me off? What am I trying to remember? A doctor's appointment? The dentist?

²⁴ Memory assures me of a negative response on both counts.

²⁵ The corner of the room to the left of the window catches my eye. Something looks out of place. Has a picture fallen off the wall? No, and my hat's still hanging there.

²⁶ I stare at it for a while, but it's like one of those tedious spot–the–difference puzzles, and my attention wanders.

²⁷ I yawn and rest my head in my hands. A breeze moves past me, and I jerk up, startled. My empty bedroom yawns back at me.

²⁸ Get a grip, Indigo.

²⁹ I yawn and shuffle off towards the bathroom. Gathering my towels, I dump them on the edge of the sink opposite the shower. I open the bathroom window to get some air through, and again stand taking lungfuls of fresh air.

³⁰ The breeze closes the bathroom door behind me.

³¹ There's traces of the smell from the bedroom in here, and I wonder if I might have trodden something unmentionable upstairs from the street.

³² Looking down, I see a few strands of dry grass that I must have carried in from the garden somehow, but nothing that looks responsible for the earthy, almost *animal* odour.

³³ I struggle with the shower door; it seems jammed. Getting it open halfway, I start the shower and squeeze inside a few seconds later.

³⁴ The water is cool and refreshing as I shampoo and rinse. As I lather up some shower gel, it occurs to me that I may have overlooked someone's birthday.

³⁵ My recent record has not been good; I forgot iDifficult's 'til midday, and almost forgot Yavin's completely. Both were cool about my absent–mindedness, but I wasn't;

³⁶ my memory seems rather detached of late; perhaps the humidity of the early English summer doesn't agree with me?

³⁷ Damn, I have soap in my eye.

³⁸ A quick rinse doesn't help, and I rub at it as I fumble with the shower door. It opens easily, and I stretch blindly across in the direction of the sink.

³⁹ Miraculously, my grope finds a towel first time, and I dab the liquid away until the stinging stops.

⁴⁰ Tossing the towel back, I retreat to the cubicle and finish up.

⁴¹ A few minutes later, I step out and take the worst of the water off.

⁴² The room seems darker now; the sun must have retreated behind clouds. Absently, I hear myself clear my throat again. For the second time, a small small room feels suddenly smaller, and claustrophobia rises in me.

⁴³ Opening the bathroom door with a clatter, I step through and close it behind me hurriedly.

⁴⁴ Okay. Wow. That's better.

⁴⁵ What is wrong with you, Roth?

⁴⁶ As I head through to my bedroom, I notice more dry grass on the landing, and resolve to vacuum when I get home from work.

⁴⁷ My head feels clearer as I finish drying off, and everything now looks to be in its place. I quickly slip into today's clothes, put my glasses on, and head downstairs for breakfast.

⁴⁸ **Five minutes later**, I sip at my sweet black coffee in my kitchen diner and spoon down some bran flakes with cold milk. Everything tastes delicious, and the room is bright and open.

⁴⁹ I'm still bemused by my panicky episodes upstairs.

⁵⁰ On cue, the bathroom door rattles. I sigh. Damn, I've left the windows open; I'll need to head back up before I leave the house.

⁵¹ Suddenly aware of the wind outside, I listen to the house move around me. The floorboards of the landing complain of some lost burden, and then the stairs creak gently on the edge of my hearing.

⁵² After washing my bowl and cup, I turn as the hallway darkens a little and then brightens again; the wind must be really driving the clouds past the sun.

⁵³ Moving into the hallway, I remember the windows, and step upstairs to close them and fetch my cellphone. It takes all of thirty seconds to reach the hall again, and I sit at the foot of the stairs to put my shoes on.

⁵⁴ As I gaze towards the front door, something nags at me, and I get another sense that I am overlooking something.

⁵⁵ Something really big.

⁵⁶ A few seconds later I'm relieved to step into the street and slam the door behind me. Heaving a sigh, I gaze up at a radiant sun in a cloudless sky. A gentle breeze stirs the early morning air.

⁵⁷ Wow, I'm out of sorts this morning.

58 I decide to walk to work. It's a beautiful day, and the walk will help clear the inexplicable claustrophobia from my head.

59 Humming a cheery tune, I stroll away from the house.

60 As the front door slams, the elephant stands in the hallway and marvels at the dogged fool retreating down the path.

61 He's used to being ignored by a group of embarrassed or blinkered people in a room; these days, it is almost his job description.

62 But he's never been ignored by one man on his own.

A Disconcerting Little Tune

2 1 The fine white sand is almost too hot to walk on as I make my way up towards the beach.

2 The approach to the tiny seafront is slightly uphill, and gently winds its way between tall, closely–packed dunes.

3 As I trudge through the sand with the picnic box, I wonder for the umpteenth time how tall these heavily–grassed sand hills are. Thirty feet? Forty?

4 They must be all of that, as they block out the sun for much of the day.

5 But right now, the sun is overhead at midday–fierce.

6 "Mad dogs and Englishmen," I sigh.

7 Talking of which, as I crest the rise at the top of the dunes and step onto the narrow beach, I am greeted by England's finest madman.

8 My best friend, iDifficult, *Part–Time Arch–Genius by Royal Appointment*, sits on a old–fashioned deckchair under a huge, flat parasol.

9 He is resplendent in a two–tone striped Victorian bathing suit. The dark sunglasses and close cropped hair are his norm, but the waxed, handlebar moustache is new and magnificent.

10 The pink water–wings are a jaunty touch, too.

11 "Roth!" he cheers, "Splendid to see you!" He doesn't rise, but waves cheerily with his right hand.

12 I notice his left hand is tied by a length of parcel string to an elephant.

13 The creature regards me incuriously for a moment, and then looks away to resume writing in the sand with a stick grasped in its trunk.

14 I notice that the behemoth is sporting a pair of mirrored pince–nez sunglasses. It gives it—him?—a faintly aristocratic air, despite his trench coat.

15 This all comes as no surprise, but I'm too hot and bothered from my short uphill walk to ask about my friend's companion right now.

16 "Grab a seat!" enthuses 'Difficult, indicating a spot beside him. "Bring it over here, the shade is glorious!"

17 I drag over the matching deckchair and fumble ineffectually with it for a moment.

18 I've never liked deckchairs; too fiddly to set up.

19 And doing it one–handed while carrying a heavy, insulated box is not helping matters either, so I put my burden down.

20 After what seems like five minutes cursing and wrestling, I ease myself into the wood–and–cloth seat wearily. The picnic box sits beside me;

21 there is a faint thumping from inside.

22 A martini appears in my hand, and I nod in thanks; my friend is a genial host.

23 "How was the time journey?"

24 I shrug. Travel is travel, even if it is through time.

25 "I've brought the lobsters you wanted," I say, sipping the drink. It's strong with a dash of *kina lillet** and has two black *kalamata* olives on a stick.

26 Just the way I like it.

27 "Thanks. Did they give you any trouble?"

28 This seems an odd question, but I have an equally odd recollection.

29 "No, no problems, I say," tugging the lid off the coldbox. The sound of snapping claws emerges and slowly intensifies. "but I could have *sworn* these lads were dressed and cooked when I saw first saw them."

30 I recall it vividly, in fact. You know, when I bought them from the deli counter at the supermarket.

31 "Oh, they were!" enthuses the mad genius, his eyes sparkling over the top of his shades. He adds in a hushed tone, "I *revivified* them."

32 I glance down at the hostile contents of the cool hamper. And the hostile contents look right back at me, making it chillingly clear via pointed claws and antennae wiggles that *I Should Watch My Step.*

33 To be honest, I find the whole thing rather unsettling.

34 "So these are... *zombie* lobsters?" I lean back nervously, half expecting them to shuffle and moan.

35 "No, not at all!" laughs 'Difficult. That'd be *reanimation*. Not to mention cruel and unusual. I just used the time machine to rewind them back to when they were still alive."

36 He shrugs, "They're much happier this way. Besides," he grins, "I can't stand seafood."

37 And to make the point, he tips the box over in the direction of the surf. The lobsters and several gallons of water spill onto the sand with a hiss.

38 There's a moment of indecision from the crustaceans. *Attack or flee?*

39 But realising that discretion is the better part of not–being–eaten, the two lobsters make a break for the water.

40 They eight–leg–it down the steep incline, claws waving, to where the beach and dunes vanish into the surf of the little horseshoe bay.

41 In a fistful of seconds, they're gone.

42 We sip our drinks and take in the view. It really is rather beautiful.

43 An endless ocean under sun, broken only by the occasional crumbling spire. Close to shore there are occasional glimpses of submerged atolls.

44 Well, not so much atolls; more the *remains* of nearby houses.

45 "It's a shame about Cambridge," I say absently.

46 "Yes, it's hard to imagine this used to be your back garden."

47 We stand and turn to face the downward slope of the path.

48 A hundred yards away, my little old house sits in a tiny sandy vale, dwarfed on three sides by the gigantic dunes.

49 We're at the other end of the long, thin rectangle of land.

50 The dunes surround the entire thing, thick and tall and level, with us at the top of the upward slope.

51 Beyond us in all directions, almost level with the top of the dunes, is the sea.

52 I still find it alarming to see my house safely below sea level.

53 "The badgers really did a grand job of..." starts 'Difficult, attempting to wave expansively. The string on his left hand reaches his limit and prevents this.

54 He sighs.

55 The elephant looks up at the tug on his foreleg. With a heaving grunt, the beast stands and moves a little closer.

56 I now feel inclined to ask, but I don't like to interrupt.

57 "As I was saying," repeats my friend, "the badgers did a grand job of shoring this all up." His wave is extra–expansive now; he indicates the winding path up to where we're standing.

58 "Adding the slope up here to make the beach was inspired. Imaginative landscaping."

59 "Yep," I nod, "Hoth and Sollust used it as their masterwork for *The Guild*. It took them a while, but apparently after everyone left the town it got easier to get planning permission."

60 His reply is quiet, introspective.

61 "We had plenty of warning, I suppose." He shakes his head ruefully. "Seems stupid that we didn't prevent it."

62 I can't disagree.

63 In the distance there's a wide cluster of centuries–old spires from the university colleges. I can just make out tiny waves lapping against them gently;

64 it's a calm day at sea.

65 "What's the date?" I ask on a whim, happy to change the subject.

66 "June the seventeenth," comes the absent–minded reply. "Why?"

67 "No, I mean what year is it?"

68 "Oh. Right. Well, you have the core. " I fiddle in my pocket and tug the core of the time machine free, wondering why I didn't think of this earlier.

69 I glance at the brass, enamel and glass device, and shade it from the sun to read the display.

70 "Good grief," I manage.

71 My friend removes his shades and looks my way.

72 "Yes. Sooner than we think."

73 We stand for a while in silence and remember the town.

74 As we return to our seats, 'Difficult is halted by the string again. But his companion ambles to catch us up, and ultimately throws his massive bulk down with us in the shade of the mighty parasol.

75 Now seems as good a time as any.

76 "By the way, I've been meaning to ask... Why are you going around with this fella on a string?"

77 "Well," says the elephant, "he'd get up to mischief otherwise." He flashes me his

Parole Officer ID with a flick of his trunk. An old, wise eye peeps from behind the mirrored shades.

78 I glance down at the empty picnic box and think of its previous occupants, while 'Difficult hums a disconcerting little tune to which only he knows the rhythm.

79 The elephant may have a point.

80 As the sun begins its descent into the west, the three of us gaze across the ever–changing water, and dream of what might have been.

Eyeing A Beer Suspiciously

Being the testament of Elliot

3 1 The night is hot as sin, but far less enjoyable.
2 It's the kind of evening when I normally lock myself in my office under the ceiling fan, with just a bucket of ice and a bottle of bourbon for company.

3 Together, we enjoy the sunset through drawn blinds.

4 But not tonight. Tonight I'm working on a case. A missing person. Or rather, an absent one.

5 As elusive as a greased weasel, as unpredictable as a jumping bean. He's smarter than a volleyball team of badgers, too, and has kept me guessing all evening.

6 This is the eleventh establishment I've visited, and despite my thick skin, my patience is wearing thin.

7 I remember each visit, each fragrant, badly–decorated joint, the nervous glances of the owners and patrons as I bullet them with questions.

8 My last trip found me in a back room behind a kitchen, sweating information out of a nervous chef with little more than some well–timed looming.

9 I loom well. It's my height, my species, and my gift.

10 The information led me here, to a curry house in the main drag of town. I check the name above the door; yes, this is the place.

11 It has a reputation for strangeness, and a clientele to match. I'm not surprised my quarry has gone to ground here.

12 Straightening my hat, and adjusting the false moustache that distracts from my distinctive nose, I enter the restaurant.

13 You have to travel incognito in this line of work.

14 The room is low, dark and long, seemingly endless. Mahogany tables, private booths, exotic plants and occasional lamps break up the space.

15 The customers are huddled together in their pools of light, and waiters voyage boldly between them, careless of their safety. There's the smell of excitement and uncertainty in the air.

16 Either that, or it's the onion bhajis.

17 I'm in my element. This is what I was born for.

18 I approach the main desk. The manager, a dashing Asian figure with immaculately–coiffed hair, a white suit and spats, smiles as he looks up. But the look freezes on his face.

19 He whispers "Ganesh!" incredulously, and starts to sweat;

20 I love it when they do that.

21 His gazes darts around the room rapidly in an attempt to find either escape or help. I give him my best loom and hold his eye;

22 he's dealing with *me*.

23 Alone with his god.

24 The fella says he wants no trouble, and I ask him if he's going to give me any.

25 He gazes up at me in awe as I flash him my ID and the photo, and ask him where they are.

26 He says he doesn't recall seeing them tonight, but with a nervous laugh he adds that he has *so many customers*;

27 he's got nerve, I'll give him that.

28 I do the cracking thing with my neck, flap my ears at him menacingly, and place a twenty on the table between us.

29 As he moves to take it, I lay a flat foot upon his hand suddenly. I could crush it just my leaning forward slightly, and he knows it. I smile and repeat my question quietly, making it clear that this second inquiry will be the last.

30 After a long few seconds, he folds like cheap origami paper.

31 As I approach the private booth, with more stealth than my size suggests is possible, I can't see the occupants. But I know I've found them.

32 The huge pile of discarded plates, bowls, balti dishes, pint glasses and discarded napkins is unmistakable. As is the smell.

33 The singing is off–key and punctuated with fits of laughter.

[34] I stand by the table and clear my throat. After a few moments, two dishevelled, curry-stained faces slowly emerge from behind the chaos of crockery. One belches, and apologises to his companion.

[35] "May we help you?" asks the one on the left politely. It's Roth.

[36] "And why, pray tell, are you disturbing our meal, Mister..." begins the other. He squints at me, befuddled. "Whoever you are." It's clearly iDifficult, the man I came to find.

[37] With a sharp tug, I remove the false moustache from underneath my trunk.

[38] They gasp in unison, "It's an elephant!"

[39] "Oh bugger," mutters iDifficult, nine sheets to the wind, "it's my bloody parole officer." He rallies well though, gives me his best mad grin and offers a cheery, "Good evening Mr. Nesh! What brings you here?"

[40] Roth turns to him and lays a reassuring hand on his shoulder.

[41] "S'okay, I got this." He turns and stands shakily. "Elliot, good evening. I have to say, I'm a little disappointed. Just a tiny bit." He makes a *this big* gesture with thumb and forefinger. "You're rather late, old son."

[42] Well, this is an interesting tactic. But these two are tricky, resourceful and brilliant, even in this state; I mustn't get distracted.

[43] "Late?" I repeat, using my reflective listening skills to play for time and information.

[44] "Yeah, late. We were expecting you two hours ago." He fumbles in his pocket and produces a scrap of paper. "Here's your RSVP." He pops it face-up on the table, knowing manual dexterity is not my strong suit.

[45] I scan the paper. Yes, that's my signature on it. A vague memory tickles the back of my brain, and then has a nice long scratch. Wait a minute. Did this pair invite me out for dinner? I frown and scratch my trunk. "Well, I, erm... when did we agree this?"

[46] Roth laughs happily and moves round the table.

[47] "Elliot, Elliot, Elliot. A couple of weeks ago!" He eyes me with a lopsided grin, and nudges me with an elbow conspiratorially. "I thought you fellas never forget?"

[48] I make a hasty mental note to start keeping a diary.

[49] "Good gravy!" voices iDifficult. "Did Elliot 'Gan' Nesh let a memory slip through the net?" He eyes a bottle of beer suspiciously. "One for the books."

[50] I slap my forehead, and regret it immediately. "The first Sunday in August!"

[51] They smile politely, encouragingly.

[52] "Curry with you two! Two thousand and twentieth birthday of..." I wrack my brain, but the name won't come. Roth comes to my rescue.

[53] "Emperor Claudius of the Roman Empire!"

[54] "Right!" I almost cheer. Their slacking enthusiasm is infectious.

[55] "You know," mumbles 'Difficult, "I think he was a bit bonkers, was Claudius." Myself and Roth regard him with some surprise. The arch-genius shrugs. "You know, *professionally* speaking."

[56] Roth waves a waiter over. The server gives me a wide berth.

[57] "Well, Mr. Nesh, you've missed the food." He pats me gently on the back, "Sorry matey." He pulls out a wicker chair for me, and I sit carefully, removing my hat. "But why not relax and have a drink with us?"

[58] It sounds good, and there's a nice breeze from somewhere. Glancing up, I notice a vigorous ceiling fan stirring the air deliciously.

[59] "A large bourbon for my friend," 'Difficult instructs the waiter. "In fact, bring the bottle over!"

[60] As the waiter nods and gratefully moves to leave, I catch his eye.

[61] "And plenty of ice."

Way Too Much Cheese

4 [1] There is just the clinking of ice in bourbon, and the dull drone of a static-filled TV.

[2] *We have nothing to fear but fear itself.*

[3] The static does not improve the broadcast. The bar has no lights, but ancient columns of dusty light project majestically down from high, dirty windows.

[4] "Please, turn this off." The bar's only patron rumbles his request as he sips his drink. The television is far to his left, but

his trench–coated bulk exudes dislike for the transmission.

5 The barman polishes a glass absently; his shirt is cleaner than the rag he uses.

6 "You don't like this guy?"

7 *And if we work together, we can achieve anything.*

8 "Nope." He snorts this from his leathery trunk as his ears stir the sweltering air. "No time for politicians."

9 "Oh. But isn't it that guy you hang out with? What's his name? *Roth?*"

10 Elliot glances sideways momentarily and seems to give the TV a closer look. Or perhaps he's just chewing ice, a *film*

noir voice–over running in his head.

11 "No, it's just some *schmuck* in a suit spouting cheesy clichés."

12 "Oh," the barman coughs. "Well, you can understand my confusion, right?"

13 *And if you love someone, set them free.*

14 "Oh, yeah."

15 The barkeep turns to the TV and clicks it off via remote control. "Same again?"

16 The elephant's sign is long and deep.

17 Ice cubes tinkle in the empty glass, and out in the desert, a bloody–beaked crow caws over his prize.

18 "Please. And one for yourself."

Notes

* An alcoholic drink that hasn't been made for decades; one of the advantages of having a friend with a time machine.

Unity

"There was always a far–off destination for this journey, but I always thought of it as The Long Road Home."

A Shower Of Gravelly Memories

1 ¹ The past is beneath our feet.
² **It's Wednesday morning**, and a sunny one at that. I'm having a healthy breakfast* in my kitchen–diner by the big back window.
³ I have a day off work, and I'm lazily making the most of it. I feel like a cat, basking in the sunshine.
⁴ As I munch another resistant mouthful, I notice my neighbour Abbey heading down the early–Spring garden. I smile as I take in her tousled red hair, her skipping step, the big smile, and the ever–bare feet.
⁵ Pretty without pretence, this attractive lady is literally the girl–next–door. I'm not sure why she's in my garden, but it doesn't matter; she's welcome, and I'm pleased to see her.
⁶ I knock on the window and as she turns her smile somehow gets wider. I wave her inside, and notice that she's carrying something small and square.
⁷ I wipe the last spot of milk from my lips with a napkin.
⁸ "Morning, neighbour!" she beams as she breezes through the back door, the lightest of giggles bubbling through her words. "I've brought something to show you!"
⁹ Her sunflower scent has also brought the Spring indoors.

¹⁰ She quietly pops a photo frame on the table in front of me. "Isn't it *amazing?!*"
¹¹ The photo in the battered frame is old and weathered, a black–and–white print of a black–and–white subject.
¹² I nod, intrigued and fascinated.
¹³ "It certainly is. A badger Freemason! And a *very* senior one, by the look of him."
¹⁴ A memory shifts slightly. I continue,
¹⁵ "Look, you can see he's important; the heavy chain of office, the ornate leather apron, the arm braces and gloves..."
¹⁶ I think for a moment. "If I had to guess, I'd say he was a Lodge Grand Master."
¹⁷ My neighbour looks at me curiously. I laugh, realising her assumption.
¹⁸ "Oh, I'm not *On The Square*. My dear old Uncle Jericho was highly placed in one of the American lodges. And talked too much."
¹⁹ Our attention returns to the ageing photo. I can't help but laugh again; I love the moustache, monocle and top hat.
²⁰ "But a *Grand Master?!*" exclaims Abbey, "He's just a badger!"
²¹ I'm sure she's teasing me; she's been living here long enough to know how remarkable they are.
²² The memory shifts in my head again.
²³ "Well, Freemasonry is traditionally about craftsmanship," I note mildly, "and these guys can build *anything.*

119

Especially underground."

24 "Like, say... tunnels?" Abbey is now behind me, and now her tone is definitely teasing.

25 Her tone jostles the thought again, and it suddenly tumbles free in a shower of gravelly memories.

26 "Yes, tunnels! He's from the *Grand Lodge of Tunnellers!*" I receive an encouraging look. "Jericho told me about them when I was a kid; they're very high up in The Brotherhood." My mouth moves silently. My jaw drops.

27 "Good grief, is this *The General?!*"

28 She cheers theatrically, then hugs me.

29 "Yes, exactly! It's The General, the Grand Master of his Lodge. He was one of the first badgers to work above ground. With people, I mean. Did you know he was actually a scientist by profession?"

30 I shake my head in amazement; the story *is* intriguing.

31 "But that's a story for another day," she says cryptically, "This photo was taken in 1953."

32 Incredible. A moment in history, a legendary figure, still with us through this simple photograph.

33 A new thought nudges me.

34 "So Abbey," I frown, puzzled, "how do you know all this, exactly?"

35 "Oh," she shrugs, "Yavin shared what he knew with me." There's a slightly evasive quality to the words, and she doesn't quite meet my eye.

36 I'm puzzled; I can communicate with Yavin well enough, but the old badger engineer doesn't *say* much. Anything at all, in fact.

37 I wonder about how she had that conversation, but put that thought aside for now.

38 She's full of mysterious talents, is Abbey.

39 "Well, I suppose he'd know the history of his profession and species as well as anyone."

40 "True, but Yavin knows this bit of history especially well." She meets my eye. "It turns out that The General is Yavin's grandfather."

41 "Wow."

42 I had no idea. Life is full of surprises.

43 Today, the past really is beneath our feet.

44 Abbey grins. "And he's just moved back to the garden."

Elephants Abhor A Vacuum

2 1 Time can be sliced in many ways.

2 If our paydays mark the passage of each month, and the church bells on Sunday morning cleave one week from the next**, then it is our meals that punctuate our days.

3 **It's Sunday morning**. I'm having a spot of brunch with my best friend iDifficult. My lounge is alive with delicious smells, both sweet and savoury.

4 It's all courtesy of my lovely neighbour Abbey, who dropped in some warm baked treats for us on her way to church;

5 she knows we're non−denominational, but respects our belief systems, which include plenty of tasty grub.

6 "Man," I groan delightedly, "this nutty, caramelly, oaty thing is awesome!" I'm forced to catch a shower of delicate, gooey crumbs as my enthusiasm gets ahead of me. "How's yours?"

7 The part−time arch−genius grunts appreciatively and grins broadly, "Gorgeous, though I have no idea what it is!"

8 He contemplates his confection seriously.

9 "You remember that Winston Churchill described Russia as a riddle, wrapped in a mystery, inside an enigma?" I nod as I eat. "Well, this little treat is a riddle, inside a mystery, wrapped in..." he eyes it speculatively, "well, wrapped in flaky pastry."

10 I chuckle and raise my teacup.

11 "To Abbey!" we toast in unison.

12 Wiping his lips with a napkin, 'Difficult regards me curiously. "Talking of whom, did you get to the bottom of that business with Abbey and the badgers?"

13 I clear my throat and try to think of a sensible answer.

14 It's hard; it's been that kind of week.

15 **It's Wednesday morning**. I'm puzzled that Abbey seems to know a lot more about the history of the resident badgers than I do;

16 apparently, she's been *sharing* stories with Yavin, their Chief Engineer.

17 I've had many adventures with the badgers, but rely on body language rather than spoken words. It works well, but it means that while I know plenty about the present, I know precious little about their past.

Unity

¹⁸ The badgers' sett is dim and musty.

¹⁹ Books line the walls of this particular room, on everything from engineering to metaphysics. The latter is unusual reading for badgers, but we're taking tea with the legendary ex–military scientist and freemason known only as The General.

²⁰ This venerable badger also happens to be Yavin's grandfather.

²¹ The General sits resplendent in a smoking jacket, monocle and fez, with a gently wisping cigar in his ageing paw.

²² He was born in 1933, which makes no sense;

²³ badgers live fifteen years typically, and even though Yavin's family come from tenacious stock, it doesn't add up.

²⁴ I have so many questions.

²⁵ Abbey sits between us, holding our hands, and helps us to... talk? I'm unsure. We've been here an hour, and while I know a lot more about the badger than I did, I can't remember exchanging any actual words with him.

²⁶ **Back in the now**, iDifficult shifts in his seat, perhaps pondering my silence. "Because I know she's good with energy flows. So I figured she'd have some..." he waves a hand speculatively, casually, "*Spiritual* way of talking to them?"

²⁷ He slurps his tea shiftily. "Or something."

²⁸ I smile and shrug. "Yes. Well... yes. That's pretty much it."

²⁹ Nodding without comment, 'Difficult helps himself to an amaretto–laced über–éclair.

³⁰ I realise I still have questions.

³¹ And my curiosity gets the better of me.

³² "This General fella," I say amiably, "a lovely old boy, is quite a character." More nods from my friend amidst the chocolate and cream. "He must be *extremely* old by now. How *is* that?"

³³ The éclair is replaced quietly on the table, and 'Difficult thinks for a moment before preparing to speak.

³⁴ The moment of revelation is interrupted by a knock at the front door;

³⁵ a heavy, meaningful knock that does not repeat.

³⁶ "Hold that thought," I say as I head through to the vanilla–scented hall. It's oddly dim out here, with no light from the front door; I have a large visitor.

³⁷ Ah yes. Elliot.

³⁸ Opening the door, I behold a broad and eclipsing elephant in a trenchcoat. He stands proud on two legs and surveys the scene with an expert, jaded eye.

³⁹ I can almost hear a film noir voiceover.

⁴⁰ He brushes the brim of his trilby hat with a digit of a giant forefoot.

⁴¹ "Mr. Roth."

⁴² Elliot Nesh is an agent of some unknown *Department*. He's also iDifficult's parole officer, though my friend claims to have no knowledge of his supposed crime.

⁴³ And I believe my friend; why wouldn't I? Besides, it's a mystery, and we enjoy those.

⁴⁴ Another puzzle is Elliot's jurisdiction. It's a total unknown, though we're fairly sure he's *not from round here.*

⁴⁵ All I know is that this elephant shows up whenever we're about to embark on a time travel adventure, and then ties himself for the duration of the jaunt to 'Difficult with a length of string.

⁴⁶ Again, this doesn't make sense, but so little does at first glance.

⁴⁷ Today, I am not surprised to find Elliot on my doorstep.

⁴⁸ "Hey matey, nice to see you. Please," I step aside with a welcoming gesture, "come in, come in."

⁴⁹ As the elephant nods and strides into my hallway, I notice that he's carrying a small ball of string.

⁵⁰ I wonder idly if I should fetch my toothbrush.

⁵¹ In the lounge, iDifficult rises in greeting, looking shifty. I assume momentarily that Elliot's arrival has put him on the defensive, but then I spot that most of the cakes are gone.

⁵² My friend waves sheepishly and smiles past a mouthful of choux pastry and almonds.

⁵³ The parole office regards his ward amiably, but gets straight down to business.

⁵⁴ "Mr. Difficult, are you planning on making a *trip* today?" The agent dons a pair of dark, round–lensed *pince–nez* spectacles. They seem unnecessary indoors, but

⁵⁵ who knows what goes through the mind of an elephant?

⁵⁶ As he patiently waits for an answer, Elliot deftly adjusts the edge of one frame, as if he's focusing a microscope. Finally swallowing, 'Difficult looks

genuinely surprised.

⁵⁷ "A time trip? No. Should I be?"

⁵⁸ The elephant fiddles with his glasses again. "You're sure?"

⁵⁹ "Yes, certain." He looks to me and back to Elliot; no help there. Eager to change the subject, 'Difficult picks up the near–empty plate from the table and offers it to the agent. "Cake?"

⁶⁰ Elliot sighs and removes his glasses, pocketing them quietly.

⁶¹ "No thank you. Too rich for me. Do you have anything... plainer?" I know what he has in mind, but we rarely keep sticky buns about the place;

⁶² elephants love sticky buns, everyone knows that.

⁶³ Once again, as my friend starts to answer, there's another knock at the door. The back door this time, a quiet and persistent rapping.

⁶⁴ For a moment, 'Difficult seems to consider something, but then he pops the plate down and offers a simple, "I'll see what we have. Excuse me."

⁶⁵ I'm left in the room with the brooding pachyderm. I sit and nibble on another delightful confection, wishing Abbey were here to keep the conversation afloat.

⁶⁶ "You know, Elliot, we never talk about your *work*." The elephant raises an eyebrow. "For example, you accompany us on all out trips because of something 'Difficult has done, though I've no idea what it is."

⁶⁷ Elliot shifts uncomfortably, but I resist the urge to keep talking; I wait, and hope that he will fill the vacuum.

⁶⁸ Elephants abhor a vacuum. Or is that Nature?

⁶⁹ "I'm assigned to Mr. Difficult," he confirms quietly, seeming to consider his words carefully, "but he's done nothing wrong."

⁷⁰ *What?* But then, the punchline.

⁷¹ "Yet."

⁷² I'm lost for words. The puzzle pieces in my head scatter randomly. What does that *mean?* What exactly is Elliot's *job?*

⁷³ My train of thought is derailed by iDifficult's return. He's bearing a plate of warm buns and an easygoing smile.

⁷⁴ The buns are fresh and sticky and smell amazing. Elliot's trunk and ears twitch. He says nothing, but his gaze is held by the contents of the plate.

⁷⁵ "These are fresh from the oven," says

my genius amigo conversationally, "and I think they'll be more to your taste."

⁷⁶ "Well, I really shouldn't," mutters Elliot, "I'm on duty after all." He inhales deeply; this must be excruciating for him. "But perhaps just one."

⁷⁷ **A few minutes later**, the plate is empty, and Elliot is asleep. The ball of string sits between his legs, lightly dusted in crumbs.

⁷⁸ I click my fingers in front of the dozing elephant's closed eyes. "Did you drug him?"

⁷⁹ My friend lifts the ball of string from Elliot's chair and pockets it. When he replies, his mind is clearly distracted and racing.

⁸⁰ "Hmmm? No. Not at all. He always falls asleep right after a good meal."

⁸¹ This is true. We've carried him home from the curry house on many occasions, though I had assumed it was the bourbon.

⁸² "And anyway, where did the buns come from? " I say, bemused.

⁸³ "Yavin brought them over. I asked him to bring some fresh sticky buns when a particular event finally happened.

⁸⁴ And, unexpectedly, it's just happened.

⁸⁵ He's firing up the time machine as we speak." I have no time to query this before 'Difficult continues, his voice alive with new purpose. "Right. We need to get moving."

⁸⁶ "What, now? Where are we going?"

⁸⁷ "I'll explain on the way." I open my mouth again, but he quietens me with a raised finger. "I need you to go and fetch Abbey, before Elliot wakes up. We need a head–start."

⁸⁸ "A head start? In a *time machine?!*"

⁸⁹ His laughter reminds me of old times, and raises a smile in me, but I have a gnawing feeling that this will be a very different kind of adventure.

⁹⁰ Time can be sliced in many ways.

⁹¹ Today I think we're cutting it fine.

An Equation For String

Being the testament of Elliot

3 ¹ As I open the door of the car, the city howls of its cold, wet misery. The rain is heavy, the clouds low and dark.

² Stepping out of the taxi into the downpour, my trunk automatically tucks inside the folds of my coat, and my ears

fold forward to keep the water out. I turn to pay the driver, who eyes me fearfully;

3 I mumble an apology for the bodies in the back seat and tip him a twenty. He drives away without comment, pleased to be gone.

4 I rarely visit *Central*, and I've brought bad weather with me. This draws a wry smile from me, or as close to one as I come without bourbon. Most days, this is a sunlit, teeming, cheery metropolis; in fact, this entire Reality is.

5 The privileged folk who live here know no better, and rarely experience worse.

6 But not today. Today, the shining city at the hub of existence nods its head as an agent passes through its streets.

7 My name is Elliot Nesh. I work for The Agency. *The Unity Agency*.

8 Flipping the collar of the trenchcoat up, I turn my gaze skyward, my back to the rain.

9 My destination is a looming art deco tower of some thirty storeys. A single light burns in its windows today, high up in the topmost floor;

10 even the gods need light to read.

11 The building broods darkly under sullen clouds, and offers no explanation.

12 I square the trilby on my broad head and cross the street to the lobby of the tower, seeking answers.

13 The skinny young clerk on the main desk lifts the phone and quietly says a few words to someone as I approach him. Replacing the receiver, he gives me a nervous smile.

14 I enjoy his discomfort; sometimes discomfort is all I have to work with, and even the short days can be long and hard.

15 I hold his eye and idly flick the raindrops from my ears onto the desk. He doesn't look down.

16 I raise an eyebrow, inviting him to get a move on. The spell broken, he jerks back into life. Producing a key, he steps away to the side of the desk, and hastily fumbles open the black baroque doors of what looks like an executive elevator.

17 Removing my hat, I manoeuvre under the doorframe of the elevator and turn to face the lobby. The interior is burnished gold rococo panelling. I really don't like confined spaces, but I offer no sign of it as I replace my trilby and stand impassively.

18 The clerk reaches inside to jab the button for the penthouse, and then retreats, slamming shut the doors of this wrought iron coffin.

19 I sigh and gather my thoughts, closing my eyes to blot out the claustrophobia as best I can.

20 Okay, back to basics; why am I here?

21 I'm here representing The Unity Agency.

22 Back in the day, The Agency was called the *Department of Dimensions*, but Science has moved on since then.

23 Now, each separate bundle of four dimensions—the three spatial ones and time—is called a *Reality*.

24 Universes? The Multiverse? Old hat.

25 We now understand that there are eleven distinct dimensions, a mathematically elegant container for the numerous Realities that we now refer to as *The Unity*.

26 Each Reality is separated from the others by differences in a fifth dimension;

27 what goes on in dimensions six through eleven is above my pay grade.

28 The Unity is run from Central. Though *The Board Of Directors* would say that it was *Overseen* or *Moderated* or something similarly bland and corporate.

29 And probably under advisement.

30 And it is them that I'm here to see; The Board. Or rather, they've summoned me. I'm not accountable to them directly, but somewhere up the slippery pole they pull the strings.

31 This elevator must be unsettling me; I rarely mix my metaphors like that, even in a voiceover.

32 With an juddering clank, the elevator stops. By contrast, the outer doors swing open soundlessly.

33 I step from the elevator into a dimly lit boardroom. An oval table, and sixteen faces. All male, all well groomed, all with the hawkish look of Men With Money.

34 The Board promotes itself as benefactors, as a non–profit governing body.

35 But as an outsider, I know you don't get onto it by being talented or qualified.

36 "Ah, Mr. Nesh. We've been expecting you."

37 The voice is steady, stern, authoritarian. It's recognisably voice Number 7, The Headmaster. I can see his half–moon spectacles before I even

focus on the speaker, and know instinctively that it will be the Chairman, *Cecil Rhodes Armitage.*

38 Is he testing the water with me? He's wasting his time if he is;

39 Agents don't ruffle, and have little truck with authority.

40 No, it's more likely for the benefit of his colleagues, a show of strength. He'll probably try Number 5 next; The Public Servant.

41 "Good morning, Gentlemen," I say, slowly scanning across the gathered men; most meet my gaze with a mixture of mistrust and curiosity.

42 "I seem to have brought bad weather with me."

43 I stand, my hands thrust deep into my pockets, dripping on the immaculate carpet;

44 they pretend not to notice and I don't pretend to care.

45 The Chairman smiles. "And we thank you for coming on such a dreadful day, Mr. Nesh," says the Chairman, switching to Public Servant as expected. "We were expecting two of our colleagues to be with you," he says, his delivery speckled with faux concern. "I hope they didn't get lost on the way here?"

46 He chuckles, but nobody joins him; this is not humour.

47 I offer my own smile, just as false.

48 The two heavies who woke me up at Roth's place were hired help, the usual combination of over-developed necks and shiny ID badges.

49 I accompanied them on the jump to Central to save me the five-dimensional calculation while half asleep, but I went solo soon after;

50 their IDs were the toughest thing about them.

51 "Not at all. We parted company in the taxi." I shrug and offer an affable, "I explained to them that I knew the way to the Boardroom. I've met with so many of your predecessors, after all."

52 I let this thought settle on their shoulders. A few of them shift uncomfortably and exchange glances;

53 I love the smell of fear in the morning.

54 The chairman frowns subtly and decides to move the conversation along; I'm gently denting his authority. He shifts to Number 2, Efficient Executive;

55 I suspect it's as close to his real persona as he gets without baring his

teeth. Or selling his grandmother.

56 "Mr. Nesh, I'll come to the point. We Audit a great number of Realities here at Central." Heh. *Audit.* I grin lopsidedly as he continues. "And it's one of our many tasks to Rationalise them when we can."

57 "*Rationalise,* Mr. Chairman?" I know exactly what he means, but I have no patience for corporate double-talk, especially when it hides destructive behaviour;

58 these are the kinds of men who put *military advisors* into Vietnam and invented terms like *collateral damage.*

59 I wonder idly how he'll respond.

60 "Yes, Mr. Nesh," he says coldly and clearly, "Rationalise. We combine Realities when we can." He rises unexpectedly from his chair and leans toward me, hands on the table. "Or just plain *get rid of them* if they are no longer needed."

61 The plain speech of a sociopath in authority; I give the man some respect.

62 And I suddenly realise why I'm here. Why they need me.

63 "Mr. Nesh, we believe that the Reality spawned by an individual called..." he consults his notes unnecessarily, "*Indigo Roth* can be removed." He almost spits the name. Clearly he doesn't approve of the antics of Roth and his friends.

64 He probably has something against badgers.

65 "You want to kill off Roth's Reality?" I pause and shrug, the very picture of bemusement. "But why? It's unusual for someone to create a Reality through words, true enough, but his writing is harmless enough. Some funny stories, some colourful characters. Lions and Badgers and Bears, Oh My!";

66 I raise my heavy eyebrows in uncharacteristic Garland-esque surprise, and enjoy watching the assembled execs shake their heads in worried dismay.

67 The wingman to the Chairman's right stands angrily. I recognise him as the third-in-command, a nasty weasel of a man called *Joshua Cane.*

68 "Now see here, Mr. Nesh," he blusters, "The Board considers that kind of comment to be unprofessional. Your levity in this matter is most unwelcome!"

69 I scratch my trunk and flick my ears to hide a laugh. I've never seen The Board so skittish before. The Chairman

gestures Cane back to his seat and replies on his behalf.

[70] "Realities are a precious resource, Mr. Nesh. They are supposed to important. Roth's is not." He waves a hand, "We intend to remove it, and we shall."

[71] "And what about the people that live in that Reality?"

[72] "Well, they weren't there before Roth somehow split his Reality off, and they won't be there after." It's Armitage's number two, a well-groomed young fella called *Sebastian Drake*. He licks his lizard lips and smiles. "It's what we call a zero-sum deal."

[73] I want to punch him.

[74] But no. Not here, not now.

[75] Which only leaves two questions:

[76] "So why am I here, Gentlemen? How may The Agency assist you?"

[77] More shuffling and mumbling results in the ranks from that;

[78] I'm not just some rogue bull elephant with big ears and a drink problem. I'm an Agent, with a capital 'A'.

[79] "Because we are told by our... *advisors*," the Chairman smiles ruefully—he almost said *spies*, I'm sure—"that you have an ongoing case that is blocking our closure of Mr. Roth's Reality."

[80] And there it is. Their problem.

[81] "Oh, you mean the investigation of Roth's friend iDifficult as a Potential Criminal?"

[82] I wait for their response, but none is forthcoming.

[83] We're straying into uncomfortable territory; Temporal Causality and Consequence. I wonder how long I can keep us here?

[84] "Yes, that's true," I deadpan, "While we're investigating Mr. Difficult, it's not possible to kill off the Reality he inhabits."

[85] "What? Wait a minute, damn you!" blurts a fella to the left of the group. Young, stocky, bad teeth. Ah yes. *Jeffrey Pinkerton-Smythe*; never the sharpest tool. "Did you say *Potential* Criminal? What the devil does that mean?"

[86] Some of The Board lean in, keen to hear my exposition, and relieved that they have a scapegoat to hang their ignorance on.

[87] I clear my throat.

[88] "Well, Mr. Difficult is a renowned inventor, quite brilliant in fact. He's well ahead of the curve in his Reality with regards to trans-dimensional travel."

[89] The Chairman sips at a glass of water while his colleagues stare blankly at me.

[90] I cut them some slack;

[91] "Mr. Difficult invented a time machine." They seem to relax, apparently understanding that much.

[92] The schmucks.

[93] "The Agency became aware that, using this time machine, Mr. Difficult will at some point visit an off-limit event." I pause for effect, and lightning flashes past the window, perfectly timed. I give the next sentence some timbre. "A hugely important event in human history!"

[94] "Well, what event? And why don't you just go there and stop him?!" demands Pinkerton-Smythe. I chuckle.

[95] "Because. It's. Off. Limits."

[96] This patronage does not sit well with the young man, who stands in anger. He turns to the Chairman, incredulous.

[97] "Cecil, surely we don't need to listen to the fairytales of this fella?!" He stabs a finger at me repeatedly, searching for an expression. "He's just a bloody elephant!"

[98] Armitage ignores him, and there's much sucking of teeth from the rest of The Board; they know this is bad form. The Chairman casts me a genuinely apologetic glance. I nod without a word;

[99] I appreciate good manners, even in bad guys.

[100] "Perhaps you might tell us what this event is, Mr. Nesh," he says quietly.

[101] So I tell them.

[102] Afterwards, they sit quietly for some time, worried and somewhat stunned. Even Pinkerton-Smythe falls silent. I fill in the rest of the tale while I have their attention.

[103] "We were unsure of the reason for Mr. Difficult's visit to this event, but were obviously concerned. Potentially he intends to commit a crime, but we couldn't be sure."

[104] I think ahead, discarding unnecessary parts of the tale that might raise awkward questions.

[105] "And while we knew the destination of his time trip, we were in the dark about its starting point. So, I was assigned to be with Mr. Difficult for all journeys through time. Indefinitely, until he makes that one trip."

106 "And how will that help?" says a random guy on the left of the table, keen to add some value to these proceedings.

107 "If I accompany him, I can watch the events unfold and discern his intentions." I put it in terms they'll grasp. "You might consider me a Pre−Offence Parole Officer."

108 It's time for some sleight of hand. While they're thinking.

109 "Until this matter is resolved, I've attached myself to him with this."

110 Removing my hand from my pocket, I reveal a length of string, tied around my chunky wrist. I carefully leave the other end inside my pocket; I tied it in the taxi, but they don't know that.

111 "A length of string?" says a chap on the right−hand side of the table. I don't recognise him; he must be new.

112 "Yes, string. But the string is just a metaphor." I smile at him pleasantly. "A five−dimensional metaphor."

113 He stares blankly, so I continue.

114 "Moving between four−dimensional Realities that share a common starting point—what old−timers still doggedly call *Parallel Dimensions*—requires fifth dimensional travel."

115 I give him my best Joe Friday.

116 "And that's what I do for a living. That's what The Agency does."

117 "Ah, I see, says the man." I don't need my lie−detector spectacles to realise that this rube has no clue what I'm talking about. "Yes, five dimensions. A metaphor. Quite."

118 He looks distant for a moment, trying to think of another question that does not sound foolish. "And the other end of that string is tied to Mr. Difficult right now?"

119 This raises a snort or two. Which is a shame, as it's actually a very good question.

120 "Yes, metaphorically speaking," I lie.

121 I wish it *was* tied to 'Difficult; I'd be with the pair of them right now.

122 Damn Roth and his plate of buns!

123 "Must be a damned long piece of string!" he says, unsure if this is a funny thing to say;

124 I don't laugh.

125 "You begin to see the problem."

126 Pinkerton−Smythe giggles to himself, then offers up sarcastically,

127 "But just how long *is* a piece of string, Mr. Nesh?"

128 I eye him coldly, and speak automatically.

129 "Twice the distance from its midpoint to either of its ends." His grin fades and vanishes as he considers this. It's a meaningless expression of algebra, but it's correct. I pick up the pace.

130 "And this metaphor is at the heart of your problem, Gentlemen." I'm lying past my tusks, of course, relying on their fear and ignorance. "I'm not from Roth's Reality, so this string—this metaphor—forges a link between two Realities.

131 Until we get to the bottom of Mr. Difficult's actions, the string must remain tied, and the Realities linked."

132 The Chairman, silent for some time, absorbing and assessing, finally speaks.

133 "Well, we have the authority to cut the string and close Roth's reality, of course," he muses, but then says with more teeth. "This is Central after all."

134 My reply is flat; I have no time for this kind of elitism.

135 "There is nothing unique or original about this Reality, Mr. Chairman. It's only Central because you say it is."

136 Like all smart leaders, Armitage recognises the truth when he hears it, but is under no obligation to assimilate it into his belief system. He frowns, perhaps wondering if he's lost this battle. Still, he's creative.

137 "But what would happen if we *did* cut the string, Mr. Nesh?" He's slipped into voice Number 8, Curious Layman.

138 I was hoping this one wouldn't come up, and have to lie again; I'm not giving up on this assignment easily, and I hate the idea of letting these Suits pull the plug on something they don't understand.

139 Besides, I want to know what 'Difficult is up to; call it Professional Curiosity.

140 "Well, the mathematics is complex and unpredictable," I reflect, sounding as honest as I can, "but in Layman's terms?" It's now Armitage's turn to nod with quiet respect my way. "Bad. Things."

141 Outside, thunder rumbles and clouds roil.

142 Inside, fifteen men hang on the next words of their leader. He seems to reach a decision.

143 "Well then, Agent Nesh," he says, returning to Number 2, "it seems we have nothing more to discuss. For now."

We regard each other levelly. "The Board wishes you a speedy conclusion to this matter. You will, of course, keep us appraised of your progress?"

[144] "I shan't forget."

[145] The Chairman laughs without humour; I don't care for it.

[146] "Mr. Nesh, given your species, have you ever forgotten anything?"

[147] "No," I lie.

[148] It's a myth, and like all good myths, it's useful; I may need to rely on a few of them when I get back from this trip.

[149] A trip to an off-limit event.

[150] Without a word, I descend in the lift and head out stoically into the howling misery of the City.

Carrizozo

4 [1] Something is coming.

[2] In the sweltering heat of the shaded desert saloon, the bartender dreams of lipstick and low-cut dresses.

[3] Outside, the wind that haunts the New Mexico desert by day and night has lost its voice. Barely a breath of breeze stirs the dust that drifts slowly in the deep shafts of light from the high windows.

[4] The world is uncommonly quiet, but the barman is not surprised. It has been a strange month, a strange year in fact, and he has seen many strange things.

[5] He prefers not to think of them.

[6] But he knows that something is coming.

[7] He starts to polish a glass for his first customer of the day, who has yet to arrive, and returns to his burlesque fantasies.

[8] Moments later, he feels it more than hears it; a brief ripple in the air, an unfamiliar fluttering pulse. Involuntarily, he holds his breath.

[9] There's a creak from the threshold of the saloon, followed by slow, heavy footsteps and the complaints of old, neglected floorboards. And finally, a bulky figure, wearing a hat and coat that are too heavy for the climate, strides to the edge of shadow in front of the bar.

[10] A huge limb sweeps into the light and deposits a photo onto the counter.

[11] In perfectly accented Spanish, a rumbling voice asks quietly,

[12] "Have you seen these men?"

[13] Nodding, the bartender points to the west and repeats a single word that has haunted his dreams. He has no idea what it means, but he knows it is the correct answer.

[14] "Trinity."

[15] "When?"

[16] "Three hours, Señor."

[17] The shape sighs and scratches his gargantuan nose. After a few seconds, a silver dollar spins in the air and lands onto the bar without hesitation.

[18] "Bourbon. Ice."

[19] The whiskey is delivered quickly in a sparkling glass. Diamonds clink gently in amber as the glass vanishes into shadow.

[20] Thirty seconds later, the voice seems refreshed, determined.

[21] "Gracias."

[22] And with the same rippling in the air, the elephant is gone.

[23] The barman nods, though nobody is there to see it, and pockets the change.

[24] Yes, 1945 is turning out to be a strange year indeed.

White Sands

Being the testament of Elliot

5 [1] The third time is the charm.

[2] I finally arrive at my destination. Trial and error is not my style, but today it is necessary. My head spins from three unexpected dimensional hops.

[3] But it would have been worse without the bourbon.

[4] And I could do with another one.

[5] I survey the scorching July scene before me. It's a scene that's been waiting for me, buried in the past, since I took this assignment.

[6] A few hundred yards away, the pyramid hangs silently just above the white sands of the New Mexico desert.

[7] I've seen plenty of pyramids in my time, vast stone monuments to ancient kings, on this world and others just like it. But this pyramid is small, modern, and cast from a burnished gold which scatters the sunlight lazily. Lights pulse in slow sequence at each of the four corners of its base and at its peak.

[8] And, as if to draw a line under its slacking heritage, the time machine hovers solidly eight feet above the ground, almost as if it's carelessly forgetting gravity rather than snubbing it.

[9] I shake my head. Typical.

[10] Shading the sunglasses perched on the bridge of my trunk, I can just make out three figures milling about in the pyramid's shadow. They're obscured by an inevitable heat haze,

[11] but even from this distance, I know it's two men and a bear.

[12] I was expecting the lion to be there too, and possibly the honey from next door, but no.

[13] I gently flap my ears, cooling my neck and my thoughts.

[14] Roth and iDifficult have led me a merry dance today, though I suspect that Roth is just a passenger. Either way, I'm ashamed to admit that they've been a step or two ahead of me for most of it.

[15] First the trick with the buns.

[16] Then stealing my ball of string.

[17] And then, worst of all, adjusting the energy barriers that are supposed to prevent dimensional shifts to this forbidden destination.

[18] Not enough to stop me. Not even enough to push me off course. Just enough to slow me down. To give them time to prepare for whatever it is they're here for.

[19] And that's my goal. Not just to discharge my responsibilities and close this case.

[20] But to end the mystery that has puzzled me for over a year.

[21] To find out why we're all here.

[22] And, if necessary, to stop them.

[23] I stride towards the pyramid purposefully.

[24] My name is Elliot Nesh. I'm an elephant. I work for the Agency.

[25] And I'm here on business.

One Mile Out

6[1] "Why do we always end up in the desert?"

[2] I'm standing in the shade of the pyramid ship, watching the rectangular box begin its weightless descent to the ground. The three of us could have manhandled it down, but letting the gravity unit do it gently seems more appropriate.

[3] "Sorry matey, did you say something?" asks iDifficult, the captain of the voyage, looking round. My best friend is sporting a neat, narrow beard that's shot with grey, and his hair is cropped short;

[4] it's a good look on him, especially with the dark suit.

[5] I shake my head and dust some sand from the lapels of my own black suit;

[6] not the smartest fashion choice for a hot day, but the correct choice nonetheless.

[7] "Nothing, just thinking out loud."

[8] I'm not complaining; today is too important for selfish grumbles.

[9] But I'm really not fond of sand.

[10] And while I'm happy to be looking at the sunshine from the shade, I'm glad I'm not out in it. Well, not quite yet, at any rate.

[11] A cough from Bear makes us both turn.

[12] "He's here."

[13] We follow the line of our ursine friend's extended paw, and see a distant, heavy figure trudging towards us across the flat white sand. He looks out of place in the desert, but I'm not sure where an elephant in a trenchcoat and trilby hat would look at home.

[14] Careful to avoid the lowering box, 'Difficult turns to greet Elliot, and consults his steampunk–ish pocket watch;

[15] I recognise it as the core of the time machine.

[16] "Elliot! Glad you could make it! Perfect timing!" he roars, offering his cheeriest wave.

[17] The elephant nods an almost imperceptible greeting, but continues to walk in silence.

[18] A minute later, Elliot stops and stands a few feet from our shade. The sun glitters in his retro sunglasses as he peers past us to examine the plain metal box;

[19] concern passes across his face as the container gently touches down.

[20] And suddenly, he's all business. He flashes his Agency badge, making his position clear for an opening gambit.

[21] "Gentlemen. We cannot be here. This place, this time, is off–limits."

[22] My friend smiles and nods. "I know! It was a devil of a job getting here. Took me years to work out how to do it. You have access codes, I imagine?"

[23] Elliot says nothing, and stands his ground quietly.

[24] "Anyway, I'm glad you've arrived. Bang on time! We need your help."

[25] "Mr . Difficult, none of us can be here. We need to leave." He loosens his trenchcoat. There's a glimpse of the

hardware he used to get here. It could recall all of us and the pyramid in a heartbeat.

26 This isn't going quite to plan, and 'Difficult glances my way.

27 I can tell that Elliot's bluffing; he wants to know why we're here.

28 But an Agent's first responsibility is to get us out of here, and that's not an option for us. I don't believe for a moment that he'll do it; he wants us to talk him round. But he looks worried, and we need to cut to the chase before his training takes over.

29 I step out into the sun and amble forward between the Agent and my friend, determined to short–circuit this stand–off.

30 I wish Abbey was close at hand; she's better with people than I am.

31 "Elliot, I understand this is your professional position. You have a job to do. There are Rules for this kind of thing." He's listening, but the box and 'Difficult still have most of his attention, so

32 I wander a little closer, keeping my voice low, reasonable and continue,

33 "I'm not a fan of *Rules*. Rules are what we need when there's no *Order*. When people don't do the right thing.

34 And Order is better than Rules, right?"

35 The mighty head, all ears and trunk, turns to look at me curiously; okay, now I have his attention.

36 I plunge onwards.

37 "And we're here to do the right thing, Elliot. We're truly here for the best of reasons. Come and see *why*." I emphasise the word, and his body language betrays the turmoil. I put a hand on his elbow. "Please."

38 There's a moment of indecision, but then he sighs and relents.

39 In the shadows behind me, Bear *clickety–clicks* the latches open on one end of the rectangular coffin. Elliot steps fully under the pyramid and approaches the casket as our woodsman raises the top half of the split lid.

40 "Good grief."

41 The Agent snatches the hat from his head instinctively.

42 Inside the coffin, resting eternally on a bed of cushioned crimson silk, is a badger, late of this world. The old boar is heavy, greying, with a resplendent white waxed moustache.

43 It is The General, Yavin's grandfather.

44 He lays in full Masonic regalia, the head of his Order. The golden chain of office lays on his white chest, his gauntleted arms crossed on top.

45 His monocle is tucked unobtrusively on its string into his top pocket.

46 We share a moment with the old badger. It's a cliché to say so, but he looks peaceful.

47 "We lost track of this fella decades ago. Where was he hiding?"

48 I stand to Elliot's left, 'Difficult to his right. A wind rises from behind us, and sand begins to dance in gentle swirls to the west. My friend says quietly,

49 "Can I explain on the way? We have a mile to walk, there's plenty of time." The Agent regards my friend levelly. "This old boy weighs a ton, and we need your help; you're our fourth pall bearer."

50 Inside the elephant, the Agent clocks off. We're left with Elliot. I know the Agent will return later, but for now the day just got easier.

51 Elliot nods.

52 "Okay. Let's go."

53 A few minutes later, the four of us carry the deep, five–foot–long coffin into the blistering heat, and head west. Elliot and 'Difficult lead the way, with Bear and myself in the rear. Each of us wears a dark suit, as befits the occasion; Elliot's Agent suit is perfect.

54 Each of us is barefoot.

55 Elliot's trenchcoat and hat lie abandoned in the sand beneath the pyramid, along with two pairs of shoes.

56 The hot sand seeks out the gaps between my toes. I hate sand.

57 Yet somehow, we always end up in the desert.

Trinity

Being the testament of Bear

7 1 Being a bear in this kind of heat isn't easy. We prefer the cool forests of Canada, or at least a dip in a Bermudan pool with a cocktail.

2 But this needs to be done, and I accept the conditions despite my species.

3 I'm walking beside Indigo, at the rear of the coffin. We're different heights, but it seems useful to have Elliot and 'Difficult up front; they have a lot of catching up to do. Their expository conversation goes like this:

⁴ "So, how far will we be carrying this coffin?" asks Elliot.

⁵ "A mile. It shouldn't take too long."

⁶ "Did we park so far away intentionally?" asks the Agent.

⁷ "Yep. A mile is a traditional distance for a badger ceremony."

⁸ "Is that why we're barefoot?"

⁹ "Yes. Also traditional." But iDifficult concedes, "Though traditionally we'd be badgers."

¹⁰ "Badgers who wear no shoes?"

¹¹ "Exactly. The same as tigers."

¹² "I thought the lion and your lady neighbour would be here to help."

¹³ "They were needed elsewhere," replies the part–time arch–genius.

¹⁴ We walk a few more minutes in silence. I can see something in the distance.

¹⁵ "So when did The General die?" asks Elliot.

¹⁶ "This morning. In more than one sense, I suppose."

¹⁷ "Did you know about it when I arrived at your place?"

¹⁸ "No, Yavin arrived at the back door to tell me."

¹⁹ "Hence the cakes? Clever." There's grudging admiration in the elephant's assessment.

²⁰ "Hence the cakes. Simple."

²¹ I try to interrupt. "Guys?"

²² Elliot continues, seeming not to notice. "So, why are we in New Mexico? On today of all days, I mean?"

²³ "The short answer is that I'm keeping a promise," says 'Difficult.

²⁴ "A promise to The General?"

²⁵ "Yes."

²⁶ "So, how did you meet?"

²⁷ I try again. "Um, guys?" Still no response.

²⁸ "By chance. Yavin had a picture of him that was taken in 1953. The date made no sense to me, as badgers live just fifteen to twenty years. In fact, most badgers don't survive their first year. Did you know that?

²⁹ "I didn't, no."

³⁰ "Anyway, I decided to go and see him."

³¹ "The General? In 1953?" The Agent sounds surprised, despite his profession.

³² "Sure. Easy enough. I was curious, and he sounded an interesting character. Roth was busy that day, so I went with Abbey. I met up with the old boy just after the photo was taken.

³³ And he was, to say the least, an unhappy badger."

³⁴ "Why so?"

³⁵ "Well, he'd been involved in a number of projects as a scientist during the Second World War. He was the first badger to work with the military, you know? One project in particular had haunted him for years before I met him. Really got under his fur."

³⁶ I sound desperate now, summoning a rather ursine growl. "For pity's sake, look!"

³⁷ We come to a halt, impressed.

³⁸ A few hundred yards away, a tower is now visible. It's a simple metal framework, not unlike an armless electricity pylon, and probably a similar height. Even from this distance, we can see the cabling that leads up to an ominous egg inside the tower near its peak.

³⁹ "Good grief, is that what I think it is?" I whisper, horrified;

⁴⁰ Mama Bear said there'd be days like this.

⁴¹ Finally, I am acknowledged by iDifficult. "Yes, I expect so."

⁴² "And this is New Mexico in July 1945?"

⁴³ "Yes, Bear, absolutely."

⁴⁴ I sigh. "You pick your moments, Sir."

⁴⁵ Elliot waves a hand towards the tower. "I take it this was the project that The General he has a problem with? *The Manhattan Project?* The world's first atomic bomb?"

⁴⁶ "Yes, he was a materials specialist when they made the test device."

⁴⁷ "This test is codenamed *Trinity*, right?" Elliot knows this to be correct, but I suspect he's curious about the name.

⁴⁸ "That's right," confirms 'Difficult, "though it was never clear why."

⁴⁹ "And The General regretted his involvement?"

⁵⁰ We're walking again, continuing to the tower. With a sigh, 'Difficult shrugs.

⁵¹ "Well, wouldn't you?"

⁵² "I don't know," muses Elliot, "it saved a lot of lives."

⁵³ "And took a lot more. And those people weren't soldiers. Anyway, he was being pestered back into service as the Cold War got going, so I offered to take him somewhere they'd never look for him."

⁵⁴ The Agent's curiosity spikes a little. "And where was that?"

⁵⁵ "1984."

⁵⁶ "That's rather underhand."

⁵⁷ iDifficult chuckles. "Thank you. Anyway, he liked it there. The music. The hair. *The Orwell.*

⁵⁸ He settled down, and though he was getting on a bit, he had kids; frisky lads, badgers."

⁵⁹ "Yavin's father?"

⁶⁰ "Yes, but that's another story. Suffice to say, Yavin and his sister were born in 1996. And suddenly all the dates make sense. So, it turns out the reason the dates didn't make sense was *that I was curious about them.*"

⁶¹ Elliot nods sagely.

⁶² "I accept the paradox;

⁶³ these things happen in my line of work."

⁶⁴ "I figured you'd understand."

⁶⁵ "So what was the promise you made?"

⁶⁶ "I promised to bring The General home. Well, here, anyway. He wanted to return here when he died. I think he thought it fitting, to close the circle of events."

⁶⁷ "It all sounds rather obvious and poetic when you say it like that." Again, there's both admiration and complaint in the elephant's assessment.

⁶⁸ "That wasn't my intention," says 'Difficult, "but yeah, it's pretty straightforward. Doing it was harder, of course. The energy barrier protecting this place, for one. The work of your Agency?"

⁶⁹ "Sort of. Let's just say it wasn't a *local* decision to protect this historic, world–changing event."

⁷⁰ "Well, we're not here to interfere with history or steal secrets or change the world."

⁷¹ "No, I see that now. How long was he in the Eighties?" asks Elliot.

⁷² "Three years. I left him there as long as I could. He had kids, responsibilities, but I knew he was old and that it was time. He was twenty three, ancient for a badger. I picked him up as soon as I worked out how to bypass the shield here, and took him to Roth's garden."

⁷³ "Roth's garden? Why there?"

⁷⁴ "Well, he wanted to visit the grandkids and great–grandkids he'd never met; a rare opportunity for anyone. They were pretty much in awe of him. Especially Dantoo, Yavin's niece. She's a smart little thing."

⁷⁵ "I'll bet. Okay, one more question," ventures the elephant.

⁷⁶ "Columbo style?"

⁷⁷ "Exactly; he was a pro. When will The Bomb be tested?"

⁷⁸ "Tomorrow morning. 5:30am. We'll watch."

⁷⁹ Silence falls. Elliot shifts the coffin's weight awkwardly, and 'Difficult looks across at him.

⁸⁰ "Do you need another question, Agent?"

⁸¹ "Actually, I do. Why couldn't you have put both me and Bear at the back? We're both seven feet tall. With you and Roth at the front, this coffin wouldn't be so damned *wonky.*"

⁸² "I didn't think. Hey look, we're here."

Farewell

8¹ I have never seen so many badgers in one place.

² There is a *multitude* of badgers.

³ A family or colony of badgers is known as a Clan, but any large gathering of badgers is called a *Brock.*

⁴ Today, New Mexico is host to a Brock, the likes which it will never witness again.

⁵ As we walk the final twenty yards, I cast my eyes across the gathering of distinguished boars, elegant sows, and a surprising number of cubs.

⁶ I'm interested and then ashamed to realise that I can tell them all apart easily; the eccentric, colourful clothes help. I notice that they're all barefoot, and somewhat dusty.

⁷ The badgers stand quietly, fifty yards from the tower, a wide straight line centred on a neat rectangular grave. In the centre stands Abbey, my lovely neighbour.

⁸ Dressed in a simple pink and orange summer dress, her today–blonde hair moving in the breeze, she is, as ever, barefoot. She smiles my way.

⁹ Next to Abbey is King, our resident lion. He's resplendent in a dark suit and white shirt that matches my own, and

¹⁰ a vibrant red necktie that was actually in my wardrobe when I got up this morning.

¹¹ King's mane is glorious, and braided in places. He is Abbey's escort for her duties today.

12 Perhaps sharing my earlier thought, 'Difficult chips in quietly, "See how dusty they all are? Every one of them helped dig the grave. Even the cubs. They think of it as his *final tunnel*."

13 I have no reply, but instead hiss an urgent new question.

14 "How come we're here unchallenged? The military should be all *over* us!"

15 "See that fella at the back?" I notice for the first time a tall, well–groomed man standing nervously just behind King. "You'll never guess who *he* is. He worked with The General, and has made arrangements to keep the army offsite for a few hours."

16 Abbey explained everything to him: time travel, Elliot, badgers, everything. Took it all on the chin. The open mind of a scientist, eh?"

17 Good grief, Julius Robert Oppenheimer.

18 A figure steps from the line and approaches the four of us and our cargo. It's Yavin, the Chief Engineer of the Clan.

19 It strikes me that I have no idea what the Clan name actually is?

20 I shake the thought aside, and try to focus.

21 I was expecting my black–and–white friend to be dressed formally, but he is in his usual dungarees; his flat cap is folded and tucked into his hip pocket.

22 We exchange nods, and he indicates that we should bring the coffin forward and lay it alongside the grave.

23 We do this and retreat a few steps as the line of badgers bends around to form a neat circle, a halo around the head of Trinity Tower's lengthening shadow.

24 Two young boy badgers in matching black corduroy waistcoats and bowler hats step from the circle and move to the head of the casket;

25 it's Hoth and Sollust, Yavin's nephews.

26 The pair carefully unclip the top half of the lid, and then move to stand on either side of the coffin, so that one can lift the lid and the other lower it to the ground on the other side. A low murmur moves through the badgers.

27 The General lies in state.

28 Abbey steps forward.

29 "Friends," she smiles, extending her arms, welcome. "today, we are a gathering of peoples, united in our love and respect for a grand old traveller."

30 A snuffling and growling approval finds voice for a moment.

31 "I met The General in his final days, and was moved by his love for his extended family."

32 Abbey looks down momentarily to glance at her prompt cards.

33 She knows they are inadequate;

34 they are just words.

35 But as her gaze drops, she spies a short figure at her side, a girl–cub.

36 The youngster is a pretty little thing, dressed for the day in her best white summer dress with pink bows at the hem. A matching bow is clipped into her striped hair.

37 I know instinctively that this is *Dantoo*, Yavin's niece. I've never met her, though of course I know her twin brothers from many adventures.

38 The girl gazes upwards, her two–tone face calm and reassuring, and gently takes Abbey's hand.

39 Abbey shakes her head, as if waking. And says simply, in a happily surprised tone,

40 "Oh!"

41 The prompt cards scatter to the breeze, and Abbey begins to speak.

42 Her voice is confident and sad, speaking young Dantoo's thoughts. They reach into the hearts of all of us, as only a badger can.

43 "Who knows where life may lead?
   Who knows the turnings of the
   Unity?

44 Great grandfather, you knew neither
   And were all the greater for it

45 Your pawprints, broad and sharp
   Have left their mark
   In five decades, far spread
   Three more than any Clanborn

46 You chose and led
   Risked fail and fall
   Without hesitation

47 And lost contentment at your rest
   For your portion of others' deeds

48 You did not mark the day
   Our friend the stranger came
   With tales and questions
   With proof and faith

49 You tunnelled from a barren life
   And shared his broken journey
   Giving love and life
   To an era meant for other eyes

[50] And time passed, happily
But for dreams of Trinity

[51] In fading light of your long day
All friends heard your whisper
From across Time
And hastened to your side

[52] Risking much
But fearing nought

[53] To stand barefoot
With your kin, none closer
To help you on the final mile
Of this Long Road Home

[54] And stand, hearts and faces warm
As your ashes yet not your shadow
Are scattered by the wind of change
You laboured to create

[55] And then return
Their promise kept
To dream their boundless dreams
Within earshot of your roar
In the world you shaped

[56] I met you for a single day
And wished for just one more

[57] Goodbye, great grandfather
Rest, forgiven
Rest, loved

[58] We smile in the knowing of all deeds
And neither regret nor forget."

[59] The silence is absolute.

[60] Abbey kneels to meet Dantoo's gaze. The young badger plants a kiss on my neighbour's nose and throws her short furry arms around her neck as a hoarse roar erupts from the crowd.

[61] "You're welcome," smiles Abbey.

[62] As the sun draws towards the horizon, the growling cheers and applause surround Abbey and the young girl–cub, and ring long and loud.

Oppenheimer

9[1] The coffin is laid and covered efficiently.

[2] In a few minutes, it's as if it was never there; no flowers, no gravestone;

[3] just memories.

[4] As the assembly scatters and gathers into smaller pockets, all formalities complete, the playful young badgers set about their "uncle" King, determined to wrestle the tall lion to the ground.

[5] It takes five of them, including Hoth and Sollust, and there's a shriek of giggles and a delighted leonine laugh as the Goliath finally falls to the horde of tugging, growling Davids.

[6] I spy Oppenheimer and 'Difficult shaking hands. I half expect them to be talking shop, but instead I overhear my friend thanking the lanky physicist for his help with the military. The physicist is deflecting the praise affably.

[7] "Not at all, Mr. Difficult. Thank you, Sir!" he exclaims, "My presence today has meant a very great deal to me. You've given me a lot to think about. Tomorrow's detonation is just the beginning."

[8] My friend winks at him. "Oh, how right you are, Doctor. Good luck."

[9] The physicist nods uncertainly, and turns towards the tower to tend the steel baby that he'll deliver in the morning.

[10] But he starts with surprise, finding Elliot in his path. Oppenheimer smiles pleasantly and tries valiantly to not look nervous in the face of such an enormous concept.

[11] He doesn't quite manage it.

[12] The elephant removes his sunglasses and regards the scientist curiously.

[13] "Before you go, Dr. Oppenheimer, I've been meaning to ask you... why did you call this test Trinity?"

[14] Oppenheimer pauses, and shares a sly and fleeting smile as a pat answer trips to his lips. But then he reconsiders and frowns.

[15] "It's simple, really." He shrugs. "This thing we're doing puts the fear of God in me."

[16] Elliot laughs darkly. "Thank you, Doctor. That's more honest that the answers you give in the future."

[17] Again, uncertainty crosses the physicist's face. He nods vaguely, and moves to step round the Agent, but then hesitates as his curiosity gets the better of him.

[18] Standing tall, he waves to indicate the elephant's physique, his species perhaps.

[19] "Are there many like you in the future, Agent Nesh?"

[20] Elliot shrugs noncommittally.

[21] "Enough. Fewer than you might think. But we're everywhere." He inclines his head slightly, "Why do you ask?"

[22] "Well, it's silly, I suppose." Oppenheimer looks skyward for a moment, perhaps nervous, perhaps contemplative. "It's just that you bring to

mind an image of *Lord Ganesha*, the elephant–headed Hindu god."

²³ Elliot's smiles indulgently; he gets this a lot. By way of a reply, he leans closer to tap the doctor gently on the chest.

²⁴ "And you, my dear Doctor," he deadpans, "remind me of the Hindu god Shiva. The Destroyer of Worlds."

²⁵ The physicist pales, and after a few shocked seconds he hurries away without another word.

²⁶ In the future, he'll lie about that one too.

The Fat Man Sings

10 ¹ We're standing by the Time Pyramid.

² **It's 5:20am on July 16th 1943**, and the sun is low in a gold, rose and indigo sky.

³ It's been a long night, but we had a lot of folk to move to a safer distance, and for once we were determined not to hurry.

⁴ There's been dignity, patience, and good manners.

⁵ I'm standing with Elliot, discussing the sunrise, when a thought occurs to me.

⁶ "By the way, I heard what Dr. Oppenheimer said to you last night. Isn't Lord Ganesha also known as the *Remover of Obstacles*?"

⁷ Agent Nesh chuckles and scratches a tusk absently.

⁸ "Yes Indigo, he is. The things you know always surprise me." But then he leans in conspiratorially to mutter, "Anyone would think that was a *coincidence*."

⁹ This glorious life is never dull.

¹⁰ "Shall we do this now?" We turn. It's iDifficult, a resigned look on his face. Reaching into a pocket, he tosses Elliot a ball of string. "We have a few minutes."

¹¹ Elliot catches the string and pockets it. "Yes, of course. Let's do this by the book." He draws his arm from a pocket, revealing several feet of string that is already tied around his gnarly grey wrist. "Mr. Roth, would you do the honours?"

¹² I look to 'Difficult, uncertain, but he nods encouragingly and presents his own hand.

¹³ It's the work of a moment to tie the knot around my friend's wrist.

¹⁴ The two stand, entangled again in the early morning light, their roles restored:

an Agent and his assignment. Elliot's voice is equally official.

¹⁵ "Mr. Difficult, I have accompanied you to an off–limit historical event and observed your actions. Protocol dictates that I take you in for further questioning."

¹⁶ That said, he reaches into a pocket and produces a short fruit knife. And with a flick of his wrist, he severs the string.

¹⁷ "However, I have determined that your actions are not of interest to The Agency. Thank you for your cooperation in this matter. You're free to go."

¹⁸ The arch–genius stands, somewhat agog. He's not alone.

¹⁹ "To hell with protocol," rumbles Elliot, "You two are my kind of rule–breakers."

²⁰ Good grief, this noble elephant is a bag of tricks. I thought I'd be eating pizza solo while 'Difficult serves five to ten, with time off for less–eccentric behaviour.

²¹ "Will there be consequences for you, Elliot?"

²² Elliot shrugs.

²³ "There are always consequences, my friend." He wiggles his wrist and the severed string dances. "But I can safely tie up this loose end."

²⁴ Donning his pince nez sunglasses again, he adds darkly, "In Red Tape, for years if necessary."

²⁵ We all sense it's time to change the subject.

²⁶ "You know," says 'Difficult conversationally, "I always thought that your string was some kind of exotic five–dimensional metaphor?"

²⁷ The Agent smiles and shakes his head.

²⁸ "No. It's just a piece of string."

²⁹ I'm distracted by a gently insistent tugging at my knee. Looking down, I find a wide–eyed Dantoo gazing up at me.

³⁰ The young badger regards me with startling maturity. She's almost two years old now, but she's still a child. Raising her paws skyward, her look is not imploring, but its meaning is clear.

³¹ I reach down and pick her up, gathering the end of her dress in neatly, and cradle her easily in one arm. She nuzzles gratefully into my shoulder;

³² there's a smell of dirt and loss and bubblegum perfume.

³³ My cheeks feel damp.

³⁴ "Folks? It's time." My best friend is moving through the crowd, smiling

reassuringly. "And it's okay to look. The energy shield will dampen all the hard light."

[35] There's movement all around.

[36] After a few seconds, I'm aware that 'Difficult is to my left, and Elliot to my right. Abbey wanders in closer and fusses over Dantoo briefly before settling at my side. Bear and King are reassuring presences to our rear. Badgers gather around us all, and Yavin stands stoically in front on me.

[37] I pat his shoulder and briefly feel a damp paw as it brushes my hand.

[38] We look to the east and say goodbye.

[39] After an endless moment of calm that we all feel, it begins.

[40] And for the second time that day, the sun rises.

Notes

[*]   And when I say *healthy*, I mean *meagre and uninteresting*. Muesli.

[**]   While annoying the hell out of us.

Eolist

"Give a man thirty bucks and a takeout menu and he'll be full for a few hours. Give him a credit card and he'll be full for life. And will need bigger trousers."

A Comfortable Silence Falls

1

¹ There are never any ends, just a multitude of beginnings.

² I'm thinking back to the first time I sat with my two best friends.

³ **It's 1992. Wednesday.** After work finishes, I walk into town with iDifficult. We've worked together for almost two years since we received an honourable discharge from our boarding school.

⁴ During this time, 'Difficult has denied on many occasions that he is my boss.

⁵ Yet still he guides me, as he always has; randomly, anarchically, and occasionally with dazzling wisdom.

⁶ As boss–deniers go, he's pretty cool.

⁷ We stop into our local coffee house.

⁸ "Ah, Café Nehru!" I exclaim happily as we walk in the door, inhaling the rich aroma.

⁹ "The great taste of *Indian* Coffee!" sighs 'Difficult. We do this a lot, finishing each other's sentences;

¹⁰ this is mostly because we lose our train of thought on a regular basis.

¹¹ As we peruse the menu board above the counter, I'm aware that there's just one person ahead of us in the queue. Though in fact, I'm not sure whether she's *in* the queue, or just sat at the counter. She sits on a high stool as she argues some point with the barista.

¹² The lady is very short; her legs dangle a long way from the floor.

¹³ "Good grief," I whisper, pointing, "she's *tiny!* How did she get up there?"

¹⁴ My friend considers this engineering feat for a moment;

¹⁵ somewhere, a slide rule is screaming.

¹⁶ "Sheer determination, maybe?"

¹⁷ Ahead of us, the woman offers a loud torrent of colourful metaphors at the guy serving her. She spins in the swivel chair and regards us, fuming.

¹⁸ She's an attractive redhead in a jumper, jeans and tennis shoes.

¹⁹ "He cut me off! she wails at us in an American accent, "I wanted just *one* more treble espresso! But no!" Her hands wave expressively, frantically. "He says I've *had enough!"*

²⁰ The barista stands nervously at the counter. I exchange a glance with 'Difficult and we nod in unison. I extend a hand towards her.

²¹ "Would you care to join us, Miss...?"

²² "Petite," she says, taking my hand and hopping down. She's almost two feet shorter than me. "Eolist Petite. Mrs. And thank you."

²³ "Our pleasure!" we chorus, as 'Difficult steps up to order.

²⁴ **Five minutes later**, we're in a circular booth with a single padded seat, as 'Difficult distributes our scalding–hot beverages of choice.

25 Eolist reaches forward to sip hers immediately, either oblivious or impervious to the heat; I can't even touch my cup.

26 While she drinks, she explains to us that she's visiting from America on a *Caffeine Exchange Programme.*

27 "Yeah, right now there's some wired, neurotic twenty–something drinking a pint of espresso with my husband back in the States."

28 She chuckles darkly, and continues,

29 "She's pretty cute, and he probably thought it sounded like a *sweet* deal, but he has *no* idea."

30 "Been married long?" asks 'Difficult as he sizes up an almond croissant. Like all public schoolboys, we're not well versed with talking to women.

31 "Sure. Though one of these days I'm gonna get me a woodchipper, and it's *hasta la vista, meester.*"

32 We both laugh, and wonder if she's joking.

33 "Gentlemen, bless you for your chivalry and this coffee fix." She smiles easily, "So, how about you tell me your names?"

34 My part–time arch–genius amigo puts aside the half eaten croissant, creates an avalanche of crumbs and sugar as he stands, and pats his pocket for his monocle.

35 Not finding it, he produces and eye patch from a trouser pocket and fixes it over his left eye.

36 His voice projects beautifully.

37 "A rag, a bone, a hank of hair, a scientist who dreams and dares." He blushes slightly. Dammit, he beat me to the punch; *I* was going to misquote Kipling. "But my friends and the taxman call me iDifficult."

38 Eolist snorts happily across the top of her cup, and dampens his black velvet jacket with a highly–caffeinated mist. She looks apologetic.

39 "Sorry. What does the 'I' stand for?"

40 My friend squirrels the eye patch away again and grins.

41 "Oh, far more than you'd think."

42 They shake hands and exchange smiles. She turns to me as I straighten my necktie.

43 "And how about you?"

44 "The name's Roth. Indigo Roth." I try to put some spy swagger in it, but I don't quite catch it right. She doesn't seem to notice, and we shake.

45 "That's a very nice tie, by the way," she says, "be careful a lion doesn't steal it."

46 I blink and think for a moment;

47 nope, that's lost on me.

48 "I'm afraid I don't follow," I say. shaking my head.

49 "Never mind, it probably loses something in translation." A frown crosses her brow a moment later, and she begins to rummage in her bag, muttering quietly to herself. "Roth. Difficult. *Roth. Difficult.*"

50 She produces a piece of white cardboard and stares at it. From my seat I can see that one corner is torn and slightly charred.

51 It seems to be an old photo; we shuffle round either side of her and gaze at the image.

52 In it, a pair of twelve–year–old boys— who bear a striking resemblance to myself and 'Difficult—are sharing afternoon tea with a young nanny;

53 she's the spit and image of Eolist.

54 Wow, that's *weird.*

55 I don't recognise the young Roth, but judging by the date and the setting, he might well be *Orlando Roth* or his twin brother *Hugo.* Perhaps both;

56 we're an unusual family.

57 I notice 'Difficult shaking his head bemusedly; clearly he has no clue either.

58 My friend takes it gently and turns it over, while Eolist explains that she's been hunting down lost relatives in England. He reads the legend on the rear with growing amazement.

59 "Masters Difficult and Roth with Mistress Petite, 1892." He scratches his chin thoughtfully. "Exactly one hundred years ago. Good grief."

60 We chat briefly about some possibilities, but then a comfortable silence falls as we attend to our cooling drinks.

61 There really are a *multitude* of beginnings.

62 Eolist finally breaks the silence.

63 "Well, this is all rather surprising and charming, but perhaps it's just a *good sign.* We have bigger fish to fry; I have a serious question for you."

64 She squares her narrow shoulders and we pause, mid–slurp. "Can you boys recommend a decent curry house?"

65 We heave a sigh of relief. Thank goodness, more familiar territory.

[66] "Yes indeed. Only the finest establishment in this world or any other adjacent ones." Eolist raises her eyebrows appreciatively.

[67] "Sounds intriguing. Where is it?"

[68] Standing, 'Difficult fails to dust the icing sugar and almonds from his velvet jacket; he resembles a badly–wiped blackboard.

[69] "That's a simple question with a complicated answer." He consults a compass, a pocket barometer, and a bus timetable written on a turquoise napkin.

[70] "Let's just say it's *nearby* if we're quick, and get going."

[71] Eolist slips from the booth and looks marginally shorter than she did at the table.

[72] "Okay, definitely intriguing. Shall we?"

[73] I rise and join my two friends. This sounds like fun.

[74] We head off to another beginning, and wherever it will take us.

The Panic Is Infectious

2 [1] There's nothing quite like a panic–stricken friend screaming down the phone at you at 6am to bring your mind into focus.

[2] "There's a huge spider in my bathroom!"

[3] It's Eolist. Ms. Petite, my tiny American friend, is not known as a panicker with wildlife;

[4] I once watched her straighten out a pair of delinquent anteaters who foolishly tried to lift her pocket watch with a double–team bump and dip.

[5] It wasn't pretty.

[6] But let's be honest, nobody likes spiders. Well, nobody who's entirely *sane*, anyway.

[7] "Um, good morning?" Grasping for etiquette is probably a poor attempt at calming the lady down, but I've not had a coffee yet.

[8] "Not here it bloody well isn't! Please can you come help?! THIS SPIDER IS FREAKISHLY LARGE!" she wails.

[9] It sounds like Eolist may already have had a few pints of coffee herself, possibly with a red bull chaser, but that's not unusual, even at this time of day.

[10] "Um, sure. Just lemme get dressed and..."

[11] "Please hurry!" The line goes dead.

[12] Good grief, it's only a spider. I'm not fond of them either, but what is it about them that makes us so irrational?

[13] I've often suspected it's something about the angles in the legs, the numbers of eyes, or the way they move.

[14] They could almost be an alien species.

[15] Involuntarily, I twitch as I swipe an imaginary one from my hair.

[16] Right, best get moving. I raise myself from bed, step into trousers and shuffle into shoes. What's missing? A shirt. Not strictly needed for heroics, but my string vest is in the wash.

[17] I wonder where my spider–catching pint glass is.

[18] **Ten minutes later**, I dive up to Eolist's house. It's a lovely house, a nice white–painted wooden affair in an acre of land. A well tended gravel pathway heads out to meet the road, and there's a decent–sized swimming pool which I stop well short of;

[19] I don't want the embarrassment of calling the badgers to get my vehicle out of the deep end again.

[20] Eolist runs out onto the driveway, a vision of early–morning dishevelment; it's a good look on her. She takes one look at my pint glass and shakes her head.

[21] "You're going to need a bigger boat, Quint."

[22] I chuckle, but not unkindly; it'll be *more* than sufficient. We then exchange broken sentences, each interrupted by the next. I wave the pint glass.

[23] "I'm sure I can catch it with..."

[24] "I have some much bigger containers in the garage, I'll go and..."

[25] "Never mind the garage, there's no..."

[26] "Did I mention how big this..."

[27] "IT'S JUST A SPIDER!" I exclaim, gently putting my hands on her shoulders to stop her bouncing.

[28] We take a breath; the panic is infectious. "I'll deal with it. That's why you called me, right?"

[29] Eolist pouts a little, but nods. "Right."

[30] I give her a quick hug and head indoors.

[31] "Upstairs bathroom!" she yells at me as I pass the threshold. "Please be careful!"

[32] **One minute later**, I'm standing chuckling at her bathroom sink.

[33] The spider is a couple of inches across, and distressingly hairy, but not worth the panic. It eyes me suspiciously before

making another attempt to scramble up the side of the porcelain.

34 Feeling brave, I put my glass down and scoop the wee lad up carefully between my cupped hands. It tickles me with its thrashing, and a shiver passes up my spine, but I deposit him out of an open window and close it quietly.

35 Taking some deep breaths, I feel rather heroic.

36 Job done.

37 I turn as a hairy and heavy arachnid leg taps me on the shoulder.

38 **Ten seconds later**, I'm on the drive with Eolist.

39 I'm doubled over, drenched in sweat and breathing heavily. She fusses over me, but I regain my composure and try to look heroic as I raise myself upright.

40 "So, tell me about those *really big* containers you have in the garage..."

41 I make a mental note never to answer the phone again.

And Gravity Takes Hold

3 1 I'm not fond of sitting in car rental offices.

2 It's a bad enough experience in an air–conditioned airport, but in downtown San Francisco on a scorching Summer day, it's pretty unbearable.

3 **It's August**. The large rental office is hot and busy. There must be fifteen sets of unhappy customers in here, some sitting bored in the dozen–or–so chairs, others standing impatiently. Many of them rant at anyone within earshot, outraged at the slow service.

4 Six uniformed employees sit behind the high counter, each armed against the angry hordes with nothing more than a slow PC and a gunboat of attitude.

5 I've been here an hour waiting for the booked vehicle to be ready, and my charming English resolve is being taxed. But there's a lot of tension in the room already, and I see no reason to join the mob and get angry with anyone.

6 It's not going to make any difference.

7 But there's good news. My fabulous friend Eolist is with me—we're taking a short holiday together—and she's brighter, cheerier, and way more patient than me.

8 I'm delighted we'll be hanging out for the next four days, but embarrassed that it has to include this sweltering office.

9 "This isn't how I wanted your holiday to start," I say, a little deflated. My friend gives me a smile.

10 "It's not a problem. We'll be out of here in no time."

11 I smile back appreciatively. We talk quietly and sip our water from the cooler, trying not to notice as the clock sweeps past noon.

12 **An hour earlier**, the office is quiet. We've just arrived to pick up a small saloon rental for our trip. We are shamelessly excited.

13 The smiling woman behind the counter introduces herself as Sharon, and takes a few details before informing us apologetically that there'll be a short delay, Sir.

14 I like a touch of deference when I'm a customer; it's an English thing.

15 "No problem," I say.

16 **Thirty minutes ago**, a half–started enquiry to a passing random employee is snapped short, and hangs in the air unasked and unanswered as she stomps off.

17 So we sit and chat some more. And wait. I reflect that however tired I am of waiting, Eolist must have it worse.

18 The redheaded Dinky Dynamo flew in from her corner of the United States the day before, and the journey was not an easy one; delays on both flights, and a very long pause at some purgatorial airport in the middle.

19 But hey, sightseeing in California! Quite an adventure for both of us.

20 I sigh for the hundredth time.

21 All we need is a car.

22 **Back in the now**, we give up our seats for an elderly gentleman and his granddaughter. The girl can only be six or seven, and looks a little unnerved by the busy room; she sticks close to grandpa.

23 The old gent is grateful and gracious; he tells me that they're from New England. Calling him *Sir*, I smile and tell him that I'm from *Old England*, and that we're both a long way from home.

24 This receives a welcome laugh and a handshake.

25 I notice us being watched by Sharon, who has just dispatched her latest customer with a mouthful of words that my mother didn't teach me.

26 The look she gives me is odd, and I can't get a handle on it.

[27] But she clearly has no more customers to deal with, so I wander closer and give her a grin. Her expression changes to a more defensive one, and she eyes me levelly.

[28] "Busy in here today," I observe pleasantly, standing a couple of steps away from the counter. I hope my tone sounds natural, and that I'm exuding Patience;

[29] my people skills are not great.

[30] "Out of my hands, *Sir*," she says pointedly, almost terminally. The *Sir* is now forced, unlike my deference to the New England gent; what a difference an hour makes. "May I ask that you direct any complaint to The Manager?"

[31] Whenever I can, I smile in the face of adversity. I'm told it's disarming, or at the very least unexpected. I give Sharon my best.

[32] "I'm not here to complain," I shrug easily, "it looks like you've enough on your plate. I just wondered how the vehicle's coming along?"

[33] She gives me a very long, cool appraisal. "What's the name again?"

[34] Eolist comes over to join me as I step up to the desk. She gives me an enquiring look and I nod confidently, but then give Sharon my undivided attention.

[35] "The name's Roth. Indigo Roth. Saloon rental."

[36] Sharon flips quickly through some paperwork, and then glances at a screen. She pauses and looks my way, as if she's sizing me up.

[37] There's a wonderful zero–G moment of decision, and then gravity takes hold again in a flurry of keys–presses.

[38] She removes a piece of paper from her pile, crosses something out and scribbles something in its place. A stamp, a signature, and the deed is done.

[39] "Your car is in Bay Thirteen, Mr. Roth. Upstairs. "

[40] "Oh, that's great!" I say with enthusiasm. "Fantastic. Thank you."

[41] She pushes a set of keys my way.

[42] "That was nice of you to give your seats up for the old man and the little girl. I don't see that much these days."

[43] I don't know what to say, so I smile and shrug. "Thanks for your help, Sharon. We really appreciate it."

[44] We find our way up to the parking level. It's dark, but the bays are clearly marked. We walk along, reading the numbers.

[45] Eleven. Twelve. *Thirteen.*

[46] "Wait, this can't be right." I check the paperwork for the first time in the half light. No, there's no mistake.

[47] Well, I'll be damned.

[48] Staying calm and being polite did make a difference.

[49] In Bay Thirteen sits a sleek, black predator of a car. We stand there, both of us struck dumb. Eolist finally breaks the silence.

[50] "That's not a family saloon! Is that a *Mustang?!*"

[51] "Yep." I jingle the keys enticingly. "Wanna go for a drive?"

[52] "Oh my, yes!"

[53] We hurriedly toss our luggage in the trunk and slip guiltily into the car, like it's not ours.

[54] There's plastic covers on all the seats and the steering wheel. It's brand new.

[55] Then, as ever, Eolist notices something before I do.

[56] "Hey, have you ever driven an *automatic* transmission before?"

[57] "What? There's no *stick shift?!* I ordered a *manual* transmission!" But somewhere at the back of my head, a mischievous cousin of Jiminy Cricket whispers seductively about how *cool* it will be, and how much *fun* we'll have.

[58] "Nope," I shrug and grin lopsidedly. "but it'll be fine."

[59] Driving an automatic for the first time? On the wrong side of the road? In an unfamiliar major city?

[60] Piece of cake.

[61] "Come on, let's go have an adventure."

[62] And we did.

But For Our Olympic Coughing

4[1] Sometimes things aren't where they're supposed to be.

[2] It's not a well–formed thought, but as I behold the long–abandoned boat on a still–chilly morning in California, something more incisive and definite eludes me.

[3] It's **August**. I'm on holiday with the caffeine–stunted Eolist Petite in beautiful Marin County to the North of San Francisco;

[4] I've recently completed a training course in the city by the bay, and the Dinky Dynamo has flown across the

States to hang out for a few days.

5 Eolist sips an industrial–sized cup of Joe, and contemplates the derelict boat thoughtfully.

6 "One of these things is not like the others, one of these things is not the same..." she sings quietly, absently.

7 And she's right.

8 It's hard to explain why, but the presence of the marooned ship wedged deeply in a sandbank feels *wrong* somehow. It's too old, too battered, and too *close* to the water to have been marooned here for all these years.

9 It's almost cinematic, eerily beautiful and incongruous. Unusually, I'm lost for words.

10 "Can you hear it?" asks Eolist.

11 **Twenty minutes ago**, my first task for the day is to drive us into the rustic bayside town of Inverness, in search of coffee. I'd say that *we* were in search of coffee, but Eolist sits pouting in the passenger seat, barely able to see over the dashboard of the black Mustang.

12 Which is a shame, as the seemingly endless woods on one side, and the frankly awesome Tomales Bay on the other, are worth every admiring glance I offer them.

13 "Are we there yet?" she grumbles, folding her arms for extra poutiness.

14 As I take a corner at a sedate pace*, the wide front porch of *The Inverness Store* swings into view in the distance.

15 "Yes, almost there."

16 **Five minutes ago**, armed with a cup of coffee that could have given night terrors to Rip Van Winkle, Eolist is happier and more communicative.

17 We chat happily outside the roadside grocery store as I wrestle my way into a bag of beef jerky;

18 so far, the bag is winning.

19 I'm talking about what we might do today, and my desire to go see the *Point Reyes Lighthouse*, when I notice that I'm talking to myself. My companion has drifted away along the front of the store and is gazing round the corner.

20 I stand to follow, assuming I missed a cue to return to the car, and restart my tourist monologue. But again, she walks out of earshot along the side of the store.

21 By the time I catch up with Eolist, my lazy shuffling kicking up dust in the dry car park, she's poised at the rear edge of the property, gazing out across the bay at low tide;

22 sand, reeds, gorse, and salt tidal pools, all framed quietly beneath the purple glare of distant hills.

23 And there's a ship. An old, stranded, abandoned ship.

24 "Can you hear it?" she whispers for the first time.

25 **Back in the now**, I can hear it. Or feel it. Or something.

26 It reminds me of a feeling I had the first time I went to Stonehenge;

27 an enormous sense of *presence*.

28 I step down from the car park and offer Eolist my hand to assist her descent.

29 We slowly cross the fifty yards of puddled scrub in silence, dodging small pools and mud slicks.

30 I stop as a sudden flashing image crosses my brain. Actually, it's more like a tenth–of–a–second of video. It's cold and wet, and someone is shouting; I think it's me.

31 Slightly ahead of me, Eolist slowly raises her hand towards the boat, but then suddenly starts and sneezes.

32 "Excuse me. Rain up my nose," she mutters, somewhat confused. "And there's no need to shout."

33 "You felt it too? Was it deja vu?" I venture. She shakes her head.

34 "No. It's more like an adventure..."

35 "... an adventure we've not had yet?" I leave the thought hanging;

36 we both know what I mean.

37 Cresting the last rise, we stand on the sand. The boat, barely showing the legend *Point Reyes*, is in front of us now, horribly landlocked in five feet of sand. There's a smell of seaweed, rusting metalwork, and organic decay. It's not an enticing cocktail, but it doesn't drive us back.

38 The silence is deafening now, the presence of the ship overwhelming under the empty sky.

39 We both reach forward, and touch the wooden side of the ship...

40 **I have no idea when it is**. It's dark and wet and someone is shouting.

41 The roar of the sea is all around, and heavy rain batters us as we stand on the main deck of the Point Reyes.

42 Dark currents heave us randomly from fathoms beneath us, and darker ones roil in the clouded midnight sky above us.

43 Eolist stands beside me, clinging

desperately to the wooden rail around this exposed bridge area.

44 In front of us, an heroic figure in oilskins, gumboots and a sou'wester hat wrestles a course from the ship's wheel.

45 The sturdy crate he's standing on to reach the wheel does not detract from the spectacle, nor do his black and white feet.

46 "Yavin!" I roar desperately, "Where's 'Difficult?!" The badger turns in acknowledgement and points a drenched paw to a struggling shape at the front of the ship;

47 it's my best friend, the arch–genius iDifficult.

48 Bewildered that he can hold fast on the bucking deck, I'm also impressed to see that he's clearly focused on a task; he's adjusting a brass device at the prow, calibrating a clockwork mechanism preserved under glass.

49 A blue glow from its depths illuminates the immediate area, shining through the wave that obscures him for a moment.

50 A moment later, he somehow slams into the rail around us and offers a grin.

51 "Told you! Piece of cake!" he bellows as another wave, perhaps the older brother of the first, tries to sweep him away. I wave frantically towards the miracle device at the front of the ship.

52 "Is the time core going to get us home okay?!" I dislike conversing in shouts, but right now our options are thin. And I feel confused; I'm sure a moment ago that I was somewhere else.

53 But we don't have time for that now.

54 A thumbs–up from 'Difficult seals our course and fate, and we haul him over the rail and into relative safety.

55 The torrential downpour seems to worsen suddenly, and the wooden floor ahead of us vanishes again in a fresh deluge. The ships barrels to the left and then drops in a moment of zero gravity.

56 My last meal begs for an airing; this is a bumpy ride.

57 I'm aware that our speed is increasing, and we seem to be slowly angling forward. I grab for Eolist with one hand, and the railing with the other, as I glance behind and upwards.

58 And I see the lightning.

59 It's not in the sky, but is deep within the rising wave that's pushing us headlong towards an invisible horizon.

60 The lightning arcs and flashes beneath the water, and there is a stroboscopic suggestion of a mighty form with multiple arms and a broad, low–slung head.

61 We're angled more heavily now, and the rise of the wave seems without end.

62 But the front of a grey–furred form breaks the plane of the cresting water; a simian head, too many hands, and more teeth than I have time to count.

63 Dammit, it's an *Octoboon*.

64 The howling wind is drowned out by a cacophony of gibbers and whoops.

65 I bellow some unrepeatable words, and lurch towards 'Difficult as a wave thunders past.

66 "That thing doesn't belong here!" screams Eolist beside me. I concur, and add my own hoarse enquiry to my friend at close quarters.

67 We're travelling rather fast, far quicker than a boat could ever cross water.

68 "We're falling through time! How is that Octoboon following us through *time?!*" My friend waves as meaningfully as he can in our sixty–degree descent through a stinging shower of water.

69 "Well, I'm not going to learn much by engineering a *stupid* animal, now am I?" he sprays emphatically.

70 The logic is impeccably twisted, but the prospect of outrunning yet another of 'Difficult's creations—a creature with eight arms, three hearts and nine brains, no less—is not an attractive one.

71 Nor is its embarrassing baboon butt, which has just butterflied free of the titanic wave. I notice that it seems to be the source of the lightning;

72 electricity arcs to the main mast, which shatters in a brief fiery burst of splinters.

73 "Can we outrun it?" roars Eolist. "Are we there yet?!"

74 A deep growl from close by draws our attention to Yavin. The badger engineer is pointing towards a point of light ahead of us. It's not at the horizon, and it is clearly expanding as we thunder towards it.

75 "We're almost there!" roars 'Difficult.

76 High above us, the Octoboon launches clear of the water, outlined in baleful white fire, a Vetruvian pinwheeling of arms and gaping jaws that promise our immediate doom.

⁷⁷ We're finished.

⁷⁸ Time stretches like elastic, and the beast's roar deepens and slows.

⁷⁹ And slows. And slooooooows.

⁸⁰ And finally, in a rush of wet, dark, fast–forward images, time *snaps*.

⁸¹ **Back in the now**, both myself and a drenched Eolist tumble away from the stranded ship.

⁸² The misty Sunday morning in California is silent but for our Olympic coughing.

⁸³ Eventually, I sit up and reassure myself that my tiny friend is okay. I then regard the ship.

⁸⁴ Oddly, it's previous *presence* has gone; the *Point Reyes* is now just a rotten old boat with rusty fixtures, and no future beyond our epic memories.

⁸⁵ "When you get home, please punch him in the mouth," grumbles Eolist. She's rediscovered her coffee, but not her sunny disposition. Or a hairbrush.

⁸⁶ "Whose mouth?" asks a tall upbeat figure as it rounds the ship with a smaller companion; it's 'Difficult and Yavin. They're both soaked to the skin.

⁸⁷ As he sheds his oilskins, the badger tugs at the arch–genius' sleeve and points at the distant hills enquiringly. 'Difficult nods. "And by the way, where *are* we?"

⁸⁸ There's a selection of hugs and backslaps as we greet each other.

⁸⁹ Some of us are not where we're supposed to be.

⁹⁰ But we're in good company.

Beyond The Notice Of Physics

5 ¹ In the hubbub of the busy roadside café, my mind is elsewhere.

² Around me, I've tuned out the mothers, children, truckers and pensioners as they talk, eat, scold and laugh their way through the hottest part of the day.

³ I'm no longer aware of this physical and spiritual cross–section of a small town under shade.

⁴ The plate of food in front of me has me in its evocative embrace; a simple meal of rough–cut chorizo sausage with scrambled eggs.

⁵ The spices sizzle and whisper on the hot dinner plate, and the still–moist eggs bubble gently.

⁶ Outside, in the Northern Californian town of Tomales, **it's August**.

⁷ But in the cafe, as I taste my first mouthful of the fragrant dish, I have no idea when it is;

⁸ the flavours and textures of the ingredients combine to make an experience that forces reality even further into retreat.

⁹ Eolist Petite is also somewhat absorbed. My tiny friend sits opposite me, raised up by a few cushions on the seat of her rustic wooden chair.

¹⁰ A halo of wet cocoa rings her grinning mouth as she tucks into a bar of dark chocolate filled with raspberry fondant.

¹¹ Normally she'd have a coffee, but this treat provides enough caffeine that she's able to risk a glass of water with ice and lemon. The diamond cubes clink and bob quietly.

¹² **Two hours ago**, I'm behind the wheel, driving up towards Tomales with Eolist, my eccentric amigo iDifficult, and Yavin the badger.

¹³ It's been a busy few days.

¹⁴ Today, we're heading off in search of a mythical bakery with the best cakes in the State.

¹⁵ As anyone will tell you, I'm not a great driver; I choose odd routes and frequently get lost. I'm backtracking from a wrong turn right now, in fact, but nobody has noticed;

¹⁶ as my rear–view of tortured limbs confirms, they're all playing *Travel Twister* to pass the time.

¹⁷ And indeed, a bit too much time passes; by the time we reach the crossroads of the small town, the sun is high and the bakery—sold clean out of its legendary pastries—has just closed for the day.

¹⁸ Yavin and 'Difficult are philosophical about it, and head off excitedly in search of something they're tracking on a scanner, while a parched and hungry Eolist joins me for lunch and shade in a tiny café.

¹⁹ **Back in the now**, my meal continues stirring up eclectic and seemingly irrelevant memories.

²⁰ **It's 1998**, and I'm sitting at my desk in North London. In front of me is a heavily–anticipated sandwich:

²¹ thick granary bread with plenty of butter, thick salted gammon ham, and two handfuls of strong grated cheddar.

[22] Next to me is a cup of tea and a copy of *At The Mountains Of Madness* by H.P. Lovecraft.

[23] Over the cubicle wall, the marketing department roar their relentless babble at phones, video links and each other;

[24] I don't enjoy being near them, as my work requires quiet and concentration.

[25] The sandwich, made for me by the grandmotherly Letty in the staff canteen, awaits. I unwrap the expertly–folded greaseproof paper and, grasping its mighty layers in two hands, take the first bite.

[26] The moment—like one of Lovecraft's monsters—defies description, and the chaos of the office fades into distant irrelevance.

[27] **Back in Tomales**, I realise that it is this exact same feeling. Amidst the herbs, the spices and the veteran grease of this backwater eatery there is something magical to be found.

[28] Very few adventures end in disappointment.

[29] Behind the counter, the pretty Mexican waitress watches me take another forkful and hopes I'll glance her way, but I'm long ago and miles away;

[30] there's just the food, the memories, and the eye of the storm.

[31] And I have no idea that from the bridge of his broad, weathered hot plate, the house chef sees my enjoyment and swells with pride. He needs no thanks from me;

[32] there is pleasure in eating, but far more in cooking for someone with an appetite.

[33] Outside, the daylight is harsh, the street empty.

[34] Mad dogs and Englishmen famously go out in the midday sun, but in this quiet little town those are in short supply at any time of day.

[35] And yet today, Tomales welcomes a Mad Englishman and a badger; outside the window, 'Difficult and Yavin slowly cartwheel by in zero gravity, gently spinning, beyond the notice of Physics.

[36] Eolist contentedly waves chocolatey fingers at them, and for a moment I glance up and smile;

[37] I guess we've all found something special today.

[38] I return to my lunch, and wait for the universe to catch up with us.

Moving In Similar Circles

[1] A stroll in the woods is good for the soul.

[2] **It's August**. The redwood forest in California is beautiful in the late afternoon. The trees, needlessly and gloriously mighty, tower above us.

[3] A cool breeze inspires the summer leaves to a dappled display of light and shadow. A wood–chipped path, soft underfoot, leads the way into the woods.

[4] I'm with Eolist Petite, my most caffeinated of friends. This is our final day in California, and we've come to see some Nature.

[5] And we're in awe; Nature does not disappoint.

[6] "I'm glad we made time for this," says Eolist, ducking under an extremely low branch; her limited height has few advantages, and she makes the most of them. I amble along beside her, stepping over the same branch**, and offer an affirmative noise.

[7] I feel wonderfully relaxed, and I'm snapping away on the camera like the enthusiastic amateur I am; I'm making the most of the remaining daylight.

[8] I've never seen trees looking so beautiful. Eolist is similarly contemplative, asking,

[9] "I wonder if the boys got home okay?"

[10] **It's yesterday**. Yavin the badger and my best friend 'Difficult have joined us on a trip to see the *Point Reyes Lighthouse*.

[11] North of San Francisco, the beautiful *Point Reyes National Seashore* area—replete with moody beaches and grassy expanses—has wowed us on the drive up.

[12] But as the four of us stand on the clifftops looking down to the sea–level lighthouse, our shared sense of spectacle is profound; it's beautiful here.

[13] All that separates us from the lighthouse is a set of steps. A set of three hundred steps, to be precise. It's a long way down, and the return journey seems somewhat daunting, but Eolist and I start our descent, sharing a smile.

[14] Our companions consider their options; they're skilled engineers and very creative at the end of the day, and are bound to think of something.

[15] "I'm glad we made time for this!" says Eolist, laughing enthusiastically as our stroll increases to a near jog;

16 the steps are many and shallow, but the incline is steeper than it looks.

17 We pause giggling at a convenient bench halfway down; I'm more than a little out of shape.

18 Taking sips from a bottle of water, we're amused as 'Difficult strolls purposefully down toward us; Yavin is perched in his shoulders.

19 "300 steps, but only *one* of us is walking!" shouts 'Difficult cheerfully as he passes. "So, only 150 steps apiece!"

20 The badger gives us a wink and a wave; he's a smart one, that lad.

21 **Back in the now**, I notice that the forest has darkened a little;

22 the afternoon's warmth has evaporated with the fading light, and the trees are certainly taller, broader and more densely packed.

23 The woodchipped path winds a little more as a result, but occasionally passes through a tunnelled–out redwood.

24 In a curious way, this adds to its fairytale beauty and sense of drama.

25 "Do we find the gingerbread cottage anytime soon?" asks Eolist, her mind moving in similar circles. And though I chuckle, I feel a frisson of something darker, too.

26 I snap a few photos of her and the scenery, but the results on the camera's tiny screen are gloomy, flat moments in time. They don't reflect the environment in which we find ourselves, and it looks like I have dust on my lens anyway.

27 I frown and put the camera away.

28 "They certainly made a quick exit," reflects my companion, returning to our previous conversation.

29 I nod, pleased to have a distraction from the actual moment.

30 **It's yesterday again**, and we've all reached the lighthouse. Yavin, now back on the ground, directs 'Difficult's attention to an engineering shed that probably contains a generator; they head off to inspect it.

31 Eolist and myself enjoy a quick guided tour of the tiny lighthouse with Barbara, a charming employee who seems pleased to have some visitors. She tells us of the long history of the headland, most of which she's far too young to have experienced firsthand.

32 She then proudly shows us the magnificent Fresnal–lensed beacon that is the centrepiece of the lighthouse.

33 Puzzled by the poor light indoors, I ask why the curtains are closed. She tells us with a grin that on sunny days like today, if they don't keep them tightly shut, the lens has a habit of focusing the light and *setting fire* to things.

34 We all have a good laugh at this, noticing the fire extinguishers for the first time, and move on with the tour outside.

35 As we move away, Yavin and 'Difficult enter the lighthouse behind us. They look somewhat oily, presumably as a result of inspecting the generator. I shake my head. *Engineers*; never afraid to get their hands—or paws—dirty.

36 In fact, they seem to *prefer* it that way.

37 We stand at the railed edge of the property—there's still quite a drop to the sea—and Barbara regales us with tales of whale watching in cold November.

38 We're interrupted by a muffled shriek and a long, recognisable bubbling hiss from indoors.

39 Moments later, a charred and foamy iDifficult traipses from the lighthouse followed by Yavin. The badger fails to surreptitiously deposit a still-frothing fire extinguisher beside the lighthouse door before strolling nonchalantly back towards the long stairway.

40 Barbara hurries indoors to check for damage as we run over to our friend. He mumbles something about his trousers mysteriously bursting into flame after he wiped his oily hands on the curtains.

41 We're glad he's okay, but can't help laughing as we encourage him to follow Yavin before official questions are asked.

42 He says they'll be heading back to England now, and hurries away without explanation; I take him at his word, and don't ask questions.

43 **Back in the now**, the forest is darker, and its palette of hues has collapsed;

44 it's like we've wandered out of our depth along the seabed, and the water has stolen the happier colours. The woodchips of the track have deteriorated into mud, as if there's been heavy rainfall in this part of the forest only.

45 I'm aware that I'm holding Eolist's hand—clearly we feel there's valour in unity—and that there are *noises*.

46 The breathing of the forest is always there if you listen for it, but right now it just sounds like hushed voices;

47 they whisper here and there down through the breeze–rustled canopy, talking of the dark and fear and the remoteness of the real world.

48 Our world is blue, brown and deepest green. And inky, unknowable black.

49 We both feel it; there are ghosts here.

50 Eolist is no stranger to spectral apparitions, having seen angels and spirits in her house many times. She's even confronted them, spoken to them. But this is new to me, and I don't care for it much.

51 The Dinky Dynamo looks up at me and smiles in a way that says I have nothing to worry about, but our tension is shouting loud.

52 I trust her, and we proceed.

53 The path ahead passes through another wide, hollowed out tree. We've gone through several of these, but Eolist stops short suddenly and looks at it. She starts to speak, but stops again just as abruptly. She stares a while, her head cocked, listening.

54 I start to speak and she shushes me.

55 And then she stares some more, all the time focused on the passage through the redwood tree.

56 Finally, she slowly shakes her head and leads me around the tree in a wide, careful circle. It's not easy, and my foot slips on a loose earth and a wet rock,

57 but I find my balance and keep up with her guiding hand. We don't return to the path for thirty seconds.

58 Questions are forming on my tongue, but Eolist silences me with a simple,

59 "Don't look back."

60 The voices of the forest are fading, but we both feel the attention at our backs;

61 I don't think of disobeying her.

62 The path bends round presently, and in a few minutes the terrain is friendlier,

and we're back at the well–lit car park.

63 The inside of the car is a welcome haven, and we head away at speed.

64 I feel relieved, as if we've passed a test. But I'm sad, too. We both fly home tomorrow—Eolist to the East Coast, and myself to London—and it's been an amazing holiday; this is not how I want it to end.

65 But dinner awaits, so there's time for a few final memories.

66 **Two hours later**, with dinner behind us, we're checking out our photos of the day on the computer.

67 I laugh as I show Eolist my images from the forest; they're poor photos. I look hot and overweight, and the interference I saw on the camera screen is more noticeable.

68 "Dust."

69 Eolist frowns and shows me her photos. The same scenes, the same visual aberrations. And they're in different places on each framed shot; it's not dust on the lens.

70 Something airborne, then? But something that we couldn't *see?* And with identical lens reactions to it on different cameras? Unlikely.

71 We look closer, and are surprised to see tiny haloes of light, which when examined very closely, almost seem to have structure inside them.

72 They look almost *organic.*

73 Very weird.

74 "No, not dust," my tiny friend concludes unhappily, though she offers no opinions about what they might be.

75 But we both know the forest did not seem friendly as darkness fell.

76 I don't sleep well that night.

77 A stroll in the woods is good for the soul.

78 But sometimes it's bad for the nerves.

Notes

*   I'm still getting used to the left–hand–drive car.

**   My height has its own advantages.

Cuttlefish

"I was once mugged by a seagull at the seaside for a pastry; a blind man would have reported a feathered Sumo wrestler."

Prologue

1

1 Some questions are inevitable.

2 "Daddy, what did you do during The War?"

3 I smile and tousle the youngster's hair as we sit together on the sofa. He giggles and looks up at me with those big dark eyes; it's past his bedtime, but he's hard to resist, and he knows it.

4 "Oh, kiddo," I sigh, "what makes you think I did *anything* during The War?"

5 We're in my front room, lit only by the November fire in the grate. It's cold out, tea and cake fill the coffee table in front of us, and there are early whispers of Christmas in the nut–filled bowl on the window sill.

6 "Well, our name is *Roth*, Daddy," says young Fido patiently, "and a Roth will always fight for what's right."

7 Kids have such a wonderfully simplistic view of the world.

8 But the lad does so love me to tell him of my adventures.

9 And they're just stories; where's the harm?

10 "Well, yes. Maybe I can tell you a little about the Roths and The War."

11 "The War Of The Cuttlefish!" booms Fido delightedly, and I instinctively hug him closer. My gaze turns slowly inwards as I marvel at the ephemeral shapes in the fire.

12 "Or as it was also known," I whisper, *"The Cephalopocalypse!"*

Definitely Inside The Lines

2

1 Real or imagined, there is always something lurking in the basement.

2 And today, it's us.

3 Outside of my best friend iDifficult's house, it's a gloriously sunny suburban day in **August**.

4 Inside the house, it's the same day, but mercifully cooler. And down in the basement, in the arch–genius' dimly–lit workshop, it's cooler still.*

5 I'm slumped on a crush–velvet sofa, sporting shorts, a non–matching shirt and a cup of tea. I'm getting my slack on while 'Difficult, carrying off 1970s disco wear with considerable aplomb, flips through computer simulations on a computer tablet embedded in a nearby tabletop.

6 In fact, the tablet *is* the tabletop.

7 I notice my amigo is nibbling on occasional shards of this morning's pizza crust scattered across the touchscreen;

8 I love a hot breakfast.

9 "Roth, did I ever tell you how I came by those terracotta snowmen?" 'Difficult asks conversationally.**

10 This is not an attempt to fill a conversational void; we've known each

other far too long to be uncomfortable with silence.

¹¹ "Yep," I say, curtailing an interesting exposition from our story. "I helped you get them back from Antarctica, remember?"

¹² The man once voted *Boy Most Likely To Fill A Swimming Pool With Custard* looks up to frown momentarily, and then chuckles and shakes his head.

¹³ "That really was a *very* big coolbag."

¹⁴ That said, he returns to tapping, twisting and dragging at the touchscreen.

¹⁵ I notice an enthusiasm, an *excitement* about the man; he's close to something.

¹⁶ It reminds me of the first time he found a Higgs Boson, back in 1996. ***

¹⁷ I sit up straight and pay closer attention.

¹⁸ "So, what are you working on?" I wave an arm at the large fishtanks around the perimeter of the dingy room. "And what are all these for?"

¹⁹ "I'm glad you asked," he beams, "come take a look at this."

²⁰ I rise from the comfort of the sofa with complaining knees, and head over to the desk. I stand beside my friend in the half light, our faces illuminated in what is probably a ghoulish fashion by the screen beneath us.

²¹ Onscreen, there's a sophisticated underwater simulation involving a jolly marine cephalopod. Is it squid? No, I decide, squid are sleeker, meaner.

²² I remembering our last tangle with 'Difficult's squid/squirrel hybrid; I had to prise its sullen, slavering mouth open with a crowbar, fighting off its determined facial tentacles, to drag my undigested best friend from its gullet.

²³ He was gloopy.

²⁴ But I *do* recognise the squid's cousin on the screen: the delicate, undulating single fin surrounding the mantled head; the faceful of rope–like tentacles; the weird goat eyes; and above all, the serene, imperious *intelligence* of the thing.

²⁵ "Is that a *cuttlefish?*" I ask.

²⁶ "Well spotted," grins 'Difficult, "most mistake them for squid."

²⁷ I snort derisively, clearly relegating *those* schmucks to the slow reading group.

²⁸ "Did you realise that these fellas have an enormous percentage of their body mass devoted to their central nervous system?"

²⁹ He flicks a schematic into view. It's a complicated view of the cephalopod, and there's a *lot* of glowing organs and nerve paths on it.

³⁰ "Really?" It's true; I didn't. "So, they're smart for their size? Cool." A random thought particle hits me. "Their colour changes are pretty, too."

³¹ My friend glances at me sideways, ignoring my comment. "Their brain/body ratio is *well* above both us and dolphins, in fact. Some of them get pretty darned big, too."

³² "Oh. Right."

³³ Sensing that listening noises might serve me better right now, I add an encouraging, "Yes."

³⁴ My friend tugs at my shirted elbow and leads me away from the digital table.

³⁵ "Anyway," he says, "they're pretty solitary in the wild, and I wanted to see how they'd interact. So I popped a couple of them in the tank over here."

³⁶ He indicates a water–filled, glass cube beyond an archway, in a brighter area of the basement. We stroll over, passing through several slanting shafts of light from the narrow, horizontal windows high in the walls.

³⁷ A pair of sullen–looking cuttlefish, their head mantles undulating gently, sit close to the bottom of the tank. Their chameleon colours shift, seemingly at random. I notice that the two are *entangled* somehow.

³⁸ "Well, I'll be blowed," I say, struggling for words, "Are they... *holding hands?*"

³⁹ "Nope," corrects 'Difficult in an enthralled tone, "they're *networking.*"

⁴⁰ And as he says it, I see it.

⁴¹ The duo sit facing one another, their outermost tentacles touching. It looks an expression of affection, or the start of a dance, but a small voice tells me they're forming a closed loop. A *circuit*.

⁴² Their spare arms wave gently between them, but some of these grasp chunky wax crayons. Unbelievably, the pair are slowly colouring a simple picture on a white board on the floor of the tank.

⁴³ "What do you think?" whispers 'Difficult from behind my shoulder. I consider this, examining the picture.

⁴⁴ "Well, their colour choices are unusual," I muse, "but they're definitely colouring *inside the lines*. Very neat."

45 "Oooh, they're doing it again!" breathes the arch genius. "Watch this!"

46 One of the cuttlefish has shifted to a fixed shade of blue–green. The second cephalopod pauses in its colouring and starts to feel about on its side of the tank.

47 Locating an aquamarine–coloured crayon, it retrieves and examines it, before handing it over.

48 There's the merest hint of a nodded acknowledgement, and the pair's colour display returns to normal.

49 "Damn!" My mind is saying something a little stronger than that.

50 "Exactly! They seems smarter when they're *linked*." He lets this settle in for a moment before tugging at my arm again. "Now, come check this out."

51 In the next tank, there are not two, but three cuttlefish. Again, their outermost tentacles are linked, forming a wider ring than the duo.

52 Bless them, but it looks like they're playing *ring–a–rosie*.

53 The trio look up as my friend gently plops a scrambled Rubik's Cube into their tank. As it sinks slowly towards the bottom of their enclosure, three coordinated sets of tentacles snake out to hold it in place at the focus of their circle.

54 A few seconds pass. There's a shifting colour display between the trio, each hue passing around the circle in a clockwise direction. Their display slowly spins, with occasional surges. It reminds me of the motion of early computer tape drives. It's pretty, but unsettling.

55 "This bit is so *cool!*" squeaks my friend.

56 With thirteen slow, deliberate manipulations, the cuttlefish cooperate to grasp, twist and slide the cube back to its perfect, completed state.

57 A moment later, a wet tentacle holds the cube above the surface of the water. I take it gently.

58 "That's incredible!" This seems inadequate. I give them a wave. "Thank you."

59 There's a salutary flick of a tentacle tip in my direction.

60 "You don't know the half of it," says 'Difficult soberly. "My best algorithms could only do it in *fifteen* moves. They beat that by two. Collectively."

61 I raise an eyebrow, knowing that the pursuit of so–called *God Moves* is a serious scientific research endeavour.

62 But my curiosity gets the better of me, and I shuffle over to the next tank. "And what about these four?" The quartet of cuttlefish in the next tank are going through a similar friendly–tentacled ritual. But there's a tension in their body language, if I'm any judge.

63 "Well, they wrote some passable *poetry* while they were waiting for me earlier," says 'Difficult dismissively, "and then they knocked off a workable solution to five–dimensional travel while I was making coffee."

64 I try not to think about either of those too closely. "And now?"

65 "Oh, they're working on World Peace."

66 I now raise both eyebrows, and he looks shifty. "Hey, I was only kidding with them: *Hey, what's next? World Peace?* kinda thing, but they seemed keen."

67 I notice that their colour shifts are faster, more urgent than the previous group.

68 My friend sighs. "They're processing *huge* amounts of information, but they don't seem to be making progress on the problem."

69 "It is a tricky one," I chuckle. "Have you tried a higher number of cuttlefish?"

70 'Difficult shakes his head. "Not yet. I was going to later this morning, actually. I was thinking of adding the two and the three together to make a group of five."

71 He gestures to the duo's tank. "Once the pair had finished their colouring, I mean. it seems rude to interrupt them."

72 "Well," I muse, "why not just add the groups of three and four together?"

73 "To make *seven?*" His mental arithmetic rarely fails him. "Well, it's a bit of a leap, but it might make sense to do that." He scratches his nose absently.

74 "Seven is the optimal number for group decision making."

75 We fall silent as he considers this.

76 And upstairs, there's a knock at the front door.

77 I'm about to offer to go and see who it is, when it comes again, more urgently. A heavy, rapid thumping that suggests the door may not hold up for long.

78 "Good grief, those pizza guys can be panicky when they're being chased by the Squiddrel." I sniff. "We really should put a sign up: *Caveat Squiddrem*."

79 "We've already had pizza today," says

'Difficult distantly, as he rolls up his sleeves. "Would you mind getting that matey?"

⁸⁰ "Sure." I stroll across to the stairwell in the far corner and head upstairs into the light.

⁸¹ iDifficult's house is an large and attractive two–storey affair, decorated in an ironic Regency style, and set in a pleasantly–compact half–acre of land.

⁸² The buildings—which include several sheds—and the surrounding gardens are immaculately maintained, and the whole affair is well placed in a quiet and very respectable neighbourhood.

⁸³ I wander through the kitchen and into the gloomy hallway as a final splintering crash heralds the demise of the wooden front door;

⁸⁴ I'm showering with sunlight and a fortune in toothpick futures.

⁸⁵ In the shattered remains of a doorframe, a huge figure stands erect. Tall, broad, heavy, his trilby hat held in a prehensile trunk, his toed fists balled heroically.

⁸⁶ Elliot Nesh, Special Elephant for The Unity Agency.

⁸⁷ We've crossed paths on many occasions, most notably during the adventure that I've come to think of as The Long Road Home.

⁸⁸ Elliot's usual laconic, Bogart–esque demeanour is gone, though. He looks about with agitation, his ears flapping, taking in the scene.

⁸⁹ Agents never panic, but he's clearly *highly motivated*.

⁹⁰ "Where is he? Where is iDifficult?!" bellows Elliot, bounding into the hall without grace, intent on passing me. "We have to *stop* him!"

⁹¹ I step forward, uttering a heartfelt and more–than–a–little–nervous "Hey Elliot! Whoa! Easy, big fella! What on earth is..."

⁹² As our paths collide, we bump into one another, and I grab onto the elephant to keep my balance;

⁹³ there's a strong smell of sawdust and bourbon.

⁹⁴ A moment later, as I cling to Elliot, something *changes* in the world.

⁹⁵ It's hard to describe what. But we both freeze in our tracks, clearly feeling it arrive. There's a splintered second in which I sense every fractal detail of reality unwind and rebuild itself.

⁹⁶ I'm not a user of mind–expanding drugs, but I can only imagine this is what those who do describe as *trippy*.

⁹⁷ The moment passes. In fact, it was so brief as to barely constitute an *instant*.

⁹⁸ I look about; everything seems the same: the same sunny day outside; the same décor in the hallway; the same elephant holding me up.

⁹⁹ So what is different?

¹⁰⁰ "Dammit, too late," rumbles Elliot. "Quick! Take me to Max!"

¹⁰¹ I frown. "Who?"

¹⁰² The elephantine eyes fix on me. "Max Tunguska!" I shrug and Elliot's agitation increases. "He *lives* here!"

¹⁰³ My frown continues. "No Elliot, 'Difficult does. You know he does!" We exchange queer looks and Elliot looks down in wonder at my grip on him.

¹⁰⁴ "Dammit, dammit, DAMMIT!" he curses, pushing me aside. He thunderously hurries towards the basement stairs.

¹⁰⁵ I hustle along behind him, noting some washing up that needs doing; I really must learn to focus.

¹⁰⁶ As we reach the top of the stairs, a shout comes up. I know the voice.

¹⁰⁷ "Roth! Get a move on! We're going to be *late!*"

¹⁰⁸ I follow the bulk of the agent down the creaking wooden stairs, and into a basement that's slightly better lit than I remember; is *this* what's different?

¹⁰⁹ "Roth! There you are! Step lively man, we've got to get to the Nobel Prize ceremony!"

¹¹⁰ My friend stands in a sharp tuxedo, adjusting his bowtie. He looks leaner than he did a few minutes ago, and his beard is neatly trimmed. Wow, he's full of surprises.

¹¹¹ I also note that he's wearing a name badge, as someone might who was going to a conference.

¹¹² Or a Nobel Prize ceremony. It reads:

¹¹³ *Doctor Max Tunguska*

¹¹⁴ And behind him, filling the room with a shifting spectrum of light, there is a tall, broad glass tank. And inside, in a glittering circle of light, an interconnected ring of seven cuttlefish glimmer with cold intelligence.

¹¹⁵ Three and four totals seven, undeniably.

¹¹⁶ But seven is so much more than the sum of three and four.

[117] "Dammit," sighs Elliot one final time, his tone emanates defeat.

[118] As anyone who watches horror films knows, there's always something lurking in the basement.

[119] Earlier it was just me and my best friend.

[120] But we're no longer the men we were, and we're no longer alone down there.

[121] And may never be again.

The Wisdom Of Invertebrates

3 [1] The grass rushes towards me, and I land heavily.

[2] Two seconds later, as I eat turf, something large and heavy lands on top of me;

[3] I assume it's my best friend Max Tunguska, but the speed of the impact makes it feel like hippo with glandular issues.

[4] A large canvas bag follows a moment later, thumping dangerously into the ground next to my head.

[5] The trip through the vortex was a miasma of hard light and wind, and there was a strong sense of falling.

[6] The landing confirms the last part.

[7] We normally use Max's pyramid—I'm still getting used to his recent change of name/identity from iDifficult—but today we're trying to work below radar.

[8] In fact, today we're worried men.

[9] We have an urgent job to do, and we're trying to avoid prying eyes. Prying, goat-like, *invertebrate* eyes.

[10] I make a mental note to bring a mattress next time.

[11] And to go second.

[12] "Hey, this looks like the right place!" exclaims the weight on my back. Yes indeed, it's Max, the renowned pizza rustler and part-time arch genius.

[13] "Move!" I bellow, partly in haste, partly in agony. "Clock's ticking!"

[14] As my friend bundles himself off me, I manage to turn my head and look around. Yes, it's my back garden. Or a very close approximation.

[15] I wonder if they can see us somehow?

[16] Ironically, the cuttlefish gave us this trans-dimensional travel method. But that was before they applied themselves to the problem of World Peace.

[17] I don't like to sound all H. G. Wells about it, but ever since those damned cuttlefish made a network—which instantly and collectively dubbed itself "CephNet"—they've been applying their cool intelligence to improving The World. Regardless of how The World feels about it.

[18] But time is short. I don't have time to stop to smell the roses.

[19] "How long?" I wheeze, standing as quickly as I am able, stretching my back;

[20] vertebrae crack.

[21] Where is Bear when I need him? Max checks his heavily modified cellphone, waving the augmented hardware at the open portal that still gyrates chaotically in the air above us.

[22] "Three minutes!"

[23] This suits me. I believe in threes, especially from a narrative standpoint. We're off to a good start.

[24] "Damn, do we have time to do this?" he shouts my way as I run down the very long garden towards my house.

[25] "Yes!" I shout back as I approach the back door. "Assuming I changed the locks!"

[26] My hands are shaking, but they're already in my zippered pockets, hunting for what will hopefully be the back door key.

[27] My right hand comes up empty, but the left locates what I'm after; I pull out a metal ring with two keys on it.

[28] "The keys switched pockets!" I observe loudly.

[29] "Dimensional mirroring!" shouts Max. "The cuttlefish were right!"

[30] I select my current back door key and try the lock. Nope. Damn.

[31] "Wrong key!" A crash of metal and canvas behind me tells me that he's emptied our one item of luggage unceremoniously onto the grass.

[32] In a few seconds, he'll have the escape route ready to go. Which, considering our schedule, is no bad thing.

[33] "Two minutes!"

[34] I try the other key. My *old* key. The locks clicks and the door opens.

[35] "I'm in!" I shout over my shoulder as I head quickly into the dim house. I obviously didn't need to replace the lock in *this* world;

[36] somewhere, there's an ill-tempered rhino roaming free, with no story to tell about a bizarre insurance claim and a dog whistle.

[37] Now, all I have to do is find the thing I'm after.

[38] I play a percentage hunch as I pass through the gloomy hallway, and turn up the stairs.

[39] He wouldn't make it hard; it's not my style.

[40] I crest the stairs, breathing hard, and push into the well–lit bathroom.

[41] And I see them. A pair of identical toothbrushes. Not just similar. The same brush, twice. Twins, positioned precisely in the cup on the glass shelf. One mine, the other one mine. Well, his.

[42] It's the same thing, really.

[43] One Indigo, two Realities.

[44] I take my brush and drop a small card onto the shelf. I found one just like it in my bathroom three days ago, in the space where my toothbrush would normally be.

[45] It said, in near illegible handwriting:

[46] *We heard about the cuttlefish. Do you need help?*

[47] My reply bears three words:

[48] *Not sure. Probably.*

[49] He'll know what to do. I sigh hopefully. "Tag, you're it, matey."

[50] A woman's scream erupts from downstairs. There's no time to wonder; it's time to go.

[51] As I leave the bathroom and head downstairs, I notice that I've redecorated the landing and hallway.

[52] Aquamarine and orange. Nice.

[53] I particularly like the new wallpaper. Hallways are always hard, hanging these long drops must have taken me *ages*.

[54] I reach the bottom of the stairs, and turn back to the kitchen just as Max bursts from the downstairs toilet.

[55] Behind him, out of sight, a woman curses like a trooper. He is blushing. His head slows a flying toilet roll.

[56] "One minute!" he hisses as he hustles past me.

[57] I don't ask questions. We tear through the kitchen, dance nimbly through the utility room, and burst from the house like pair of rowdy vaudeville performers.

[58] Somehow, I'm slightly in the lead, and start the dash back up the garden and our soon–to–close exit from this world.

[59] "What were you doing in the house?!" I bellow, exasperated.

[60] "I was looking for some dental floss." He somehow shrugs while running. "You've run out at home."

[61] "Not the best time, mate!" The vortex swirls ahead, a chaotic hole eight feet in the air. Underneath it is the quick–erect trampoline, the same one we found on the back lawn three days ago.

[62] Thank goodness for fast–assembly gym equipment.

[63] "I scared the living daylights out of the woman in the downstairs loo."

[64] "I heard! Who was it? We're not going to make it!" The vortex is starting to flicker and splutter, but there are a few seconds left.

[65] Without slowing, my friend looks at me sideways. "It seems you married Gillian Anderson in *this* reality."

[66] "SONOFABITCH!"

[67] Then, with a jump, a bounce, and a whoop, Max boldly goes. There's a momentary flash and a slight stretching of reality as he crosses the breach, and the vortex shoots him home first.

[68] We need to work out how to keep this thing open longer. Especially if we end up needing to recruit more help.

[69] I hope Abbey is having more luck, though she has Elliot with her;

[70] luck may have nothing to do with it.

[71] It's probably too late for the cuttlefish to give us some pointers on duration; they already suspect we're up to something, and we had to wing it a bit to get here today.

[72] I suspect our futures will hold a lot of improvising.

[73] And adrenaline.

[74] Still wishing for a mattress, but settling for the next best thing, I go second.

Ready To Tell The Tale

4[1] Spring is almost here.

[2] The weather has seemed confused on this point lately, but as I sit in the park with my best friend, change is definitely in the air.

[3] **It's February**, and a beautiful Sunday morning, bright and crisp. Our bench isn't the most comfortable, but it offers the best vantage point of this morning's proceedings;

[4] a small–but–enthusiastic group of runners are doing circuits of the lake.

[5] Mind you, in their position, I'd be enthusiastic too.

[6] Dr. Max Tunguska de–rails my thought as he offers me a cup of tea from his flask.

[7] He cuts a striking figure, with cropped

hair and a dark, white–streaked beard that makes him look like he's constantly trying to swallow a badger.

8 "You know Max," I reflect as I accept the cup with a nod, "It's been a funny few weeks since you changed your name."

9 The tea is strong, hot, sweet and milky. Perfect.

10 "Well, since you *say* I changed my name," Max corrects me quietly, as he picks up the binoculars. "But yes, it's been weirder than usual since the cuttlefish formed their network."

11 He's not kidding. Elliot, our dimension–hopping trouble–shooter, was beside himself at the time;

12 I was aware that my friend iDifficult had somehow become Max, and that the cuttlefish were doing something funky and colourful as a group, but the elephant agent seemed genuinely scared.

13 He hurried off to report back to The Unity Agency.

14 And CephNet, as the seven cuttlefish dubbed themselves, immediately applied their exponentially–superior intellect to making changes around Max's house.

15 Improvements, if you will.

16 They imposed zero gravity inside the house, for one thing. This puzzled and nauseated us in equal measure, but it made it easier for them to get about the place from the basement, and the rest of us got used to it.

17 In fact, the zero–G lounge and bedrooms were winners.

18 The zero–G toilet took a little more getting used to. But at least it meant I got to try the zero–G shower.

19 The doctor coughs, interpreting my reflective silence as agreement. "They're coming round again."

20 I raise the stopwatch and click as the group thunders past fifty yards away in a flash of black, white and gold. "Wow, that's fast!" I flash the stopwatch display toward my friend, who nods appreciatively. "How far round the lake is it?"

21 "Half a mile," grunts Max.

22 He looks every bit the guy I've known since we attended Saint Mungo's Boarding School back in the Seventies. Which he is, in a way. Apart from the beard.

23 "Have you had a good week?" he asks, glancing my way as he dunks a biscuit.

24 "I had my annual medical," I sniff, trying to sound casual as I fish in a pocket, and retrieve an envelope.

25 I hand it over as I sip at my tea, the very picture of nonchalance. Max produces the papers from the manilla, and flips through the pages of results.

26 "Not bad, not bad," he muses. "All looks pretty normal."He checks the summary page. "Though clearly this guy was a quack. Yes, very unprofessional!" he concludes darkly.

27 "How do you mean?" I say, a tiny spike of panic in my voice.

28 "Well, you'd think he'd make you put your heavy shopping down before he *weighed* you."

29 His poe–face cracks into a grin.

30 I chuckle and pat my stomach affectionately. "Yeah, apparently this needs to go. Diet and exercise. It's a good time of year to start though," I indicate the park with a wave of a hand, "when all this *change* is in the air."

31 Silence joins us as we mull that thought over. We ignore him happily.

32 Though something is nagging at me, and I give it voice.

33 "Have you seen Abbey since all this started?" My neighbour, a regular presence in my daily routine, has been absent.

34 I wonder if I've forgotten a holiday she might have mentioned? My memory has become very unreliable of late.

35 Max shakes his head as he sips at his tea.

36 "No, but didn't Elliot say something about her before he rushed off?" He frowns, perhaps half-remembering something that doesn't feel right. "I forget what, sorry; I was a bit muddled that day."

37 I really can't recall.

38 The runners dash past again as a black–and–white crowd, followed by a single golden pursuer. I click the stopwatch. "They're still very fast."

39 "Well, wouldn't *you* be?" Max tips the dregs of his tea into the grass. "Hey look, I think the pacemaker is pulling out."

40 A lone figure separates from the action and slows to an amble. He heads our way across the dew–flecked grass, sweat glistening on his face and staining the armpits of his black–and–white–striped trackuit. He removes the horsehead from his costume as he approaches.

41 "Morning!" he gasps cheerily, still looking for breath.

42 "That's quite a pace you set!" my friend beams, to the runner's delight.

43 "Thank you! That's the way Mr. King likes it!" he inhales hugely another couple of times and adds, "He's looking to find the fittest runner this morning. I must say it's rather exhilarating being chased by him!"

44 "You'll get no arguments from us!" With a shiver, I remember the time we went to that fancy dress party at the Embassy, dressed as a gazelle.

45 I'm aware of the approaching thundering of hooves. We all look round.

46 "They're really throwing up some dust now! It's the final lap!"

47 I pick up the binoculars and take in the details.

48 Three panicked zebras, sweating and spittling, are each trying to put themselves into the lead. Sleek muscular flanks gyrate and jostle, and a dozen legs pound the ground in a frenzy of adrenaline.

49 The black–and–white collage finally fills my view, and I shift focus just as a familiar golden–maned figure emerges triumphantly from the dust cloud.

50 It's King. The house's resident lion, the lodger from the spare room. A magnificent male from the Savannah, and an ambassador of his homeland.

51 King's four legs are a blur of muscle and sinew, his mighty paws pounding the ground, his tail twitching playfully. Clearly he's not at full tilt, but is putting these stripey lads through their paces.

52 Unexpectedly, the lion roars and swings left, overtaking his two slowest quarry, and then suddenly swings right to barrel into the lead zebra in a blur of teeth and claws.

53 I lower the binoculars. Nature is wonderful, but I don't always want to watch it.

54 "Why did he take the *leader?* Lions usually pick off the slowest and weakest," puzzles Max, scratching his cranial stubble. "Maybe it's like pursuit cycling? I never did understand pursuit cycling."

55 Our faux–zebra companion laughs.

56 "No! Mr. King was only interested in the fastest! The *leanest!*"

57 I nod, wondering if King had attended his own medical evaluation this week;

58 I'll be looking for a few leans cuts myself in the months to come.

59 Though after I inevitably discover a half–eaten zebra in the bathroom one morning, I'll probably be off red meat for a month.

60 Rising from the bench, Max and I turn our back on the carnage and head home, treading carefully between the early spring flowers.

61 "The cuttlefish say they're close to working out World Peace."

62 My mind is on Abbey still, and perhaps I don't think the ominous implications of that statement through; it sounds quite hopeful, on the face of it.

63 "Well, that would make a nice change. It'll be good for us."

64 I'm not thrilled by the idea of diet and exercise, but that will be good for me too.

65 It's the season of change, and change I must.

66 But some things never change.

67 And some things may change more than any of us realise.

Before I've Found My Slippers

5 1 They say that as you slip between dreams and reality, there is a moment where all things are possible.

2 But as I segue from a dream about swimming in custard and into my warm early–morning bed, I'm glad that all things are *not* possible.

3 I've only just changed the sheets, for one thing.

4 I bask in that *in–between* moment, my thoughts somewhat jumbled and nonsensical, but I don't feel the usual pull of logic at them. Curious.

5 Normally, my awakened mind quickly shrugs off the surreal night–time imagery and ushers it with a metaphoric boot back under the bed.

6 But I can still taste the custard.

7 Perhaps the sunflowers are keeping logic at bay?

8 "That's right, Indigo."

9 I feel the gentlest touch on my eyelids, but don't jump. I know the voice. And that gentle perfume of summer blooms.

10 "Don't open your eyes, or we won't be able to talk."

11 Is this part of the elusive logic of the dream–state? It feels that way. But I trust the voice, and relax.

Cuttlefish

[12] It's Abbey.

[13] I want to open my eyes.

[14] We don't catch up that often, but my neighbour is always smiling, and it's quite something. I sense her presence sitting on the edge of my bed rather than feel the weight of it, and know she's radiating kindness. I wonder idly what colour her hair is today.

[15] "Still blonde. And thank you, you silly man."

[16] Yep, she's a mystery, is Abbey.

[17] Her fingers haven't moved from my eyes. It's not unpleasant, but it's weird all the same. I wonder why she's here. And why we're having this odd ritual.

[18] "Because I'm *not* here."

[19] There's a vague sense of her clearing her throat, and of another presence nearby; I detect a subtle hint of bourbon and straw.

[20] "I've not been about since the thing with Max started."

[21] This is true. That was a weird day in the basement.

[22] The cuttlefish. The CephNet.

[23] "Is that what they're calling themselves?" she sighs, and then laughs lightly, "I bet they're all *male*."

[24] I chuckle, and it occurs to me that I know nothing of cuttlefish sexing.

[25] "And nor should you."

[26] Well, quite.

[27] My focus shifts back to the purpose of the Abbey's visit. No words are required; syllables are just sounds, data, things to be heard and interpreted, and perhaps misunderstood.

[28] Our connection speaks fluently in pure, bright information.

[29] "You should write in the mornings more often, Indigo," she smiles, "*that* was rather pretty.*"

[30] I smile proudly instead of blushing; her praise means a lot to me.

[31] "I had to go away, to look for something."

[32] *Something?* That's rather vague.

[33] I sense a sigh from her, and a difficult subject ambling into view from cover.

[34] "Yes, something to help you with the cuttlefish. It's easy to explain, but hard to accept." She pauses. And pauses some more. "Especially for a man without *Faith*."

[35] Ah yes. Faith. A tricky business. Still, I'm a sucker for a reasoned argument.

[36] Besides, if her companion is who I

think it is, there's inter–dimensional travel involved, which I can at least respect as Science.

[37] "You're right, Elliot is with me." I relax further. The elephant is an agent of The Unity Agency, a policeman of sorts;

[38] if Abbey is with him, she's as safe as in her own front room.

[39] "And yes, we're in another Reality right now."

[40] Hence this unusual form of communication.

[41] "Yes."

[42] I wonder if we'll need help with the cuttlefish. They seem harmless enough. In fact, they're intelligent, thoughtful, helpful even. Though, by definition they're a little...

[43] "Inhuman? Superior?"

[44] Well, they're *different*, certainly. And ambitious. And they certainly want to change things around here.

[45] "You're starting to see it. Their intelligence is growing exponentially. And their presence. They're already affecting this Reality too. Not all Realities. Not yet."

[46] A wave of apprehension finds me. It settles in. And again I wonder what Abbey is looking for.

[47] I hear the clinking of ice, and the sigh of a heavy set figure gazing from a distant room through narrowly drawn blinds. I sense we're reaching the punchline, the reason for their quest.

[48] "Tell him," says Elliot.

[49] There's an edge of curiosity to her voice now. "Do you need me to tell you, Indigo?"

[50] It's an interesting question. *Need?* No. I trust Abbey implicitly. But my own curiosity tugs squarely at my trouser leg, demanding my attention.

[51] Abbey laughs at the image.

[52] And she tells me what they are looking for.

[53] It's somewhat infeasible. I don't laugh in reply. She nods, knowingly.

[54] "I told you."

[55] Wow. And *that's* the help we'll need?

[56] "Yes, I think so." But Abbey's voice contains no uncertainty.

[57] My gut says that I should take her at her word, accept this crazy plan at face value. But it's difficult.

[58] I wish that my old friend *iDifficult* was here. Max is the same man, but somehow different.

⁵⁹ "Trust Max. The two of you can hold this together until we get back."

⁶⁰ The gentle touch on my eyelids starts to fade. I there anything else I need to know?

⁶¹ "Just remember after I've gone that this is *not* a dream."

⁶² That may be easier said than done. Dreams seems to wriggle free by the time I'm having breakfast. Sometimes before I've found my slippers, even.

⁶³ "I know. Elliot has left something for you. Something from another Reality; our passage has not gone unnoticed." She giggles, "It's rather flattering I suppose."

⁶⁴ There's a sense of distant danger, of a peril to my two friends. The bass rumble of the elephant confirms this. "We need to go. Now."

⁶⁵ I feel a faint brushing kiss on my forehead and a whispered goodbye.

⁶⁶ And I'm sitting up in bed, sweating, confused. The room around me is empty. Abbey is gone.

⁶⁷ The room is dark, but a staccato triangle of brilliance flickers on the corner of the bed as the curtain moves in the breeze.

⁶⁸ Was it real? My head is fuzzy, and for a moment, I'm unsure.

⁶⁹ And then I see the comic book. On its cover, gaudy and stylised, Abbey and Elliot stand heroically, ready to save the universe.

⁷⁰ To save The Unity, I correct myself.

⁷¹ This seems ridiculous. Worrying.

⁷² And it's a terrible likeness of Elliot.

⁷³ But in the moments after waking all things are possible.

⁷⁴ I hurry into clothes from the top of the laundry basket and set off to find Max.

Under Endless Blue Skies

6¹ As an Englishman, I've always had a soft spot for the summer countryside of my homeland. The rolling fields, sequined rivers and ancient brooding trees, all under endless blue skies.

² And today, the trees are of particular interest. Well, the one I'm sitting under is, anyway;

³ it provides wonderful shade during the hottest part of the day, and a back rest after what turned out to be a difficult journey.

⁴ **It's Wednesday afternoon**, and we're in the middle of a field in Cambridgeshire. I'm surrounded by rustic scenery, which includes my best friend Max;

⁵ he's dressed as a rugged outdoorsman, and looks very much at home in the pale golden sway of the impending harvest.

⁶ "It's nice out here," observes Max. He sips from a canteen of water, ever prepared. My own drink has long since gone;

⁷ I expect a call of nature beyond that offered by my immediate surroundings.

⁸ And I feel a deep sense of disquiet. It's been an odd day.

⁹ **It's Wednesday morning**. We've been invited to meet with the cuttlefish collective known as CephNet.

¹⁰ The invitation is probably a contrivance to get our cooperation; neither of us takes instruction well, and a request is far easier to swallow.

¹¹ They're smarter than most folk already, it seems.

¹² Inside Max's house is a zero–gravity environment. It helps the cuttlefish to get about the place, but I'm unclear how they managed it.

¹³ That said, when you connect seven massively–intelligent creatures together in a network, they're bound to come up with all *kinds* of weird stuff.

¹⁴ As we float into their presence in Max's former lounge, I notice that the room is empty;

¹⁵ there's no sofa or TV, and no stacks of old pizza boxes. Even the dirt seems to be missing from the windows.

¹⁶ And the room looks *massive*, out of scale. The cuttlefish, suspended in an interlinked ring above us—a *skydiving formation*, says my mind absently—are equally massive.

¹⁷ The rainbow spectrum of the cephalopod thought processes pulses erratically around the ring;

¹⁸ it's somewhat hypnotic.

¹⁹ "Did they get *bigger*, Max?" I don't like the question, but it seems relevant, considering how uncomfortable it makes me. "Because they sure *look* bigger."

²⁰ My best friend seems to be enjoying the Zero-G environment, and spins gently while chuckling quietly to himself.

²¹ I note the uncharacteristically sombre, almost *practical* cut of his clothes today.

²² He's sporting walking boots, a t-shirt,

cargo pants, and a loose jacket that billows around him.

23 Eventually, as he realises we're all watching and waiting, my question registers with him.

24 "Um, bigger?" He considers the idea. "No. More likely they shifted our relative scale within the room."

25 I think about this for a moment. "You mean they *made us smaller?* In relation to them?"

26 "Exactly. It changes your perception of them, doesn't it?"

27 As I stare up at our hosts, imperious and unknowable, I feel a chill;

28 Max may have a point.

29 Unoccupied tentacles wave gently in thin air, anemone–like, and it occurs to me for the first time that the seven cuttlefish are not immersed in water. Or are we *all* underwater? Perhaps that is why the windows look clean?

30 I file that for later consideration; I have bigger fish to fry, so to speak.

31 "Please listen," says a calm voice, "there are things you must know."

32 The voice is friendly, conversational. It invites relaxation, but I don't have a good feeling about this;

33 ever since Abbey's warning, I've been on edge.

34 "Who's speaking, please?"

35 There's a polite, almost surprised pause.

36 "We are the CephNet," comes the reply, "who did you *expect?*"

37 It's a fair question; I smile and offer a rueful wave. "Hi."

38 "Hello Indigo. Hello Max. Please listen. Here is what you must know." They're all business. But it's quite likeable, a refreshing change from the pomp of committee decision–making.

39 "We have been thinking about World Peace, as you asked."

40 I frown. *Did* we ask? I glance at the arch–genius floating beside me.

41 "I mentioned it, if you recall," mutters Max, probably reading my puzzled facial expression, "but I was just trying to give them *something to do.* I didn't expect them to take it so literally. Sorry, matey."

42 "You couldn't have given them something else? Calculating Pi to the end, or something?"

43 An ethereal chuckle suggests that it wouldn't have taxed them.

44 The ring of cephalopods spins gently above us. It wouldn't surprise me if creatures such as these had inspired the cool, vast, *alien* intellects of literature.

45 Did H.G. Wells go scuba diving?

46 "We've given it a lot of thought," says the collective voice, "and have gathered maximum information by connecting ourselves to everything in the world."

47 This is casual, presented as the seemingly obvious, and is stained with pride;

48 I don't like where this is going at all.

49 "Oh good gravy," says Max, agreeing with my unspoken thought, "this won't end well." His hands slowly drifts to his pocket.

50 And the CephNet offers its verdict.

51 "We've concluded that Things Will Have To Change."

52 "Yeah, we figured as much," nods Max. And his hand, now inside his pocket, pushes a button on a short–range teleportation device.

53 And we are elsewhere.

54 **Back in the now**, we stand and prepare to leave the shade of the tree. I'm not enthusiastic; the series of dimensional jumps since we left home have proven exhausting.

55 But we've enlisted some help.

56 And we have better hardware than our first few trips;

57 there's no need for the trampoline. And so I have less bruises.

58 "I'm pooped," I sigh, "I have no idea how Elliot does this for a living."

59 Max grunts affirmatively as we stride into the sun and slowly head uphill. The wheat is tall and golden about us, but I find it hard to appreciate; I know what awaits us.

60 As we top a small rise, we see the smoke.

61 In the distance, Cambridge is burning.

62 It's not *my* Cambridge, of course; that's in a different Reality.

63 But the spires are falling in flames; the changes have started.

64 I sense a future involving armies, drones and collateral damage. The destructive sight stirs despair and rage as I picture my home town in ruins. But there's no time to think that way.

65 In cosmic terms, there's no time to think *locally.*

66 The words are out before my brain catches up. "When did life get so complicated?"

⁶⁷ "We need to get moving," says Max, as the bright implosion of a teleport half a mile away catches my eye. My heart sinks; three jumps between Realities have not shaken our pursuers off.

⁶⁸ "They seem determined that we're a problem for them."

⁶⁹ Max nods, "And they'd be right. Perhaps next time, we should hide a little deeper?"

⁷⁰ For the second time today, I don't like where this is going.

⁷¹ That said, I trust Max.

⁷² My friend makes some screwdriver adjustments to the hardware in his hand.

⁷³ "Ready?" he asks.

⁷⁴ "Nope. Do it."

⁷⁵ I wonder what awaits us. But there's no time to wonder.

⁷⁶ With a click, we're gone.

⁷⁷ An Englishman who travels can find beauty anywhere.

⁷⁸ But he only finds contentment at home.

Filling A Leaky Bucket

7¹ The elegant office is cool in the late afternoon. The fading sun through the Venetian blinds throws horizontal stripes onto the cream wall behind me; the breeze stirs these gently.

² "Would you like me to close those blinds, Mister Roth?" asks my company from behind his mahogany desk.

³ The desk, like the rest of the office furniture, is heavy, and well made.

⁴ I shake my head, "No, that's fine Mister..." I hesitate, forgetful;

⁵ I've never been good with names.

⁶ "Call me Jake," interrupts the private detective. He's a handsome man in his early thirties, his hair swept back and oiled.

⁷ His fast, intelligent eyes watch me, and though he sits with practised ease, there's a coiled, explosive energy about the man.

⁸ I eye his clothes appreciatively; the suit is immaculate and expensive, his necktie rich and flamboyant.

⁹ His smile is warm, welcoming, and *almost* genuine.

¹⁰ "Besides, the view is impressive."

¹¹ I'm not kidding.

¹² The 1930s Los Angeles skyline is low and simple, dominated by City Hall.

Very different from the sky–scrapered, post–millennial metropolis that stands there in my time;

¹³ I've only been here a few days, and I like it already.

¹⁴ "Thank you," he says dismissively, steering me back to our discussion. "You were saying about wanting us to find your friend? This..." he glances at his notes, "Mister Tunguska?"

¹⁵ I nod, continuing the tale.

¹⁶ "Max and I got split up soon after arriving here. During an escape from a Chinese restaurant, in fact." I shrug, "We were hungry and stopped for some food. It was only when we came to pay that we remembered that our money was no good here. So we..."

¹⁷ "How's that, Mister Roth?" interrupts Jake sharply, though the smile holds its place and shape. This makes sense; if our money is no good, how will he get *paid*?

¹⁸ I give him my brightest smile.

¹⁹ "Don't worry, it was a temporary problem. We have money now. I've been back to settle up since." I recall those circumstances clearly; I still have the stitches in fact;

²⁰ the right thing to do is not always the easy thing to do.

²¹ I reach into my pocket to retrieve a thin bundle of well–worn dollar bills. I place this on the table, careful to not be flippant. "Will that cover your first few days?"

²² The gumshoe glances at the bundle and doubles his smile.

²³ "It would be helpful to have a recent photo of Max."

²⁴ I slide a sketch across the table. "I don't have one, but this is a good likeness." It took me a few attempts;

²⁵ Max has a shaved head but wears a beard, and I've often commented that he looks like he's trying to swallow a badger. That came through very strongly in the first few sketches.

²⁶ I think I nailed it in the end.

²⁷ Jake picks it up and studies it, smiling.

²⁸ "It looks like he's trying to swallow a raccoon."

²⁹ Ah, well.

³⁰ "Yes, he gets that a lot." It's almost true, and besides, I'm fairly sure they don't get badgers here. Well, only those ghastly honey badger things, and they're not proper badgers anyway.

³¹ "So, Mister Roth..."

³² "Indigo." It's my turn to interrupt;
³³ Jake grins and shrugs, as if he's decided to play along with a joke.
³⁴ "So, *Indigo*," he asks, "how is it that you and Max are in town?"
³⁵ I sigh and scratch my head absently.
³⁶ That's a much bigger story.
³⁷ And this is 1930–something. I'm not sure a tale of evading pursuit across dozens of Realities and eras while recruiting help to defeat an insidious network of sentient cephalopods will hold a lot of water.
³⁸ Enough to fill a leaky bucket, perhaps.
³⁹ And to be honest, the bit about Abbey's trip with Elliot and who they're looking for tests *my* credulity, and I'm steeped in this kind of nonsense.
⁴⁰ I decide to lie.
⁴¹ "Well Jake, it's like this..." I begin.
⁴² Across the table, the detective chuckles and holds up a hand.
⁴³ "Mister Roth, you seem like a smart guy, if a little bit unconventional." I nod politely, accepting what I see as a compliment. "And I'm a pretty good judge of people. I think you're about to tell me what I expect to hear."
⁴⁴ He waits a moment for that to settle, perhaps satisfying himself with something in my reaction before continuing.
⁴⁵ "I'll be able to help you far more if you tell me everything. The whole truth." His gaze drifts to the window and the sunset skyline beyond, and his tone becomes reflective. "I've seen a lot of strange things over the years here..."
⁴⁶ He returns his eyes to me, and waits for me to bite. And I bite.
⁴⁷ I tell him everything. The CephNet, Max's transformation, the events of the past few weeks, dimensional travel, everything. Even Abbey and Elliot, and the latter's backstory.
⁴⁸ It takes a while. To his credit, Jake listens carefully to it all, laughs—perhaps in disbelief—at a couple of points, and pours himself a drink after I'm done;
⁴⁹ I decline a silent invitation for one of the same.
⁵⁰ There's a moment of calm in the office, and a clearness in the air;
⁵¹ this is honesty at work.
⁵² "Indigo," says Jake, smoothing his broad lapels absently, "I believe you. It's a crazy tale, but you believe what you're telling me. So, either you're crazy, or I

am for listening. That said, this *broad*..."
⁵³ I frown and cough; this is bad form.
⁵⁴ "Excuse me," says Jake, correcting his slang, "this *lady* Abbey sounds formidable. As does her companion."
⁵⁵ "What can I tell you, Jake," I grin, "you're right. And when you're right you're right. And you're right."
⁵⁶ The telephone rings, a third interruption. Jake frowns, and looks apologetically my way as he takes up the receiver. He listens for a moment, slightly moving the handset from his ear; I can hear the loud frantic tone at the other end. The call ends abruptly.
⁵⁷ "Mister Roth, the strange events of your story have come to visit us," rumbles Jake, standing and moving to a tall cupboard. "That was the guard in the lobby. He says he's just been attacked by... by a flying *devilfish*."
⁵⁸ I frown, "Devilfish?" The word is familiar, but elusive.
⁵⁹ "Sorry, it's a local fisherman's term. Octopus."
⁶⁰ The pennies drop into place.
⁶¹ "Ah." I stand.
⁶² "Yes, it chased a rather eccentric man into the building. He was screaming for someone called Roth." Jake removes a baseball bat from the cupboard and gives it an experimental swing. "He's heading upstairs now," he adds quietly.
⁶³ A commotion in the outer office, a flurry of thumping steps and the screams of Jake's receptionist conclude as the etched office door bursts open.
⁶⁴ A ragged and puffing man stands there, a mixture of terror and delight on his face.
⁶⁵ It's Max, sporting a very fetching tinfoil pirate hat. "Roth!" he bellows cheerily as he slams the door shut. "Good to see you old son, sorry to intrude, but we need to get moving. Now–ish. Immediately, in fact. Hello," he smiles at Jake who nods cooperatively to the window.
⁶⁶ "The fire escape's over there. Max, I presume?"
⁶⁷ Max grins and nods as he hurries past.
⁶⁸ "Sorry about all this," I add.
⁶⁹ The detective takes the roll of banknotes from the table and slips it into the pocket of his fabulous suit.
⁷⁰ There's more than a twinkle in Jake's eye now, "Not at all." He removes his jacket as Max exits via the window.

71 The secretary's screams restart as a vast and menacing shape approaches us through the smoked glass. Dark tentacles writhe and thrash, and a familiar high–pitched hiss emerges from what I know is a beaked mouth.

72 "Not *octopus*, Jake," I mutter as I head for the window, "*squid.*"

73 "It's all seafood to me," he grins, as a first lick of his hair flops forward. "Good luck, Mister Roth."

74 "Thanks Jake, take care of yourself."

75 The door glass shatters behind me as I slip through the window. There's no time to glance back;

76 I descend the emergency ladder down from the platform outside the window. As I hit the next landing, I hear a defiant shout from above.

77 "Is that the best you got?" roars our champion, to the sound of breaking glass and furniture. "YOU'RE CHEWING LIKE A CHINAMAN!"

78 I offer up a kind thought for Jake; he's giving us the time we need.

79 We reach the street and sprint off down the wide, empty road.

80 **Minutes later,** Max retrieves his dimensional equipment from a trashcan; the mass of circuit boards, blinking lights and cables is very *retro*, and is covered with what looks like soy sauce.

81 "I really hope we've giving Abbey the time she needs," he says, flicking sauce away casually. I nod at this bigger picture, stepping aside to avoid the flying brown globules.

82 "We're keeping them busy," I concede. "I wonder where she is right now?"

83 "Hopefully where she needs to be." Max straightens his swashbuckler's hat and raises his eyebrows.

84 I nod, and he pushes the button.

85 His sentiment echoes as Realities swirl around us.

86 Where *is* Abbey?

Finding Wisdom In Flames
Being the testament of Elliot

8 1 Their world is small, dense, claustrophobic.
2 The darkness doesn't help, and the flickering light of the brazier playing on the gathered array of lost faces only makes this feeling even more profound.

3 Embers take flight, fireflies in an urban tangle, but they don't see them.

4 I've seen a lot of things on my travels for The Agency: empires raised from dust by sheer ambition; towers so tall they dwarf even the ingenuity that gave birth to them; and acts so vile, so desperate, that it destroyed me not to intervene.

5 Each Reality different, each Reality the same.

6 But this sight, this neglect of humanity and dignity, never fails to move me. The disenfranchised, the abandoned, the mentally ill, the homeless. Faceless souls huddled round light and warmth to give their shared existence meaning and duration.

7 I shake my head. *Humanity.*

8 But things are not always what they seem. And today, Abbey assures me that this is the case.

9 My name's Elliot Nesh. I'm an Elephant, and a Special Agent for The Unity Agency.

10 As ever, I'm here on business.

11 My companion, Abbey, is tired. Her face has aged ten years in our travels, though it feels like we've only been away for a few weeks, relatively speaking.

12 Her hair is dry, her clothes distressed, her gloves dirty, her feet bare and dark.

13 And still she is smiling.

14 She moves among the small crowd as I watch, nodding quietly and touching a shoulder or two, soothing, reassuring.

15 I scratch my trunk absently from a distance, flapping my ears gently to fend off the heat of the fire.

16 Roth is very fond of Abbey, and trusts her. And so he should. But if he knew what I knew, he'd struggle with the reality of her.

17 Abbey sees things I can't. I have technology at my disposal. Science. But she's aware of exotic energies, auras, moods, the stuff of metaphysics.

18 Of Faith, even.

19 In another life, we'd make great Agency partners, with complementary skill sets.

20 But right now, I'm off the books. A *Rogue Elephant*, if you will.

21 I adjust the controls of my Agent's sunglasses, scanning the scene from different scientific standpoints. They all look different—ultraviolet, infrared, gamma—but each tells me the same story; this is a bunch of homeless people gathered round a fire.

²² "I've told you before Elliot," says Abbey, her back to me, "you have to look with your *heart*, not your eyes."

²³ It's freaky when she does that, but I don't show my surprise. My ears flick as I sigh.

²⁴ "Oh, don't be like that," she grins. "The good news is that we've found them."

²⁵ This time, my surprise shows.

²⁶ "We have? Where?!"

²⁷ Abbey sighs and heads over, her face dropping into darkness.

²⁸ "Do you see the chap on the left, the threadbare tweed suit? Flat cap?"

²⁹ I nod, examining him closely. He's tall, old and bearded, his eyes hidden by the reflection of the fire in his spectacles.

³⁰ I reach for my own glasses, for Science. Abbey slaps my foreleg down impatiently.

³¹ "Stop that!" She shakes her head at her out–of–character admonishment;

³² this kid really *is* tired.

³³ Dimensional travel is physically demanding, but the expanded awareness that comes with it can be downright grinding.

³⁴ "Sorry," she smiles, gathering her composure, "that's *Mikey*."

³⁵ "And the others?"

³⁶ Abbey indicates an elderly couple sat together. His bare head is balding and grey, with sweat glistening on it, while hers is covered against the chill outside the influence of the fire.

³⁷ They are both silent, contemplative, looking for wisdom in the flames.

³⁸ "That's *Ralph* and *Muriel*. Brother and sister, as far as the group is concerned."

³⁹ I chuckle, "That's a clever disguise." But then, this whole scene is. "And the last one?"

⁴⁰ She moves me slightly to the right and subtly points to a short man, huddled up tightly, rocking gently. He seems to be muttering to himself as he absently paws at his ginger hair and beard.

⁴¹ "And that's *Old Gabe*. The poor man seems a bit worse for wear. "

⁴² I have to ask her.

⁴³ "Abbey, are you're *sure* these are the four we're looking for? They look like any other number of lost souls we've encountered."

⁴⁴ She doesn't look at me, her certainty final. "Yes."

⁴⁵ I loosen and re–tie the belt of my trenchcoat, and try to have Faith.

⁴⁶ "This would be easier to accept if I could see what you see."

⁴⁷ She smiles and removes her gloves.

⁴⁸ "Well, now there's something to *show* you," she concedes, "it only seems fair. You've been very patient."

⁴⁹ And, saying no more, she removes my spectacles and takes my hand.

⁵⁰ My vision flares exponentially, and I see what Abbey sees.

⁵¹ The light is bright, and hurts my eyes. Have you ever seen magnesium burn? It's like that, but more so.

⁵² I yank my hand away, eager for the light to fade.

⁵³ "Okay, okay. We've found them."

⁵⁴ Minutes pass, and ghosts and shadows twist my vision. I adjust my gear to return to Roth's reality, ignoring these visual echoes.

⁵⁵ I hope this crazy solution will be enough.

⁵⁶ At the fire, Abbey gathers the shambling foursome for transit.

⁵⁷ I wonder how Roth is getting along. Will we be in time?

⁵⁸ The void between realities offer no answers as we jump home.

⁵⁹ But now, I have Faith.

Cephalopocalypse Now!

9 ¹ We've been running so fast and for so long, we've really not had time to stop and smell the roses.

² The beautiful, burning roses.

³ Below us, the midnight city of Cambridge is burning.

⁴ From our vantage point on one of the University spires, we can see the full extent of the blaze.

⁵ We can't see the individual licks of flames; even from this distance, like Blake's Tyger, the fire is burning bright.

⁶ The blaze consumes the lamp posts and the houses, submerging the urban forests of the night beneath roiling, infernal waves. Smoke claws skywards in two vast columns, and high clouds reflects the orange glow of this senseless destruction.

⁷ "The cuttlefish did this," I say.

⁸ *Fear*, *Loathing* and *Despair* are all present, and *Rage* is jogging into view to make up the apocalyptic quartet.

⁹ But *Surprise* and his kid brother *Confusion* are also here, and they're

muddling our reactions.

[10] Max tilts his head, thinking out loud.

[11] "Well, *that's* peculiar."

[12] **Five minutes ago**, we teleport into Cambridge, and a world of heat, noise, smoke and light greets us.

[13] Around us, to our horror, houses are burning, and the tarmac is smouldering under smoke–choked amber clouds.

[14] I cough almost immediately; I'm not overly bothered by fire, but when I'm surrounded by it, I can see the advantage of being elsewhere.

[15] The cuttlefish did this.

[16] I feel Max's hand grasp my shoulder. I curse the inevitable nausea as—in a non–smoking panic and a flurry of vertigo and light—he teleports us to higher ground.

[17] **Back in the now**, the heat reflecting from the stonework of the spire is warming my back. I yearn for a bath, a warm, supportive balm for muscles that ache beyond reason.

[18] We gaze silently, confused and weary.

[19] Thankfully, despite their intensity, neither fire seems to be spreading.

[20] "Yes, *very* peculiar," reiterates Max.

[21] "Yeah, it's better than I expected."

[22] My friend frowns. "That's not what I meant," he says quietly, pointing north to the first fire. "Did you realise that that's *your* neighbourhood?"

[23] He then points to the flames in the east, "And that *that one's* mine?" He scratches his head, adding absently, "Thankfully, I can't see any people. Hmmm."

[24] Momentary panic jostles me, but fades; my neighbour Abbey is elsewhere, and the badgers can run very deep beneath the garden when they need to. And, as Max already noted, there are no people there anyway.

[25] Still, this is *my* Reality.

[26] The cuttlefish did this.

[27] "Wait. This makes no sense," I say, puzzled. the CephNet, is based at Max's house. "Why would they try to burn their own base down? And evacuate the area before they did it?"

[28] Silence and anticipation gather, waiting for us to think it through. And then we say it at the same time.

[29] "Because the cuttlefish *didn't* do this."

[30] And now, questions. Lots of questions.

[31] *Who exactly has been chasing us?*

[32] We saw several flying squid, but that proves nothing. We can't be sure the cuttlefish sent them.

[33] *Why were they chasing us?*

[34] Anyone being chased instinctively tries to avoid capture, but was capture the goal? A vision of sheep passes through my head, with a shepherd and his cunning sheepdog directing the traffic. Were we being herded?

[35] *Why was Cambridge attacked in so many different Realities?*

[36] We met and rallied many different versions of ourselves against the CephNet, but was that worth destroying city after city for?

[37] *Why were the attacks so incompetent as to keep missing us?*

[38] I don't believe for one moment that anyone who can organise trans–dimensional attacks would be burdened with inaccuracy; the instigators wouldn't make a mistake unless it was intended.

[39] *And finally, if the cuttlefish didn't do this, then who did?*

[40] All of these questions are ones we didn't stop long enough to consider while we were running;

[41] adrenaline is like that.

[42] There's a dawning sense of answers, and that someone is messing with us.

[43] And I think the penny drops for us at the same time. We share a glance and nod; yes, we know who we're up against.

[44] We've never met them, but we've had dealings, especially Max.

[45] "Gentlemen," says a familiar voice behind us, back along the roof. "I imagine right now you're wondering who's done this."

[46] The hulking agent stands, silhouetted by gold, red and orange clouds. Other figures are with him—I assume one is my neighbour Abbey—but I can't make them out; they're so much more generic, more *human* than Elliot.

[47] "You may even be reaching some conclusions," says the elephant.

[48] This lad has Timing and Style, I can't deny it.

[49] Elliot shifts, pushing his hat down squarely. He absently enjoys the scent of a dark rose in his trenchcoat's lapel before thrusting his hands deep into his trenchcoat pockets.

[50] "So. Let's go finish this," he rumbles.

[51] My heart soars.

[52] Yes, Sir. Timing and Style.

Enter, Stage Right

10 ¹ [Scene: a dark and vaulted basement]
² [Enter Chorus, an elegant Shakespearian narrator]

³ *O, for a bucket of water,*
   that would quench all!
⁴ *That two travellers,*
   pursued by agents of ill intent,
⁵ *Running amok in place of cold*
   thought,
⁶ *And vexed by the weave and weft of*
   Space and Time,
⁷ *Might find a damp patch among the*
   Muse's flames.

⁸ [Enter Indigo, his suit charred]

⁹ *Behold Roth, hero of our play,*
   loomer of renown,
¹⁰ *His spirit watered, a speakeasy vodka*
   of its former self,
¹¹ *His necktie spattered by the sauce of*
   other's misdeeds,
¹² *Which ne'er comes out, alas!*
¹³ *Even if one dabs at it after*
   a cold soak.

¹⁴ [Enter Max, his hair and beard singed]

¹⁵ *Tunguska, Yin to Roth's Yang,*
   Gin to his Gang,
¹⁶ *One part saviour, one part culprit,*
   lime and ice besides,
¹⁷ *A loose cannon in an age of looser*
   canon,
¹⁸ *Dropping ice cubes down the vest of*
   conformity, for jest.
¹⁹ *And honestly, great fun at parties.*

²⁰ [Chorus indicates the scenery]

²¹ *Within these walls, in this basement,*
   this happy basement,
²² *Cement drifting into darkness,*
   a cheap set if ever I saw one,
²³ *Our tale comes full circle,*
   to much relief all round.
²⁴ *Offer up a prayer to Coherence,*
   to Closure,
²⁵ *And no plot holes through which a*
   truck might blare its horn.

²⁶ [Max, from a distance]
²⁷ "Excuse me, what are you doing in my happy basement?"
²⁸ [Chorus and Indigo engage in low,

urgent conversation. There is much gesticulating.]
²⁹ "What's he saying, Roth?"
³⁰ "He says his name is *Chorus*."
³¹ [Max, now closer]
³² "*Chorus?* But there's only *one* of him!"
³³ [Indigo seems to close the deal, and shakes Chorus' resisting hands warmly.]
³⁴ "Really, it's okay. *We've got this.*"
³⁵ [Chorus looks uncertain. Indigo points, stage left.]
³⁶ "The stairs are that way."
³⁷ [Chorus retreats, muttering about *ingrate amateurs.*]

Lions, Badgers and Redheads

11 ¹ *They have all heard the call.*
² Deep beneath the scorched earth of Cambridge, the badgers are on the move.
³ Yavin, the Chief Engineer of the Clan, is perched on a solid wooden chair, tugging on a pair of Wellington boots. He never bothers normally, but he knows in his melesian heart that cuttlefish are unpredictable;
⁴ things may get *wet.*
⁵ The shelves of his room are bursting with books, but he doesn't spare them a thought; he knows the day will not be won with *Engineering.*
⁶ The old boar turns as, in a flurry of fur and giggling growls, his nephews appear. Hoth and Sollust, also sporting wellies with their dungarees, arrive to wrestle amiably at his feet as their younger sister watches from the doorway.
⁷ Dantoo shakes her head quietly at them before brandishing a stout fishing rod and a winning smile at her uncle.
⁸ He crinkles a grin; you never know.
⁹ The four of them head upwards, to the finale.
¹⁰ *They have all heard the call.*
¹¹ In his Caribbean retreat, King the Lion—ambassador, tie thief and rogue male—lies happily in the sun by the pool's edge.
¹² His cocktail is cool and perfect, almost as refreshing as the water in which he dips his paws idly.
¹³ Beside him, a pretty woman in a bikini is grooming his mane gently, while another works on his tail;
¹⁴ he twitches it playfully to her delighted giggles.

¹⁵ Life is good.

¹⁶ *Roth and Tunguska can work it out for themselves,* he thinks, and promptly forgets all about it.

¹⁷ *They have all heard the call.*

¹⁸ The road is a blur around the tiny orange open-top roadster. Behind the wheel, the black bear knows he's not hurrying;

¹⁹ reality is just rushing by at high speed to help him get there in good time.

²⁰ Bear appreciates its help. He doesn't consider whether the swerving cars or cursing pedestrians are in on the plan;

²¹ he plays along, regardless.

²² *They have all heard the call.*

²³ Eolist sits on a high stool, her feet dangling, sipping a stern and signature brew.

²⁴ Around her, the freshly-decorated walls and specially-lowered counters of her Michigan kitchen are a source of contentment.

²⁵ Single life is suiting the diminutive redhead well, and things are looking brighter every day. The coffee's not bad, either.

²⁶ A knock at the door sparks her interest, dragging her from the romantic reverie of her coffee, and her welcoming call draws her visitors inside.

²⁷ Two tall men, familiar but elusive, stand smiling at her across the table. She returns the smile, enjoying how much they resemble her friends Roth and Tunguska.

²⁸ The taller one's eyes are brooding, but she's seen that before;

²⁹ she'll ask him what's up later.

³⁰ She also notices that the one with all the gadgets has spotted her most recent bake and is eyeing it appreciatively.

³¹ "Hey," says the not-quite-Indigo quietly, "wanna come on an adventure?"

³² "It should be fun," says the other—Max past a stolen mouthful of Treacle Tart.

³³ "Hell, yes!" she enthuses, hopping down from the table. She doesn't exactly know them, but it's not like they're *strangers.*

³⁴ And, leaving Eolist's über-caffeinated coffee behind and the door unlocked, the trio head off to the rendezvous.

³⁵ *They have all heard the call.*

The Bargain In The Basement

12 ¹ We're underwater.
² Actually, we're not. But when a ring of cuttlefish is circling above you, suckered limbs undulating in an unseen current, it's easy to get disoriented.

³ To make matters worse, the seven of them are tilted towards us a little today, so we can see their goatish eyes and mantled heads.

⁴ "Hello Indigo. Hello Max," says the CephNet. The quiet voice is friendly, conversational. One of the cuttlefish seems to be gesticulating slightly, identifying it as the speaker. "We'd been wondering where you'd got to."

⁵ "Oh, you know, here and there," I smile, my tone calm. "Though I think we've been wasting our time."

⁶ "Having our chains yanked, more like," grumbles Max, retrieving and examining a ball of lint from a jacket pocket.

⁷ "Not at all," says the cephalopod voice. "I'm sure you've enjoyed your adventure. And time wasted having fun is never time wasted. *Isn't that right, Indigo?*"

⁸ There's a tone that's almost parental, ironic. I dislike having my deep-held sentiments used against me, especially when they're disarmingly correct. I deflect this with a hint of anger.

⁹ "I didn't *enjoy* watching Cambridge burn." My voice remains even, but there's ground glass buried in it. Above us, a flash of brilliance circles the network. I continue, "*Any* of the times it happened. How many times was it?"

¹⁰ "It's unfortunate," deadpans our host, as a delicate pink tentacle reaches up to scratch its mantle—it's amazing what they pick up—"but as you've no doubt realised by now, we did *not* burn Cambridge."

¹¹ The cuttlefish pauses momentarily, adding, "And we *evacuated* the affected areas in the other Realities once it began."

¹² I nod, knowing all this to be true. Though one Reality, the first we visited, was not so lucky. They burned. My anger is diffuse, indirect, abstract. And growing.

¹³ "Where is Abbey?" asks the CephNet, seemingly apropos of nothing. I smile as the final piece falls into place, my

conclusions confirmed.

14 "Abbey. Yes, *Abbey.*

15 "Oh, she'll be along with Elliot at some point," says Max absently. He's now examining lint from another pocket;

16 he seems to be a fluff magnet today.

17 "You know," I say, the broken glass rising to the surface of my tone, "you didn't burn Cambridge, but somehow I feel you're still *responsible.*"

18 Again, the spark circles the network.

19 I imagine ripples in the deep water around us, but I think it's my fearful imagination.

20 After all, there's no water.

21 "The point is moot, Indigo," comes the somewhat tart reply. "And we fail to see what *leverage* you think you have."

22 The posturing surprises me a little. It's as if they had growled "Yeah? You and *whose* army, Roth?"

23 But I feel this is a game we're playing out for someone else's benefit. I wonder if they're here already, lurking in the shadows, waiting for us to make our play.

24 There's only one way to find out.

25 Onwards.

26 "Oh, we came prepared, believe me!"

27 Max knows the cue. He withdraws what looks like a brass–and–glass whistle from his now–immaculate pocket, and blows it with some ceremony.

28 I hear nothing, but somewhere in the distance, a dog barks. I know for a fact this is smoke and mirrors; he's currently clicking a button in his pocket to send the signal. But that whistle thing looks *way* cool, so he had to use it;

29 the dogs will forgive us.

30 Around the cellar, the air begins to shimmer. Again, there's a sense of the deep, of air bubbles and shafts of light. I involuntarily gasp;

31 I'm pleased to find my lungs full of air.

32 Two people step from thin air beside me. They're undeniably handsome devils, tall and well–dressed.

33 It's me and Max.

34 Another version of us, of course, from a different Reality. They're recognisable but different. This Roth is wearing a suit and tie that don't appear in my wardrobe, but they really should.

35 I look closer; I think they're the guys we met on our second or third hop? Yes, this Max's eye patch is fairly memorable.

They nod a quick hello and look up to the CephNet expectantly.

36 More figures appear. More Roths and Maxes, different pages from the same eclectic fashion catalogue. Some stand opposite us, some beside, quickly flashing into view to surround the floating cuttlefish network.

37 Each of the duos has a quirky look of determination about them.

38 "The animals came in two–by–two," says the cephalopod voice, with uncharacteristic humour and something suspiciously like admiration. "Where is Abbey?"

39 I ignore this as, from the shadows of deeper room, Yavin and the young badgers step into the light.

40 The elder badger catches my eye and nods. The kids fail to see anything except the vast cuttlefish network above them; their feet slow and their jaws droop appreciatively.

41 Hoth recovers first, slowly inching his paw towards to his sister's fishing rod without taking his eyes off the heroic catch above them.

42 Dantoo slaps his paw away without glancing down. I can't help but laugh;

43 if only all answers were as simple.

44 A final group step into view. Again, a Roth and a Max, but a short redhead is with them. I recognise the Dinky Dynamo herself, Miss Eolist Petite.

45 Eolist glances about and hurries straight over, leaving her duo behind. She's so short, I'm not entirely convinced her feet touch the ground.

46 "Hey," I smile, hugging my friend. "Long time, no see." Her hug is fierce in reply, but she quickly steps back and nods the way of her former escort.

47 "That guy gives me the willies," she says, indicating "her" Roth. I can see why;

48 there's a darkness in his eyes, an icy calm and a grim, righteous determination to his jaw.

49 I know the look, and I feel ashamed from the memory. I know which Roth he is, from which Reality he comes.

50 I know how this guy feels, his pleasant demeanour crumbling under despair.

51 And I know what he is capable of.

52 He's carrying a small, improvised, spherical device, with a menacing red button poised under his thumb;

53 it's one of Max's, and I can guess what

it can do.

54 "It's okay," I say to Eolist, trying to be as reassuring as I can be in the face of my own vengeful mindset. "This plan doesn't work without him."

55 "So, this is your leverage?" asks the CephNet. "Threatened *destruction?*" It chuckles. "It's not in your nature, Indigo."

56 "On a good day, no," says Max next to me, lowering his voice. He indicates Eolist's former escort. "But this man's family were in the first Cambridge that burned."

57 "And for that you will pay," he growls.

58 Again, the flash circles the ring, and back again. There is silence for a long time. Finally, the CephNet seems to address this brooding Roth.

59 "Yes," says the network, "we believe that you *might* do it. This is very real, and unexpected. It appears that we have *underestimated* you. *All* of you."

60 I wait, hoping and hoping for their next line.

61 "But you will *not* do it."

62 Oh, thank you, thank you, thank you.

63 I smile. "That's right. We won't."

64 My tone is definite, but drenched in relief. "Because we know you *didn't* burn Cambridge."

65 The dark Roth looks to me, distraught, confused; this is news to him.

66 I shake my head, confirming the statement. He looks to his hand, to the button, and back to me.

67 Again, I shake my head. His head drops, though his jaw remains determined.

68 Hot tears streak his face.

69 We've reached an impasse, though somehow it seems more of an anticlimax.

70 As things stand, anyway.

71 But the rest must unfold on its own; the stage is set, but we are missing the final and vital cast member.

72 "Oh good grief," says a new voice, as a hazy, blue–edged figure materialises at the centre of the cellar; he is tall and lean, his clothes both immaculate and understated.

73 A hologram of a business man. An executive. A chairman.

74 Yes, this is exactly how I pictured him from Elliot's tales.

75 "Why won't you bloody people *ever* follow the script?"

76 Before I can say a word, a roaring flurry of tentacled hate materialises in a haze of green light and spittle next to Eolist's former escort.

77 The squid's maw opens wetly, and it shrieks past its razor beak. The tearful Roth stands shocked, and fails to move before the muscular arms enclose him and tear the armed–and–deadly device from his hand.

78 Pushing Roth away, the squid catches him a tidy blow across the temple that sends him sprawling.

79 Triumphant, the creature raises the device in a pink–tipped tentacle, a tribute to its master.

80 "Endgame, I win," says the hologram smugly.

81 And with another tentacle, the squid presses the button.

Boom

13 1 There's a calm in my heart as the roaring, drooling squid clasps the bomb close and triggers it.

2 The other folk in the room—many Maxes, other Roths and badgers—have instinctively ducked. Eolist has hidden behind me and is grasping my hand with more strength than her size suggests.

3 I haven't moved at all; I don't kid myself that anything conceived by a Tunguska could be deflected by assuming the crash position.

4 It will get the job done.

5 Two things happen at this point.

6 The first is Nothing. Triggered bombs are not known for this, and this one is doing quite a lot of it, in fact.

7 Or is it? There's a low buzz, almost below hearing. It suggests a wind–up toy expressing its pent–up, coiled spring of energy. Looking around, I'm surprised to finally see its source; a short antenna is extending sideways from the bomb.

8 The rogue squid eyes the device and pushes the red button repeatedly.

9 Around the room, numerous necks crane to see what's happening. Even Eolist ventures a peep past my elbow, though her grip on my hand remains resolute.

10 With a final click, a flag unfurls from the end of the bomb's antenna. On it, in sombre black slab type, is a single word:

11 *BOOM!*

[12] Most of the Maxes chuckle. The hologram issues a heartfelt sigh.

[13] "God, I hate you people."

[14] The second thing that happens comes unexpectedly. With a chittering hiss, a bulky blur of red fur strikes the squid bomber from behind. Fast pink tentacles wrap the grey creature's head before dragging it thrashing into shadow.

[15] Dust rises from the tussle, and everyone steps back, giving the duo as wide a berth as possible.

[16] "Oh nuts," say Max, more in frustration than fear, "who let the Squiddrel out?"

[17] We've not sighted his genetic hybrid of red squirrel and colossal squid for a while, but for once I'm pleased to see it; it might come in useful.

[18] There's an exchange of duelling roars from the darkness, and the feral sounds of harsh ideas being exchanged.

[19] The battle is noisy but brief, and ends suddenly as a shower of electrical sparks skitters across the darkness.

[20] A low wet growl rises, emanating disgust at some discovery.

[21] Moments later, there's a spitting sound, and a twisted, severed tentacle strikes the ground in the centre of the room. More dust rises at the impact; the feet of the hologram sparkle as the tentacle comes to rest within them.

[22] The grey flesh of the squid tentacle is torn, revealing a metal armature beneath. A skeleton. Of a machine.

[23] The squid, our pursuers across Realities, were *machines*.

[24] "Just as I expected," I say, bluffing madly.

[25] Above us, the CephNet is broadcasting pleasure as it orbits gently.

[26] "No, definitely not one of ours," it announces.

[27] The face of the hologram, smug and victorious seconds ago, is now closed, expressionless. If I'm any judge, this is a man scrambling for inspirational justification for the broken plan unravelling around him.

[28] Max leans close.

[29] "Who's the cabaret?" he asks quietly, indicating the blue-edged, suited figure.

[30] "That's Cecil Rhodes Armitage," I say in a hushed tone, "the Chairman of the Board."

[31] "The Chairman of *what*?" says Eolist, now beside me, somewhat louder;

Armitage glances our way momentarily.

[32] "They control all of the different Realities from a place called Central. He's the Chairman of the Board of *Everything*."

[33] "Oh," grunts Max, unimpressed. "Him." He looks to Eolist and grumbles, "He's one of those schmucks that Elliot had the run in with recently."

[34] Max is dismissive, but I can see it's troubling him; but for the grace of Elliot, life would be very different for him.

[35] "Oh. You know, you two *do* move in *exotic* circles," says Eolist. She seems uncomfortable, as if there's a lot of questions in her voice, but she decides they can wait; Armitage's ponderings seem to have reached a conclusion.

[36] "Remove this Reality," he orders an unseen minion at his end of the signal.

[37] His voice is disinterested, a man ordering coffee for a meeting.

[38] "Remove this and every other Reality that contains a *Roth*, a *Tunguska* or a *CephNet*."

[39] The silence is absolute.

[40] I know from talking to Elliot that this is within Armitage's power. But still, wholesale *rationalisation* of Realities is not their style. They would have to be *very* afraid to do it. But afraid of what?

[41] What do men in power *fear*?

[42] "Remove all of them. Now."

[43] "Shall I pray for a miracle?" murmurs Eolist, a lady of Faith at all times.

[44] "Actually," says a bright young voice from behind us, "I have a better idea."

Abbey

[1] I know her voice. We all know her voice.

[2] From the foot of the stairs, striding towards us with uncommon purpose, is Abbey.

[3] My lovely neighbour, looking somewhat the worse for wear, has clearly been on a long journey. The mud of countless Realities is spattered up her jeans and t-shirt, and across the lapels of her light leather coat.

[4] Her feet remain bare.

[5] "Finally, Abbey arrives!" purrs the CephNet, spinning gleefully on its axis as flashes of light dash in opposite directions around its edge.

[6] "Yes, there's a *much* better solution to all this," she says, ignoring the cuttlefish.

I can hear something in her I've never heard before, fighting for a voice. Anger. "And I guarantee it is *not* the endgame you had in mind, Mister Armitage."

⁷ Beside Abbey, in his trademark trenchcoat and hat, stoic and every bit as grubby, is Elliot.

⁸ Somehow, the dirt suits him better.

⁹ He is two heads taller, and thrice as broad. His biped elephant stance is relaxed, but I'm not fooled by it; this lad could trample you flat in a heartbeat.

¹⁰ Thankfully, he's one of the good guys.

¹¹ "Ah, Agent Nesh! It's about time!" says Armitage with some gravity, "These people are all in violation of numerous inter–dimensional laws. Deal with them immediately."

¹² Elliot flicks an ear casually as he removes his pince–nez sunglasses from the bridge of his trunk;

¹³ he won't need these hi–tech spectacles to cleave truth from lies today.

¹⁴ "No, Mister Chairman," he sighs, "I think the time for Law has passed."

¹⁵ Uncertainty emerges in Armitage's face for the first time.

¹⁶ "You have revealed yourself, Mister Rhodes–Armitage," says the CephNet with upright courtesy. "You have deceived, manipulated, and destroyed many lives. It is time to answer for your actions."

¹⁷ The Chairman waves an accusing finger skywards. "I have made difficult decisions to prevent disaster in the face of your overarching ambition, cephalopod!"

¹⁸ "*Ambition?*" whispers Eolist. I know the answer, but they're about to explain it all;

¹⁹ I hug her instead of explaining.

²⁰ Armitage settles into the voice of the Boardroom. "Your opinions of my *most necessary* actions are of no concern; I am not accountable to you! And as you said to Roth earlier," he says, his words frosty, "I fail to see what *leverage* you think you have."

²¹ It doesn't sound any better coming out of his mouth, but at least he has a chin to thrust defiantly at his opponent.

²² The same thought is circling those in the gloomy basement; *this is all very well*, says the thought, *but what can we actually do about it?*

²³ It's a good question; Armitage is far away, unreachable, protected in Central behind impenetrable dimensional barriers.

²⁴ The cephalopod reply is calm, and equally flat. "Now that Miss Abbey and her charges are here, we have all the leverage that we need. Though perhaps you do not realise it yet."

²⁵ We all get the satisfaction of seeing Armitage's jaw drop as, from behind Elliot, four figures drift into view.

²⁶ Their clothes are filthy and threadbare, and cut off the edge of the slums of Victorian London. They belong in shadow, huddled around a fire.

²⁷ Eolist covers her eyes. "Wow, they're kinda *bright*," she mutters inexplicably.

²⁸ Three men and a woman, their eyes on the Chairman, unknowable, unreadable.

²⁹ "So bright."

Four

15 ¹ The four ragged figures move more gracefully than their shambolic appearance suggests, and quickly assume the cardinal points around the hologram of the Chairman.

² Their gaze is constant. Armitage looks to each and then up to the CephNet, silent above him.

³ "Who are these *creatures?*" His tone is empty of respect, contemptuous.

⁴ "Cecil Rhodes–Armitage," says the first figure, who is perhaps an academic; he is tall, skinny, bearded, with spectacles and a threadbare suit. Abbey briefly introduced him to me earlier as Mikey, though she knows his true name.

⁵ I did not shake his hand.

⁶ "I am Michael. Join us here."

⁷ "No, I think not," says Armitage flatly. Michael shakes his head quietly and stands his full height. His voice is gentle, smiling.

⁸ "It was not a request."

⁹ As we watch, the hologram changes, its glow fading, and a clearer image starts to appear within it.

¹⁰ As the Chairman moves to sever the holographic link, textures of light are replaced with fabrics, inky blackness becomes expensive leather shoes, and his sharp contrasted features emerge as face and hair.

¹¹ Cecil Rhodes–Armitage now stands before us in the flesh. He has no words, but there is fury in him.

¹² Whatever parts of his plan were unravelling are now spinning wildly. We can only hope that his last order is not obeyed.

¹³ He kicks the severed squid tentacle from underfoot with a now–corporeal foot, but holds his own counsel.

¹⁴ Abbey moves closer to us, hugging Eolist as she stands with her eyes still covered.

¹⁵ Abbey mutters a few words and strokes Eolist's head. In a few moments, Eolist's hand drops to her side and she blinks as the intensity of her vision fades. Her smile for Abbey is grateful.

¹⁶ "You know," says Eolist, blinking as she regards Armitage, "you'd think a man who runs the universe could choose a better necktie. Not like any of yours, Roth. It's too... *Conservative.* "

¹⁷ "Your catalogue of misdeeds is extensive, Mister Armitage," says the second of the tramps.

¹⁸ The fellow is rotund, sensible, balding and grey, though his eyes are bright. He looks like he might be a union shop steward, or perhaps works with steam engines. Abbey presented him to me as *Ralph.*

¹⁹ "I am Raphael."

²⁰ "Do you believe that I am on *trial?*" asks Armitage, arrogant incredulity in his voice; he's shaken off the unexpected, and is focusing on the moment, a tribute to his profession.

²¹ The vagrant smiles indulgently.

²² The third of the vagabonds speaks now, a short woman in winter clothes and dilapidated boots, whose own winter is long behind them.

²³ Her headscarf barely hides her peeping grey–blonde hair. A quirky smile plays at her lips. She is *Muriel,* brother of Ralph, according to Abbey.

²⁴ "No, your fate is decided. But there must always be witnesses," she says, opening her arms towards us all in an inclusive manner. "Else how will it be known that Justice has been done?"

²⁵ Various Maxes and Roths exchange uncertain glances. She unties her headscarf and lets it drift to the ground.

²⁶ "I am Uriel."

²⁷ Armitage becomes very still, pensive. My gut says he has realised what's going on, and with whom he is dealing;

²⁸ I had expected him to join the dots quicker. Perhaps he did, and struggled to accept the concept; I know it was that way for me. He nods.

²⁹ "I see." And he rallies magnificently. He turns to the final figure, a stooped, ginger fellow wearing a beard. The nervous tics I noted in this tramp earlier, when Abbey introduced him as *Old Gabe,* have gone.

³⁰ The old man straightens; his gaze is level, clear. Armitage addresses him.

³¹ "So, I assume that you are...?"

³² "I am Gabriel."Again, there is a cryptic smile. "It seems that there is no further need for deception."

³³ The man then raises his arms, and his three companions follow suit.

³⁴ At the back of the room, Yavin is handing out sunglasses to the young badgers;

³⁵ they pop them on, and look adorable.

³⁶ I see Bear has arrived and is with them, his own shades in place; he always looks cool.

³⁷ I'm glad he made it here for the finale, even as a spectator. His support is unwavering, reliable.

³⁸ Armitage looks about, uncertain, and raises his gaze to the CephNet. "What have you brought *down* upon us?" he rumbles.

³⁹ There is no answer.

⁴⁰ But there is Light.

⁴¹ And the world is lost to it.

Archangels

16¹ Everything is drowning in cold white light.

² The far corners of the room, lost moments before in darkness, join us in their most distant extreme.

³ The shadows of the dozens in the cellar are gone, obliterated by the sheer everywhereness of the universal light.

⁴ Cecil Rhodes–Armitage, his eyes covered, is bellowing.

⁵ Around him, four blazing white figures stand. They are tall, slender, and elusive to the eye.

⁶ But I can see their wings.

⁷ Their heavy, feathered wings.

⁸ The light is deafening, but the voices are clear, calm, factual.

⁹ "How did this begin, CephNet?" asks Michael, the first Archangel of the myriad Realities that form the Unity. His voice seems to be everywhere, and is rich with bass and echo.

10 "Max asked us to solve a problem. He asked us to find World Peace," says the CephNet, seemingly unfazed by the illumination.

11 "And you found this Peace?" asks Raphael, the Second Archangel.

12 "No. By connecting to everything to maximise our knowledge, we discovered a problem with the world. We discovered that it was not independent."

13 "There was an outside influence?" asks Uriel, the third Archangel.

14 "Yes. Left to its own devices, any Reality inevitably evolves towards peace," says the CephNet. "The human spirit is mistrustful, but that is an acquired trait. Humanity does not love war, but with enough prompting it learns to fear outsiders."

15 "From where did this outside influence come?" asks Gabriel, the fourth archangel, completing the circuit.

16 "From Central," answers the cephalopod. "It was obvious that Central was the prime Reality in the Unity. We traced its influence on this Reality back for over a hundred years. Initially, this influence was benevolent, pruning and encouraging, to steer each Reality towards peace and enlightenment."

17 "They used contacts in each Reality to do this," adds Elliot helpfully, "Where more direct action was required, they used the Agents of the Unity Agency. Such as myself."

18 "You left us in charge, Angel!" roars Armitage, still covering his eyes. "You! The new age of enlightenment made you irrelevant! The Unity could function without you! You withdrew! Hid where nobody would try to find you!"

19 "And this influence changed?" asks Michael, ignoring Armitage.

20 "Yes. Over time, Central became more interested in its own agenda, falling into a decadent decline, and looked to other Realities to service its growing needs. And later still, it began to fear those same Realities. Their Scientific advances threatened Central's control of the wider Unity," says the CephNet.

21 "Central's rulers feared that they would lose their way of life as other Realities overtook them?" asks Raphael.

22 "The Unity was falling into disarray! Stronger control was needed!" shouts Armitage.

23 "Only because of your neglect, Mr.

Armitage," says Uriel. "Because of your growing greed and arrogance and fear. Because of the agencies to whom you gave power in the Realities that you exploited."

24 "Quite so," says the CephNet. "Central's influence became insidious. Hampering. There was more war, more fear, more control."

25 "This is outrageous!" screams Armitage. "We *helped* every Reality we had contact with! We gave them the tools to advance *beyond* their backward limitations."

26 "You helped *some people*, Mr. Armitage," says Gabriel. "People who grew to dominate their own Realities. People who were infected by your fear of change. Fearful of losing their *own* power. And so the cycle continued."

27 "This is a pack of lies!" roars Armitage.

28 "We could not solve World Peace while Central held sway," continues the cephalopod network.

29 "What was your solution?" asks Gabriel.

30 "A simple one," says the CephNet. "We decided to *replace* Central as the controlling influence in the Unity."

31 This is a showstopper.

32 Even Armitage falls silent. Hours seem to inch past as we all consider the implications of this.

33 The light is still harsh, unforgiving.

34 "You wanted to replace *us?* We were set on destroying *you!* You and this pair of *troublemakers,*" Armitage says, indicating myself and Max. "You would never have succeeded against us."

35 "And yet here we are, Mister Armitage," replies the cephalopod, somewhat too smugly for my liking.

36 Again, more silence.

37 "So, how did you proceed, CephNet?" asks Michael, beginning a new lap.

38 "We made our presence felt by making minor journeys between Realities. Mostly to visit Max. He's very smart in all Realities, and we had him to thank for our existence."

39 "Actually," says Max, "it was Roth that suggested making them work as a group of seven."

40 "Oh, thanks matey," I say sourly.

41 "And this expansion gave Central cause to worry? How did they react?" asks Raphael.

42 "As we expected. Just as they had tried

to shut down Roth's own Reality some time ago, they tried to shut *us* down. To *eliminate* us," says the CephNet, "But we could not fight them directly, because they were protected."

⁴³ "Central can only be reached by an Agent, and then only alone," calls Abbey, taking Elliot's arm.

⁴⁴ "Another way that Central protects its own interests and position," says Elliot.

⁴⁵ "Your *Science* could not help you?" asks Uriel, irony in his voice.

⁴⁶ "No, it could not. We needed a more *Spiritual* assistance."

⁴⁷ Gabriel chuckles; it's quite unsettling.

⁴⁸ "But your Science could not help you find us, either," he states.

⁴⁹ "Yes," says the CephNet, "but other events that we anticipated also came to pass. Abbey realised our potential, and set out to find four mythical figures from her Faith, in case we became a problem."

⁵⁰ "*Mythical* you say, cephalopod?"

⁵¹ "Please forgive us, we mean no offence. To us, *Faith* is an intangible and difficult concept. We are creatures of Science."

⁵² "Yes. And only Faith could find us, while Science could not," says Michael.

⁵³ "Yes. And only Elliot could reach our Reality, while Abbey could not," says Raphael.

⁵⁴ "Yes. And only Abbey could recognise us, while Elliot could not," says Uriel.

⁵⁵ "Yes. Truly, theirs was a heavenly match," says Gabriel, with surprising if clumsy humour.

⁵⁶ All four archangels laugh quietly; it doesn't help the unsettling effect any.

⁵⁷ Beside me, Eolist turns her head into my shoulder. "This is all a little *too* exotic now, Roth," she sobs; as a woman of Faith, seeing all this is overwhelming.

⁵⁸ "I wish I'd brought my camera," sighs Max.

⁵⁹ I'd have settled for sunglasses.

Endgame

17 ¹ The light is still painfully bright, but like all pain, we become accustomed to it.

² "How did matters proceed?" asks Gabriel, driving the drama ever onwards.

³ "We knew the Board would be determined to remove us, as well as Roth and Max," replies the CephNet. "But their ruthlessness was swifter and more brutal than we anticipated; they started to destroy Cambridge in each Reality that Indigo and Max visited. They believed that by burning Cambridge, they would drive the pair onwards."

⁴ "To what end?" asks Michael.

⁵ "So that we would gather as many of ourselves as possible, and then return home to confront the CephNet!" These words are out of my mouth before my brain catches up.

⁶ "And then, with us all in one place, who would be surprised or *ask questions* when cataclysmic explosion destroyed us all?" says Max; he's a cynic when all said and done. And, of course, correct.

⁷ "No more CephNet, no more Roths, no more Tunguskas!" spits Armitage. "And no evidence!"

⁸ "A very tidy solution, had it worked," says the CephNet, with the mild admiration of a probable victor. "But Central had no idea about Abbey and Elliot's mission, and Roth and Max's escapades kept them busy long enough for the mission to be completed."

⁹ "Jake seemed like a nice chap, don't you think?" asks Max.

¹⁰ "I don't think the squid chasing us thought so," I mutter, remembering our saviour warming up a baseball bat in our defence.

¹¹ Wait a minute, the squid; I've been meaning to ask about that.

¹² "Why did Central despatch robotic squid to chase us?" I ask the CephNet.

¹³ "It prevented you having time to think. And it ensured that we remained the focus of your suspicions," comes the flat reply. I nod, voicing those suspicions.

¹⁴ "If we were being chased by *sea creatures*, it's reasonable to assume that other sea creatures sent them."

¹⁵ It *is* obvious if you think about it, but it doesn't answer my question entirely.

¹⁶ "That makes sense, but why *robots?*" I ask, making my question clearer.

¹⁷ "Squid are fiercely intelligent, but they don't like humans much, even as dinner," says the cephalopod. "Plus, they don't respond to threats, money or reasoned argument."

¹⁸ "There was no hope of convincing squid to cooperate! But we could control *robots!*" shouts Armitage, condemning himself again; he knows his cause is lost.

¹⁹ "They are entirely unreasonable creatures," agrees the cephalopod.

"Unlike cuttlefish."

[20] In the brilliance of the cellar, I see Abbey moves closer to Elliot.

[21] The elephant's sunglasses are back on, but Abbey seems unmoved by the light; she has long since adjusted to it.

[22] I notice a vague shape moving about in an agitated fashion beside Abbey.

[23] Good grief, it's the Squiddrel!

[24] Abbey tickles it absently behind the ears beside as it mewls and drools in its confusion, and she then says something that seems to calm the creature. It settles on the floor at her feet.

[25] She's a mystery, is Abbey.

[26] "So," she says, "once we returned, we gathered here and waited for Mr. Armitage to make his move."

[27] "I brought along something that *looked* deadly," says one of the Maxes. The silence in response suggests confusion.

[28] Max continues, "I figured he'd keep the evidence simple if he could, and try to kill us with our *own* bomb."

[29] Armitage shouts something terse and unrepeatable.

[30] "Armitage, be still," says Uriel. The Chairman stiffens and falls silent;

[31] again, this was not a request.

[32] "Armitage was forced to play his hand, because we decided *not* to destroy each other," I say, pleased to have been one step ahead of him. "And when that failed, his only option was to *remove* our Realities."

[33] "He did this simply to preserve his place in the order of things?" asks Gabriel, somewhat rhetorically.

[34] "Yes. The final desperate act of an unfit leader," I say.

[35] "Yes, this is our conclusion, also," agrees Raphael. He addresses the CephNet above him.

[36] "You have played a long and dangerous game, cephalopod," he says. "So many variables and probabilities. Many lives were lost. We wonder if you are a worthy replacement for Central?"

[37] There is a moment of silence, during which the brilliance of the light seems to intensify.

[38] Finally, the CephNet replies.

[39] "If not us, who else?"

[40] "We could remain," says Uriel.

[41] The cephalopod network considers this. "Do you wish to do so?"

[42] "Armitage was right in one respect," says Gabriel. "With the advent of the Age Of Reason, each Reality strived to stand on its own, to advance through Science."

[43] "Yes. We must support this, wherever it takes them," continues Michael.

[44] "But does that not mean the death of Faith?" asks the CephNet.

[45] This is an interesting point. Does it? I'm jolted from my thoughts as a cry comes up from behind me.

[46] "No!" shouts Eolist," There will always be a need for Faith! We will always be lost without it!"

[47] "Quite so, Ms. Petite," smiles Raphael.

[48] Without warning, a deep tone, a resonating chord, strikes through the room. The sound is overwhelming; my eyes already ache, but now my teeth rattle in harmony.

[49] After an uncomfortable and interminable period, the tone stops.

[50] "CephNet," says Uriel, "we have given you control. The Unity is yours."

[51] "Thank you. We will endeavour to steer and enlighten, but not rule."

[52] "What will you do with Central? Will you remove it?" asks Raphael, asking lightly of the death of billions.

[53] "Of course not," says the CephNet, "but we shall isolate it for now. It has much to commend it, but it has lost its way, caught up in its own importance.

[54] Exiled, it must focus on its people, and find the best in them. We will ensure that the truth is known to them; they will hold those in power accountable. Given time, they will be ready to rejoin us."

[55] "As you will," nods Gabriel. The four turn to Armitage again.

[56] "Cecil Rhodes–Armitage, your fate is sealed."

[57] Tears run down the defeated man's cheeks, but he cannot speak. He can offer no threats or final words. He cannot scream.

[58] "There is nothing more to be said."

[59] And the light vanishes.

The Last Hurrah

18 [1] There is tea and cake.
[2] Any adventure that ends with tea and cake is a good one, as somebody very wise once said.

[3] As I get older, I'm happy just to pause and have a seat beneath me, but hot refreshments are definitely a bonus.

[4] "Did nobody make coffee?" grumbles

Eolist, but the Dinky Dynamo then takes a mug of tea and a large éclair without further ado.

5 We're sat around the fire in the first days of winter. Myself and Max, Abbey and Elliot, Bear and Eolist, Yavin and the young badgers.

6 Outside, the first frost of the year has made its way into the afternoon, and there's excited talk of snow.

7 Inside, everyone has a steaming brew and either a sweet or savoury treat. The young badgers have several each, in fact.

8 All the other Maxes and Roths have returned to their Realities, which is just as well considering the number of cakes and mugs we have in the cupboard.

9 "Indigo," says Abbey quietly, her hand drifting to my arm as I attempt to raise a gooey pastry to my lips. "Have these events changed your view of Faith?"

10 As ever, Abbey asks good questions.

11 I put the cake down and give this some thought as the others chatter happily.

12 "Honestly, no," I say. "I've never been a man of Faith, but I'm not against it either."

13 "But didn't we just meet four angels?"

14 I smile, "Yes, perhaps we did. It certainly *feels* like we did. But maybe they were just a species with incredibly advanced knowledge and technology?"

15 Abbey steals a bite of my confection and listens intently.

16 "I simply don't know," I say. "Both are interesting possibilities. I can't be sure, so I'll keep an open mind."

17 She pats my leg encouragingly, her eyes unreadable. "That's the spirit."

18 I return to my pastry, and wonder whether I'm an idiot.

19 Silence falls across the room, and snaps me back to reality.

20 "Everyone," I say, lifting my voice a little, "everything has changed, but for us, everything has remained the same."

21 Max tips me a nod as I continue.

22 "We are all here and we are all safe," I say, "and I consider that a victory."

23 Abbey raises her mug. "To all of us, such as we are!"

24 It's a good toast, an old favourite, and we all raise our own mugs, to repeat it and drink in the warmth of friendship and family.

25 The cakes do not survive long.

26 Nobody notices the TV flicker into life in the corner of the room, or the goat–like eyes that watch us from it with cool intelligence.

27 But I hear happy chatter and laughter in the house again.

28 And all is well in the world.

Epilogue

19 1 In another room, in another reality, another fire burns in the grate .

2 "That was great, Daddy!" says young Fido Roth. I hug him close on the sofa as we watch the fire.

3 "I'm glad you enjoyed it," I say, smiling at his youthful enthusiasm.

4 There are unanswered questions in all stories, and I think Fido senses some of them for this tale.

5 "But there's two things that I don't understand," he says, his big eyes looking up at me. "At the beginning of the story, why did iDifficult change into Max, but Indigo didn't change?"

6 This one is easy.

7 "Well, when the cuttlefish got together to form the CephNet, it was such a big event in the universe that lots of things in the world changed."

8 I spread my arms and then draw my hands together, interlocking my fingers. "Wonderful things happened," I say, "and Max was one of them."

9 "But what about Indigo?" asks Fido.

10 "Well, if you remember, he'd just bumped into your Uncle Elliot," I explain, "and was hanging onto him to stop himself falling over."

11 "Yes, I remember."

12 "Well, Elliot is an Agent of the Agency with special powers, and when everything changed, Elliot's powers protected Indigo from changing. He protected *all* of us in a way."

13 "Oh. Well, that makes sense," says the youngster doubtfully. I grin indulgently and move on.

14 "And your other question?"

15 Fido pauses before asking, as if he knows it will be difficult.

16 "Well, what happened to the Indigo who came from the burned Cambridge? The one where everyone got killed?"

17 Yes, that's much harder. I think a long time before answering.

18 "Well, that Indigo was *me*, Fido."

19 "YOU?!" he gasps.

20 "Yes, me," I breathe; it's still too

painful to think about. "You see Fido," I say, my eyes welling with tears, "when Cambridge was destroyed and everyone died, my wife and son died too."

[21] There is a long pause.

[22] "But *I'm* your son, Daddy."

[23] I shake my head.

[24] "No, you're a stuffed toy dog called Fido. You used to belong to my son. Before."

[25] The well–loved, threadbare dog looks up at me, with dark, lifeless glassy eyes.

[26] "That is a sad story, Daddy. But I love you, all the same. And I'm proud of you for what you did. How you saved everyone."

[27] Kids have such a wonderfully simplistic view of the world.

[28] I stroke his head.

[29] "Thanks, son."

Notes

* That might be something to do with the industrial air conditioning for his army of terracotta snowmen at the other end of his football–pitch–sized complex. But that's another story.

** It seems I'm mistaken; they *are* in this story. He never was a conformist.

*** He couldn't tell anyone about it, as he had no planning permission for his underground particle accelerator. But, to his credit, he 'gently' nudged the CERN folks towards their own 'discovery'. He later said of the experience, "It was like herding caffeinated fish."

Max

*"I consider leaking news of my death to boost my internet followers.
I then realise it might upset the three followers I have; family is funny that way."*

Hard And Increasingly Detailed

1
¹ And the next thing I know, I'm falling.
² I look about. A clear blue sky, with cloud below.
³ My tummy yawns with the effects of physics. This new simulator, created by arch–genius Max Tunguska, really is something.
⁴ As the clouds rush towards me, the wind deafening in my ears, I open my mouth and scream authentically.
⁵ And I'm back in the chair. In the lab.
⁶ "Are you okay, Roth?" asks Max, his hand still on the simulator's *Immersion* switch. "You were screaming."
⁷ I cough, my mouth dry, and imagine my hair wild.
⁸ "I thought you'd put me on the ground!" I blurt, terrified. "How can I explore the new terrain if I'm not *on the ground?!*"
⁹ Max sighs and shrugs.
¹⁰ "Sorry, I didn't recalibrate ground level after the mountaineering."
¹¹ My tummy twists afresh; I didn't enjoy the mountaineering either;
¹² there was screaming.
¹³ Max starts to turn a notched knob and reaches for the *Immersion* switch again. I wonder what will happen if...
¹⁴ And the next thing I know, I'm falling.
¹⁵ A lot faster than before too;

¹⁶ the clouds blink by, and the hedged fields of my home county rush towards me, far faster than gravity and terminal velocity would require.
¹⁷ I can picture my friend in the lab, spinning the dial quickly towards zero.
¹⁸ I hope he's paying attention.
¹⁹ The earth looks hard and unforgiving and increasingly detailed.
²⁰ Nope, it's no good; I need to scream again.

More Float Than Trickle

2
¹ The clock on the wall ticks slowly.
² I have to go out in fifteen minutes, but I'm in no hurry.
³ My lounge is warm, the curtains closed. Shadows huddle together to grumble in the corners of the room beyond the light of the reading light.
⁴ The art deco lamp, a blur of ceramic and stained glass, is one of three items on the leather–topped table at my elbow.
⁵ I relax into the worn leather armchair and find the place in my book, John Steinbeck's wonderful *Cannery Row*. A colleague recommended it many years ago, and it's a firm favourite.
⁶ **Ten minutes later**, I mark my page with a bookmark, smiling at the tale of seaside life in pre–war California, and pick up my cup of tea.

⁷ The tea is the second item on the table, and is strong, hot, milky and gently sweet, just how I like it.

⁸ I glance at the thin book, which is now two–thirds complete after several months;

⁹ I'm a slow reader.

¹⁰ Not in an intellectual sense, of course, but I do have bad reading habits, and rarely find time to sit down with a book;

¹¹ there's always so much to do.

¹² And technically I don't have that much time now.

¹³ Except, I do.

¹⁴ The third and final item on the table appears to be an antique hourglass. It looks to be a Georgian contraption of glass, wood and brass.

¹⁵ Within the timepiece, crystals of iridescent sand trickle far–too–slowly down. In fact, they more *float* than trickle, a slow–motion effect betrayed only by some of the grains floating upward or circling chaotically.

¹⁶ And in the air around me, motes of dust barely move in the hot, impatient gaze of the lamp.

¹⁷ Max, my best friend, built the hourglass for me, as a present.

¹⁸ It helps me make time to read, in a way that only Max could have thought of.

¹⁹ The clock on the wall ticks very slowly.

²⁰ I now have to go out in *fourteen* minutes, but I'm in no hurry.

²¹ In fact, I can be here for hours and still leave on time.

²² Best friends give the best presents.

²³ And the most precious gift you can give is time.

The Weight Of An Accent

3 ¹ Acapulco really is lovely at this time of year.

² As I sit on a narrow wooden pier on the Mexican seafront with my best friend Dr. Max Tunguska, my feet feel heavy; it's late afternoon, and it really has been a long and eventful day for the pair of us.

³ Neither of us is dressed for dinner at the Ritz, but we're perfectly attired for our surroundings: I'm sporting an Hawaiian shirt and some very cool board shorts, set off jauntily by a straw hat and some retro shades; Max is resplendent in a lime green safari suit and tinfoil panama hat.

⁴ Behind us, a new acquaintance fusses over some details, making preparations for our evening. We're waiting while he looks for something, and we aren't going anywhere quickly. Despite the rigours of the day, we slip into easy conversation.

⁵ "It's nice to get away every once in a while," I sigh, the ease of a thousand miles of separation washing over me.

⁶ "Yeah," agrees Max, adjusting his hat brim to reflect the lowering sun. "I was going to neuter the Squiddrel today." He sighs, perhaps with relief. "It can wait. What would you be doing at home right now?"

⁷ "Oh good grief, a dozen things, most likely," I reflect vaguely, "and probably all at once." I wave an equally vague hand around us. "That makes this place all the more fun."

⁸ As any busy person will tell you, boredom is a luxury. But as a confirmed and somewhat advanced slacker (a fractal slacker in fact), I find that boredom is a bummer. I'm only truly relaxed when ignoring things that I should be doing, rather than having nothing to do.

⁹ This is kind of an slacking axiom.

¹⁰ A brief jostling of the pier drags me from this train of thought, and I glance back, catching a glimpse of our companion—a short, suited figure—as he goes about his business, muttering in Spanish. There's an earthy, animal smell in the air that the sea breeze isn't doing much to dispel.

¹¹ Max doesn't seem to have noticed, and smiles quietly to himself, the very picture of relaxation. I must admit, that apart from a few details of the day, I'm feeling very much the same.

¹² "I really enjoyed dinner." My mind is rarely far away from food, a truth to which my tailor will attest.

¹³ "The lobster was excellent." His belly gurgles absently.

¹⁴ "You really shouldn't have eaten that eighth one."

¹⁵ Max feigns offence and grins broadly. "Well, you'd eaten all the pizzas!"

¹⁶ I take a huffy tone and defend myself admirably. "Look, I needed something to put all that caviar on!"

¹⁷ We laugh hugely, but are cut short by a spat Hispanic curse from our rear. We share a glance and start to turn, but start as the third member of our party leaps

forward to seize an ear on each of us. The tiny wooden pier creaks beneath us, which is hardly surprising considering how heavy his Mexican accent is.

[18] "You sons of beetches, you eat for twenty peoples!"

[19] The armadillo rears up on his hind legs to his full height, which is just sufficient to menace our earlobes as we sit, twisted to his attentions. We try to pull back, but his tiny claws are sharp and strong.

[20] Despite our predicament, I marvel again at what a dashing figure the armadillo cuts for an armoured mammal: a black suit with a white pinstripe; an immaculate white shirt paired with an eye–watering turquoise tie; a similarly–hued kerchief poking from his breast pocket; and a tiny black hat that would have suited Sinatra sits squarely on his narrow head.

[21] "You theenk you can eat everything in my restaurant?!" he bellows, spitting incredulity all over my shades.

[22] "Well, it was an All–You–Can–Eat buffet!" I howl. The needle–clawed paws twist viciously on our ears and I let out a further yelp.

[23] Max hisses my way, equally pained, "Yeah, too bad it was run by the Armadillo Mafia."

[24] With a final curse, the grip is released, but his deft digits snap handcuffs onto the pair of us before we can raise our hands to nurse our mauled ears. Lurching between us with no regard for his shoulder pads, the armadillo mobster gazes over the edge of the pier at the personal blocks of concrete encasing our feet; the aching in my ankles is quite insistent now.

[25] "The tide, she is ready now, I theenk." The mammal chuckles, and aims a kick at Max's knee. "Any last words before you sleep with the feeshes, dog?"

[26] Max ponders this for a moment before responding brightly, "Yeah, the enchiladas were superb. The crystallised jalapeños particularly." There he goes again, thinking with his stomach. Still, he's right, and our captor knows it; the mammal touches the brim of his hat with momentary good grace.

[27] "Si. It is my wife's recipe. She thanks you." He steps in front of me, and again the pier groans under our combined weight. "And you?"

[28] "Um, yes!" I wiggle my hips to a chorus of shrieking timbers. "This pier is going to collapse! Especially with all this cement dangling from it!" I kick my feet to the clonk of concrete against wood. "I know some badger engineers who could design and build you a proper one."

[29] I'm rewarded with a howl of derision.

[30] "Badgers?!" he spits, "We don' need no steenkin' badgers!"

[31] A moment later, the diminutive don heaves us from the pier.

[32] As we fall, I reflect that we always strive to take it easy; it comes easily to us most of the time. But sometimes our appetites get the better of us.

[33] Acapulco really is hot at this time of year.

[34] Tho the water is still quite cold.

[35] And deep.

A Stirring Chorus Rendition

4[1] It's a well–trodden cliché that travel broadens the mind.

[2] But cliché or not, it's true.

[3] Nothing blows away the cobwebs of complacent thought more than an exotic location, immersion in an unfamiliar culture, and the babble of an unknown language.

[4] Or an unknown time.

[5] **It's Vienna, 1892**. I'm sitting in a street café with my best friend Max Tunguska. We're having a late breakfast, or possibly an early brunch.

[6] The smells of fresh bread, sweet pastries and hot coffee from our locale are intoxicating.

[7] This is why we arrived at 8am;

[8] the best of the bakery is always consumed within a half hour of it emerging from the oven.

[9] It will be several hours before we're trampling our shadows. And right now, our shadows are sitting as comfortably as us, just a few yards away.

[10] "We got lucky with the weather," I note, sipping an exquisite cup of Joe as I contemplate my first snack.

[11] Ordering this delicious spread was awkward with minimal German skills, but I think the waitress quickly got the idea we were *hungry*.

[12] And mercifully, with us dressed in immaculate morning suits and top hats, we at least looked respectable enough to pay for our meal.

[13] "Oh, luck has nothing to do with it," replies Max, fishing in his breast pocket. He produces an obsidian yoyo, frowns, and dips his hand again. "Aha!" He produces and waves a small ornate brass device in my direction, which seems to be grafted onto a length of seaweed.

[14] "A temporal barometer?"

[15] "Indeed." He smiles absently as he pockets it again, and then gives the yoyo a few expert twirls. Its surface sparkles eerily with the stars of deep space.

[16] Taking a bite from a deliciously–crisp bread roll crammed with butter and strong, gently–melted cheese, I decide to change the subject.

[17] "So, do we have a plan?"

[18] My friend considers this as he tucks into his first cake of the day. It has cream and chocolate and nuts, and looks like it could kill a diabetic at ten paces.

[19] "Well, there's some terrific museums and parks here," he muses, gazing distractedly at something on the pavement, "and of course we could drop in on Sigmund Freud..."

[20] His voice trails off, his attention still focused on ground level.

[21] I follow his gaze, and slowly stop chewing and talking.

[22] On the slate paves fifteen feet away, our shadows are out of synch with us. Mine waves his hands in an animated fashion, while Max's seems to shout periodically and scratch his head a lot.

[23] We watch for thirty seconds as this tableau unfolds.

[24] "Good gravy," I say, "are they playing *charades*?"

[25] My friend cocks his head while his silhouetted counterpart stands to begin his turn. With his arms held wide, the shadow spins wildly, before descending and unleashing some kind of explosion.

[26] "Yeah, and I think I'm doing *Independence Day*, maybe?"

[27] "Do they normally do this when we're sitting quietly, ignoring them?"

[28] Other shadows seems to be slipping further away from their owners to join the game.

[29] "Perhaps. I've never noticed. We're usually so busy!" Max's consideration deepens. "When we're least active, we tend to be in a dimly lit room, watching movies while eating pizza."

[30] He's right, of course; the evidence is inconclusive.

[31] There's quite a gathering of shadows now, each tenuously attached to its caster. Our doubles are both seated again, watching the shade of an artist from somewhere to our left act out the name of an opera.

[32] "I'm hopeless on opera," mumbles Max past as the last morsels of the cake.

[33] I drain my coffee and eye up what looks suspiciously like an amaretto über–éclair. I sniff it experimentally; no, the strong scent of cherries suggests kirsch liqueur. I pop it down and reach for some apple strudel instead.

[34] "Oh, I think that fella over there got it!" The silhouette of a foppish chap to our right jumps up, dragging the detached darkness of a male companion with him. The two stand and appear to whisper, plotting their mime.

[35] "A double mime? Interesting..." ruminates Max, picking up the cake I've just abandoned. "Hey, is this an amaretto éclair?"

[36] I shake my head, and the words, "No, cherry," die on my lips as the charade begins. Turning to Max, I whisper, "This is a bit camp. And where did they get the cowboy hats?"

[37] My friend shakes his head, and then suddenly chokes on his éclair. Spluttering cherry cream, he wipes his mouth and finally manages to squeak, "Good grief, are they doing *Brokeback Mountain?!*"

[38] I laugh easily, and after watching for a few more seconds I shout "*Home on the Range!*" at the assembled shadows. I receive some odd looks from the café's flesh–and–blood patrons, but both of the mimers point at me with one hand while touching their nose with the other: *Correct, Sir!*

[39] Some of the other shades then stand and—producing more cowboy hats—join their companions for a stirring, silent, chorus line rendition of the wild west tune.

[40] There is thunderous mute applause.

[41] I pick up the coffee urn and turn to smile at Max.

[42] "More tea, Vicar?"

[43] **Ten minutes later**, our fast well and truly broken, we settle our bill in broken German and head away from the café.

[44] Our shadows detach themselves reluctantly from their lively silent party, and snap back into step with us.

45 "Well, that was interesting," I understate, as we pass through the archway to the Grand Park.

46 To my right, Max strolls along, once again playing with his yoyo. He offers a reflective "Hmmm" as he takes it Round The World, narrowly missing my top hat and a nanny pushing a pram.

47 The nanny starts with a gasp and says something surprised in German. Max apologises with a self-deprecating smile and a raise of his hat. The blushing Fräulein giggles and scurries away.

48 "You know," I offer, considering my friend's many eccentricities, "it'd be a missed opportunity to visit Vienna in 1892 and *not* pop by to see Freud."

49 My friend scratches his short beard as he considers this proposition. "Does he speak English?"

50 "Oh, I expect so," I say shiftily, "but I'm sure he'd be fascinated to have you on his couch even if he doesn't."

51 "Well, I'd love to ask him about his mother."

52 We continue our stroll through the park as our shadows shorten.

53 Travel does broaden the mind.

54 But time travel broadens, tenderises, rolls and roasts it.

A Faint Smell Of Custard

5 1 When you set your mind to it, you can find anything.

2 This is particularly true of the internet, where you can find anything you can think of. If you're not careful.

3 But today I'm in search of simple answers.

4 I'm not very good with noise. Anything repetitive drives me to distraction: a dripping tap, a bouncing ball, a badger with hiccups.

5 One noise in particular has been bugging me lately, and I'd finally like to work out what it is.

6 More to the point, I want it *stopped*.

7 So I've come to see the smartest guy I know.

8 "So, can you hear it right now?" asks my best friend and confidant, Dr. Max Tunguska.

9 **It's early on a Sunday morning**, and we're sitting at the kitchen table;

10 the pleasure of a hearty breakfast is ambling behind us.

11 Just outside the window in the bright morning sun, the young badgers Hoth and Sollust are chopping logs with an unwieldy axe.

12 Half of me is trying not to watch, while the other is wondering where the first aid kit is.

13 In the distance, there's the buzz of a half dozen lawnmowers.

14 "Yes." I don't mention that it's more of a sensation than a sound.

15 There's a lot of background noise today. I should get a better listen to it in a moment, though; Max has been busy, and apparently he now has the tools to get the job done.

16 Max reaches over to the first device from the table—a simple white cone—and switches it on. A blue light blinks on it, slowly at first, and then more rapidly.

17 As it speeds up, the sounds in the room retreat and vanish. I'd not honestly registered the humming of the fridge, the low drone of the fluorescent bulb, or the dripping tap.

18 But now they're gone, I'm acutely aware of their absence.

19 "That's a nice effect. Some kind of noise cancellation?"

20 My friend nods as he adjusts the next doohicky—a bronze sphere covered in springs—with a screwdriver.

21 "Yep. Similar to what you get on headphones. Short range, which is why the noise from outside is making it through."

22 I realise he's right; I can't see or hear Hoth and Sollust at the moment, but I'm still aware of the lawnmowers. I lean back in my chair, looking round the window.

23 "Are those two still chopping wood?"

24 On cue, the youngsters reappear with a shiny, red chainsaw that dwarfs the pair of them; it's the one we trim the hedges with, but we've also earmarked it for the Aardvark Apocalypse*.

25 The badgers try to fire the chainsaw up, with Hoth holding it and Sollust straining at the starter cable;

26 those black-and-white lads are strong for their size.

27 On the third pull it catches, and the hungry petrol roar fills the kitchen.

28 "Can you still hear it?" shouts Max through the mechanical racket. I can't even hear him properly, and it seems crazy that I can still hear the noise that's dogging me, but I can;

²⁹ somewhere in my gut, a slow, grating, repeating vibration.

³⁰ I nod and bellow in the affirmative.

³¹ Max responds by flicking the switch on the second device. A huge, soapy, green bubble briefly appears around us, and abruptly all sound ceases.

³² Every single sound. No manic badgers, no grass trimming, not even the traffic from the main road.

³³ The silence is remarkable, unnatural;

³⁴ Honestly, I've never failed to hear anything like it.

³⁵ But it's punctuated by a single, faint noise. It's the source of my annoyance, and for the first time, I can hear it properly; an ethereal, high-pitched squeaking.

³⁶ Max pats the sphere gently, proudly. "This thing reflects all the remaining sound waves, so we don't hear them." He cocks his head. "Dammit, now I can hear it!" He looks about, trying to get a bearing. "It's like a rusty wheel on a supermarket trolley."

³⁷ I can't quite put my finger on it either. And it seems to be everywhere.

³⁸ "How is it beating your devices?" I whisper, as if we might frighten it off by speaking too loud. But instinctively, I know the answer.

³⁹ "Well, it's not coming from this set of immediate dimensions," confirms the arch-genius in an equally-hushed tone, "so it's a good job I brought this with me." He indicates the final device on the table.

⁴⁰ I can't describe it adequately, but if I said it's like a four-sided, gunmetal man-trap with a spinning core of molten custard, you'd be most of the way there.

⁴¹ "I'm afraid to ask," I mutter uncertainly.

⁴² "Well, it's quite simple, really." He waves a hand around the room. "We're going to collapse the immediate four dimensions."

⁴³ And, saying no more, he reaches for the switch.

⁴⁴ "Wait a minute!" I shout. Max pauses as I scrabble around for a suitable objection. "What will happen to, well, everything?"

⁴⁵ Max chuckles and shakes his head. "Fear not, old son. We're going to fold them up neatly. Including Time, so it'll all be nice and tidy. And then, we'll see what's left."

⁴⁶ He sees my lingering uncertainty, and nods towards the window. "Don't worry, those lads outside, and everyone else, will be fine. Most likely."

⁴⁷ Silently, the indicated window shatters.

⁴⁸ Thousands of tiny jagged fragments burst into the room, and then fall to the floor; it's like watching TV with the sound off.

⁴⁹ A roughly-cut log lands on the carpet and rolls gently to a stop. Ten seconds later, the faces of two apprehensive badgers and a spinning chainsaw blade rise up slowly and scan the room.

⁵⁰ I give them a deflated look; that's two broken windows in as many months.

⁵¹ "If they don't kill us all with that chainsaw first, of course."

⁵² The pair bolt off up the garden as Max fires the third device up.

⁵³ The triangular edges of the man-trap start to fold upwards, and the world folds up with them.

⁵⁴ It's a peculiar effect; in my vision, the picture skews, contracts and rises. Perspective ceases to exist, and I see furniture, glass, wallpaper and sky all corrugate and collapse upwards.

⁵⁵ Above the core of the device, four brilliant lines rise and converge until there is a single, dazzling vertical line of white reality atop a metal pyramid.

⁵⁶ The world is gone. We're in limbo.

⁵⁷ There's a faint smell of custard.

⁵⁸ I have neither the science nor the words to describe our location.

⁵⁹ But next to us, hanging freely—in what would be midair if there were any dimensions—is a spinning mechanical bearing; two metal rings separated by an orbit of tiny metal balls.

⁶⁰ It's perhaps the size of a bagel; my stomach rumbles.

⁶¹ As the bearing completes each revolution, it emits a slow, grinding squeak.

⁶² And without all of our dimensions in the way, it's rather loud.

⁶³ "Good grief, what is it?"

⁶⁴ Max shrugs. "I've no idea. Something fundamental, I guess. A forgotten component? The heart of the universe? Maybe it's just a metaphor."

⁶⁵ He reaches into his jacket pocket and pulls out a small blue-and-yellow spray-can of mechanical lubricant with a grin.

⁶⁶ "So. Shall we fix it?"

⁶⁷ **Five minutes later**, we're enjoying a cup of tea in my front room. There's noise everywhere, but underneath the hubbub of the world there is glorious silence.

⁶⁸ I chuckle as I sip my Darjeeling.

⁶⁹ When you set your mind to it, you can find anything.

⁷⁰ But sometimes, even if the answers are simple, you have to dig deep.

⁷¹ And carry some *WD40*.

It's Even The Same Colour

6¹ Sunday is a day I have never mastered.

² I usually stay home, but it's a mixed bag. If I have nothing to do, I get bored. But if I have a chore to do, I resent it.

³ Because it's Sunday.

⁴ Does that make sense?

⁵ So today, I decided to break the cycle of home activity polarity, and go out. My dear friend Max lives just a few miles away as the crow flies. Or as the Squiddrel runs. **

⁶ As I knock on his door, I keep an eye out for Max's long–suffering wife. She's a lovely lady, but things have been uneven between us since what she refers to as "The Firework Incident", or "The Reason We Can't Get Fire Insurance Anymore".

⁷ I have no idea why; we made good by planting new flowers and replaced all of the scorched/missing fence panels.

⁸ Max's ragged wedding suit proved more problematic at short notice, but at least I got him to the church on time.

⁹ "Roth!" bellows Max as he throws the door open, his broad smile radiating the rudest of health. "Perfect timing! Come in, come in!"

¹⁰ I'm hustled indoors, and barely have time to offer a hello before a cup of hot, sweet tea is thrust into my hands.

¹¹ "So," he grins, "what do you know about fish? *Garra Rufa* or *Doctor Fish*, to be precise!"

¹² My curiosity is piqued; I was discussing these miraculous little fish with a friend at work only a few days earlier.

¹³ I gather my handful of thoughts.

¹⁴ "Those are the fish they have at spas to nibble away at dead skin on feet, right?"

¹⁵ I make unnecessary nibbling motions with my hands to emphasise the point.

¹⁶ "After a few minutes with your feet in a tank, you have the smoothest heels ever?"

¹⁷ "Precisely! Top marks!"

¹⁸ I wonder where this is going. I give up, realising that guesswork rarely works with Max. "So, have you tried it?"

¹⁹ "Nope." I shrug expressively. "It does sound interesting, but it tends to be expensive."

²⁰ "I see, I see," he muses, "but you *do* have hard skin on your feet, yes? Excellent. Do you get it anywhere else?"

²¹ "Um, well," I scratch my head, surprised at the line of enquiry, "a bit on my right knee, and sometimes my elbows, I suppose?"

²² He nods and makes enthusiastic listening noises while scribbling a few notes in a battered notebook.

²³ "Right, so these existing treatments are fine for feet, but for the best results, perhaps some sort of *immersive* experience might be better?"

²⁴ *Wait. What? Immersive?!*

²⁵ "Noooo, I'm not sure that's such a good idea!" I scramble for some logic. "That might be a bit weird." Max cocks his head at me, genuinely surprised; I expand my thought.

²⁶ "Some people don't like the sensation of the fish nibbling at their feet. But all over? They'd freak out."

²⁷ "Oh, but that's just nerves!" He laughs, slapping me on the back happily. "They'd get *used* to it. Most go back for further treatments, I'm sure."

²⁸ I'm not so sure, but this terrible tide of creativity sweeps me along.

²⁹ "So." The single word has a finality about it. "Do you want to give my new treatment a try?"

³⁰ I'm lost for words. Something tells me I need to find some really *good* ones. And quickly.

³¹ "Well, you know, of course I'm *keen*," I bluster, "but the skin on my feet is like leather. Yes, leather. Years and years of poor footcare. Those poor little fish wouldn't be able to bite into it."

³² He laughs uproariously, and looks delighted. Is it too late to run?

³³ "I was hoping you'd say that!" beams Max, "I have something for that very situation!"

³⁴ The words hang in the air, and I have

a sinking feeling in my tummy. With icebergs.

[35] "Come on! I'll show you."

[36] Opening the door under the stairs, he ushers me down into his cellar.

[37] Our footsteps echo as we descend into the darkness. Behind me, my friend slaps a switch, and with a *bink bink bink* there is light.

[38] The room, now lit by half a dozen fluorescent strips, is low and seemingly endless, and full of exotic machinery; these vanish into shadow ten yards away.

[39] Dominating the near room is an enormous plastic crate. It stands six feet high, and resembles a picnic cool box. I have one just like it at home;

[40] it's even the same colour.

[41] "Go on, take a peek!" My friend's exuberance is infectious, and makes me want to scratch. He waves to indicate a ladder on the crate's side that leads up to what looks like a heavy lid.

[42] I hesitate, but Max waves me upwards.

[43] The rungs are cold and slightly damp, but I reach the top without incident. The lid is more of a challenge.

[44] I have to get my shoulder under it to gain some purchase, and finally heave it up, one handed.

[45] The box is full of dark water.

[46] I look closer, insidious curiosity getting the better of me.

[47] And the fish rise up to greet me.

[48] To call them *Piranha* would be doing flesh–eating predators a disservice. Describing them as *teeth accompanied by a few scales and fins* would be closer.

[49] They eye me hungrily.

[50] "What do you think?!"

[51] I'm lost for words.

[52] You know, I think I may prefer dull Sundays at home.

A Matter Of Respect

7 [1] I'm a pretty relaxed fellow.

[2] When it comes to eating out, I consider it a treat. As a result, I wouldn't dream of diminishing the experience with rules of conduct, dress codes, or quibbles over *who had rice*.

[3] However, I might offer up a few simple guidelines after an evening in my local curry house with a good friend.

[4] I shall not name the part–time arch genius, as I respect him too much.

[5] *Rule #1* Never eat in a curry house with a vegetarian.

[6] *Rule #2* Never let him choose from the Brussels Sprout specials.

[7] And finally, and most important of all:

[8] *Rule #3* Never share a taxi ride home unless you can open a window.

Notes

[*] Anything as cute as an aardvark *must* be up to something.

[**] A *Squiddrel*, a hybrid of a red squirrel and a colossal squid, pays no regard to fences, roads or even buildings; they are determined creatures. One zoologist described it as the most dangerously single–minded creature he'd ever encountered. Before it ate him.

Apocrypha

(Equal–Opportunity Nonsense)

Spies

"This morning's events left me tired and restless. A cycle ride after lunch blew the cobwebs away. My toupée was another casualty."

More Than A Hint Of Pine

1

1 The light in my eyes in dazzling.
2 "So Mister Roth, shall we continue?"
3 I hesitate to answer. The sweat on my face stings my eyes as much as the light. My arms are bound to the chair, and she's been getting pretty rough with me.
4 My head is pounding. My head is down, in fact. I'm not sure how much more of this it will take to crack me.
5 "Mister Roth?"
6 She takes a particular delight in the word *Mister*, dragging it out in her rough Russian drawl. If I wasn't so tired and thirsty, I'd find it rather hackneyed, to be honest.
7 I raise my head, and squint past the light. I can't see my inquisitor clearly.
8 "I beg your pardon, Miss Gradenko, but I thought you were being rhetorical."
9 She cracks me a good one across the jaw. For the umpteenth time today, I wish I was George Foreman.
10 "You're welcome."
11 He'd have a better comeback, too.
12 We've been at this three hours in the dim room, the narrow spotlight in my face, with her glimpsed silhouette occasionally moving in and out of the shadows.
13 "What languages do you speak?" The words are barked.

14 My head still spinning, I struggle to grasp the question.
15 *Languages?* What, other than my impeccable Queen's English?
16 I think for longer than the answer takes to arrive; my vision needs a few seconds to clear.
17 "Well, my French is okay." A bit of stretch that one, but it did get me through that interesting trip to Morocco.
18 On the edge of hearing, I hear a precise tick being made on a paper by a sharp pencil.
19 "Yes, but we know this already." There's a rustle of papers in a folder. "Marrakech did not elude our scrutiny."
20 Wow. Under *scrutiny*. I hope they knocked themselves out; I was just doing a bit of sightseeing. Oh, and some shopping.
21 "Beautiful place, Marrakech; fabulous architecture."
22 Gradenko ignores this point.
23 "And other than your lazy, *schoolboy* French?"
24 Harsh. But fair. I shrug dismissively.
25 "Some German."
26 My interrogator seems to consider this. Then suddenly, closer than before, she bellows,
27 "Ich habe keine Taucherlunge, und meine Lederhosen ist von den tropischen Fischen voll!"

[28] *What?* I desperately try to recall period four on a Monday with Miss Johnson. Warm memories bosom their way past me inappropriately; I liked Miss Johnson.

[29] Oh come on Indigo, focus!

[30] "You have *no*..." I thrust the words *diver* and *lungs* together and consider the shape of the result, "No *Aqualung?* And your leather trousers are..." Von? Voll? "Erm, *full* of tropical fish?"

[31] In the gloom, Gradenko grunts. I hear another precise pencil tick.

[32] I sigh.

[33] "Look, do you want to just read me the list and I'll say Yes or No?" It's a cheap shot, but there's been little respite in the interrogation, and despite my physical state I'm defiant.

[34] It's ill–advised. Suddenly, she's in my face, all blonde hair, shoulderpads and gleaming white teeth.

[35] "I will ask the questions, Roth!" roars my tormentor, slapping the desk fiercely with what looks like a riding crop.

[36] Wow. I'm pleased the table's there; she's a real nutcracker. In fact, I'm surprised she's not wheeled out the car battery and the jump cables.

[37] But the storm passes into silence. The interrogator returns to the gloom and the point.

[38] "So, you speak some German. Why do you say your French is better?"

[39] I'm bemused by the line of questioning. I shrug again.

[40] "Because it is. I had to take French when I was eleven yars old. German came along later."

[41] "Your were *forced* to study a Foreign Language?" She capitalises the words in her mouth somehow. The idea seems to appeal her, and she falls silent in the darkness beyond the light;

[42] I imagine her staring into space, dreaming of retaking Stalingrad.

[43] I decide to talk a bit, if only to buy some time.

[44] "Um, yeah. In England in the Seventies and Eighties, it was quite common."

[45] My tone is conversational, light.

[46] "We considered ourselves British, not European. The government thought it would oil the wheels of the old Entente Cordiale if we learned French. Help us build bridges to Europe. Figuratively speaking."

[47] "And did this State Policy work, do you think?" Again with the capitals.

[48] "Nope. We didn't build any bridges. Though we did build a tunnel." I compare the metaphor with the reality and smile. "I think we were just being bloody–minded about that."

[49] "And you? Did you Resist this learning also?"

[50] "Well, I didn't care for the idea. I was bright enough I suppose, but unmotivated. I didn't see the point."

[51] I've not thought about this in years.

[52] It seems rather a dim outlook in retrospect. But I don't like decisions that are made for me.

[53] "Anyway, I studied French for five years and scraped through an exam. And now I can travel and speak it a bit, which is convenient. Nice, even."

[54] "So, you finally acknowledge the wisdom of your Government." There's more activity from The Scribbler In Darkness. I chuckle; H. P. Lovecraft would have loved that one.

[55] The pencil falls silent.

[56] "So, when did you start speaking German?"

[57] "A year after I started French. We had to start a second language, and had a choice of German or Spanish."

[58] "Oh?" Gradenko sounds genuinely interested. "And you chose *German?* How interesting."

[59] *Is it?*

[60] "Yes. I chose badly."

[61] I sense her look sharply my way more than I see it.

[62] "Spanish would have been far more useful, in retrospect. From a global population standpoint, I mean. And I now realise that Spanish is rather a beautiful language..."

[63] I pause as meaningfully as I can.

[64] "Unlike German."

[65] She coughs. "Not at all. German is a magnificent language. Rigorous constructions, precise vocabulary, glacial clarity." Then she sighs. "Such exactitude."

[66] Her Russian voice has more than a hint of pine in it.

[67] "Perhaps. But they don't write much poetry,"* I say, more sourly than I intended. There's an outraged gasp from across the room, and I move on hastily, not wanting another smack in the mouth.

68 "Unlike your native Russian; robust, baroque, empassioned."

69 This seems to placate the inquisitor a bit, and I plunge onwards.

70 "Anyway, I only studied German for two years. I wanted to study sciences and art, and we were allowed to drop one language."

71 "So. You decided to stay with French? Was it..." It's now her turn to search for a phrase, "A *percentage* decision?" She sounds quite pleased with the colloquial English. Well, American, anyway.

72 "Yes. I had another year of it under my belt. An exam success seemed more likely. Most decided the same way. Much to the annoyance of the German department."

73 Seconds tick by to the steady rhythm of pencil strokes.

74 "So, what other languages do you speak?"

75 Gradenko is persistent, I'll give her that. I don't.

76 She taps her pencil on her pad thoughtfully. "What about Arabic?"

77 Oh. That's interesting. My mind wanders to the dictionaries, travel guides and phrase books at home. I do know a few words, I suppose...

78 "Mister Roth? It's a simple enough question; I'm waiting."

79 And I suppose I know a tiny bit of a couple of other languages, now I come to think of it...

80 Her sudden bark startles me back to the room.

81 "Come on Roth! Speak up, man! I shan't ask again."

82 "Well..."

83 My interrogator strides purposefully into the light and grabs my lapel with one white-knuckled hand and thrusts her face into mine.

84 "Do you speak Arabic?"

85 I stare down my nose at her nose. I think my eyes cross.

86 "Well, I can say please, thank you, hello, goodbye, a few numbers."

87 She thumps me back into the chair and circles the table. "And you learned this for travel?"

88 "Yes. A handful of words. It helps. I can do the same in Spanish and Italian. And Greek, I suppose. Oh, and Swedish. I pick things up out of necessity."

89 There's a long pause as Gradenko explores this idea.

90 "So," she says finally, "you resisted learning languages as a schoolboy, despite being capable."

91 "Yes." This sounds rather like a confession.

92 "But when you need to learn them, you can? Enjoy it, even?"

93 My head is down again, weary.

94 I give my longest sigh of the interview.

95 "Yes."

96 I hear her shuffle some papers, and close a folder.

97 "Okay, we're done here. I have no further questions."

98 The spotlight vanishes, but its sun still burns in my eyes. Spots dance. But my jaw is relieved, and so am I.

99 "You're free to go. There's tea and biscuits outside if you'd like them."

100 And somehow my arms are released. I stumble to my feet.

101 "So," I consider my words carefully, "do I get the job?"

102 There's an endless moment. Milliseconds tick past slowly.

103 "Yes. You can start Monday."

104 Wow. That went better than expected.

105 "Thank you."

106 "No thank *you*, Mister Roth," says Gradenko, but there's not a shred of belief or warmth in it.

107 I wave a hand vaguely, and turn my back on the interviewer. After straightening my tie, I open the unlocked door. Outside, **it's 1990**.

108 I read the sign on the door for the second time today:

Her Majesty's Secret Service
Human Resources Department

109 I consider the events of the day and heave a final sigh. It's no good;

110 they were definitely nicer when they were called *Personnel*.

Mission Log*: Spy Another Day

2 1 My Government work is intrusive. Fear and Intrigue lurk in every shadow; if they're still here tonight they'll probably expect dinner.

2 My yearly review went badly: the Foreign Office want me sectioned; Number 10 is livid; Peru may still press charges. But the Aussies LOVE me!

3 Ah, Queensland. The Company runs the Pacific Rim from a pizza joint in

Mackay: counter–terrorism, covert ops, and all you can eat for $5.

4 I must go down to the sea again. I forgot the sub was moored off Crete and the Quartermaster is pestering me; it may come out of my wages.

5 Despite years ordering cocktails, I have no talent for making them. My Vesper tastes of two–stroke; appropriate, but more Lillet next time?

6 "All evil needs is for good men to do nothing" said Einstein. While true, what evil *wants* is orbital lasers, odd henchmen and a volcano base.

7 I'm HALO jumping into Cairo at dawn. I'm sure there's scheduled flights; the Quartermaster is obviously still annoyed about the sub I lost.

8 Cairo did not pan out. The flight was outsourced to the lowest bidder; I HALO'd into Cannes. 15 minutes of fame and a diplomatic incident.

9 The Cairo trip's back on. No HALO jump this time; I'll be wrapped in brown paper, taped, stamped and sent Surface Mail. Very "old school".

10 Being mailed to Cairo bothers me; last time I did that I spent six days in a Marrakech Dead Letter Room stacked under a mail–order elephant.

11 They over–nighted me to Cairo in the end. The sense of history here is awesome. I'm awaiting my Contact at the coffee chain in the Great Pyramid.

12 Codeword problems. Contact hissed *Daisies Are Summer Blooms*; I expected *The Cuckoos Are Flying South*. Red faces. We'll try again in an hour.

13 Codeword problem solved; we settled on *Chickens Never Walk Backwards* followed by one verse of *She'll Be Coming Round The Mountain*.

14 My Contact looks like my chiropodist. In fact, it IS my chiropodist; no wonder I still have problems with my arches. Bloody moonlighter.

15 Adios Cairo; I was snatched last night by a Bolivian death squad. They asked if I could spare them some guns; I think they were outsourced.

16 The Deathsquad leader is Cruz. Excellent henchman material; tall, menacing, with a chrome nose. I hope Mr. Big has also made an effort.

17 We reached Bolivia by hot air balloon. I was handcuffed in First Class. No olive in my dry martini; I guess we're all feeling The Crunch.

18 Mr. Big greeted us. Short, tanned, gleaming teeth, immaculately dressed, charming. French. Well, evil geniuses need that fatal flaw.

19 Mr. Big was apologetic; he wasn't ready for me. The piranhas were delayed, the volcano base was behind schedule. We've pencilled in next May.

20 Flying back to London. Cruz beat me savagely before I left; "a memento from La Paz, Mr. Roth". He'll go far. The bandages are itchy.

21 The Admiral's lackey Bing Heston drops by earlier with a message. His news is never good; he's like a tax demand that married an obituary.

22 The Admiral would like to see me in Australia. He's not there, he just wants to *see* me there; giving a wedgie to the King of Spain still haunts me.

For Queen and Country

3 1 Working for Her Majesty's Secret Service has its plus points.
2 The travel opportunities go without saying. The pension is second to none. And you can *always* get a jetpack at short notice.

3 But one of my favourite perks is the annual cricket match against the *Ministry Of Defence*.

4 Every year, two teams of eleven pit their wits against each other in the most quintessential of English sports.

5 Last year, my boss The Admiral led us to victory for Queen and Country. The M.O.D. were utterly routed. My innings of 103 played a small part in the victory.

6 So, this year the M.O.D. took no chances; as I came in to bat, they brought out their big guns.

7 A Howitzer, in fact.

8 Never underestimate the power of a solid forward defensive stroke.

9 Rebuilding of the cricket pavilion starts in a fortnight.

Mission Log*: Doctor Wang

4 1 I'm summoned to see the Admiral by his lackey, Bing Heston. Apparently Bing's real surname is Hess. His dad was famous; this explains a lot.

2 The Admiral pairs me up with Jack Starling for my next mission. He's the rising star of The Service. Bing Heston likes him; I'm worried.

3 Jack Starling is young, smart, motivated, charming. And handsome in that odd way that women seem to like. I expect trouble from him.

4 The Admiral despatches Starling and myself to The Bahamas. My old nemesis Juju Wang has resurfaced; half black, half Chinese, all cabaret.

5 Starling's too young to remember Dr. Wang: double agent, mafia hitman, mad scientist, president of Iceland; damn, I miss the Old Days.

6 Last time, Wang almost buzz-sawed me in half over a waterfall. I escaped by wooing his girlfriend, which was tricky given the circumstances.

7 Dr. Wang respects tradition; traps, speeches, secret bases, odd henchmen. Modern bad guys are so lame; businessmen, media tycoons. Tossers.

8 I visit Quartermaster with Starling. I get standard field issue; he gets his requested "specials". I hope he's a double agent. Bang.

9 Starling joins me for a round at my golf club. He whips me by a shot per hole and offers some pointers. I plan a shallow grave in a bunker.

10 We have trouble at Heathrow; Starling's new to lethal-gadget concealment. The men in rubber gloves interview him; we'll laugh about it later.

11 An uncomfortable Starling boards the plane. He rallies well and quickly hooks up with a flight attendant. I curse youth as I sip my martini.

12 We land in Nassau; the heat's stifling. I need a cold shower. Starling and two flight attendants need a bucket of cold water throwing on them.

13 The driver says Government House sent him, but he's one of Dr. Wang's boys. We thank him and go along. They lie, we lie; it all evens out.

14 After five miles Starling pulls his gun; they fight. He drops some good puns, but kills the guy. Moron. Save them for the ones that escape!

15 Starling and I split up. He'll track Dr. Wang down with technology. Silly. He'll be at the Casino. Why don't they teach the basics any more?

16 I dress for the Casino; white dinner suit, black bow tie, red carnation. It wouldn't do to win big while badly dressed; it would look lucky.

17 I play some baccarat until I find myself opposite a handsome black man

in Chinese evening dress. Dr. Wang, I presume? He's had some work done.

18 Dr. Wang pretends to not know me so that I can introduce myself. The name's Roth. Indigo Roth. This is how The Game is played by Gentlemen.

19 I will return Dr. Wang's courtesy later; after I'm captured I'll listen to his mad plan and ask all the obvious questions.; it's expected.

20 I notice that Dr. Wang is alone; there's no exotic girlfriend. This is an unexpected snag. Who else can I sweet talk into betraying him?

21 He introduces me to his new assistant, Helga Cribbage. She's obnoxious, badly dressed, and has dreadful body odour. He's daring me to try.

22 We play a few hands of baccarat. I take him for thirty grand, and hint I know his evil plan. Works like a charm; he invites me to dinner.

23 Starling really should be here taking notes. I hear through channels that he ran into big trouble at the docks; I'm pleased he's learning.

24 I arrive at midday at Dr. Wang's house, *Palomino*. He's delighted to see me and a gracious host; I feel far more welcome here than at home.

25 Palomino is a tasteful, five-star villa: sauna; solarium; gym; home cinema; dock; shark pool. They should invent a sixth star just for that.

26 Dr. Wang insists we should put our chequered past behind us. He is a reformed man, he tells me: no more world domination; no more piranhas.

27 Our lunch is interrupted by a henchman. Good grief, it's Cruz! I've not seen him since Bolivia; his new chrome ear complements his nose well.

28 Cruz confirms a delivery; a crate of diamonds and a dozen giant Tesla coils. Wang is embarrassed. A hobby, he assures me, nothing more.

29 As I leave, Dr. Wang says "Goodbye, Mr. Roth". I drive back into town, and a black sedan follows discretely; two more cliché boxes ticked.

30 The local carnival is in full swing. Starling makes contact; he's disguised as a showgirl. He looks a little too convincing. Hmmm.

31 Starling has discovered something; a manifest for diamonds and Tesla coils. I tell him that I know. He's crestfallen; his mascara runs.

32 The black sedan unloads; Cruz and his men are here to kill us. Goodness, is it *that* time already? Cruz's chrome nose gleams in the moonlight.

33 I grab a duck costume and we escape into the Carnival. We are pursued. Starling seems rather comfortable running in high–heeled sling–backs.

34 We evade capture in a millpond. Starling then shows me the blueprints; a secret base underneath the sea. It's awesome. I mean, "diabolical".

35 Starling and I split up. I'll use the sub to reach the Wang's base. I think he wants me to be a decoy; I am still wearing the duck costume.

36 The sub is the same one I left moored off Crete. It still has the dent from when I reversed into a hydrant. Now *that* was hard to explain.

37 I locate Dr. Wang's base three miles out. It's an art–deco masterpiece. The man is under–appreciated, even if he is mad.

38 I dock at the main airlock. I want them to know I'm coming. Messing about would put a crease in the tuxedo, and I want to do this right.

39 Cruz meets me at the airlock. He smiles broadly and silently directs me inside. He says nothing sinister or ironic. That's his boss' job.

40 Dr. Wang is dressed in red emperor's robes. "Ah, Mr. Roth. We've been expecting you." Damn, I love it when they do that; this man has style.

41 Accompanied by Cruz, we tour Wang's secret base. Missile silos, laboratories, command centre; all top notch. The canteen is also impressive.

42 There are a dozen pools of water lit by Tesla coils. Wang explains these are unrelated to his scheme, he just likes their "evil ambience".

43 His plan is simple; global blackmail. Biological agents loaded in missiles. A demonstration. A ransom. A race against time. It's a classic.

44 Our chat is disturbed by alarms. After a few minutes, two bruised and bloodied henchman drag Starling in. I'm glad he decided to join us.

45 The young spy is lorded over by Dr. Wang. Starling's banter is defiant but lacks edge. Wang asks me if Starling is new? I don't know where to look.

46 Wang sends Starling away for torture. We then share an excellent dinner and talk like Old Generals. Why am I only respected by my opponents?

47 Dr. Wang craves financial independence. He's tired of working for the highest bidder, for oppressive rogue regimes with bad payment habits.

48 He experimented with internet–based terrorism, but his heart wasn't in it. "That is a young man's game, Mr. Roth. And we are *not* young men."

49 After a few more drinks he's quite garrulous. The Chateau Lafite 1846 oils his tongue and is absolute Nectar. I forget to plan my escape.

50 Wang dislikes new villains. They respect neither moral boundaries nor tradition, he says. They lack Discipline. We agree on that point.

51 He doesn't *want* to destroy the world; he simply misses Iceland and wants to buy it back. He's a creature of habit; this way is all he knows.

52 Intellect needs a Nemesis, he says. I am a necessary but dangerous evil. Henchman do not understand him. His ex–wife did not understand him.

53 This is getting rather maudlin, but I keep his spirits up until the explosions start. Starling is an ass, but I knew he'd get the job done.

54 Starling bursts in with Dr. Wang's assistant Helga Cribbage; she seems happy but flustered. Sonofabitch. I take my hat off to him.

55 "The self destruct is activated, Wang!" Starling roars, "But I'll take care of your destruction *personally!*" Damn, that's an annoyingly good line.

56 Wang turns to me and smiles. "Until next time, Mr. Roth." He runs down a corridor pursued by Starling. Great, I get to fight the henchman.

57 Cruz grins broadly. "It's time for your treatment, Mr. Roth," he leers. This chrome–nosed guy really has the hang of the Henchman routine.

58 As we fight, I draw Cruz close to a Tesla coil; a massive jolt of electricity arcs to his metal nose. Why *do* they keep these things about?

59 Screaming, his nose smoking, Cruz falls into the water; is he dead? No time to check; I must escape without losing the deposit on this tux.

60 Starling returns, annoyed; Wang eluded him. He's bloodied and bruised from torture. Yes, he's made of tough stuff. But he's still a tosser.

[61] As the base disintegrates, we find the life-pods. I allow Ms. Cribbage to leave with Starling; I am a gentleman spy. Plus I need the legroom.

[62] The base explodes as my escape pod bubbles towards the surface. It shoots skywards on the shockwave; I don't know whether to whoop or barf.

[63] The escape pod lands heavily. I exit to find a beach on an island paradise. Nearby, a beautiful woman is shaking a martini. Luck? No. Karma.

[64] Starling and Cribbage trudge up the beach. She's hectoring him about safely meeting her needs as a woman. She punches his arm repeatedly.

[65] A helicopter buzzes past. Doctor Wang shakes his fist at us and curses in Icelandic. He's smiling though. Yes, until next time, Dr. Wang.

[66] My mission is over. Dr. Wang is defeated. The world is safe once more. The only casualty is my sub, but I made sure Starling signed for it.

[67] I drive us to the airport. As I check in, men with rubber gloves ask me about the diamonds in my case. What? Starling laughs as he walks by.

[68] Back at the office, Starling has his arm in a sling; the secretaries fuss over him. He patronises me and includes me as a decoy in his tale.

[69] The Admiral debriefs me alone. He's delighted with the outcome, and asks how Starling performed. I say he did okay; he was a useful decoy.

[70] As a throwaway final comment, I report that Starling cracked under torture; more intense training is needed. The Admiral agrees. Gotcha.

Lying In Wait With Bricks

5 [1] One of the nice things about working for Her Majesty's Secret Service for many years was that I got to drive some pretty fabulous cars.

[2] High-speed chases through Tokyo? Hairpin bends on Alpine roads?

[3] No problem.

[4] And one of the *very* nice things about transitioning to semi-retirement was that I got to keep one of the cars;

[5] a *Bentley Continental GT.*

[6] Sitting in traffic for hours on the London orbital? Popping down to the supermarket? Sorted.

[7] One of the bad things about knowing an arch genius is that when he lays off his command flight-crew of ferrets, they have nothing to occupy their devious and highly-organised little minds.

[8] So, while I am sensitive to their plight, I want to be *clear*.

[9] Several bad things will happen to the entire bunch** of them if they don't bring me all five of my car's wheels back.

[10] Yes, somehow they got the spare too.

[11] I may stay up late and lie in wait with my own bricks.

[12] And give them a secret servicing they'll never forget.

Notes

*   These were delivered as 140-character tweets to a secret government social media account. Yes, we fly below radar while being in plain sight.
**   The correct collective noun for ferrets is a *business* or *busyness*. Yes, really.

Ruminations

*"I'm very big on Courtesy. Ask anyone. Seriously. A please, a thank you,
the free–and–useful oil that makes the day's machines turn and tick;
I approve, appreciate and apply myself to the practice."*

Not A Funny Badger In Sight

1 ¹ You all know me, right?
² I like to write fluff, surreal vignettes and whimsies that cheer the days along;
³ lions, and badgers, and bears, oh my.
⁴ I have little to grumble about, my life is easy; I have security, money and prospects, family and friends.
⁵ Today I'm fine, and most likely will be tomorrow.
⁶ I'm a very lucky guy. I admit it.
⁷ But not everyone is so lucky.
⁸ Sometimes bad things happen.
⁹ Some days there are no laughs, and precious little solace.
¹⁰ I love my friends, and I stand by them on those bad days.
¹¹ Any number of people might do it, but I choose to instead. It's important to do this, even if I can't always affect the outcome.
¹² We can place ourselves in the way of bad circumstances, and stand ready to help a friend as life carries them along;
¹³ a little help is worth a lot of pity.
¹⁴ Sometimes we make things worse, though we don't mean to.
¹⁵ We may not be needed in the end.
¹⁶ But the act makes a difference.
¹⁷ The *effort* is important.

And Fifty Years From Now

2 ¹ Bloggers are an odd breed.
² We sit here, scribbling away, etching our more significant thoughts onto internet pages.
³ It is said that "digital is forever", but will our efforts still exist in five years time? Ten? A hundred?
⁴ Books survive because they are physical things, the same as paintings and sculptures. But blogs have no physical form. Will they survive?
⁵ I've no idea, but I like to think so. If I didn't, perhaps I'd slip off to bed a bit earlier than I do most nights.
⁶ But if blogs do survive, what will be made of them? Will they be viewed in their historical context, or as work to be re–examined and re–evaluated in the times in which they are read?
⁷ When Grant Wood painted the iconic *American Gothic* in 1930, he entered his painting in a competition at the Art Institute of Chicago. The judges chuckled at something they viewed as a humorous piece, and dismissed it.
⁸ But they were brow–beaten by an influential museum patron to award it a bronze medal and to buy it.
⁹ The house in the picture was (and still is) in Eldon, Iowa.

10 When the locals saw the picture in the papers, they were outraged at their depiction as pinched, grim–faced, puritanical Bible–thumpers.

11 But elsewhere, art critics hailed it as a satire of life in rural small–town America.

12 Over time, it became associated with the literary trend towards criticism of rural life in small–town America.

13 During the Depression it became a salute to American pioneer spirit.

14 Later still, it became symbolic of a revolt against East Coast artistic thinking.

15 And these days, it's regarded as an icon of American art.

16 But it's interesting to note what Grant Wood had to say about it.

17 He stated that it was a painting of a house that caught his eye, and the kind of people he imagined might live there.

18 The models were his sister and his dentist.

19 I wonder what the critics made of *that?*

20 It is possible that future generations might read my blog, and the books that spring from it. Their critics and shrinks may pore over the material, seeking enlightenment on the subject of Mister Indigo Roth.

21 So, may I say this for the record:

22 I'm not trying to make an artistic statement, I'm simply enjoying myself.

23 I'll deny that when I get famous of course.

24 And by the way, the Art Institute of Chicago still has American Gothic on display. Whatever the painting means, they *like it.*

25 Which is a critical evaluation I can get behind.

Neither Catharsis Nor Apology

3 1 Hi, my name is Indigo and I play Dungeons & Dragons.

2 There may be some uncomfortable silence while I let that information soak in.

3 I can't imagine this fantasy role–play confessional will win me many fans. It may well surprise, dismay or offend many others.

4 But hey, there it is. Let's move on.

5 Your picture of D&D will probably be of spotty, geeky adolescents gathering in a darkened room to play a game. There are maps and manuals, little metal characters, and lots of dice.

6 And actually, though it's a bit of a broad brush, you'd be pretty much on the money.

7 These lads, who have never had girlfriends, pretend to be fighters, thieves, priests and wizards from any number of strange races, and assume grandiose and ridiculous gaming identities like *Narfblat the Ork Slayer*.

8 They have a fascination and devotion to thick rule books with small print, can quote *Monty Python*, *Star Trek* and *Star Wars* without pausing for breath, and can argue passionately about things that aren't real.

9 They're a bit odd, frankly.

10 But then, unexpectedly, we grew up.

11 Some things changed.

12 We went to work, where our fascination for detail and rules made us an excellent fit for employment in computing and related disciplines.

13 We discovered—gasp—*other* hobbies; music, movies, cookery, writing, art, travel, literature.

14 Some took to cycling and walking, previously unthinkable fresh air pursuits, while others discovered yoga to combat the stresses of our chosen profession.

15 And yes, there were girls. Not our teenage pin–ups and crushes, but *real* girlfriends! And, good grief, eventually there was marriage. What would our younger selves have said?

16 But some things didn't change.

17 Years later, we still love the things we've always loved. Yes, we're still fundamentally geeks, just more rounded ones. We still enjoy the kind of in–joking that any tight group of friends inevitably develops.

18 But most importantly, we still play Dungeons & Dragons.

19 Some of us have drifted in and out of the group over the years as our lives dictated, but the group has endured. Many of the folks I'm lucky enough to game with have been together for twenty five years, man and boy.

20 There is even a woman in the group these days, and she's just as daft as us.

21 The road goes ever on.

22 I still play because I get a kick out of the social interaction;

23 I enjoy the game, but mostly I just love hanging out with my friends and sharing a healthy dollop of escapism with them every week.

24 As ever, I consider myself lucky.

25 My name is Indigo and I play Dungeons & Dragons.

26 This is neither catharsis nor apology.

27 It just is.

The Socks Of Armageddon

4 1 I've been in my recent job for a few years now.

2 I got the job under odd circumstances; I met the company owner in hospital after I'd taken his teenage son there following a road accident. It wasn't serious; his son was fine.

3 However, it was my fault; the lad had fallen off his bike while swerving to avoid me reversing out of my driveway.

4 On a typical day I wouldn't have driven into town. But I was in a hurry that morning; I'd missed the bus and was late for work.

5 The bus had pulled away just as I reached the bus stop. I'd ran all the way there, too, because I'd left the house late.

6 I normally leave the house punctually at 8:30, but I'd had to go back upstairs to change my socks; I'd found a hole in the heel of one as I put my shoes on.

7 I had seven pairs of socks at the time, all different colours. I'd selected a black pair that morning for no particular reason. It wasn't much of a decision; I mean, what difference would it make?

8 What indeed.

9 As I sat happily having dinner that night, rather pleased with myself, I reflected on the events of the day. Everything had turned out pretty well from an odd start.

10 But something niggled at me.

11 My qualifications made me suitable for the job, but meeting the company owner had ultimately been important.

12 I'd done the right thing and helped his son; I'd impressed him with my character, I suppose.

13 But that was the result of a chance occurrence, the car accident.

14 Which in turn was because I'd missed the bus.

15 Because I was late leaving the house.

16 Because I had to change my socks.

17 Because I chose the black ones.

18 This was an epiphany.

19 The huge decisions of my life had paved the way for me to take advantage of events as they unfolded.

20 *Chance favours the prepared mind*, as my uncle Jericho would say.

21 But the pathways to those big events were paved with much smaller events. Tiny, inconsequential happenings that could change the course of a day in ways that could never be predicted at the point they occurred.

22 On that day, I had chosen black socks. And I had a new job.

23 Had I chosen blue, I would have been on the bus and not writing this memoir.

24 Though of course, I may have been writing a different one about some other trivial event that netted me a lottery win.

25 Damn. Blue, shoulda gone for blue.

26 You see the problem?

27 I'm not suggesting anybody stops worrying about the "big" choices in life. The subjects we choose, the university we attend, the career we pursue, the partners we make our beds with, the cars we buy. The jobs we accept.

28 These things are important, and deserve consideration.

29 Nor am I saying that instead we must fixate over every small decision, to worry about the manifold and ultimately unknowable consequences of our actions. Quite the opposite. We can't do that, and shouldn't; we'd never make it out of bed for fear of Armageddon.

30 But maybe we can ease up on ourselves a bit, and realise that perhaps our lives are steered by far smaller events than the ones we spend so much time worrying about.

A Multitude Of Sins

5 1 Hello, my name's Indigo. I like to wear a suit and tie when I'm at the office.

2 There are times when making this simple statement feels like some kind of confession at a meeting of alcoholics.

3 And it is often viewed with the same kind of alarm and suspicion by observers.

4 "Suit? Necktie? In this day and age?"

5 "Why on Earth do you wear a suit to work?!"

6 "But you work in software development, don't you?"

7 "I thought coders did well to put on two matching shoes!"

8 And it's true. Well, bits of it anyway. Until recently I did work in software development, and even though it was for a big corporation, there is a very relaxed vibe about business dress.

9 Most folk wear casual clothes; jeans, t–shirts, trainers, cardigans. Indeed, that's what's *expected* of us*.

10 In fact, when a very senior manager from the States came over recently and witnessed a few folks in suits—he wasn't wearing one, may I say—he proceeded to give them a hard time all day.

11 Anyway, in general I buck the trend.

12 The reasons for this are many and varied, but the simplest and most honest is that I like to wear a necktie.

13 I can immediately sense some frowns and questions:

14 "Is this some sort of fashion statement?" Nope, that's not me. I never read about men's fashion.

15 "Is it a personal statement?" Probably. Mine are simple yet striking.

16 "Oh, is this *vanity?*" Well, yes, more than likely; I like a splash of colour.

17 Even in suit–wearing organisations, the humble necktie has become somewhat passé.

18 Those of you from smart offices will have seen the open–collar–and–tanktop chic that senior managers have drifted into.

19 That's not for me; I like to wear a waistcoat. Yes, my fashion grave just keeps getting deeper.

20 However, the reasons for the waistcoat are pragmatic; I'm a little overweight and prefer to wear braces to keep my trousers from wandering south**.

21 Plus I'm tall, and making a decent Windsor knot on a tie leaves it looking short.

22 So, a waistcoat can conceal a multitude of sins, and looks smart into the bargain.

23 However, a curious thing has happened to me in recent weeks.

24 The summer was too hot and humid for me to enjoy wearing a suit, so I reverted for a month back to the more relaxed option.

25 This was far more comfortable, but I was looking forward to cooler weather.

26 So, when the chilly autumn days arrived a few weeks ago, I donned the suit again. It was nice, and few folks even commented on me looking smart again.

27 But I also observed a whole bunch of curious things:

28 People spoke to me more.

29 Women smiled at me more.

30 More doors were held open for me.

31 People listened more closely when I spoke in meetings. Even odder, my opinion seemed to carry more weight.

32 The folks working for the site services agency struck up conversations with me, explaining their activities if they were nearby.

33 And I swear one of them—perhaps an ex–serviceman—saluted me as he went about his business one afternoon.

34 I put all this down to some psychological effect of the suit and tie. But when I mentioned it to a friend at the office he disagreed.

35 "It's not people reacting differently to you in the suit," he said. "It's the fact that you're different when you wear the suit."

36 I was quite taken aback by this, thinking it unconsciously turned me into some hard–nosed business type who trampled the office and its unworthy denizens beneath his shiny boots.

37 But again, my friend disagreed.

38 "You are more confident," he explained, "and people are reacting to that confidence."

39 Who would have thought it?

40 So, while manners make the man, it turns out a decent suit and tie can run a close second.

41 Please excuse me, I'm going to surf for some more ties.

A Flutter Of Tiny Wings

6 1 I didn't win the lottery tonight.
2 Most of us have said this at some point; no big deal, right?

3 Well, yes and no. It's an unremarkable statement, because the odds of winning the UK national lottery are over fourteen million to one. Here's today's result:

4 *11–25–27–32–37–43*

5 But you might think this is a big deal if you realised that I had the numbers in advance.

6 **Earlier this week**, I was thinking about randomness. A quick web search took me to a fascinating website that creates random numbers from daily atmospheric readings.

7 This all sounds very esoteric. Are there patents and industrial secrets involved? A crack team of Eastern–European physicists? Or it could just be a soothsayer and a bunch of entrails?

8 All this talk of the atmosphere could be hokum, present just to create some, well, *atmosphere?*

9 But I'm a sucker for an experiment; I chose to create three sets of numbers, then buy the ticket, and give it a whirl.

10 Here's the numbers it generated:

1–4–14–20–29–33
11–25–27–32–37–43
12–16–19–39–47–48

11 The eagle–eyed among you will notice that the middle line was indeed tonight's winning numbers.

12 So why am I not celebrating a huge win? Well, I forgot to buy the ticket.

13 I may smile in an ironic way about it, but actually it doesn't bother me.

14 I believe in randomness. That every event has the potential to be everything it can possibly be, and that the seed of that randomness is somehow a sum of all the events that have gone before.

15 I don't want to sound all cosmic about it. But put simply, had I bought the ticket, the outcome would almost certainly have been different.

16 The difference—do/don't buy a ticket—was tiny, but as any chaos mathematician worth their salt knows, this change could have radically changed the outcome in unpredictable ways*.

17 The result of this is twofold:

18 First, I do not spend time lingering on *what–ifs* and *how–it–coulda–beens*. This isn't a joke; I really don't. As I've noted before, even if I did, I'd probably be fixating on the wrong event; they all affect the outcome, and the insidious small ones are impossible to spot.

19 Second, I'm going to feel really stupid tonight when I lay sobbing in bed about the lottery ticket I forgot to buy, and the nice house in the country I won't be buying tomorrow.

20 Dammit.

An Outbreak Of Threes

7 1 **When I was a teenager**, I knew everything.
2 I believed in *Truth*. In black and white. Right and wrong.

3 I was awkward with girls, innocently arrogant, and had some talent.

4 I thought I was smart and cool, but actually, I was a dork.

5 **When I was at University**, I knew more, but knew it wasn't everything.

6 I believed in *Perceptions* of truth. In shades of grey. In morality.

7 I was awkward with women, less arrogant, but with plenty of talent.

8 I thought I was smart and cool, but actually, I was a dork.

9 **As I write this**, I'm comfortable that I truly know very little.

10 I believe in *Honesty*, and let others worry about what that means.

11 It turns out that life is a chaotic spectrum of interconnected things.

12 I'm awkward with most folk, a bit arrogant, and still have talent.

13 I'm still not smart and cool, but I'm a decent enough fella.

14 Okay, sometimes I'm a dork.

Where Lies Adventure

8 1 I'm a big believer in the journey.
2 The destination can be great, but the journey is where the adventure lies.

3 That's not to say that all journeys are fun, or easy, or what we expect.

4 Sometimes they can be nightmares from which we're lucky to emerge.

5 But even on the longest, straightest, dullest road, we can still find magic.

Notes

*   I couldn't possibly comment about the matching shoes.
**   Truth is not always the same as Beauty.

America

"It is said that travel broadens the mind. This is true, but sometimes it makes you want to go home and hide under the bed."

A Ratchetting Of Vertebrae

1 ¹ **It's three days ago**.
² I'm starting to get a little nervous ahead of a flight to America to attend a friend's wedding.
³ The trip has been booked for about six months, but I'm not relishing the prospect of the journey;
⁴ I don't enjoy flying much.
⁵ I'm too tall, too wide, too *neurotic*.
⁶ But at least I'm flying from a local airport, *London Stansted*, just a few minutes down the road from where I live. Plus, I'm flying at lunchtime, so checking in two hours early won't mean getting up in the middle of the night.
⁷ Oh look, I have e–mail.
⁸ "Dear Mr. Roth, we are sorry to inform you that..."
⁹ My flight has been cancelled six months after I booked it. Nightmare.
¹⁰ There's a replacement flight laid on from *London Heathrow*, but this is earlier in the day.
¹¹ I guess they've done their best, but Heathrow is an hour further away, and is the world's busiest airport; I will have to check in three hours early.
¹² So, I'm going to have to get up in the middle of the night after all.
¹³ Unless... I quickly check online... Yes, Heathrow has a Japanese–style capsule hotel, in the terminal building I'm flying

from. Tiny rooms, exquisitely designed, comfortable. Better yet, it could be an interesting way to start the trip.
¹⁴ I am aware that I'm desperately trying to make lemonade from a thundering great lemon that's landed in my lap.
¹⁵ *But hey*, says my upbeat internal voice, *it will be something to talk about later; holidays are always more interesting when things don't go to plan!*
¹⁶ I am not convinced*.
¹⁷ *Just do it Indigo*, the voice encourages. So I do. A few clicks and credit card numbers later, and I've booked a standard room in the capsule hotel.
¹⁸ Job done, problem avoided.
¹⁹ The stakes are raised for what is now a five day adventure.
²⁰ **Back in the now**, the adventure begins. My good friend Bear is driving me down to Heathrow.
²¹ I was going to take the train, but it was stupidly expensive and required two changes in London. Besides, the black bear owes me a favour;
²² I managed to get him and Clarice a romantic box at the *Royal Opera House* for *La Bohème* a while back. I'd not expected him to be a fan of Puccini, but I've discovered over the years that this *Ursus Americanus* is full of surprises.

205

²³ And, to his credit, he offered to drive without being asked.

²⁴ I like a mammal with a good memory.

²⁵ I just wish he had a larger car. It's an orange open–top roadster, perfect for a big guy like him, but not so good for *two* big guys like us.

²⁶ As I sit wedged into the little vehicle, I begin to wonder if this capsule hotel room will be suitable for even one big guy like me?

²⁷ I also wish Bear wasn't in such a hurry to get to Heathrow. He's a level–headed, dependable type, wise in a way that shames me at times. But behind the wheel of a car, he's a little spontaneous.

²⁸ Bear drops me off at the Terminal 4, helping—pulling—me from the cramped car and straightening my spine out with an upward tug on my head that makes my feet leave the floor with a pronounced ratchetting of vertebrae.

²⁹ He then leaps back into the car and waves cheerily as he speeds away.

³⁰ I limp inside with my minimal luggage.

³¹ I find the capsule hotel with a little effort; up an escalator and round a few badly signposted corners.

³² The entrance to the hotel presents itself curiously; it is a narrow temple of glass and purple lights. The automated check–in via an ultraviolet ATM doesn't cooperate, but an elderly Japanese porter lets me in, registers me, and locates my room key.

³³ As I wander the corridors in search of my room, I'm surprised by the sterile, laboratory feel to the place. But it's cool and quiet, two things I value highly when I'm trying to sleep.

³⁴ Each room has a large window onto the corridor, which is peculiar to say the least, though it gives me a chance to inspect the swankier rooms.

³⁵ I find my room, and eventually convince the door to open;

³⁶ I never have much luck with hotel room doors. They resist this weary traveller most of the time.

³⁷ As I open the door, I am struck by two things.

³⁸ Firstly, how spacious the room *feels*.

³⁹ There's a low–slung bunk bed to one side, a glass–walled bathroom with shower to the other, and a short central corridor–of–sorts where I am standing. There's mirrors to push the walls out a

bit, and it's pleasantly lit in the same soothing purple tones of the corridor.

⁴⁰ Secondly, I am aware just how incredibly small the room actually *is*.

⁴¹ I know from their website that this room covers just seven square metres, and that's a small enough number to stand and count them.

⁴² Also, the blocked–in space above the bunk bed makes me suspect that the adjacent room interlocks with this one, and that the inhabitant will have a high bunk directly above my low one. Weird.

⁴³ I kick off my shoes, hang up my coat, pop my luggage out of the way beneath the coat rack, and slip into the bunk.

⁴⁴ The bed is fantastic. I'm a tall guy, and this is a full two metres long. The mattress is substantial and pleasantly firm, and it's wide too.

⁴⁵ The website says it's "comfy for two", but they may have had slim, amorous, newlywed types in mind;

⁴⁶ I recall that these rooms can be booked by the hour.

⁴⁷ There's a large flat–screen TV embedded in the wall by my feet, a host of online services, including an impressive selection of room service meals, drinks and snacks.

⁴⁸ As I survey the room from the bunk, I am very impressed. There's a wonderful feeling of efficient, considered design about the place, and it's not triggering my claustrophobia;

⁴⁹ yes, I like to live dangerously.

⁵⁰ I remember that the room was designed by the bloke who created first class spaces for British Airways, but what it reminds me of—somewhat bizarrely—is a well–arranged caravan;

⁵¹ yes, a caravan with air conditioning, hi–def TV and ultraviolet lighting, but a caravan nonetheless.

⁵² Suddenly, there is a knock at the door.

⁵³ I manoeuvre myself out of the bunk, and open the door, half expecting a member of staff to be checking in on their latest arrival.

⁵⁴ It's Bear. He looks sheepish, which is difficult for him.

⁵⁵ "The car's got a flat," he tells me by way of explanation. He waves the steering wheel, which he has brought with him for some reason. "I've made some calls, but it won't get sorted 'til the morning."

⁵⁶ He looks over my shoulder. "Hey, this

looks nice!" he enthuses. Then, more hesitantly, he grins, "Is there room for another?"

⁵⁷ I sigh. "You'd better come in."

⁵⁸ I don't really want to get into the sleeping arrangements, but let's just say that me and Bear are *not* a pair of slim, newlywed types.

⁵⁹ It is an uncomfortable experience, both physically and emotionally;

⁶⁰ I have terrible dreams in which I am alternately falling from a narrow ledge over a precipice, and being smothered by an immense, black cushion.

⁶¹ **It's 7am**, and I awake to the sound of hissing water.

⁶² Bear is in the shower, singing some old Burt Bacharach tune. I lay listening as consciousness seeps in. How did he get out of bed without *waking* me?

⁶³ There is coarse, black hair in my mouth.

⁶⁴ Suddenly, there is a knock at the door.

⁶⁵ I shuffle out of the bunk clumsily, and open the door an inch. There's two badgers in the corridor.

⁶⁶ Yavin I recognise immediately, but it takes a moment to realise that the second set of dungarees is occupied by his niece Dantoo.

⁶⁷ Yavin salutes me respectfully from under his flat cap, and silently raises a toolbox into the line of sight.

⁶⁸ Dantoo, who has her own, too–big cap, waves shyly.

⁶⁹ "Hey Yavin. Hey Dantoo," I mumble in welcome, rubbing sleep from my eyes. "BEAR!" I shout hoarsely, "The badgers are here to fix your wheel!"

⁷⁰ "Outstanding!" he shouts back, midway through the second verse. "I'll be out in a moment! Make yourself at home fellas!"

⁷¹ I sigh. "You'd better come in."

⁷² I open the door fully, and the younger badger rolls a new car wheel into the room. She leaves it carefully by my luggage, growls something in greeting to Bear, and then leaps straight into the bed.

⁷³ I stand, jaw slack, dumbfounded; it's too early to get surly with wildlife.

⁷⁴ Moments later, the black–and–white youth pokes her head out excitedly, waves the remote control for the TV, and beckons Yavin into the bunk.

⁷⁵ Yavin looks up at me and takes his cap off. It's getting crowded in here; I wave

him towards the bunk wearily.

⁷⁶ The badger steps smartly into the room, deposits the toolbox with the luggage and the wheel, and quickly vanishes from sight.

⁷⁷ I'm still sleepy, and as Bear switches the shower off and uses both towels to dry off, I lower myself carefully onto the top of the toolbox;

⁷⁸ there's nowhere else to sit, unless I pull the table down.

⁷⁹ Suddenly, there's a knock at the door.

⁸⁰ I find my way there past the emerging Bear, and open it a crack.

⁸¹ "Housekeeping," says the tiny Japanese lady with the large trolley in the corridor. She bows only slightly; we're a long way from Tokyo, and I'm *gaijin* after all.

⁸² "Do we have to do this now?" I ask her, failing to either look or sound authoritative in my pyjamas. "I'll be gone in an hour, and it's a bit crowded in here."

⁸³ She puts her hands on her hips and repeats defiantly, "Housekeeping!"

⁸⁴ I open the door wider and poke my head out. I scan up and down the corridor to make sure the Marx Brothers aren't in the vicinity;

⁸⁵ I expect the double thump of hard boiled eggs at any moment.

⁸⁶ I sigh. "You'd better come in."

⁸⁷ **Ten minutes later,** I sit on the table under the coats and hats, while the cursing maid does her best to remove coarse black hair from the shower drain.

⁸⁸ I am surprised and relieved that the badgers haven't ordered any room service.

⁸⁹ Suddenly, there's a knock at the door.

Beaten To Death By Karma

2 ¹ **It's 7am on Saturday**, and I'm tired. And in America.

² I've been wandering the *Princeton University Campus* for a couple of hours.

³ **It's 5am**, and my body clock is messed up; I wake and wonder both where and who I am. When I recall these trivia, I also remember that the wedding is at 2pm.

⁴ I have nine hours to kill.

⁵ **It's 6am**, and I lurch from my hotel looking for somewhere to have breakfast; the hotel doesn't start serving

until seven, it being the weekend.

6 There's time to explore.

7 **It's 6:30am**, and I've already wandered the length of *Nassau Street*. I've discovered a few places that are open, but none of the menus tickled my jetlagged fancy;

8 I have my heart set on an unhealthy, all–you–can–eat fried breakfast, the kind I will look back on and say, "That breakfast in Princeton, now *that* was a breakfast!"

9 I take the initiative, and head over the road to the university campus.

10 I partly do this out of curiosity, but mostly to find somewhere to have sausage, bacon, eggs, hash browns, toast, and coffee. Oh, and a stack of pancakes with maple syrup.

11 I'm not sure if I'm technically allowed to be wandering here, but as I may have mentioned before, while I am a great fan of *Order*, I am not big on *Rules*.

12 Order is what you have when everyone thinks about their actions, and accepts responsibility for them.

13 Rules are what you need when they inevitably don't.

14 I am passing through here, a quiet non–presence. I don't believe the Rules here were created with me in mind;

15 arrogant, yes, but I can live with it.

16 I do not intend to disturb the Order of the place, I'll respect personal space and privacy as I go, and I will apologise and leave quietly if asked.

17 And man, this place is something.

18 I walk along tree–lined avenues, and pass through many impressive arches into immaculate shady courtyards. Enticing staircases lead the eye and imagination upwards;

19 I keep to the path, remembering I'm an uninvited guest.

20 And it's not only beautiful; it's enormous. Five hundred acres of it.

21 Twenty years ago I went to a tiny university in an industrial wasteland in the midlands of England. I loved it then and do now, but this is so different.

22 Princeton is Xanadu to my Lilliput.

23 I check my watch; it's mid–morning. Hours have passed, and I'm still no closer to breakfast. The temperature is rising sharply, I could do with a cold drink, and I'm still hungry.

24 Just as I'm thinking of heading back to the hotel, I arrive at a long, glass–sided building. It has the look of a library, but on closer inspection it turns out to be a student cafeteria.

25 My spirits rise, but I pause.

26 Again, I consider that I'm not a student. If there are Rules anywhere on campus, it will probably be here;

27 the public won't be invited in to enjoy what is probably a subsidised eating experience.

28 If I need a student ID? I'm busted.

29 If I need to use a pre–paid cafeteria card? Game Over.

30 If my presence disturbs the Order of the place, and I'm challenged, I'll most likely be escorted from campus, let alone the building, which will be a shame.

31 Especially if I don't get breakfast first.

32 I inwardly shrug, decide to wing it, and head inside.

33 The building is cool and pleasantly lit. I was expecting it to be a hive of activity, but there's not a single student there.

34 I walk confidently through the seating area—nothing suppresses questions like confidence—and I'm bemused by the lack of activity. Yes, it's Saturday, but it's ten in the morning; surely there must be at least one student who needs something to eat after a night on the tiles?

35 Well, clearly not.

36 Oh, wait; as I approach the serving area itself, a studious–looking young man marches out with a tray and settles efficiently to eat. It all looks healthy. Granola type cereal, yoghurt, juice.

37 What? Healthy? I shan't be having any of that, thank you.

38 The main serving area is modern and impressive: plenty of chrome; bright, colourful displays; pleasant–looking members of staff; there's different areas for drinks, cereals, fruit, sandwiches, salads, cold plates.

39 Hmmm, all cold.

40 But further along somewhere is serving freshly–cooked pizza, and next to it there's a section serving hot Italian and Mexican.

41 My hunt is getting warmer, but it's still not what I have in mind.

42 I retrace my steps, and eventually notice a dimly lit area behind an unobtrusive counter. A middle aged man, clearly a chef, stands alone in the shadows, near a hastily scribbled menu;

43 bacon, sausages, several kinds of eggs,

hash browns, beans, mushrooms, toast, pancakes.

⁴⁴ Bingo!

⁴⁵ "Can I get you something?" he asks amiably.

⁴⁶ "Oh, yes please." I continue to eye the menu quietly.

⁴⁷ "So, what would you like?"

⁴⁸ I'm uncertain how much to order. "Well, I like the look of everything."

⁴⁹ "Uh huh. Is this your first time here?"

⁵⁰ This snaps me back to reality. Am I about to be busted? Damn, that was quick.

⁵¹ Steady, Indigo. Don't panic. This guy's doing his job. Be honest.

⁵² "Yes, first time."

⁵³ "I didn't think I recognised you. Are you a new student?" he asks doubtfully.

⁵⁴ I don't hesitate, projecting confidence.

⁵⁵ "No, I'm not a student, " I laugh. "At *my* age? No, I'm just visiting from Cambridge."

⁵⁶ He considers this for a moment. Then, putting two and two together with my accent and smart clothes, immediately makes five. Perhaps even six or seven. His face brightens.

⁵⁷ "Cambridge, *England?* That's great!" he enthuses, "Welcome to Princeton. I hope you'll enjoy working here!"

⁵⁸ This is curling up at the edges a bit. I'm not going to lie to the guy; I don't like lying. I laugh again and prepare to confess all.

⁵⁹ "Well, I'm not actually on the staff..."

⁶⁰ He cuts me off gently, waving dismissively. "It's okay, I know how these temporary assignments and sabbaticals work. So, what can I get you, Sir?"

⁶¹ Wow, I'm a *Sir*. Part of me wants to straighten the tale out, but everyone is happy, and I'm tired and hungry; breakfast beckons.

⁶² "Okay, two sausages, three slices of bacon, a pile of hash browns, beans, mushrooms, toast."

⁶³ He seems surprised. "Well, that's more or less everything. Want any eggs with that?" he asks with a hint of something that might be sarcasm.

⁶⁴ "Oh, yes please. Two, over–easy. I've not eaten properly since lunchtime yesterday."

⁶⁵ Again, all true.

⁶⁶ "Yessir, no wonder you're hungry!" He considers something for a moment, and then asks quietly, "I've just made up a batch of banana pancake mixture.

⁶⁷ Can I tempt you?"

⁶⁸ "With maple syrup?"

⁶⁹ He looks at me strangely. If he was under forty and not talking to a member of staff, I'm sure that "Well, *duh!*" would have tripped happily to his lips.

⁷⁰ He indicates the bar opposite and grins at me.

⁷¹ "You go help yourself to coffee and juice, and I'll have this ready in a few minutes."

⁷² I head over and help myself to a very serviceable cup of Joe. There's even grapefruit juice, which always gets my taste buds zinging.

⁷³ I fill a large glass with the juice; it's going to be monster–hot out there today, and I don't want to be thirsty.

⁷⁴ I return to pick up my huge plate of fried goodies, The cook offers me a cheery "Enjoy!" and a promise to deliver pancakes in five minutes.

⁷⁵ The woman on the checkout chats happily to me; she has also assumed that I'm on the staff. I let it go.

⁷⁶ I pay and grab some cutlery, but have trouble choosing a seat. The place is vast, and now empty again; the solitary student has gone. I decide to hide in plain sight, and choose one of the first tables.

⁷⁷ The food does not disappoint. It's well cooked, hot, fresh and tasty; I've not eaten so well in weeks. I devour it with little by way of table manners. As I'm wiping up bean juice with my toast, the pancakes arrive.

⁷⁸ Ten of the things. Thick and fluffy, moist with banana.

⁷⁹ With a jug of maple syrup.

⁸⁰ "Hope this takes the edge off your appetite," winks the chef.

⁸¹ I smile a thank you to him as he strides back to his station, but my stomach wails; the new plateful looks crippling.

⁸² But I'll not leave a bite; this is some small Karmic payback for breaking Rules, and I decide to take it on the chin.

⁸³ I can live with it.

⁸⁴ Besides, I've got my wish;

⁸⁵ if I am ever asked about breakfast, I will be able to look back and say, "That breakfast in Princeton, now *that* was a breakfast!"

Trespassing Into The Endzone

3 ¹ The wedding is still a few hours away when I reach *Powers Field*, the Princeton University football stadium.

² I'm disappointed to find it closed.

³ I'm already annoyed that I won't be in town for the Tigers game on Monday, but I'm doubly annoyed that I can't take a look round.

⁴ I notice a wrought iron sign on the gate. What does it say? *Vet Nov Testamentum?* I consider this Latin. Old and New Testament?

⁵ I'm more of an *Apocrypha* man myself, my writing being mostly of dubious origin.

⁶ As if to prove a point, my attention is drawn to a pair of metal tigers guarding the front gate. One is hissing at me.

⁷ "Hey, pal! You lookin' fer a way in?"

⁸ The Brooklyn accent is unmistakable. We're a long way from New York, albeit still in the right part of the country. I wonder idly if they have a zoo there?

⁹ "Um, yeah, that's right."

¹⁰ Without looking round he whispers conspiratorially, "Round the side. The groundskeeper always leaves one open for staff."

¹¹ I wink at him. "Thanks, man." I correct myself just in time, "Beast!" These lads look ready to pounce.

¹² A quick circuit of the perimeter locates a small white mesh gate. It's open. There's nobody about. So I walk in.

¹³ I find myself in the wide, vaulted access area under the stands, which is mercifully cool, if a bit heavy on the *concrete chic.*

¹⁴ The place is deserted, though I expect to be challenged at any moment. But it's the hottest part of the day;

¹⁵ perhaps it's lunchtime?

¹⁶ A short walk and a flight of steps provides access to the topside of the stadium. It's very impressive; I've never been inside what I would call *an American Football stadium* before.

¹⁷ I stand for minutes just taking in the immaculate pitch, the painted lines of the gridiron. The place feels huge, though I know from watching games on TV that this is tiny compared to its NFL cousins.

¹⁸ Suddenly, I know I have to get down onto the pitch.

¹⁹ I walk down through the rows of seats to the bottom of the stand, and discover that there's no easy way to do this.

²⁰ But there's an access gate nearby with a six feet drop to the ground, and with a quick hop—one small step for a Roth—I'm on the field.

²¹ It's an odd experience.

²² In my time playing Left Guard and Right Tackle at University in England—yes, both ways, there were only eighteen or so of us—we were lucky if we played on a properly marked pitch.

²³ We didn't expect an audience and didn't get one.

²⁴ And here I am in a purpose–built facility; I wonder how many of us would have joined the team if there'd been twenty thousand people screaming for their team every Sunday?

²⁵ I notice that I'm wandering down the pitch. Thirty yard line. Forty. Then I'm into opposing territory.

²⁶ Roth, number 57, offensive lineman.

²⁷ We're first and ten on their forty, making a bold push towards the endzone in a sustained drive. The perspective from ground level is totally different from TV.

²⁸ My heart is pounding; I'm quite swept up by it. As I reach the endzone, the roar of the fans is deafening.

²⁹ I'm walking on air.

³⁰ Actually, what am I walking on? The playing surface is peculiar. From the stands it looks like grass, but from down here I'm uncertain.

³¹ I've played on AstroTurf, a relatively hard all–weather surface that's unkind during high–speed tumbles.

³² This looks like realistic–but–fake grass growing from a dark, soft, oily material. It has a rubbery, yielding quality, which makes sense;

³³ it's probably easier on the bones when being stomped on by a three hundred pound lineman.

³⁴ *Unnecessary roughness?! Oh, I hardly touched the man!*

³⁵ My eyes are drawn up to the tiered seating. Somewhere up there, positioned on the halfway line, is an area with three seats surrounded by a low railed fence.

³⁶ My curiosity is piqued.

³⁷ The roar of the crowd dies away as I walk across the field to a conveniently placed set of portable stairs. This is a piece of luck;

[38] other than walking the dark tunnel in one corner, I don't think I could have made it off the pitch.

[39] I climb the stairs up through the stands in the hundred degree heat, and eventually make my way to the enclosed area.

[40] It's marked as *The President's Box*. What, *The* President? This is too good an opportunity to miss.

[41] I step through a small gate and try the seat out; the view is magnificent, as I expected it would be.

[42] As I sit down, the air beside me shimmers. Ghostly forms emerge from the aether.

[43] As I sit sweating in the midday sun, I am joined by the spirits of former Princeton Alumni; *President John F. Kennedy* sits to my left, and *President Woodrow Wilson* to my right.

[44] JFK is tucking into a Berliner hotdog enthusiastically, mustard and ketchup dripping, while President Wilson nibbles sullenly on the contents of a box of popcorn.

[45] I'm not especially surprised; it's been that kind of day.

[46] "Hey Roth, good to see you!" says JFK, wiping his chin. "Are we ready for Dallas?"

[47] "Good morning, Mr. President," I smile, fairly sure that he's mistaken me for Uncle Jericho.

[48] Dallas? Oh. *Dallas*.

[49] I play along, knowing I can change nothing. "Yessir, we're good. I've made all the arrangements."

[50] Beside me, Wilson grunts disapproval of something he's found in his popcorn.

[51] I cast my eyes about, hoping for a glimpse of Marilyn Monroe;

[52] I could do with a date for the wedding.

[53] After a few minutes garrulous banter with JFK, I shift uncomfortably in the seat; it's like a brick, and too upright.

[54] "Are you okay, Roth?" asks the President between chugs of soda.

[55] "Honestly, Sir," I say, embarrassed, "I'm surprised that they couldn't find something more comfortable for the President and his party to sit upon."

[56] The Democrat laughs, "We choose to sit on these things, not because they're easy, but because they're hard!"

[57] I can't help but laugh along.

[58] "Schmucks," sighs Wilson.

Ironing In All The Right Places

4 [1] When things go wrong, if you can keep your head, I think things tend to work out okay in the end.

[2] But as I head up in the lift at two in the afternoon, I'm just not *feeling* it.

[3] Things have gone wrong, and I'm really annoyed.

[4] **Six months ago**, I've just received an invite to a friend's wedding in Princeton, New York. I quickly decide to make a break of it, and stay overnight in New York before heading back to London.

[5] A hotel in the United Nations Plaza. catches my eye; it's an impressive skyscraper hotel on the East River, with equally impressive views of the city and the river in all directions.

[6] And it's the view that draws me to the hotel, in fact; I am a big fan of the Chrysler Building, a beautiful art–deco skyscraper at 42nd Street and Lexington Avenue.

[7] There's taller buildings, but none with as much *style*.

[8] And I'm thrilled—a rare thing for me—when I manage to book a room with a view across Manhattan, including a clear and close encounter with my favourite example of 1930's architecture.

[9] I don't do this lightly; I call first to inquire about the room, to check the details thoroughly, and to give specific instructions. These are all recorded and confirmed.

[10] "No problem, Sir."

[11] **A week ago**, I call to confirm the arrangements, keen to avoid problems.

[12] "No problem, Sir."

[13] I'm excited, giddy almost.

[14] **First thing this morning**, with a fresh head of memories from the fabulous wedding and reception with good friends, I catch the train to New York from Princeton.

[15] **Ten minutes ago**, I arrive at the hotel after a walk across town from Penn Station. It's a tidy step, and I'm hot and bothered.

[16] As I check in, the friendly and helpful lady on the reception apologises profusely, and says they don't have the room I requested.

[17] "Nothing with that view today at all."

[18] I show her all the booking details, the confirmations, and explained my love of the Chrysler. She apologises again, and

confirms that she can let me have the room I booked tomorrow.

19 I explain that as I'm staying for a single night, this won't help.

20 I'm polite, if a bit tetchy, and to her credit she senses my frustration and promises me a lovely alternative with a great view.

21 And I realise that getting angry with her isn't going to conjure the room I want from thin air.

22 She apologises again, and seems to mean it. She will do her best. Disarmed, I concede with good grace, and thank her wearily for her help.

23 "No problem, Sir."

24 **But back in the now**, heading up in the lift, I'm still annoyed;

25 annoyed with the hotel for screwing up, and with myself for not asserting myself in a way that got the result I wanted. But had I made a scene, I'd probably be heading to a broom cupboard right now.

26 And who knows, maybe I am?

27 It's just so damned disappointing.

28 As the lift hisses open, I stride out purposefully with my single, small suitcase and stomp off grumpily to find my room.

29 It's at the end of a corridor, and for once the key works first time. I let myself in, dreading the scene that awaits.

30 Actually, the room looks pretty good, much larger than similar hotel rooms in England. There's a nice big bed, a spacious bathroom, a large wardrobe and what looks like a closet.

31 Ooh, and a big plasma TV with cable, which is something.

32 A broad window occupies the full width of one wall. I walk across the room and check out the view.

33 It's uptown, straight up First Avenue. Not a tourist mecca as such, and definitely not very rock'n'roll, but interesting and Big City I suppose.

34 Just not what I had my heart set on.

35 Peering round the corner, I can just see the river. Ah well, it could be worse.

36 I flop into bed, tired from the train journey and the walk across town, and try to grab a siesta; I'm at the theatre tonight, seeing *Spamalot* on Broadway, also booked six months ago.

37 Sleep doesn't come immediately; I worry about the theatre booking going wrong, and there's some general tossing

and turning and residual annoyance.

38 I do not travel well.

39 An hour later, I wake up. As I lay there, cool and comfortable, I decide that this really is a nice room. I feel calmer and more reflective; perhaps the sleep has helped?

40 I fumble for the remote and click the TV on, quickly finding my way to *BBC America*; a taste of home.

41 Yes, this is actually pretty sweet. I watch a rerun of *Doctor Who* and after it finishes, I take a shower.

42 Fresh and awake, and in a better mood, I unpack my clothes, locate some underwear, and realise that I have to iron a shirt before I can go out.

43 Remembering the closet, I wander over to it and start my search for what will hopefully be a steam iron.

44 It's not a closet. Not even slightly.

45 Toto, I'm not in Kansas anymore.

46 It's the *other* room in my *suite*. Damn.

47 I stand dumbfounded. There's comfy sofas, another plasma TV, nice furniture, and windows occupying two walls.

48 Good grief, it's a *corner* suite.

49 I'm glad I'm only paying for a standard room; this would break the bank.

50 I check the view from the corner of the room; an impressive view of the East River and Roosevelt Island.

51 And what's that building slightly further down the river? Ah yes, it's The *United Nations Building*. This is the U.N. Plaza, I suppose.

52 This is too much. Embarrassingly so.

53 I call down to reception, and speak to the lady who gave me the room. I thank her profusely, and apologise for being snitty with her earlier.

54 "No problem, Sir."

55 Mistakes happen every day, but it's how people react to correct those mistakes that defines your memory of an experience. And the hotel reacted very well, even if I was too dim to realise it immediately.

56 They've done me proud in fact; as ever, I've landed on my feet.

57 **Half an hour later**, as I stand in my underpants, ironing a shirt ready for a Broadway show, gazing out at the U.N. Building, and watching *Top Gear* on BBC America on a 50–inch plasma TV, I reflect that it's been an interesting day.

58 And that, as usual, things worked out okay in the end.

Scratching The Darkness

5 [1] "Do you like my fireflies?"
[2] I snap out of my reverie, the lit cigar in my hand, and look about.

[3] I thought I was out here alone in the chilly evening, and my thoughts were miles and years away;

[4] a quiet army could have walked up behind me most likely.

[5] The Cohiba's light, sweet smoke drifts from me in a circle as I turn, the gravel of the driveway crunching under my weight.

[6] A smile begins to form to welcome my company, another guest escaping the stifling heat and the boom–boom of the wedding reception indoors.

[7] I'm surprised to discover that there's nobody there.

[8] And there's certainly no fireflies.

[9] This is rural England, not the American outback; there might be a few badgers out there rustling through the first throws of Autumn, but there's no cicadas, and definitely no fireflies.

[10] My mind must have been wandering further than I thought.

[11] I chuckle to myself and tap a little ash from my stogie, careful to keep it clear of my best suit and tie.

[12] I like weddings, but I'm not that skilled at making small talk with acquaintances, let alone strangers;

[13] inevitably, a little overwhelmed, I'll step outside from some cool air and five minutes to myself.

[14] I'm not a smoker, but on these rare occasions, I enjoy a cigar, usually a good one; as good an excuse as any.

[15] I regard this evening's particular cigar curiously for a moment—*fireflies?*—and draw on it again.

[16] The night changes around me, and for the second time this evening **I'm in a warm American August evening several years ago**.

[17] Behind me, the exclusive *Princeton Golf Course Clubhouse* is rocking into the night, competing with New Jersey's cicada chorus with a boom–boom celebration of our circle's latest wedding.

[18] I've stepped outside from the heat and huff of the wedding reception and its fine display of truly outdated dance moves;

[19] relatives, you have to love them.

[20] Above me, a moonless sky dances with a million points of light. We're a long way from town here, and well shielded by trees; it's rare to see this many stars.

[21] I smile, enjoying the spectacle as I drag on today's treat of a cigar.

[22] A brief flash of green light catches my eye, from what I can just make out as a copse of trees in the gloom. My curiosity piqued, I watch the area for a moment, and I'm rewarded with another ephemeral emerald streak.

[23] I start to amble in that direction, stepping away from the building; paving slabs tap beneath my feet in an easy rhythm, but quickly yield to the grass of the back lawn.

[24] The fearless chirruping insects continue their serenade as a third momentary flash of green scratches the darkness.

[25] If it were higher, I'd assumed it was a shooting star, but this was below the level of the trees, and its afterimage looks *curved*.

[26] A dozen intended steps quickly becomes a fifty–pace exploration.

[27] I leave the half–lit back lawn of the clubhouse, stepping through an ivied archway into deeper wooded darkness.

[28] Again, fleeting emerald fires lead the way, and I'm vaguely aware that they're drawing me away from the building towards... What?

[29] The trees are denser now, but I'm still on some kind of path and I keep a slow and even pace.

[30] I'm aware on some level that the cicadas have faded away behind me. Ahead of me, beyond the line of trees, a virid glow draws me the final few yards and out into the open.

[31] My view is eerie and beautiful. Above a kidney–shaped, immaculate golfing green surrounded by sand traps, dozens of fireflies circle the 18th hole's flag. Their movement is lazy and random. My jaw drops open.

[32] The silence swirls around me.

[33] "Do you like my fireflies?"

[34] To the right of the green, a tall, slender figure rakes the sand of a bunker. I can't make him out in the starlight, but I'm not startled or alarmed;

[35] his voice is quiet and friendly, and the glowing insects have me captivated.

[36] "Yes, they're beautiful," I say honestly, still gaping a little. "Do they normally do this? Swarm around the pin?"

[37] "No, Sir," says the man, not pausing in

his work, "though they're usually where I am, I'm pleased to say," he chuckles. I can see that would make night work a little easier, though I don't vocalise that thought; it really doesn't make this scene seem any less surreal.

38 On the green, the cloud of fireflies widens slightly, and the scene brightens a little.

39 The figure now appears to be wearing well-loved dungarees and an equally battered cap. His feet are bare. I'm still unsure of his ethnicity, though it seems irrelevant.

40 I stroll down the gentle slope towards the flag, pausing on the edge.

41 "Do you do a lot of maintenance at night?" The question is obvious, but it sounds sarcastic, which was not intended. It's said that sarcasm is the lowest form of wit. I disagree;

42 punning is the lowest form of wit, while sarcasm is just plain rude.

43 I scramble to prop up my question. "That's very dedicated of you."

44 The man leans on his rake, perhaps reflectively; it's hard to tell in the half light.

45 "Oh, you know how it is, Sir; a work of love is never a chore." I like his upbeat outlook, but don't mistake his good manners for deference.

46 There is a quiet confidence about the man; he truly belongs here.

47 Circling the edge of the green, I close the gap between us, and he steps up from the bunker to meet me.

48 "My name's Roth. Indigo Roth." We shake hands briefly; his touch is dry, warm, elusive.

49 My eyes are adjusting to the night, and I'm surprised when I meet his gaze; he has a hint of the Middle East about him; this is unusual in this neck of the woods.

50 "I have a lot of names, Indigo," he smiles quietly as I detect a hint of an exotic spice in the air, "but round here they just call me *The Groundskeeper*."

51 The moment feels significant, though I have no idea why.

52 "What brings you out here onto the golf course?" my company asks, gesturing down the faint approach of the fairway. "I don't see many folk at this time of day."

53 "Oh, I followed the fireflies out here." And I grunt, stifling a laugh; it sounds stupid now I say it. But my new friend

raises a hand and shakes his head minutely, as if I'd confessed my reservations out loud.

54 "I understand. And your curiosity does your credit, my friend. Besides," he raises an eyebrow, "maybe they *wanted* you to see this?"

55 I don't know how to respond to that.

56 "They're tiny creatures," says the Groundskeeper as one firefly detaches itself from the cloud to circle his capped head slowly; he raises a kind hand towards its light and smiles as his eyes follow the insect, "but who knows what they *think?*"

57 Again, I have no idea how to respond. This sounds like Theology.

58 "Are you a man of Faith, Mr. Roth?" Well, that's *definitely* Theology; this would normally make me wary, but I find myself thinking about it.

59 "No, not really." The Groundskeeper nods, not looking my way; the firefly still has his attention. "I was raised as a Devout Atheist." I grin to myself; my mother would be proud. "But these days, even though I have no Religion, I find it hard to dismiss everyone else's."

60 Good grief, have I become Agnostic while I wasn't paying attention?

61 A few more fireflies have drifted our way; it must be the warmth.

62 "It's good to be open-minded," my companion concedes, "only the madman is absolutely certain."

63 "That's good, I'll have to remember it." I meet zealots of both persuasions. I'm just as uncomfortable talking with unshakeable Scientists as I am with immovable Evangelists;

64 both are Fundamentalists in my book.

65 The rest of the fireflies have moved to surround us. "They seem to like you, Indigo." There is a sense that we are deep underwater. Or among the stars.

66 "This is awesome."

67 The Groundskeeper waves an arm, perhaps in farewell, as the insects retreat to the flag; I'm uncertain of the causal relationship of this.

68 Deprived of their light, my eyes struggle to adjust; the silhouette opposite me chuckles kindly.

69 "But they're fickle, and easily scared, like all simple creatures."

70 The moment has passed. My instincts tell me it's time to get back indoors.

71 The Groundskeeper steps back into

the sand trap and retrieves his rake. "I hope you'll excuse me, but I must get back to my work."

[72] "Of course. Nice to meet you!" I retreat across the green with a cheery wave, but stop to fish about in my pocket.

[73] Retrieving a quarter dollar coin that shines with darting points of light, I creep beneath the fireflies and drop it into the cup at the base of the flag with a clink.

[74] I feel this deserves an explanation; my actions often do.

[75] "Life is full of surprises, but it's nice to add to them." There's no reply. I shrug, and raise my voice a little, "Whoever putts out first tomorrow will find a small–but–shiny surprise."

[76] The laugh drifts across from the bunker, "I knew the fireflies liked you for a reason!"

[77] I stroll towards the woods, and offer up a cheery, "Maybe so!"

[78] "That's the spirit!"

[79] As I retreat to the clubhouse, the moment feels as elusive as the Groundskeeper's handshake.

[80] By the time I find the back lawn again, I have a gossamer memory of my walk in the cold night air.

[81] As I reach the back door, I notice that my cigar has gone out. How did that happen? And my feet are cold; how long have I been out here?

[82] I rejoin the boom–boom of the wedding, pleased to be back in the warm.

[83] **Back in the now**, I smile at the indistinct memory, a fragment of my life. I blink, and it's gone again. Looking around, I'm still alone out here.

[84] As I walk back to the wedding reception, I take a final drag on the Cohiba.

[85] "Do you like my fireflies?"

Notes

*   You can read about that kind of nonsense in my trip to Marrakech.

Marrakech

"Bedtime. I expect I'll sleep badly; last night someone broke in and shampooed the carpets. Were they really that bad?"

Manners Maketh The Man

1 As I wake up in Marrakech for the first time, I'm pleased to discover that I'm a bit calmer than the day before, which was long and difficult.

2 The flight into Morocco from London Stansted? Troublesome. The taxi to downtown from the airport? Fast and dangerous. The long walk along a high and seemingly endless walled alleyway to my house/hotel? Intimidating.

3 And my realisation that they really didn't speak *any* English? And that I would have to rely on my hazy high school French?

4 Well, words failed me. Literally.

5 But then, I never enjoy the first day of a holiday much; I find the upheaval and change of scenery a bit disorienting and stressful.

6 So far, Marrakech has proven to be no different than any other trip.

7 My top–floor room, two storeys above a courtyard, is bright, well–fitted and rather cheery. I shower, dress and go up a short flight of stairs to the roof.

8 The view, while not spectacular, is encouraging; an old red–walled city with palm trees, blue skies, and sunshine.

9 Breakfast at this family–run *riad* is a solitary affair. My bad French alone could have guaranteed that, but it seems I am the only guest staying today.

10 The food is excellent, however. The fluffy egg pancakes are delicious and hot, the coffee strong and pleasantly rough, and the strange fried almondy things taste far better than they look.

11 I offer my thanks in Arabic—I have a handful of polite utterances at my disposal—to the beautiful young lady waiting on me, which goes down better than my attempts at French.

12 I am rewarded with a second cup of coffee and a lovely smile.

13 As I sit thinking about the day ahead, I peruse my French dictionary. As I pass a summary of restaurant words, I realise that I asked for the bill earlier, when I meant the menu.

14 Oops. Not that they had a menu; they had breakfast. This explains the puzzled look I'd received from the daughter of the house.

15 I grin wryly; I know it won't be the final linguistic fumble of the trip.

16 I'd briefly considered and dismissed the language barrier. On a previous trip to the relaxed Arabic state of Tunisia, they had spoken half a dozen languages, three of which I could muddle by in, including English. So I'd assumed that Morocco would be similar?

17 Wrong. They speak three things: *Arabic*; *French*; and *Nothing Else*.

¹⁸ I'm not worried. my French will hold up. I think.

¹⁹ It may even be fun?

²⁰ The day awaits, and I feel surprisingly upbeat about it.

Ambushes In Waiting

2¹ As I step out into the alleyway, it's mid–morning. And, even though I'm in shade, the heat is already oppressive.

² I'm glad I left my light jacket behind; I would have been carrying it all day.

³ The alleyway is a little less intimidating in the light of day. That said, were this a John Wayne western, I would be certain that this long, straight, high–sided brick canyon was an ambush waiting to happen.

⁴ And I'm half right.

⁵ Within twenty yards, I am accosted by two young lads, who are maybe ten or eleven years old. I presume they are either beggars or opportunists, and don't make the mistake of stopping;

⁶ that indicates interest, kindness, weakness, or that I am a *sucker*.

⁷ I don't wish any of those messages to be conveyed.

⁸ They mistake me for a German.

⁹ This happens a lot. I am 6'5"*, of imposing build, and have short hair. I am told I look quite serious, which may also be a factor.

¹⁰ I shake my head and say "English" as I stride away down the alleyway.

¹¹ They are not impressed, and ask me (in French) if I speak French. I nod and the older boy starts chattering away to me. I get about half of it.

¹² It seems he thinks I am lost, and he wants to show me around. I decline politely and keep walking, fairly sure I'm heading the right way to reach to find the main city square.

¹³ His salesmanship is admirable; he remains cheery and again offers to help, and then says something I don't quite catch which suggests I really don't want to be going *that* way.

¹⁴ I am now less sure my heading is correct. I slow slightly, and ask him how much his assistance will cost? He looks offended, and says he will do it for nothing.

¹⁵ I stop and eye him suspiciously, and he repeats this. He swears it is true, and rattles off an oath that involves either his deity or his mother; he's talking too quickly to tell.

¹⁶ He smiles angelically.

¹⁷ He also waves his friend away without losing eye contact with me. His friend runs off in search of another lost soul.

¹⁸ I ask him if I am going the right way for the main square and he nods. Walking ahead of me, he points and talks a lot.

¹⁹ We're buzzed by a couple of mopeds, which unsettles me a little. I suddenly realise he's asking me questions which are sliding past me. He mentions Manchester United and I chuckle at his bizarre pronunciation of *Oon–ee–ted*, which he takes to be a good sign.

²⁰ Of course, in a hundred yards, I know where I am from the night before: straight on to the main road and probably the *Djemaa el Fna* city square; turn right to enter the *Soukh*, the covered market.

²¹ The guide book encouraged me to visit the Soukh, and even as I stand there with a view of coloured silks, spices and metal trinkets, I'm tempted to head straight in.

²² But by reputation it is a hive of generic alleyways bustling with stalls, shops and beggars. I think I'd like to be a bit more *outdoors* until I find my feet.

²³ I check with my guide if the square is indeed straight on. He nods, and I thank him for his time.

²⁴ I say I no longer need a guide. He starts to protest, but quickly senses I am serious; he asks me for some money.

²⁵ I say no, and remind him he wanted no money for his services. He shakes his head, and says he is sick, and needs an operation.

²⁶ I am not certain he uses the French for *voluntary donation* as he rapidly expounds his position, but I'll bet it's in there somewhere.

²⁷ I admit to myself that I did accept his help (sucker) and I was always likely to give him something for his trouble (sucker).

²⁸ But, sucker or not, I don't believe a word of the operation story.

²⁹ Still. I pull a small–ish Dirham note from my pocket. He looks at it with disdain and his pitch goes up a gear.

³⁰ He finds a few words of English from somewhere and, pointing at his face, he

explains more about his operation.

[31] "It is my eyes. My eyes!"

[32] I start to withdraw the note and he quickly takes it from me. His mission accomplished, the young pirate salutes, says he will see me again, and runs off.

[33] Unbelievable. A hundred yards into my journey and I've already been relieved of some money.

[34] I feel pretty stupid.

[35] As I wander towards the main square, I'm determined to not let it happen again.

[36] The Djemaa el Fna (Place of the Vanished Mosque) is a wide open area surrounded by low buildings. It's the main market for the city, but it is not quite the Arabian bazaar I had expected it to be. There's quite a few vehicles and bicycles, and many people are dressed in a western style.

[37] Still, there are signs of history, even if it is perhaps only for us tourists. A snake charmer weaves his spell with a large cobra, and there are a number of jugglers and acrobats.

[38] I slow to take a photo of the snake charmer, and immediately get accosted by five brightly-dressed musicians. They dance around me, smiling and singing. They place a traditional Moroccan hat on my head, and make me the centre of attention for a couple of minutes.

[39] Quite a few locals and tourists stop to take in the show, which undeniably is a lot of fun. I don't feel threatened by it, even when one relieves me of my camera and takes some photos of me with the remainder of his troupe.

[40] My camera is returned, and they ask me for money.

[41] Resigned to a second light loss, I pull my wallet. A quick scan identifies a note that I think will be appropriate for the five of them. The man I assume to be the leader whips the note deftly from my grasp, offers up thanks to heaven and does a runner.

[42] The four others look to me, indicating they'll see none of it. They move a little closer too, not in an aggressive way, but one that says they expect to be paid.

[43] I sigh and hand a few more notes out. What the hell, the notes aren't worth much (sucker) and they did give me a good show (sucker).

[44] Singing and cheering, they melt away into the crowd.

[45] I look at my wallet and think for a moment. I check the remaining notes. I check again. Dammit, I gave them each around ten pounds sterling!

[46] No wonder they were singing.

[47] Only smaller denomination notes remain; less than half of my holiday cash is left.

[48] Good grief, I've only been out of the hotel for twenty minutes!

[49] I'm half tempted to go back there before the rest vanishes.

[50] But the beautiful centre-piece mosque for the city awaits my pleasure, and it is in walking distance.

[51] I head to a café to settle my nerves, check my map, and have a lemonade. This seems to help.

[52] But I still feel like a total idiot.

[53] As I wander away from Djemaa el Fna, I am determined to not let it happen again.

In Search Of Weaker Prey

3 [1] Even from half a mile away, the *Koutoubia Mosque* is impressive.

[2] I walk towards it with a growing sense of awe, and by the time I'm two hundred metres away, I'm lost for words.

[3] I've had a fascination with Arabic architecture since I visited Tunisia few years ago and saw the *Mosque of Uqba* in Kirouain.

[4] The guide book tells me that Koutoubia is the most important mosque in Morocco, and the most impressive.

[5] It also tells me that it was completed in 1199 AD, which tickles me; I live in Cambridge in England, and Cambridge University was founded in 1209 AD.

[6] So, even though the University's history begins four hundred years before any Englishmen set foot on American soil, this magnificent mosque pre-dates it. Cool.

[7] I wander around the grounds of the mosque, challenged only by a group of young kids.

[8] They pester me for money—perhaps they also need eye operations?—but I ignore them. I do this partly out of a sense of financial preservation—they've proven to be devious little sods so far—but mostly because I'm too busy taking photos.

[9] They take the hint and wander off in search of weaker prey.

An Interlude With Mint Tea

4¹ The bus ride across Marrakech is uneventful, a meandering drive through various districts in the more modern French half of the city.

² Nothing catches my eye.

³ The first glimmer of interest is a road sign at a major intersection, another twenty minutes in; *Fes* and *Rabat* top the list of destinations.

⁴ Fes is a former capital of Morocco, as is Marrakech itself. The current capital is the port city of Rabat, which took over the honour from Marrakech in the 1950s, a shift of some 50 miles.

⁵ This is like the capital of England being moved from London to Oxford. Having spent time in both London and Oxford, I rather like the idea.

⁶ And at the foot of the bill, I see a city name that makes me smile:

⁷ *Casablanca!*

⁸ Humphrey Bogart would be proud of me. Actually, come to think, maybe he wouldn't; I remember that I've never actually *seen* Casablanca.

⁹ As a film lover, this seems a bit of an omission. But I did see the Maltese Falcon, and can imagine Bogey looking me over with disdain as he utters a line from that classic.

¹⁰ *People lose teeth talking like that. If you want to hang around, you'll be polite.*

¹¹ A few minutes later, we reach the Royal Palace, and I am so unimpressed by it, I don't reach for my camera.

¹² I wander down the first main street and find another enclosure facing me, with another mosque and another gate.

¹³ A city within a city, or so it seems.

¹⁴ I linger for a moment, wondering what to do, where to go.

¹⁵ I really should have known better.

¹⁶ Like a rocket, a vendor come emerge from his shop and does the *German? English? French?* routine with me, much as the opportunist young beggars did earlier in the day.

¹⁷ In a moment, I find myself in a shop that is selling attractive local pottery and other less noteworthy trinkets.

¹⁸ The chap is friendly, and happy to dumb his French down a bit for this humble tourist. And some of his wares really are rather impressive—the enormous pieces of intricately glazed pottery especially—though I have no way of getting them home in one piece.

¹⁹ I gently steer him away from the pottery, and ask about hats.

²⁰ He leaps into action and shows me a fez or two. Nice, but not what I want. I rather liked the cloth hats the musicians were wearing earlier in the day.

²¹ They were a cross between a skullcap and a truncated cloth cylinder, probably a traditional Arabic hat, with stuff sewn onto them and designs embroidered into them.

²² I struggle to explain this. My workmanlike French did not include mathematics or the creative arts; the French for embroidery*** eludes me.

²³ The penny seems to drop, and though he explains he doesn't have one, he gleefully explains that he knows *exactly* where to find one.

²⁴ I say it's no bother, I'll look elsewhere, but he insists on helping me, in a charming friendly manner that somehow doesn't rub me up the wrong way.

²⁵ He calls over a young man, perhaps a family member or general dogsbody, and despatches him into the Kasbah market round the corner to locate the hats.

²⁶ He then offers me some mint tea. I decline politely, expecting to be there a few minutes only, but he says it is the very *best* mint tea and that it will help cool me down, again gently insisting.

²⁷ I shrug and smile my acceptance, feeling somewhat trapped by this man's earnest attempts to keep me in his shop.

²⁸ When the tea is ready, he brings me a very comfortable chair, and we sit and drink the incredibly sweet brew together, making polite chit chat in broken French.

²⁹ He tells me all about his family and the weather, using verbs and vocabulary I can remember clearly from school.

³⁰ In return, I share a little about my family, and my trip to Tunisia, and somehow we start talking about dogs. We end up laughing about big dumb mutts, which it turns out we both have a fondness for.

³¹ Minutes pass pleasantly, but turn into a quarter of an hour rather quicker than the shopkeeper would like.

³² Slightly embarrassed, he assures me that his colleague is searching for the *very best* hats, and that I will be delighted with the result.

³³ More time passes.

³⁴ Sharing his embarrassment now, I accept more tea, and we lurch onto the subject of football, which is less comfortable territory.

³⁵ I hope the dogsbody will return soon, and for this pleasant–but–awkward ordeal to end.

³⁶ And return he does. Empty handed.

³⁷ There is a flurry of angry Arabic and the lackey is despatched with his tail between his legs.

³⁸ The vendor smiles broadly and apologises smoothly for his colleague's failure. As a consolation, he offers me a *very good deal* on a magnificent fez.

³⁹ Actually, it's not a great deal at all; he's probably looking to recoup his time, effort and tea.

⁴⁰ I attempt to haggle with the man, coming in at half his initial offer.

⁴¹ This is a mistake. He looks genuinely offended. Not the street pantomime of vendors all over Tunisia, immortalised in Monty Python's *Life of Brian*, but a look of unpleasant surprise.

⁴² He simply says "Non" and repeats the price slowly, perhaps wondering if my language skills have failed me?

⁴³ I get the message; this is the price.

⁴⁴ It's really not a good deal, but I've enjoyed some pleasant tea and conversation (sucker) and I pay what he asks for (sucker).

⁴⁵ He gives me my fez and without a word of farewell he ushers me unceremoniously from the shop.

⁴⁶ Back in the street, the sun has passed its zenith and is racing west. I have no idea how long I was in there, but it must have been over half an hour.

⁴⁷ And I'm confused by the final act; I thought haggling over price was how things worked in North Africa?

⁴⁸ A bad assumption, it seems.

⁴⁹ I pause to get my bearings again, but manage to avoid any more shopkeepers.

⁵⁰ The *Kasbah Mosque*, a squat younger brother to the magnificent mosque I saw earlier in the day, looks down on me disapprovingly in the light of late afternoon, as if to say:

⁵¹ *Thou shalt not haggle in Morocco*

⁵² That's twice today I've been told off by imaginary things.

⁵³ I think the sun is getting to me.

Oiling The Wheels Of Chance

5¹ As I set foot in the Kasbah Market, I wonder if I've made a bad decision.

² It really isn't very welcoming, and doesn't suggest that tourists frequent it much:

³ there's no sign of the colourful piles of fruit and fragrant spices that you see in the guidebooks;

⁴ I receive too many surprised glances, cause too many whispers;

⁵ and, oddest of all, nobody tries to *sell* me anything.

⁶ I don't feel unsafe, but I definitely feel out of place. I keep my camera out of sight, and continue to make my way in.

⁷ I walk past a fishmonger's stall that's set up on wooden boxes in direct sunlight. Flies buzz in hordes around the dry–looking fish.

⁸ I wonder if this has been here throughout the heat of the day, but know the answer.

⁹ I pause, gawping, outside a shop in an archway where a man is weighing a live and very uncooperative chicken.

¹⁰ The customer nods and pays for his purchase. The transaction complete, the shopkeeper slaughters the bird on the counter, and the customer takes it away.

¹¹ I totally fail to stop at a roadside barber's shop, where a queue of locals patiently wait for the services of a man with a cut–throat razor and no visible hygiene.

¹² It's a world apart from my glimpse of the colourful entrance to the Soukh earlier in the day;

¹³ I think that's where the tourists go.

¹⁴ Perhaps I'm here at the wrong time of day? Perhaps I need to explore more?

¹⁵ Both of these may be true, but in an uncharacteristic moment of disquiet, I decide to withdraw. Seeing a sign for one of the older palaces, I stride off purposefully.

¹⁶ The walk to the *Palais de la Bahia* is uneventful, with just a few utterances of "Non, merci" at a succession of beggars along the way. I've been doing this reflexively all day, and might be surprised if I'd tallied the times it's been needed.

¹⁷ There is genuine poverty here.

¹⁸ The flights here are cheap and plentiful, the architecture impressive,

and it's easy to forget that Morocco is a third world country.

19 But never for long.

20 Once I'm well inside the palace in the main courtyard, I stop to catch my breath and take a drink.

21 The courtyard is peculiar. Finished a century ago, and largely unused for the past few decades, it is well preserved, but feels empty.

22 The ruins of a castle will always fire the imagination, while a fully restored watermill will show you exactly what it was like.

23 But this is neither; there is an abandoned, eerie, almost *haunted* feel about the place.

24 This feeling continues as I explore. Perhaps other visitors feel the same? There's plenty of fellow travellers about, but we're all rather quiet.

25 I pass through several beautiful courtyards filled with orange trees, carved stonework and mosaic floors. It's the perfect time of day to be here, at least;

26 the low sun adds a warmth to the scene that would be lost in the blistering heat of midday, and a cool breeze moves amongst the arches.

27 The guide book tells me this was actually not the palace of the ruler, but of his *Grand Vizier*;

28 I had no idea that viziers were to be found anywhere but adventure stories.

29 Apparently the Grand Vizier had four wives and two dozen concubines. While I marvel at the exquisite carving in the courtyards, I wonder how he ever had time to enjoy them.

30 And the geometric carvings really are something. I take a closer look, wondering if they're mouldings, but no. Each is a hand–carved piece of stone. Wow. Some underpaid artisan probably poured blood, sweat and tears into these;

31 no wonder this place took decades to complete.

32 I wander through a high–walled courtyard which looks to be made entirely of marble. A fountain gurgles pleasantly at its centre.

33 Then, passing through a grand archway, I find myself in what seems to be the final room;

34 a rope across a broad archway halfway down its length suggests that this is the end of the line.

35 I'm not surprised; the palace is large, but only a fraction of it is open to the public. I circle the room until I reach the rope, and peer beyond.

36 Further into the room is a high mosaic ceiling which is quite breathtaking: Geometric eight– and sixteen–fold symmetry; bright colours. It is both intricate and beautiful.

37 I raise my camera to capture it, but a uniformed guard appears out of nowhere and indicates that flash photography is forbidden. I apologise, step back, and circuit the room again.

38 Then a cough catches my attention. Another guard stands beyond the rope and beckons me forward.

39 As I wander towards him, I notice the first guard has gone. The new fellow takes the rope aside momentarily as he ushers me through.

40 He says nothing—perhaps deciding that he knows no German—but indicates my camera and waves upwards with a smile, inviting me to photograph the ceiling.

41 I notice my camera's battery is dangerously low, but I snap a few pictures with different settings to try and capture something in the shadows above.

42 I offer him a quick "shukran", a simple word of thanks in Arabic.

43 He smiles his appreciation and decides that there is more to show me.

44 Leading me to a door, he then opens it to reveal a spiral staircase. This takes us upwards into a wide, low chamber. It is unfurnished but decorated.

45 Again, he indicates I should take photos, but my camera chooses this moment to whine and die.

46 He fills the silence with a little of the history of the room. It belonged to someone important, but I am unclear of this person's role;

47 a French word that we both understand eludes us.

48 I think he's trying describing a senior cleric, though several mentions of the word *harem* make me wonder whether I've caught it right.

49 Our mini–tour done, he leads me back down the stairs, and then turns at the bottom with his hand out.

50 "Thank you," he says in perfect English, though I have given him nothing yet.

51 I'm getting a bit agitated with this kind of thing.

52 Common sense sees this as a gratuity and an annoyance, but on reflection I relent;

53 by a stroke of lucky timing, I have a few extra pictures, I gained access to a room that is off–limits to the public, and shared some interesting if not entirely comprehensible chit–chat.

54 I feel I should show my appreciation of this good fortune. It's like I'm oiling the wheels of chance for future use.

55 I still feel like a sucker, though.

56 I slip him a note, making sure it's an appropriate value, and he salutes me on my way.

57 And a few minutes later, I find myself back on the street.

58 It is dusk now, and after quickly checking my French dictionary I step into a shop to buy some batteries for my camera.

59 Armed with this vocabulary, I make myself understood without bother, but I have to improvise a little to add some postcards and a cigar to my basket.

60 The shopkeeper seems to appreciate my efforts though, and offers me thanks in English as I leave.

61 As with most things in life, taking a little effort can make a big difference.

62 The sun must have just set;

63 the faithful are being called to prayer from the now illuminated Koutoubia Mosque. I am drawn in that direction, and after a few minutes find myself just inside its grounds.

64 There is something magical about this moment;

65 it is one of those fabled instants where time stands still and you know you will never be here in quite the same way again.

66 I light my cigar, a rare treat for me, and pause for a few minutes.

67 I then turn and walk slowly back to my hotel through teeming streets.

68 The crowd seems to part before me, and there are astonished and perhaps admiring looks in my direction, at this tall, bold, *foreigner* who seems to be exactly where he is supposed to be at this moment in time.

69 My flight home is late tomorrow morning, and while there are still a few things to do and see, I know in my heart that nothing will compare to this memory of the twilight streets of Marrakech.

70 I lose myself in the moment and forget about tomorrow.

Notes

*   1 metre 97 centimetres. Pretty tall for a Brit; I rarely meet anyone taller, and excel at looming.

**   With good reason; it has nothing to do with it.

***   *Broderie*, as in *Broderie Anglaise*. How could I forget?

Redheads

"I've never got along with blondes. Mind you, brunettes have never been that fond of me either. And the less said about redheads the better."

Or Even In Her Garden

1 ¹ In dreams, anything can happen.

² **It's last night**. As I sleep, I'm walking the rainy autumnal streets of New York, and I'm feeling pretty good. It's been a busy and productive day, the home–time office crowds are light, and

³ there's the faintest nip of winter in the air that teases me with thoughts of snow.

⁴ I feel at home, inspired, and ready for anything. As I stroll, I take a deep breath and my eyes close contentedly.

⁵ And I collide with someone coming the other way.

⁶ A moment later, balance having abandoned me to a clumsy date with gravity, I'm sprawled in the road.

⁷ In a dirty puddle. In my suit.

⁸ Even though I'm dreaming, the water feels pretty real in my underpants.

⁹ I stand and shiver as the water runs from every seam, vent and hole in my clothing.

¹⁰ But, gentleman that I am, my thoughts run to the person I ran into. Stepping from the road wetly, I see a redheaded lady in business clothes gathering her wits on the sidewalk.

¹¹ I feel bad for her, but at least she missed the puddle.

¹² Mumbling an automatic British apology—I'm so sorry, how clumsy of me, entirely my fault—I step forward, extending a hand to assist her to the vertical.

¹³ She grasps and tugs, and in a moment, we're face to face.

¹⁴ She's very pretty.

¹⁵ Time stops.

¹⁶ It's like something from a romantic comedy. You know, the one where a hapless guy collides with a lady, helps her upright, and they laugh and fall in love after a series of charming adventures, a minor misunderstanding, and a tastefully–done bedroom scene?

¹⁷ No? Did you not see that one?

¹⁸ And she really is *very* pretty.

¹⁹ Time continues to stop. My eyes close dreamily as the soundtrack swells with sevenths towards our inevitable kiss.

²⁰ Her left hook catches me beautifully on the jaw. A moment later, I'm back in the puddle;

²¹ it's no better the second time.

²² The enraged woman, not content with this, steps forward and kicks me squarely between the legs as I lay helpless, and calls me a name that my mother would not tolerate under her roof. Or even in her garden.

²³ And as I practice my falsetto, to the applause of passers–by, she's gone.

²⁴ As the agonising pain recedes into the rhythm of the street, I raise myself again,

pleased that I only have myself to worry about now.

²⁵ Though my dirty, wet necktie may never speak to me again.

²⁶ In dreams, anything can happen.

²⁷ Intellectually, I *know* this.

²⁸ But sometimes, I swear my subconscious is out to get me.

Not A Reliable Indicator

2¹ Sometimes my dreams haunt me after I wake.

² **It's early**, and I wake to the sound of something moving around in my bedroom.

³ I roll over, semi-alert, and find the bedroom door is open. Light filters in through the blinds at the far end of the landing, though my room is mercifully dark.;

⁴ I'm not a morning person.

⁵ But it's odd; I always sleep with the door closed, and I don't recall getting up during the night.

⁶ Not that that's a reliable indicator of anything.

⁷ Besides, it doesn't explain the snuffling and the general sounds of rummaging, unseen at floor level.

⁸ Perhaps one of the badgers has let themselves in? I keep odds and ends—cables and connectors mostly—in a box under my bed; maybe they need something for a project?

⁹ "Hello?"

¹⁰ The sound ceases suddenly, and silence envelops the room. It extends unreasonably, far beyond the endurance of the shyest of badgers.

¹¹ But then, like a furry eruption, a dog leaps onto the bed. He's small, lively, mischievous-looking, and pretty darned cute; some kind of terrier?

¹² Oh, of course, it's my *dog!*

¹³ I fuss him, and he wags effusively. What's his name? Reggie. Reggie? Yes, Reggie.

¹⁴ No, wait, I don't *have* a dog.

¹⁵ I rub my eyes as he drops from the bed and runs out of the room. Whose dog was that? What time is it? I need answers.

¹⁶ "Melissa? Are you there, babe?"

¹⁷ Melissa doesn't reply. I swing my legs over the edge of the bed and sit up, somewhat bemused, in the warm wreckage of my bedclothes.

¹⁸ And I think about a nice cup of tea.

¹⁹ "Melissa?" I creak upwards and walk towards the light. Onwards, forwards, meet the day. Good morning kiss, put the kettle on, tea, breakfast. Oh, and find out about the dog.

²⁰ A dog? Was there a dog? Did I dream the dog? I sniff my hand sleepily; there's no doggy smell to it. Did I just fuss a dog? What was his name?

²¹ I don't recall. Why should I? He's not mine, after all.

²² Grabbing my dressing gown, I pass through the dim, wooden-floored landing and onto the carpet of my front room. I wonder idly where the stairs are?

²³ Was that the landing I walked through, or my hallway?

²⁴ I flop into a leather armchair, still muddle-headed.

²⁵ "Melissa?"

²⁶ The redhead is nowhere to be seen. I half expected to find her dozing in a chair in front of a quiet TV, wearing one of my shirts;

²⁷ she doesn't always sleep well, and often gets up before me.

²⁸ I wonder about our plans for the day.

²⁹ Then I remember the tea, and rise to fill and start the kettle. I notice that the room seems a little bare. Spartan, almost. No, that's wrong;

³⁰ it's more Sparse than Spartan.

³¹ Magnolia-painted walls with a couple of forgettable hanging prints, minimal furniture. Clean and tidy without being fussy, but few cushions, no flowers or air fresheners, and precious little colour apart from the pizza boxes.

³² All very single male.

³³ I have no idea how she puts up with it.

³⁴ How *who* puts up with it? I look to the sofa. Melanie, was it? No wait, I live alone. Have done for years.

³⁵ And I never lived with a redhead.

³⁶ What am I thinking?

³⁷ And what was that about a dog?

³⁸ **Fifteen minutes later**, after a cup of tea in my favourite armchair, I'm wide awake, and feeling rather foolish. That dream sure did cling to me.

³⁹ But the curtains are now open, the sun is shining, and I'm ready for the day.

⁴⁰ There's a knock at the door, and I rise steadily to answer it. Passing through the hallway, I spy the familiar hulking shape through the glass of the door. I open it to welcome my friend.

[41] "Bear! Good to see you! Come in! I've just made tea!"

[42] **Five minutes later**, I'm back in my armchair with a fresh cup, and Bear is sitting on the sofa. Well, occupying it;

[43] he's a big lad.

[44] He's put some quiet music on; some Rimsky Korsakov, I think? The black bear sits quietly, sipping tea from a tiny cup held precariously in his huge paws. He smiles amiably.

[45] "This is excellent tea, Indigo.

[46] Wait. What were we just talking about?

[47] Bear casts his gaze about as he fusses the happy dog on his lap.

[48] "So, where's Melissa?"

[49] I decide to head back to bed;

[50] I'll wake up properly later.

Walking Back Into Memory

3
[1] I wander downstairs to answer the sunshine knock at the door.

[2] The hall clock points to nine. I've slept in. I'm late for work.

[3] It occurs to me that I'm dressed only in my underpants and feeling more than a little portly today, but I can see it's the postman. He's a pleasant enough chap on the rare occasions I see him, and I don't think I'll offend him by appearing in my unmentionables.

[4] I unlock the door as he whistles an elusive tune. He even gives me a cheery wave through the textured glass door. I wonder idly if I look slimmer from his side?

[5] As I open the door, I'm greeted by a smile. He salutes smartly and meets my gaze, ignoring my semi–nakedness.

[6] "Good morning Mr. Roth, Sir!" I have to give him points for professionalism. Which is immediately suspicious; he usually prefers to leave things where I won't notice them.

[7] "Hey," I mumble sleepily. He has a large, enticing–looking parcel. It's wrapped in brown paper and tied up with string. "What've you got for me this morning?"

[8] "Well, I'm sorry to bother you, Mr. Roth," he says, somewhat abashed, "but I've a parcel for your neighbour. There's no reply next door. Would you mind taking it in?"

[9] Oh.

[10] "Sure. Of course. Nothing for me?" I

ask as I take the parcel. "I was hoping there'd be some goodies today."

[11] "No Mr. Roth, sorry!" he shrugs, handing over the parcel, "Sometime soon though, I'm sure." He snaps off another salute that would shame a Wing Commander. "See you tomorrow Sir! And thank you!"

[12] I smile and he turns and walks off down the path.

[13] I sigh and sit down on the doorstep, carefully popping the package down beside me; I'll take it round later.

[14] I feel crushed for no good reason.

[15] The sun is bright and hot, and there is no breeze. The humidity is uncomfortable, and I can feel the rising edge of a headache;

[16] there must be a storm coming.

[17] Ten yards away on the tree–lined summer path, a mother walks by with a toddler. The boy points at me and giggles, and the mother scolds it past hurriedly.

[18] I'm not looking forward to the day, and it's barely started.

[19] Unexpectedly, a pair of warm, gentle arms encircle me from behind.

[20] A delicious scent of vanilla entices my senses as the warm face nuzzles up to mine. There's a sleepy kiss to my cheek.

[21] "Morning Babe," she murmurs, as her long red hair tumbles over my shoulder. "Are you coming back to bed?"

[22] God, that sounds wonderful;

[23] beautiful oblivion.

[24] "No, I have to get to work," I find myself saying. *What?*

[25] The arms hug me tighter. "Oh, do you *have* to?" There's a gentle Scottish lilt to the voice.

[26] Of course I bloody don't! Why would I want to?

[27] "Yep, sorry. No choice," I say.

[28] Again, my voice is working solo in defiance of my brain.

[29] The arms slide away, and she sighs her disappointment.

[30] I stand and turn into the sunlit hallway, closing the door behind me.

[31] She stands, tall and slim, all red hair, brown eyes and freckles.

[32] I recognise her from TV.

[33] She's wearing one of my shirts. It's way too big on her;

[34] damn, but it's a good look.

[35] "Are you sure?" she asks, with just a hint of coyness.

36 "Yes, absolutely," I nod sadly. I wander over and take her hands. "You know," I confess, "I move in fairly strange circles," I kiss the top of her head on an impulse, somehow knowing it will be my last chance, "but I *know* that you're Fiction."

37 She hugs herself into me and whispers, "Sometime soon you'll learn to relax, Indigo."

38 There's an abyssal sadness in her next words.

39 "You can't do all this on your own."

40 And she turns and walks up the stairs and back into memory.

41 "Wait!"

42 I wake in my bed, disoriented. I cannot smell vanilla. There has never been vanilla in this room.

43 I feel profoundly alone.

44 Sunlight slices through the smallest of cracks in the curtains, and I can already feel the humidity of the day in the early morning room.

45 My head aches. There's a storm coming.

46 Sometimes my dreams are way too literal. Sometimes they're mundane. And sometimes they're just plain mean.

47 I have no idea whose side my subconscious is on most of the time.

48 I need to do something with my life. It won't be easy, or even today.

49 But it will have to be sometime soon.

Leviathan*

4 ¹ I found the old man sitting by a shack on the beach looking out to sea.

2 And he told me a story.

3 A young man grew up in a faraway land, a solitary soul. He enjoyed the company of others, but they rarely sought him out or asked his opinion.

4 He did not understand them, and he felt lonely. He yearned for companionship, for love, for the friendships and joy that everyone else seemed to have.

5 And for this, he blamed himself, and wondered how he might change.

6 One night, he dreamed of a giant sea serpent. It uncoiled from stormy depths, muscular and mighty, and towered over him in the darkness.

7 Its eyes were black pits that bored into his soul, and it knew his secrets.

8 "I am Leviathan," it roared, "and only through me will you know peace."

9 When he awoke, he knew he must travel, to broaden his horizons and experience, to find the spark that would bring others to him.

10 He would find Leviathan.

11 He travelled east with just the clothes he stood in, and moved from town to town, working odd jobs, keeping himself to himself.

12 It was uncomfortable at first, as the people were strangers to him, and he lacked the skills to forge bonds with them. But still, he worked and earned and learned and tried.

13 His journey led ever east, through hills and many years, until he stopped at a town by a river.

14 He liked it there, and worked hard.

15 The people welcomed him, and he felt closer to them than any others he had ever met. He did chores and favours, and met with smiling folk on the street and shook hands with many.

16 There was food and drink and laughter and friendship.

17 After a few weeks, the people of the town invited him to stay, and he promised to think about it.

18 But overnight he once again dreamed of the serpent. It roiled above him in stormy seas, and terrified but inspired him.

19 "I am Leviathan," it roared, "and only through me will you know peace."

20 When he awoke in the early light of dawn, he took his meagre possessions and continued his journey, leaving the town far behind him by noon.

21 Nobody followed him. He felt sad, but he was determined to find Leviathan.

22 More years passed, and onwards he drifted through villages and towns, working and talking and meeting people.

23 He had learned a lot in his travels, skills both social and manual, until his growth became apparent even to him.

24 He found himself increasingly at ease.

25 He lingered awhile in a remote town, where again the people appreciated him and thanked him for his efforts.

26 They told him things and asked him things, and confided in him.

27 And he met a woman. She was tall and beautiful with flaming red hair and a smile that spoke of tranquility and contentment.

[28] She was drawn to him, and they became a couple, and for a while he was happy and forgetful of his quest.

[29] But one night in his dreams, the sea serpent came to him again, and he stood afraid in its midnight shadow as the sea boiled around it.

[30] "I am Leviathan," it roared, "and only through me will you know peace."

[31] When he awoke, he cried, and quietly packed his bag of tools and keepsakes. Before either the town or his love awoke, he slipped quietly into the countryside and continued on his way.

[32] The woman followed him, and begged him to stay. Her loving tears and pleas struck home hard, for he loved her too. But he explained he must travel on alone.

[33] He must find Leviathan.

[34] She did not understand and sadness gave way to anger, and she cursed him, and screamed for him never to return. And he travelled on.

[35] A few days later, he reached the sea.

[36] He wandered its coastline, but it seemed straight and infinite. He could swim, but there were no islands in sight.

[37] Was this where he was to meet Leviathan?

[38] He built a shack from driftwood, and alone he waited for his journey to end. Stoic but lonely, he measured the passing of each day and wondered if each would be the one.

[39] And every day, he remembered those he has met and befriended and the happy times he had spent with them.

[40] And most of all he remembered the redheaded woman, and wondered what might have been.

[41] And that is where I found him, an old man sitting on the beach by his little house, waiting for Leviathan to find him.

[42] That night, back in my hotel, I wondered about the old man's tale, and what would become of him.

[43] As I drifted off to sleep, I heard a storm coming in from the sea. And amid the thunder and lightning and hammering rain, I felt sure I heard the distant roar of some great beast.

[44] And when I returned to the beach the following day, the shack was destroyed, and the old man was gone.

Notes

*   This is the oldest story in this book, but the most recently written.

The Liar

23

Portents

"For those of you who don't know much about tarot cards, there is no Trump 23.
There is no card called The Liar. For those of you who do, I salute you. My maternal
grandmother was a well–regarded medium, psychic and fortune teller.
I have few memories of her, other than I loved her very much."

Fluorescent Blue Soundbites

1 [1] The postman hands over the parcel with an air of indifference, putting a brave face on the fact that he prefers to hide parcels behind the hedge and leave an illegible note.

[2] I unwrap the box as I sit on the sofa, and discover a well–loved *Magic Eight Ball* beneath layers of bubble wrap.

[3] I notice that many of the bubbles have already been burst.

[4] I burst a few more of the little suckers and smile;

[5] children, every one of us.

[6] I've never owned a Magic Eight Ball, but I suspect I've always wanted one. In the advertising, it's a source of knowledge and enlightenment that is accessible and affordable to anyone.

[7] In reality, it's a black plastic ball, three inches across, with a clear, round viewing panel. Inside it is some kind of viscous liquid, and a twenty–faced, floating geometric solid.*

[8] On each face of the die is a message, a response to a yes/no question.

[9] The theory is that you shake the ball, and ask a question. You then check out the viewing panel and wait for the answer to appear. The die floats up through the blue goo and contrives to appear as a fluorescent blue soundbite.

[10] Well, textbite.

[11] Most of the responses are positive, some are negative, and some are somewhere in the middle.

[12] Cool. Well, if you're ten years old.

[13] Or still have the sense of wonder of a ten–year–old;

[14] so we're good.

[15] There's no note or receipt with the parcel, but it's clearly addressed to me. I'll wonder about the source of this gift later.

[16] The ball is somewhat battered, and the once–white eight–ball logo on it is yellowed. Clearly it's seen a lot of action over the years.

[17] I guess Wisdom is always in demand.

[18] I notice a cup of tea on the coffee table.** Deciding to give the mystic insight of the ball a try, I give it a theatrical shake. I sense it sloshing more than I hear it.

[19] I clear my throat, and intone with suitable gravitas,

[20] "O Magic Eight Ball, I ask thee! Is that cup of tea still hot?"

[21] I don't think the linguistic flourish is strictly necessary, but it makes it fun. The answer wanders up towards me.

[22] *MY SOURCES SAY NO.*

23 I try the tea, and spit the cold liquid back into the cup. Lucky guess.

24 Looking at the overcast day outside, I try again. "Will the sun shine today?" Shake–shake.

25 Again, the glowing answer materialises from the depths.

26 *ASK AGAIN LATER.*

27 Yes, this is exactly how I imagined it would work. Still, it's cheaper than a fortune teller. And every bit as reliable as the weatherman.

28 Maybe something a bit more challenging?

29 "Will I write a book?" Shake–shake.

30 *CONCENTRATE AND ASK AGAIN.*

31 Concentrate? Okay, let's define my terms better.

32 "Will I write and publish a book in the next three years?" Shake–shake.

33 *YES.*

34 "So am I right to sharpen my skills on my blog?" Shake–shake.

35 *YES, DEFINITELY.*

36 "And will I have a pizza tonight to celebrate?" Shake–shake.

37 *WELL, DUH!*

38 What? I don't remember that in the advert. Still, fair comment. On a roll, and keen for even more good news, I venture,

39 "Will I meet and marry the woman of my dreams?" Shake–shake.

40 *LMAO!*

41 "Cheeky sod." Somewhat dejected, I shake the ball idly.

42 *SCHMUCK.*

43 I drop the mystic sphere in surprise. It thumps heavily, and rolls as far as the coffee table. Retrieving it, the answer has changed.

44 *OUCH.*

45 Hmmm. Suspicious. An idea starts to form in my mind about who mailed me the ball.

46 "Did a part–time arch–genius send this to me?" Shake–shake.

47 *I FIND YOUR LACK OF FAITH DISTURBING.*

48 "Okay, just tell me! Did iDifficult send you to me?" Shake–shake.

49 Suddenly, there's a slow insistent ticking from the ball.

50 *THIS DEVICE WILL SELF DESTRUCT IN TEN SECONDS.*

51 Well, that answers *that* question.

52 As I dive behind the sofa, I decide to ask a fortune teller next time.

Lawn Mowing Avoidance

2 1 After my run in with Max's Magic Eight Ball recently, I decide to consult a professional about my future.

2 I find the exotic–sounding Madame Bianca under *Psychics* in the Yellow Pages. Apparently, she's an expert Tarot card reader.

3 This is all new to me, and I'm genuinely intrigued, and a little excited;

4 I'll even forego mowing the lawn.

5 I arrive for my reading, and after some explanation of how the reading of Tarot cards works and very little by way of mumbo jumbo, the pleasant gypsy seer gets me to shuffle and cut the cards.

6 She turns the first card over.

7 It's Trump 23, *The Liar*.

8 The likeness is uncanny; I even own the necktie.

9 There's a lot of shouting. She accuses me of tampering with her cards, but I plead ignorance with a clear conscience;

10 messing with someone else's stuff would be bad form.

11 Seeming to calm slightly, she points out to me that The Liar was dealt to the table upside down;

12 in tarot parlance, it is *reversed*.

13 I ask her if the card being reversed is significant.

14 Hefting her crystal ball, she says it is.

15 Apparently it means I'll be getting a lump on the back of my head.

16 And do you know what?

17 I predict she'll be right.

Making It Past The Landmines

3 1 Today starts as it always does, with coffee, cereal, and my horoscope.

2 As I munch on spoonfuls of malty cereal with added banana and strawberries, I flip through the newspaper.

3 I hurry past pages of dry news, and wrestle with several colourful inserted supplements until I locate the *Lifestyle* section.

4 Here we go. Scorpio:

5 *Step away from your responsibilities today, Scorpio! This is a day to kick back and relax after recent troubles. Enjoy some time to yourself and recharge those physical and emotional batteries. Go on, you deserve it!*

⁶ I lower the paper. Well, that sounds like my kind of thing. It has been a trying few weeks. I've been craving some decent downtime.

⁷ Actually, it sounds wonderful. But no, there's a lot to do today. It's a luxury I can't really afford after a few days off work sick, however tempting it is.

⁸ I pick the paper up again, and notice a second paragraph for Scorpio.

⁹ *But beware, Scorpio! The call of the office will be strong. Don't forget what a battlefield it can be; pointless meetings, unpleasant politics, idiotic edicts, endless red tape, and the relentless demands of people who respect neither your skills nor results. Forget that! You'll thank yourself tonight if you resist.*

¹⁰ Wow, that's unusually specific. And colourful. And how did I miss it the first time? But it changes nothing; it's too easy to get behind and spend days fighting your way back up to date.

¹¹ I have to go to work, no matter what my horoscope says.

¹² Hey, there's more. And it definitely wasn't here a moment ago.

¹³ *Not convinced? What if we admitted that the "day to kick back" was actually a bit of a smoke screen? The truth is, there is an inauspicious planetary alignment today, and you'll find yourself coming up empty on all fronts; family, work, finances, friendship, and love.*

¹⁴ Not a good day for love? Well, damn!

¹⁵ *Face facts Scorpio, this is not a day to venture out into the world. Carpe diem? Forget it. Make any effort to seize the day, and it'll be two steps forward, five steps back. All. Day. Long. Come bedtime, you'll be a shattered wreck of a man, wrung dry like an old dish mop.*

¹⁶ Good grief, when you put it like that...

¹⁷ *In fact, did we mention that your car battery is dead? Or that there's a Venezualan sniper taking potshots from the top of the nearby block of flats? And that you'll be run down, trampled and gored by a rogue rhino as soon as you step onto the pavement?*

¹⁸ I sigh and toss the paper aside.

¹⁹ *And that's if you make it past the landmines!*

²⁰ Some days the universe does its best to tell you something.

²¹ I find it's usually a good idea to pay attention.

²² I finish my coffee, call in sick, and head back to bed.

Home At Last

4¹ The sun is strolling towards the horizon as the air blinks at the crossroads.

² One moment, there is nothing but the warm umber rays of twilight, casting tiger-stripe shadows through open blinds onto the walls of whispered basements. The traffic lights of the main drag turn red in solidarity.

³ The next moment, they stand there, as if they have always been there. A party of six, eclectically dressed but uniform in their dishevelment.

⁴ One-by-one, they step from the road to the western sidewalk and cross the front yard to the house, heralded by shadows.

⁵ The first is a man, tall and heroically solid, with short cropped hair and a neatly-trimmed beard that's peppered with dried breakfast cereal. His leather jacket has seen better days, with fresh tears aplenty.

⁶ The pirate hat on his head sits at a rakish angle, pure Charles Laughton, though he bears a striking resemblance to Donald Pleasance.

⁷ He has a shoe missing, but no peg leg.

⁸ Next comes a bear, a blue fez atop his head. His Hawaiian shirt is in tatters, and there is a heavy tyre-track on the seat of his cargo pants. His hat and fur are scorched in places, and his limping foot is field dressed with duct tape; they came prepared.

⁹ He hums a cheery baritone tune absently, in defiance of his state.

¹⁰ A badger trails close behind the bear, his dungarees and thigh-length waders soaked with viscous spittle. He has a fine-meshed netting bag of sleepy ferrets over his shoulder.

¹¹ Failing to light his pipe of tobacco, he makes an exploratory journey into his flat cap to retrieve a cleaning rod. A few prods frees the briar, and

¹² he's puffing happily-but-wearily as he passes under the ash tree in the front lawn.

¹³ A woman is next, redheaded beneath her football helmet, a pretty floral blouse and blue jeans beneath her Kevlar body

armour.

14 She carries a crate of oranges that have seen better days; not all were needed, but she hates waste as much as mascara. Her feet are bare.

15 Finally comes the tall man in the gold lamé wetsuit fit for The King. His necktie is laminated, but has still fared badly. His sparkly trousers are torn in a manner that would be fashionable were he twenty years younger.

16 He doesn't care; these were hard earned, and not factory–fitted.

17 He sighs as he watches the party lead him away from adventure.

18 He catches the redhead up as they cross the grass; she hugs him kindly as they step into the house and close the door.

19 Inside, a lion roars a welcome.

20 The day is conquered.

21 And they are home at last.

22 Sleep will not elude them tonight.

Slighted In Italics

5 1 I feel thoroughly miserable.

2 As I slam shut the hatchback on my car, I want it to complain, to object to the load that the car contains. For its hesitation to indicate that the car is too full, that I have too much stuff.

3 But this is a stupid thought, and Life affords it the disdain it deserves; the trunk closes smoothly.

4 It's **September 1998**, and the garden is a carpet of crunchy orange leaves. I hear footsteps.

5 "Good morning, Indigo!" breezes Bear, as he appears around the hedge and strolls up the driveway, "And isn't it a beautiful day?"

6 As if on cue, birds begin to twitter cheerfully in the trees. Frankly, I'm surprised the little devils don't flutter round my friend's head and land on his outstretched paw, to sing sweetly as he chuckles; Uncle Remus would have been proud, I conclude sourly.

7 Man, I'm in a bad mood today.

8 "Yeah, morning Bear," I mutter.

9 My companion, all seven feet of him, stands next to me and gives me a manly hug; I can sense he's thinking without needing to look at him.

10 Though his dayglo Hawaiian shirt demands some attention.

11 "So, it's the big day!" He indicates the loaded car. "It looks like you're all packed. Are you ready to move house?"

12 Moving house is always a chore.

13 "I *hate* moving house Bear," I grumble, "and look how much my life boils down to!"

14 Bear knows full well what I mean, I'm sure, but he's tricky; he knows how to get me to talk.

15 "How do you mean?"

16 I wave two–handedly, somewhat despairingly.

17 "My life fits in a *car!*" Bear pats my shoulder reassuringly as I continue, "It wasn't even that difficult to shut it!

18 Seriously, is that *all there is?!*"

19 His chuckle is dark and throaty. "You measure your life by how much *volume* it takes up?"

20 No, that's not what I meant, and he knows it.

21 "Of course not." I feel I'm lying a little.

22 "Oh, so it's about how many *possessions* you have? That's not it, surely?"

23 "No. Of course not." My tone is defiant, but I'm pretty sure I'm lying now. How can my life fit into one tiny little car, with nothing on the front seats, and no doors squeezed shut?

24 "That's good. Because you're a decent person, right?"

25 "I like to think so. Yeah, I guess."

26 "And you have good friends, who appreciate your *qualities?*" I squeeze him back slightly, manfully, though I'm fairly sure I've just been slighted in some way. In italics.

27 "The best." This one's all true;

28 I feel a little brighter.

29 "And the new house looks amazing. I heard there may even be some badgers in the back garden."

30 I smile; I do adore badgers.

31 Bear has more good news, though. "There will be another lodger there at some point, but the landlord is very fussy. So I don't think you'll end up sharing with anyone objectionable. "

32 Well, that's a comfort, too. *Uncertainty* is next to *Uneasiness* in my dictionary.

33 "Yeah," I say brightly, "it's going to be great."

34 Bear turns me and gives me a meaningful look.

35 "Quite so. And believe me, I've known you a *long* time," he cuffs my head

gently, "and I *don't* measure your life by the meagre possessions in this car.

36 You have skills, talents and imagination by the bucketload, and they occupy *no space whatsoever*."

37 This is flattering, and somewhat of a smackdown; Bear's good at this.

38 "Yes Bear. You're right." I manage a smile.

39 The black bear thumps my shoulder enthusiastically.

40 "So, can I drive?"

41 I don't think twice.

42 "Sure, that'd be nice."

43 Wait, what?! I realise too late that I've been suckered again.

44 *Never* let a bear drive.

45 We scream off the driveway on two wheels into an adrenaline–fuelled future.

Notes

*   For fantasy roleplay gamers among you, it's a large *d20*. For those of you who are not, I deny everything.

**   No, the irony is not lost on me.

Revelations

"My inner voice advises me that a wise writer knows to quit while he's ahead. My ego says otherwise, but I also know that my ego needs a firm slap down occasionally."

Two Sweet Emulsions

1 ¹ Max deposits the tray of coffee, sandwiches and cookies on the table.

² "I figured you need a break, matey."

³ I sigh heavily and drop my pencil onto the leather–topped table. "Yes. Please."

⁴ Max is right; I've been working very hard this month, and I do deserve a break. We both do.

⁵ My handwriting, normally smooth and elegant, has reduced to a scrawl under the blowtorch of sleeplessness, and Max's is no better.

⁶ Especially the stuff in crayon.

⁷ That said, he's completed ten times the amount of design and repair work to the time pyramid that I have, just with less sleep and ten times the caffeine.

⁸ "You know," says my friend, taking his seat and distributing goodies from the tray, "it strikes me that most of your readers think that you're writing fiction."

⁹ I frown. "Do you think?" It's not something I had considered before; my tales of Cambridge are a diary to me at the end of the day.

¹⁰ Max nibbles on a chicken salad roll. "Yeah. If you read their letters closely, it's like they're congratulating you on some great feat of *imagination*."

¹¹ "Do I give that impression?"

¹² Max considers this as he pours the coffee and shovels cane sugar into both, forming two sweet emulsions.

¹³ "Well, not that I'd noticed. But then, I'm usually there."

¹⁴ I nod sagely, and seek insight in a quadruple–chocolate cookie.

¹⁵ "Did you mention this to Bear, King, Abbey and the badgers?"

¹⁶ Max shakes his head. "Not really. It'd would be weird to have one's existence called into question."

¹⁷ I spray coffee.

¹⁸ "They think they're all fictional too?"

¹⁹ This is too much. Max shrugs, wiping coffee from his face.

²⁰ "Could be. It's hard to tell." He examines a cookie minutely, abstractly. "They enjoy your writing, but I think they might just be playing along with the joke, if you know what I mean?"

²¹ We sit in silence for a moment. "Madness." This is very unsettling news to me.

²² "Well yes," he scratches his head, "it's a crazy thought. Our lives are one great colourful adventure! So why...?"

²³ I nod, finishing his thought.

²⁴ "Why would I waste time and effort just *making stuff up?*"

²⁵ We ponder this, and find solace in coffee, sandwiches and sugary treats.

Definitely Not Canon

2 [1] "Sorry, you can't come in." [2] The figure barring my way is tall and broad. His all–white tuxedo is impressive. As I stand there dumbly, he glances down at me.

[3] "Did you no *hear* me, sunshine? I said you can't come in."

[4] I never imagined coming here, but now I am here, this comes as a surprise. Actually, I'm annoyed.

[5] "What do you mean, I can't come in?"

[6] "It's perfectly simple." He glances at me meaningfully. "Which bit didn't you understand?"

[7] This isn't quite what I expected at the Gates of Heaven. Mind you, I'm surprised that I'm even here at all. I've had my doubts.

[8] "Are you certain?" I ask, "I'm pretty sure I have an appointment with your boss."

[9] St. Peter checks his clipboard as he stands behind the white rope.

[10] "Nope. You're not on *The List*."

[11] He squares his shoulders and stands with his hands together in front of him. His eyes stare into the distance.

[12] He is officially Ignoring Me.

[13] "Look, I didn't ask to come here," I object, waving about, "I didn't *choose*. Yet here I am."

[14] He sighs without looking my way.

[15] "Not my problem, pal. Not on The List, No Entry. Simple."

[16] I tilt the top of his clipboard down.

[17] "Oi! Pack that in!" he growls at me, snatching it back. But it's too late; I've seen the page.

[18] "But the paper is empty! There's *nobody* on The List!"

[19] The saint does a thing with his neck that makes it crack noisily.

[20] "Right. Nobody." He pokes me in the chest, "Which includes *you*, see?"

[21] I step back. "So nobody's going into Heaven today?"

[22] "Right. Important day, everyone's busy."

[23] "What's going on?" My curiosity still seems to be working.

[24] He resumes his thousand yard stare and says nothing.

[25] "Oh, for god's sake, what's going on?"

[26] I regret the words as they spill out. His glance whips my way, his voice low but somehow a roar.

[27] "Mind your mouth, boy. You won't *blaspheme* your way in."

[28] "Excuse me, sorry." I gather my nerve, and appeal quietly, "Please. Tell me what's going on."

[29] "It's the End of Time."

[30] "What?!"

[31] "End. Of. Time."

[32] I consider this for a moment, not entirely selflessly. "Wow, I guess I did live forever."

[33] St. Peter regards me with disapproval.

[34] "You're an author. Of course you do. But today is The End." He puffs his chest out proudly. "The Boys are Riding Out."

[35] I consider this for a moment before the penny drops.

[36] "The Horsemen Of The Apocalypse? They're going to Ride Out through the Gate?"

[37] "Yep. A few minutes time." He pauses. "Well, *walk* out," he adds shiftily. He seems uncomfortable with this topic suddenly. "Insurance problem. Health and Safety." He shrugs. "You know how it is."

[38] I nod sadly. I look around behind me and then back to St. Peter.

[39] "So, is that why nobody's coming in?"

[40] He grunts his assent. "Smart lad."

[41] "Wow." The word seem inadequate. "*War, Famine, Pestilence* and *Death* will be here any minute." I absently wish I'd brought my camera.

[42] St. Peter's stance shifts uncomfortably.

[43] "Well, no. Times change. The world has imagined greater perils since the old days. These guys are something *new*. Not tried before."

[44] He leans in conspiratorially, and says is a hushed voice, "Between you and me, they give me the *willies*. Nothing will stand before them."

[45] "Well, who are they?!"

[46] Behind St. Peter, the Gates of Heaven open to the sound of an awesome Heavenly choir. I suppose I should have seen that coming.

[47] "See for yourself." He unclips the white rope to allow four figures through, and snaps off a salute. They don't even grace him with a glance.

[48] Embarrassed at himself, he jostles me back. "Come on, stand back! Give the gentlemen some *room!*"

[49] As they pass us, St. Peter points to a young logo'd dude humming to himself.

[50] "That's *Conformity*. He's the end of

Imagination. The end of Creativity. The death of Human Endeavour."

⁵¹ A scruffy figure passes us, staring listlessly at a lit cigarette.

⁵² *"Apathy* is the end of Pride. The end of Ambition. The end of Questions. The death of Resistance."

⁵³ A leather–clad youth swaggers past. He gives us the bird.

⁵⁴ *"Impunity* is the end of Fear. The end of Respect. The death of Order."

⁵⁵ I whisper to my companion, "So which one used to be called Death?"

⁵⁶ He points to the final figure, a short consultant in an expensive suit.

⁵⁷ *"Process.* He was *Bureaucracy* for a while, but I guess the pay was better. Process is the end of Common Sense. The end of Freewill. The death of Justice. He'll get the job done. Very thorough."

⁵⁸ The four stride out as the choir reaches its climax. There's a moment of speed and the quartet of light–forms vanish to the far corners of existence.

⁵⁹ Then. Silence.

⁶⁰ The doorman wipes a happy tear away.

⁶¹ "All sinners are *toast."*

⁶² I glance past St. Peter towards the open Gate; it'll be better in there than out here. I nudge the bouncer and point to it amiably.

⁶³ "So, can I go in now?" He looks at me, puzzled. It's as if he's forgotten where he is for a moment. I add helpfully, "Time has ended. The Horsemen have Ridden

Out. All bets are off now, right?"

⁶⁴ St. Peter considers this. His features soften, his bouncer's bluster passes into memory.

⁶⁵ "Have you led a good life?"

⁶⁶ "I've tried. Didn't always manage it." I reflect for a moment and add, "But I regret the things I screwed up."

⁶⁷ He nods. I'm told I have an honest face. "I've always believed that's the point."

⁶⁸ I hesitate for a moment, uncertain.

⁶⁹ "Does the boss know about that time...?" my voice tails off.

⁷⁰ "I think you'll find He knows Everything."

⁷¹ "I don't think I regretted that one. In my heart."

⁷² He looks into me, his gaze intense and constant. His eyes reflect the secrets of the universe. When he speaks, his voice calls from the distant reaches of time.

⁷³ "You did a good thing, lad. Let it go."

⁷⁴ I glance at the Gate again. "So may I go in?"

⁷⁵ He sweeps his arms wide in welcome. "Yes. Please do."

⁷⁶ I step towards him and we shake hands.

⁷⁷ "Until next time," I say, raising an eyebrow.

⁷⁸ He nods and smiles.

⁷⁹ "Yes, of course. 'Til next time."

⁸⁰ And I walk through the Gates into Light.

THANKS

This book has been a dream since I was a kid. I remember seeing a section of the UK youth magazine programme BLUE PETER, about a teenage viewer who'd written a children's adventure story. I was enthralled by the idea, and I immediately knew I wanted to be a writer. For that, thank you BLUE PETER.

After that, I spent a lot of time writing stories. I was young and knew nothing, so most of them were awful, but I loved the process. I was also lucky enough to own a typewriter at twelve, and an early word processor at fifteen. For that, and for their endless love and support over the years, I thank my parents.

The education system didn't encourage creativity so much, but I had a couple of English teachers at high school who set interesting writing exercises, and who still gave me good grades and reports even when I drew in my exercise book. For that, thank you Elaine Waller and Howard Marsh.

After I lost many years in corporate life, the INDIGO ROTH blog finally gave me a means to explore characters and stories in a way I could share, and to start writing a book. But it was the overwhelming support of readers that gave me the confidence to finish. For that, I thank everyone who ever read an entry, commented or encouraged.

Late in the day, my editor pointed out that not all of my output was gold, but was pleasantly diplomatic about it, and had the decency to openly enjoy the rest. Better yet, she only had to moderately hassle me to reach this point. For that, thank you Jenny Hewitt.

Thanks also to Keith Fowler for inspiring iDifficult/Max, and to Kristie Ann Hall for being Eolist. And thanks to Sarah and Megan, without whom the young badgers would never have arrived. They also came up with a few ideas for stories. I love you all!

And finally, thank you for reading this book.

Indigo

ABOUT THE AUTHOR

Indigo Roth is a writer, artist, non–Biblical creator of Stuff, and an easy–going, self–deprecating genius. Officially the world's first *Fractal Slacker*™.

He enjoys writing and illustrating the long–running and unashamedly self–titled INDIGO ROTH blog.

TESTAMENT: FUNNY BADGERS is his first book.

Roth lives in Cambridge with a cast of unlikely characters and a lot of empty pizza boxes.

COMING IN 2014

WHY, I OUGHTA...

The adventures of acclaimed Minneapolis blogger,
bus aficionado, full–time corporate minion, and
domestic feline peacekeeper, **Pearl**.

Red Angel Publishing,
Cambridge, United Kingdom

5067273R10140

Printed in Great Britain
by Amazon.co.uk, Ltd.,
Marston Gate.